About the Author

The author is a retired police officer who has had a lot of life experience. He was married to his first wife for thirty years and they raised four children. Following a divorce, he married again and divorced just three years later. Apart from writing, he plays the piano, loves gardening and has carried out a lot of DIY building projects in his spare time. He is a 'people person', and has always taken a keen interest in behavioural psychology and relationships.

Bruno Beaches

TIL DEATH WE DO PART

For Samantha

I hope that you thoroughly enjoy this book.
Thanks for your interest

Bruno Beaches

Promotional Copy No 8.

AUSTIN MACAULEY PUBLISHERS™

LONDON • CAMBRIDGE • NEW YORK • SHARJAH

26/3/21

A CIP catalogue record for this title is available from the British Library.

ISBN 9781398408456 (Paperback)
ISBN 9781398408463 (ePub e-Book)

www.austinmacauley.com

First Published (2021)
Austin Macauley Publishers Ltd
25 Canada Square
Canary Wharf
London
E14 5LQ

Chapter 1

Pablo walked up the short path to the front door. It was a ground floor maisonette on a small, mixed estate that used to be council housing. It was a very quiet neighbourhood. The tiny front garden was overgrown with grass, cascading over itself from the potential height of eighteen inches, yellowing, and going to seed already. The front window was large but obscured on the inside with a combination of curtains and a blanket. It was broad daylight, and the sun was out on this warm, early summer's day. He stood at the front door and observed the dull creamy paint peeling off the wood like bits of old, dry, onion. He noticed the remnants of a door knocker. The plate was there, but the hinged knocker was long gone. He looked at an electric doorbell buzzer which was hanging by a black wire on the door jamb, with a lonely tail of red wire hanging loosely beside it. That obviously wouldn't work.

He knocked on the door window with his knuckles. Not too hard. He didn't want to sound aggressive. As he awaited a response, he pondered the state of the place. Addicts' homes were usually like this. Neglected. Really neglected. The extent of neglect was in direct correlation to how long it had been since someone who actually cared about the place had lived there. Addicts spared no money or effort to look after themselves, let alone somebody else's property. This was one of the side effects of their addiction, where the reward system of the brain had been hijacked by drugs. Things that normally made people feel good didn't work for the brain that was in thrall to heroin. He felt a little apprehensive, as always in this situation, not knowing quite what to expect. There was no response. He knocked again, this time a little harder.

A few moments later the door opened slowly and slightly. The occupant appeared cautious and wary, as expected. Pablo looked at the half a face partially hidden by the door. It was murky behind him. A lot of addicts blanked out windows with curtains or blankets all day long. They didn't want the world looking in on them, and they didn't want to look out on the outside world. That was a part of their escape. A young man with pale skin and shabby clothes answered the door, squinting into the bright daylight.

"Yes?" he said nonchalantly, using the door as a shield.

"Mark Foster?" Pablo said it like he was asking, but to him it was really a statement. He recognised the half of the face he could see. He had seen his picture many times on the daily computer intelligence screenings.

"Who wants to know?" Mark answered, waiting for Pablo to state his business, and sounding not a little apprehensive. Pablo handed him a business card which he politely reached out for, opening the door a little more to do so.

"Pablo Pinkerton", He replied. "I'm a local police officer, but what I do is very different from what you're used to Mark. I work with addicts to get help with their addiction. Can I come in and explain how it works please?"

Pablo stated his role as succinctly as possible, always trying to make it sound relevant before the potential client had a chance to reject him. He always sneaked their first name in too. That came across as friendly. He wouldn't conduct a conversation on the doorstep. If they weren't willing to let him in, he'd try another time when maybe they would. Of course he tried to look as relaxed and non-threatening as possible, always wearing casual non-uniform clothing.

Mark replied rather cheerfully.

"I've heard of you. you've been to see some of my mates."

Pablo liked to hear that. It made the initial breaking of the ice so much easier. He knew he was already working with quite a few of Mark's associates, which helps, but even when there was no prior link, he was always surprised at how readily he was allowed the opportunity to state his case to these drug-addicted criminals. They tended, in general, to be withdrawing, private, and wary people, shy of exposing themselves to the world at large. To mainstream society, they were not exactly invisible, but they definitely weren't a part of it. They were on the periphery, or in the underbelly, with their bad habits and undesirable lifestyles. They were not regarded kindly or with understanding. They were, after all, mostly criminals. For Pablo however, they were his work, and he saw them foremost as unfortunate people. To him, they were a complex challenge. He was surprised that over the past two years, he had only been refused entry on just two occasions. He had found to his surprise that after he had come to know them better, he didn't dislike them at all. He disliked their criminal activities, and he had no time for their addictions, but he didn't dislike them as people. They were really just like any other group of people; some smart, some not; some humorous, some not; some friendly, some not. After he had learned their stories, usually about messed up neglected or abusive childhoods, he actually felt quite sorry for them.

Mark opened the door more fully and retreated into the house.

"Come in" he said brightly.

Pablo stepped inside, slowly, allowing his eyes to adjust to the dim light. Inside the narrow hallway was clutter; discarded clothes, bags, shoes, and a bicycle. There was a stale smoky smell in the air mixed up with the distinct sweetness of cannabis. The place desperately needed some fresh air. He was always circumspect on entering an addict's home. There was usually more than one person there. In their own way, they were quite a sociable bunch. They didn't work, so they had a lot of time to kill each day, and spending it with like-minded associates made that easier. Additionally, they had to be in a small reliable coterie to ensure a reliable constant source of the drug of their choice. They mixed freely with their own kind. Pablo liked to know who exactly was there.

Some addicts or their associates were anti-police, and as he operated alone, he had to watch his own back.

Mark led him into the lounge where he sunk into a dingy armchair at right angles to, and on the other side of the sagging sofa. The sofa directly faced a large TV screen which was blaring out some dispute between two enraged people in a courtroom setting. It was only by visiting other people's homes that Pablo had any idea what day-time TV was like. He was always respectful inside someone else's home, of course, but he also seriously disliked competing with the noise of a TV when talking, and from what he could tell, such programmes were often on just for the sake of it. Now that he was there, it was unlikely that anyone was going to pay much attention to it anyway. Before mentioning the TV, he took in as much visual information as he could about the other fellow in the room. He was sitting in an old armchair to the right of the sofa. He looked to be of a similar age to Mark, but he didn't look emaciated like Mark did, which meant that he wasn't probably too much into heroin, yet, if at all. Pablo didn't recognise him, which was unusual. His research was extensive and he usually recognised subjects and their acquaintances before he was introduced to them. The lad looked relaxed, his face resting on one hand, studying him. Pablo didn't get the feeling that he might be a threat. He looked very directly at him and said "Hi".

"Hi" the lad said back. Somehow that was enough for Pablo to discern that he was feeling curious, rather than threatened. And Pablo was, after all, very good at reading body language. That came from twenty years of police work, bringing up four children, and being married to a woman of very few words. The only place for Pablo to sit was on the sofa, with Mark on his left and the other lad on his right. He didn't prefer to sit with one on each side. That was not a strategically strong position in case anything kicked off. He instinctively weighed up the risks according to his police training; Size of potential combatants, likely skill levels, overall physical fitness, likelihood or evidence of weapons, level of agitation or intoxication, any apparent injuries or disabilities, environment, mood etc. He saw no warning signals in particular, and according to his intuition and experience, he didn't consider himself at any particular risk. He would have to look out for spent needles left lying around and maybe blades too. He couldn't remain standing. That would not be conducive to generating the kind of relaxed non-threatening atmosphere he needed, in order to achieve the best outcome of this meeting. Mark was not known to be violent. Both lads were relatively lightly built, and he himself was highly trained in the art of self-defence techniques, and so, as he weighed things up, he was comfortable that he wasn't taking any undue risks by staying, and sitting. He sat down on the sofa, and rather sunk into it. He was a little concerned that he wouldn't be able to leap up particularly rapidly if he had to, but he forced his face to look relaxed, not concerned. He maintained peripheral vision to his right as he addressed Mark to his left.

"Mark, would you mind turning the TV off for a while please?"

As usual, there seemed to be some surprise when he asked this question. Presumably the TV went off so rarely that it was a bit of a shock to the system.

"OK" Mark muttered as he fumbled for the remote, which seemed to be buried somewhere down the side of his chair. Pablo looked directly at the lad to his right.

"I don't think I know you do I?" he queried.

The lad smiled. "Don't you? Well I am just a friend of Mark's." A predictably coy response.

Pablo just smiled back at him and left it at that. With the poor light in the room, Pablo's eyes were taking time to adjust. Even though it was the middle of the afternoon, natural light was being blocked out, and the single, dull, dirty light bulb that hung drably from the centre of the ceiling gave a low light. The glass coffee table in front of the sofa was adorned with no end of clutter; opened beer cans, used coffee mugs, spoons, a tobacco pouch, roll-up cigarette papers, fag stubs, lighters, a bong, scraps of folded paper, crisp packets, scrunched up sweet wrappers, and a few coins; no obvious weapons.

"Would you like a cup of tea?" Mark enquired brightly.

"Thank you for offering, Mark" Pablo replied, " but I'm fine thank you."

He wasn't normally offered anything, but in any case, he never accepted offers of food or drink inside client's homes. Apart from the unlikely event of something being spiked, the usual absence of hygiene was enough to put him off.

"Well" Pablo commenced, "is it ok for me to discuss police matters about you in front of your friend here?"

"No problem" Mark said, smiling. This didn't surprise Pablo. He well knew that the drug-taking fraternity were actually quite close, and they all seemed to know each other's business, which is why people like him tried to tap people like them for intelligence on others.

"Ok, I'll explain to you what I'm here for. As you well know Mark, my colleagues stop you regularly to check for drugs or stolen items. Sometimes you get arrested. Over the years you've been in and out of court, with various penalties imposed. Sometimes you're on probation. Sometimes you're not. But what you definitely are, is stuck in a vicious circle. It's my job to help you break that cycle if you want to, but only if you want to. I can't force you to do anything, but on the other hand, if you cooperate with me, I can help you get help, and it will take a lot of the heat off you from my colleagues."

"You talking about MEND ASS?" Mark queried.

Official bodies tended to shorten titles to acronyms, but this acronym had obviously been given a slightly comical twist. It was actually ENDDAS which stood for End Drug Addiction Services.

"That and a few other things Mark. If things went well, I might even be able to get you some training which could lead to a job."

Pablo realised that talking to someone like Mark about work was about as realistic at this time as talking about pigs flying, but he threw it in anyway. He wanted to sound as potentially helpful as possible. Addicts always needed quite some encouragement to try engagement.

"I've tried MEND ASS before. It didn't work." Mark used a tone that made it sound like there was no point in going on.

"Yes I know that Mark, but nobody succeeds the first time. It often takes a few attempts."

He didn't want to get into statistics, which were really rather depressing, but some addicts did eventually succeed, but it was probably more to do with where they were at mentally the time of engagement than anything else. They really needed to be totally fed up with the complications of their life to have any chance of success in rehabilitation. This sometimes happened when a close friend of theirs died from an overdose, or perhaps when they finally realised how close to death they were.

"Do you mind if we go through your story Mark so I better understand how you came to be where you are today? Then we'll be more able to determine what could really help you." Pablo had been very surprised when he first started this role, at how easily addicts opened up to him. It was partly due to his easy-going nature and that he seemed trustworthy, partly due to his years of police experience in interviewing people, and it seemed, partly due to the fact that most addicts liked to tell their story. Perhaps it was because no one normally took any interest in them. He had found that each one was quite different despite a lot of common background threads. He wanted to get Mark to open up personally. That would help build rapport. It would also undoubtedly demonstrate that whereas Mark claimed to have tried with ENDDAS and failed, he would be able to present the case that he hadn't tried hard enough or for long enough. It was well known that clients fell out of the system for the most trivial of reasons, and that they really did benefit from having a mentor to encourage them keep re-engaging, and it was the process of falling off the wagon, and getting back on that worked in some cases, eventually. Of course, some would suffer fatal overdoses in the meantime. Addicts who were cleaning up were more vulnerable to an accident than consistent users. They didn't always seem to grasp that if they had been clean for a while, their tolerance levels would have lowered, and a previous safe dose could now be fatal. A lot of overdoses were because of this effect. Sometimes of course, it would simply be down to bad luck; a batch of heroin was far stronger than usual, or had been diluted with a toxic substance. Users never knew how much a product had been cut, or thinned out, with something like talcum powder, chalk dust, or worse. They were always dicing with their lives. From a police perspective, if addicts were in treatment they committed a lot less crime, and that's why Pablo was paid to do this work.

Mark's mobile rang. The ringtone was some raucous pop song. He answered it but said nothing other than a few 'yeah's and a few 'no's, and then put the phone back in his pocket. Word had probably gone out that Mark had a visitor, and someone was ringing to see if things were ok.

Pablo spent about half an hour chatting with Mark, getting to know his pathway through various children's homes, peppered with occasional short stays with foster parents, and the journey of substance abuse. The important thing was that Mark was willing to receive help. Pablo had outlined the process and what the goals would be. He finished by reminding Mark that he would be monitoring his progress with the other agencies, and would be dropping in on him unannounced regularly, to see how he was getting on.

"You ok with that Mark?"

"No problem."

He seemed genuinely pleased that someone was interested in helping him. Pablo stood up and they shook hands. As he left he took one more good long look at the other lad. He didn't want to forget his face, and then he saw himself out. He re-emerged into the bright daylight, and was dazzled by the light as he took in the quietness and pleasantness of the estate. It was a sedate cul-de-sac with the houses built around a huge empty green. He thought to himself that you don't see that kind of waste of space any more on new estates. They really cram them in now.

The freshness of the air delighted and relieved him. When he was a kid, this would have been called a council estate, but these days that wouldn't really apply as a lot of these sturdy pragmatic but rather plain houses and maisonettes had passed into private ownership. He walked back to his car, trying to look reasonably anonymous, his shoulder bag hanging over his shoulder. A bag that contained a few essential props, like a gas canister, a retractable baton, and a set of handcuffs, just in case things ever turned nasty. He was a big muscular man, well able to handle himself, and he carried an air of confidence about him which reflected his training, experience and self-belief. But he also believed in not tempting fate, hence the hidden weaponry. He also always wore a thick stiff leather coat; much less chance of being pricked by a stray abandoned used needle. He had been doing this job for about two years, and he loved it. It was right up his street. It was challenging, interesting, independent, and he felt that it made excellent use of his interpersonal skills, and the rare success story made it really rewarding.

A toddler on a bike with stabilisers wobbled towards him. He stood still and pulled himself back against an old privet hedge to allow the toddler to pass.

"Sorry" a young podgy mother said as she walked briskly behind the toddler, fag in one hand, mobile phone in the other.

"No problem" Pablo replied pleasantly, smiling at her. It interested him that for so many families on this estate, life went on so normally. Yet, one or two here diced with death itself on a daily basis, and they were the sons and daughters, brothers and sisters or cousins of some of these families.

Mark was local to the station where Pablo had his own office, so he drove straight back there. As he entered the building the stark contrast hit him. Orderly, clean, with personnel dressed smartly and cleanly in uniforms or suits. Generally he spent very little time in his office. To be honest, he felt it was an unnecessary luxury. He could access his files on any computer throughout the force. He opened up the computer system and wrote about Mark whilst the information was still fresh in his mind. He kept meticulous records of visits, and made comprehensive notes of what he had learned from meetings before things slipped out of his mind. He didn't make any notes whilst with a client. That would seem too police-like, and would probably worry them, so he had to exercise his memory instead. One of the many things he liked about this role was the lack of paperwork. He only made notes as he wished, and he only had to make one written report per month to his district commander about progress. Bliss. And he enjoyed writing his reports anyway. He was proud of the amount of work he did, and the rapport he was building with his client group.

He phoned Cathy at ENDDAS

"Hi Cathy. Got another one for you."

She sounded a little bemused as she answered.

"Which one this time?"

"Mark Foster."

"Mark Foster" she slowly repeated as she entered his name into her system.

"Mark Foster, Mark Foster, there he is. We had him for a few months in 2006. Looks like we had him on a script, but he kept using, so he got binned."

"Ok" Pablo simply replied. "Well, if you can book him in for a triage, I'd be grateful, and I'll do my best to help keep him engaged this time."

"Ok" she agreed. "Give me his mobile and we'll contact him for an appointment. I'll let you know when it is."

"Cheers."

He felt that this inter-agency cooperation was such a good step forward. The police could do a lot to help channel addicts into the programme. ENDDAS provided the expert counselling and chemical alternatives to street drugs, namely Subutex or Methadone scripts. The users wouldn't need to commit so much crime to pay for their drugs and they would get healthier. It was a win-win situation. The client would have to submit to weekly counselling sessions preceded by urine tests to ensure that they were not then still using heroin. The Subutex was a blocker, deleting any effect heroin would normally have, and Methadone was a safer alternative to heroin, which under their supervision, would be prescribed in smaller and smaller doses over a suitable period of time, in the hope of weaning them completely off. Not surprisingly, the vast majority of addicts went for the Methadone option.

There was a tap on his door as a familiar face peeked through the doorway.

"Ok to come in for a mo, mate?"

"Of course Steven. It's good to see you mate. Come in."

He and Steven had worked together on response a few years earlier, and had got on really well. Steven was a younger officer, but he was mature and sensible beyond his years. Pablo thought he looked a little grey and tired, but he didn't say anything.

"Still enjoying cosying up to the criminal fraternity?" Steven enquired mischievously.

"Loving it mate. Nobody gives me any hassle, and seriously, it is a worthwhile role. You know that."

Most fellow officers regarded Pablo's role with suspicion, considering that it involved such close liaison with high-profile offenders. They didn't consider it a role for a police officer, but Steven was one of the few who saw its value. He himself had lost a nephew to a heroin overdose a few years earlier, so he was particularly sensitive to these issues.

After some banter and small talk, Steven got to the point.

"Pablo, have you seen Jack Bruges yet?"

"Give me a chance mate. He's only been out for a couple of weeks, but he is on the list. Anyway, surely he's POU?"

The Prolific Offender Units had been introduced about four years earlier at the same time as Pablo's role was devised. Their role was to deliver a major part of the new Offender Management Programme. They were multi-agency units comprising staff from the health authorities, the probation service, and the police service. Ordinarily these organisations were not geared up to communicate with each other, with an ingrained reluctance to share, borne out of fear of reprisals under the data protection act. However, now the government was directing them to talk to each other and to share information under the auspices of reducing crime. This was about breaking glass walls between different organisations, and encouraging them to let down their barriers for the greater good. It took a big push from government at high levels within these organisations to bring about a sea change in attitudes, but it was a sensible and useful step forward.

"No, he's not. He's just released on licence, which means he's pretty much free as a bird."

"He sees probation."

"Big deal."

He gave Pablo a look that reflected his disparaging view of probation.

"Ok. So what's your beef with him?"

"He's pushing hard drugs into the comp' where my daughter goes. My missus is livid, and I promised her I'd try to do something."

"Fair enough buddy. I'll make him a priority. I remember nicking him once quite a few years ago for an assault. He was a right arse in front of people, but when you got him on his own, he was like a different bloke, quite reasonable really."

"Thanks mate."

They shook hands affectionately, and Steven left looking a little happier than when he had walked in. Seeing him reminded Pablo of the overdoses. Over the past two years, he'd had five. And in fact none of those five had actually engaged in the process of rehabilitation. They were simply people who had accepted his occasional contact, but who were not ready yet to engage properly. He had built up some rapport with them, but was still trying to persuade them to try something remedial. His very first client was a lad handed over to him by his predecessor. A lad called Jo. He was just about to finish a prison sentence for possession, and a placement in a residential rehabilitation centre had been earmarked for him. All Pablo had to do was visit him in prison to sell him the scheme. This he tried his very best to do, but it was like talking to a brick wall. Jo couldn't see how lucky he was to be offered a place like that, which really was like gold dust. He generously said he'd think about it. Pablo tried to get across the seriousness of his choices; either to try to get or stay clean, or go back to the old ways, which were fraught with danger. Jo didn't get it. It was so frustrating. He was released without taking up any help from Pablo. Just two days later he was found dead in a public toilet with a needle hanging out of his arm. The tolerance reduction effect.

Then there was Emma. A young lady who through no fault of her own had been passed from institution to institution as a child and had never really known love or proper parenting, and like many others from a similar background, had never learnt her self-worth, or how to self-discipline. In time she drifted into alcohol and drug abuse, which soon spiralled into heroin abuse. One sad day she unwittingly took a dose too strong for her, and it put her to sleep like a terminally sick animal. Then there was Brian, a guy aged about forty who resided in a doss house occupied solely by drug addicts and alcoholics who had all been taken off the streets. Pablo visited him regularly there, but he could not squeeze even a tiny amount of optimism into him. Brian was so disillusioned with life. Heroin blocked out the hopelessness and the penetrating sense of total loss. Once upon a time, he had been a 'normal' guy with a home, a family, and a respectable job. The marriage breakdown and the loss of family life was the start of the complete crumbling of his life, which in a few short years brought him into this miserable, shameful existence. He was deeply embarrassed and humiliated, and he regularly 'accidentally' overdosed, but each time so far, someone had called an ambulance, and a shot of adrenalin bought him yet another chance of life. Pablo would challenge him about this brinkmanship, but this guy was genuinely past caring. He looked Pablo straight in the eye, and said without passion or regret,

"I don't care what happens." He really didn't.

The day arrived when the ambulance was called too late to save him.

The next casualty was just like the first. A man in his late twenties called Steve who was really popular and full of life, and criminally active. He was a heroin addict, but a decent spell inside prison cleaned him up. On his release, he was apparently determined to stay clean, and it did seem to his family that he possessed the strength of character to see that commitment through. Unfortunately shortly after his release, it was his birthday. Well, you can't refuse a little treat on your birthday can you? Trouble was, the old tolerance issue again. His birthday meant a very special journey, to meet his maker.

Finally there was Robert, the thirty five year old cocaine addict. He had been arrested so many times that he regarded himself as mates with all the staff at the local old-bill. And he was a very personable, co-operative guy. It's just that he had to mug people to pay for his habit. And he'd had this habit for too long. His heart protested and he died of a heart attack whilst out pushing his bicycle up a hill one sunny afternoon. Thirty five years old, but his heart had been worn out by the repeated hyper stimulation of drugs.

These things sharpened up Pablo's act. He had to do what he could. It really was a matter of life or death.

Chapter 2

Pablo may have loved the variety and the cut and thrust of challenging police work, but his home life was quiet, and that's how he liked it. He and his wife Delilah lived in splendid isolation in gloriously quiet countryside. At work, he was dealing with demanding people and challenging situations in the city, and he did like the feeling that his people-skills were being put to great use. When he was off work however, he liked to recharge his batteries by being quietly creative, alone. He loved gardening and DIY. These things took a lot of time and they absorbed him. Over the decades, he had developed a very wide skill set from the practical challenges he undertook and accomplished earlier in his life. When their four kids had been younger he loved to do things as a family, but now the three boys had grown up and left home now leaving only the youngest child at home, Sarah, in her late teens, and that left him free to take on ever more demanding projects.

He and Delilah were like a well-oiled machine. They had worked well together in all their projects, and in bringing up four wonderful people. They had run businesses together. She had made a fantastic mum and homemaker. As far as she was concerned, that had been her one and only calling in life. She had never wanted anything else. Unlike Pablo, she was a great cook and she always provided lovely meals for him when he got home. They had an old-fashioned relationship, and they were both fine with that. He was the breadwinner, and she was the home maker. They say opposites attract and that was certainly the case for them. He was a large strong man. She was a slim delicate woman. He was rather gregarious. She tended to be shy. He was impulsive, she was cautious. She noticed things visibly around her very keenly. He walked around with blinkers on, yet he was the one who could readily visualise what a wreck of a house could look and feel like after improvements, whereas she could only literally see the mess and struggled to see hypothetical potential. They had different complementary strengths and with the deep love they felt for each other and their children, their relationship was a symbiotic sanctum.

Strangely, neither of them expressed love in a verbal effusive way. They had both come from homes where love had never been expressed verbally, and that seemed to have influenced both of them in their adult lives. Instead, they demonstrated their love for each other in practical ways. Her primary love language was acts of service, and that's how she demonstrated her love to him; cooking, being a home-maker, and being a faithfully keen sexual partner. His primary love language was physical touch, and he was very affectionate and tactile with her. They had a lot of sex. They treated each other with consideration, commitment, devotion, practical support, and quality time together. They had met when he was just sixteen, and she was fourteen. They had grown into adulthood entwined in each other, and now they had been married for twenty nine years. They were both very proud of their staying power.

Of course, no relationship is ever perfect. He had always found her somewhat closed and emotionally distant, and for her, she found him painfully open and over-friendly with all and sundry, and over the years, this had made her feel insecure. It was an issue that they had never properly confronted and dealt with. Instead they counted their blessings, and they were entering a new exciting era. The previous summer, they had been blessed with their first grandchild, and they hadn't even reached their fifties. Pablo still thought of Delilah as beautiful, even after so long together. She was exceptional in many ways, and one was that she still weighed the same currently as she had done on her wedding day nearly thirty years earlier, so it was easy for him to still see the attractive vibrant teenager in her that he had fallen deeply in love with so long ago. He was four stone heavier, and she sometimes teased him about that. All in all though, he felt that he lived a charmed life in many ways.

One sunny day, he visited his first-line supervisor, a CID sergeant half his own age, called Caine. Caine shared an office with Inspector Framlin who supervised several departments, including the Prolific Offender Unit to which Pablo was loosely attached. Generally, Caine was preoccupied, and had much better things to do than take any real interest in what work Pablo was doing. He had never been out on a visit with him, or discussed his role with him, or enquired about progress. Pablo regarded him as a supervisor on paper only. He was one of those ambitious savvy types who concentrated on what looked good on his CV. There were a lot of those types in the police service, and they're the ones who progress quickly through its ranks. If you were exceptional in the role you performed, that was classed as just doing your job. To get on, you had to be able to manipulate the system, and that was a different skill entirely. Caine wasn't essentially conscientious about his actual work. That was only important and relevant in relation to how it could make him look good on paper and nudge up his future promotion prospects. However, he was pleasant enough, and for Pablo, it was nice to be left alone to do his job as he saw fit with no interference. He only ever saw Caine if he made the trip to his office for some reason. On this occasion he needed to arrange some time off. Caine would have to authorise it. They chatted in a jovial amicable care-free fashion. Caine was saying how the boss was rather stressed out at the moment because he was under pressure to lose one of his staff back to 'response'. Policing priorities changed regularly, depending mainly on government dictates. Flavour of the month might depend upon current Home Office perception of public concern. Or it might be that senior officer reshuffling would lead to new initiatives being churned out by people new in post, keen to make their mark. Presently, shoring up officer strength on immediate response units, the guys at the cutting edge, was being prioritised at the expense of specialist roles. It's what the public wanted, understandably. Support roles were theoretically subordinate to 'response', but in practice, support roles were regarded as the cream, involving as they did, more sociable hours, less stress, less unpredictability, fewer urgent demands, specialist training, extra qualifications and therefore more kudos, usually less danger, and often more financial perks and the privilege of plain clothes to boot.

Caine suddenly changed his countenance from relaxed and unguarded to measured and earnest. He had just realised that he had said too much. He continued defensively.

"Of course Pablo, your role is safe. He's not considering changing your role at all."

He was full of reassurance and succour and Pablo's only thought was 'he doth protest too much'. They moved quickly and efficiently onto the topic for which Pablo was visiting. They booked his annual leave as requested, and he left Caine in peace to carry on working on whatever was good for his promotion prospects. As he walked away from the office he wondered what would happen to him now that his role was going to be terminated.

It was a full week later that he was summoned back to the office to see the boss. He met with Mr Framlin on his own. There was always a large dose of decorum when meeting with a boss. All officers over the rank of sergeant were referred to as 'Sir' and had to be deferred to, so unlike American cop films where all ranks seemed to be on first name terms and were all very blunt and rude to each other. He sat down demurely opposite Mr Framlin, the desk between them symbolising the existential divide, and respectfully waited for Mr. Framlin to start the proceedings. He was a portly amiable man in his late thirties. He was always business-like in a manner befitting his rank, but he nevertheless managed not to be officious, distant or overbearing, unlike many others of his rank or above. Pablo admired and respected that about him.

"Pablo, you know that all specialist departments have got to find personnel to go back to response don't you?"

"Yes sir."

"Well, I've got to find two. One from POU and one from prisoner-handling."

"Yes sir." He was being subdued. He knew what was coming.

"I'm afraid that the axe is going to fall on your role. We're not allowed to reduce our POU personnel by law. I'm sorry. I have no choice."

He looked vexed but he had chosen to cut straight to the chase. Pablo sat stony-faced looking at him, feeling so disappointed. He so loved his role. He felt defiant. He had to fight for this role. Mr Framlin continued explaining his plan.

"'m not putting you back on response Pablo. I'm moving one of the POU officers back and I want you to replace him on the POU. You're very good at what you're doing, and your skills and experience will fit in perfectly in the POU."

He rightly presumed that this would be far more preferable to Pablo than going back on response with its earlies, lates, and nights.

"Thank you sir, but I'd like to make an appointment to see the Superintendent please."

"I can arrange that if you want Pablo, but if it's about this move, I can assure you it won't make a blind bit of difference. He has made his mind up about this. There's nothing you can do."

Pablo studied his sincere face for a few moments while he mulled over the corner he was in. He wasn't feeling selfish. He was feeling disappointed because his role was amazingly productive, and from a policing perspective, it was a crime to abolish it.

"He doesn't know what I do, does he sir?"

"He does Pablo, but not everybody believes that this is the best way to use police resources, and now that the pressure is on …."

Pablo didn't believe that this superintendent either knew much about what he did, or cared. Senior officers these days were more involved in managing budgets and making sure the right boxes were ticked, than concerning themselves with directly fighting crime per sae. Pablo sat there looking dejected. Then he said appealingly

"Does he know that for each addict I help get into a programme, that individual stops committing burglaries or thefts, or whatever else it was that he was doing to fund his habit? That's a hell of a lot of crime reduction."

Mr Framlin looked equally frustrated. He knew that what Pablo was saying was true, but he had to maintain a fixed approach.

"I'm sorry Pablo. You start on the POU a week on Monday."

He looked at Pablo with that sympathetic but determined look. Pablo capitulated.

"Is that all sir?"

"Yes Pablo. We'll be very happy to have you working on the POU."

He looked relieved that this little ordeal was over now.

"Thank you sir" Pablo replied mechanically, and he left.

So disappointed. He had lost his dream job.

Pablo knew the POU office. It was established on the ground floor of the Probation offices. Because of his close involvement in the drugs scene and his loose attachment to the POU, he already regularly attended their weekly meetings to help provide insights into developments out in the field, and to give first-hand accounts of his interaction with particular individuals of interest. Therefore he had come to know a little about his fellow police officers on the unit too. Debra was from CID; an old-school, long-in-the-tooth, and very much feet-on-the-ground type. She had a lovely dry, cynical sense of humour. She always seemed to be in a good mood. She had been a police officer for many years and had been on the POU from its inception a few years earlier. The other partner who was remaining on the unit was Alan, a young-in-service thirty-year-old cocky so-and-so. Pablo's only experience of him had been during these multi-partnership meetings, where this young officer with just three years' service, came across as very full of himself. He seemed much more self-assured than his experience justified. He spoke as if he had many, many years of experience, and was the most knowledgeable person present. That irritated Pablo rather. He considered it disrespectful. He didn't expect to get along with Alan too well.

In his last week in his independent role, he visited all of his clients, explaining the changes and letting them know that he wouldn't be able to supervise them as he had been doing. Strangely they were quite disappointed, but also fatalistic. For them this was life. They were accustomed to being let down, especially by organisations, and they accepted it as second nature. He explained to the ones that he felt would most benefit from his involvement that he would continue to maintain some contact if at all possible, but at this stage couldn't say how much or how often. As far as the police service was concerned, there was no ongoing duty of care towards his clients. He had been moved from one box to another. End of story. Simple. Clean-cut. No consequences. However, he was a human being, not just a faceless cog in an unfeeling organisation, and he didn't share the organisation's nonchalance. He would do what he could to maintain a little support for these people. Real people. He had come to care about them, and even to admire the efforts they were making to change their lifestyles.

On the Monday of his transfer, he attended the POU office and found his new desk directly opposite Alan's. This was going to be confrontational. Alan wasn't the best person for him to be sitting opposite. The health staff in the unit had their own offices down the corridor, but the police members shared a large open plan office with half a dozen probation officers. There was also a young team-helper called Aurora who was responsible for helping everyone with administrative tasks, such as finding things, copying things, contacting people for meetings, updating diaries and computer records etc. She wore her heart on her sleeve, reacted theatrically to everything, and was the source of much good-natured amusement. She was undeniably sweet and lovable, but unavoidably comical too. Every office needs someone like that in it as an antidote to the mundane. Debra sat at a desk behind him, with a probation officer in front of her.

She brought him up to speed in her inimitably dry and whimsical manner; their job was to interrogate the police intelligence system on a daily basis to keep on the ball with the current state of play with all the prolific offenders, of whom there were about thirty in their district. They worked closely with their colleagues in probation and health and had a duty to share their intelligence with them. It was the police personnel who would conduct weekly home visits to offenders who were on licence from prison, and either they or their probation colleagues could make visits to offenders in prison. These normally occurred shortly before their release on licence to explain the conditions of the licence on them - basically that the POU had them by the balls until their licence expired. They also worked closely with a partner charity called Roofed who found accommodation for offenders. They also liaised with an agency known by their initials of WTFN who tried to find training and jobs for problem cases such as recovering drug addicts and prolific offenders. Part of helping offenders reduce their offending was to help them achieve settled lives, and that included accommodation and, if at all possible, honest work.

Occasionally a police officer on the unit would accompany probation officers during one of their routine interviews with a visiting client at the probation offices. There were also the multi-agency meetings to attend here in the probation offices, and the weekly police strategy meeting held at police headquarters where their input would be invaluable because of their direct personal involvement in Prolific Offender cases. It all sounded pretty busy but easy-going to Pablo. In his now defunct role, he had needed to resort to his charm and powers of persuasion to get results. Here they simply used the carrot and stick method. The offenders would be offered a lot of practical and very useful support, but on the other hand, if they failed to co-operate sufficiently, they would be simply arrested and taken back to prison, their release licence being summarily revoked.

Pablo asked Debra a few questions.

"Who decides if a licence is to be revoked?"

"Their probation officer really, but if we ask nicely, they'll do it for us no problem" she added with a knowing smile.

"Are we answerable to anyone here?"

"Not really. The bosses sort things out at their level. The probation boss, Mr Harris, is absolutely lovely. You couldn't ask for a better boss. He takes a lot of interest in what we do here. Only Caine and Mr. Framlin give us any kind of supervision."

"Caine?" he queried.

She immediately knew what he was saying.

"Yeah we don't see much of him, it's usually just the boss. It's quiet here Pablo. Keep your head down, do your job, and no one bothers you." She smiled again. She obviously liked it here.

"One final question" he added.

"Go on."

"Why is that girl named after part of a nipple?"

She smiled broadly. "I think you're getting Aurora and Areola confused."

"Oh yes. Silly me."

They both smiled. They liked each other.

Over the next few weeks he slipped seamlessly into his new role. Debra only worked three days a week, and on some of the days when she was not in, Alan and he had to cover meetings and visits between them. It was on these days that Pablo managed to get out on his own, and often he would make time to drop in on one of his old clients. He wanted them to know that someone still cared about them.

Alan had made it clear that he thought that home visits were a waste of time. He was more than happy to cover the meetings, when he could give everyone else the benefit of his deep insights and wisdom. Between the three of them they had to find a harmonious way of managing their joint role. Initially this revealed deep-seated conflicts between Pablo and Alan. Pablo had firmly brought his mentoring style with him from his previous role, and he wanted the role to be as dynamic as possible. Alan by contrast was cynical and uncaring. He saw the clients more as a challenge to be heavily managed and censored. Debra was ever the diplomat valuing both sides of the argument. The result was a lot of heated arguments between Alan and Pablo in the first few weeks together, each trying to justify their opinion to the other. One might have expected them to have become the best of enemies. They were both very strong characters. They were both opinionated, and yet after these contentious early weeks, they resolved their differences quite happily, and to everyone's surprise, they grew to respect and like each other. They became good friends, despite their initial mutual misgivings. Their loud strong exchanges seemed to have cleared the air between them, although they had caused much alarm and consternation amongst the probation officers who had never witnessed such heated arguments between two staff members before. Probation officers were clearly a very different breed to police officers.

Chapter 3

One dull but dry late winter morning in March 2008, Pablo was at the office with Debra. It was about lunchtime, when they got a phone call. Debra had handed him the phone saying dryly that it was the boss, for him. Why would the boss want to speak to him? That was unusual. The boss regularly attended the probation offices and spoke to all three of them, usually as a matter of routine after some other engagement there. He took the handset rather gingerly.

"Hello sir, Pablo here."

"Pablo, I know you've got training this afternoon, but I want you to come into my office first, ok?"

"Ok sir. Just me?"

"Yes Pablo. Just you."

"Ok. I'll be there shortly."

He replaced the receiver. It seemed strange that the boss wanted to speak to just him and not his two colleagues as well. Maybe it was something to do with the training, but why didn't he say over the phone? Pablo felt a little uncomfortable. The boss's office was at the police station, a ten minute walk away from the probation service premises where Pablo was. He didn't know if there was a problem. He wasn't aware of anything. He hadn't heard any rumours. He marched on. He would find out soon enough. When he arrived at Mr Framlin's office, the door was open, and he was sitting behind his large desk. Pablo stood in the doorway and politely tapped the door to announce his arrival.

"Come in Pablo and shut the door behind you."

He sounded business-like as usual, his voice was controlled and even, but nevertheless, Pablo sensed something ominous. Mr Framlin didn't look directly at him. He was looking intently at some paperwork on his desk directly in front of him. Pablo entered, feeling that the need to shut the door was a bad sign. There was nobody else present. That was a good sign. He had worked under Mr Framlin for about nine months. The bosses got moved from one department to another quite regularly, so he'd got to know quite a few. Mr Framlin was a reasonable and fair guy who took a genuine interest in his staff. He invited Pablo to sit in the chair in front of his desk. Pablo sat down rather tentatively, obviously wondering what was going on. It always seemed that the bosses had taller chairs than the ones on this side of the desk. Mr. Framlin got straight to the point. No small talk first.

"Pablo, I'm afraid I have to inform you of a complaint made against you."

Pablo froze. Thoughts began to race around his head. He felt his insides floating up and down. Anxiety was not a feeling familiar to him, but now he was feeling strange butterflies fluttering around inside his stomach. People say butterflies, but butterflies are pretty, and this didn't feel pretty at all. He felt ever so slightly sick. Mr Framlin cut to the chase, as was his style. He read out the details of the complaint in full, firstly that he had unlawfully harassed Miss Cassie Woolridge in writing, by telephone and by email in an effort to engage her in an unwanted relationship, and secondly that between March 2007 and February 2008 he had accessed police records pertaining to Miss Cassie Woolridge for a purpose other than in accordance with his police duty. He finished with the official caution, 'you do not have to say anything,' etc, which was so familiar to Pablo because it was what he said to suspects when he was dealing with them. He then invited Pablo to make a reply if he wished to do so. Pablo was a pretty clear-thinking person normally, but he was so shocked at the charges, that his mind wasn't functioning properly. He was processing that he had suddenly changed from being an investigator to being the investigated. He shockingly suddenly found himself on the wrong side of the equation. And he was confused. The complaint might be concerning Cassie, but surely she wouldn't have been the one to make it. She had been one of his former clients, and was someone he had formed a genuine friendship with, although he hadn't seen her for over four months. He was struggling to believe that she would make any allegations against him. Why would she? They had always got on so well. Pablo looked up briefly at him, trying to focus better. He hoarsely whispered.

"Who is the complainant?"

"Cassie Woolridge" Mr Framlin repeated.

Surely it had been her boyfriend Marlon? He thought this because there was a history to this story. But Mr Framlin confirmed it was actually Cassie. He was still shocked. She was a heroin addict, but she had done so well after accepting his help.

"I can't believe she'd make a complaint against me" Pablo said quietly, more to himself than Mr Framlin, looking puzzled and probably confused. His face pointing towards the desk, but his eyes were somewhere vacant in the middle distance. He knew that this was not the time and place for him to make his representations. As for the bit about accessing police records he just thought that that was complete bullshit. It was his job to be familiar with police records, particularly about drug addicts. He wondered why some office-bound former police officer comfortably ensconced in a plush office in the internal affairs department somewhere, drinking coffee all day and carrying out his duties at a very leisurely comfortable pace, would conjure up that kind of accusation for no good reason. He must have been in his rarefied environment too long, and had completely lost touch with reality.

Mr Framlin completed his official duty as supervisor by handing Pablo a form nine which was the official record of service of complaint. Then he kindly said

"I'm really sorry Pablo. I don't enjoy having to do this."

He was being totally professional, but it was nice to see a little pain in his eyes. He then did his best to be helpful. He firmly instructed Pablo to see his federation representative as soon as possible. He also said that pending the investigation being completed, Pablo would be suspended from his normal role. With an air of appreciation for the traumatic nature of this event, Mr Framlin told him to go home now and come back in the morning when he would find him something to do behind the scenes until the complaint had been dealt with.

"Prisoner handling probably" he added.

Pablo got up slowly, feeling rather dazed, fazed and alarmed. He was experiencing a confused mixture of emotions. He felt the urgent need to act defensively. As far as he was concerned, he had done nothing wrong. He was undoubtedly a man of integrity. Even when no one was watching him, he always did the right thing as far as he was concerned. Trouble was, the organisation and he didn't always see eye to eye. He tried to suppress his bubbling fears. He felt guilty until proven innocent. He felt trapped, like there was nothing he could do. How do you prove a negative?

He thanked Mr Framlin politely and quickly left his office. He retraced the ten minute walk back to the probation offices in something of a trance. He hoped that Debra wouldn't still be there, but she was, still busy with her computer. She looked up at him quizzically.

"I thought you'd gone off to training for the afternoon?"

He tried to seem nonchalant, normal, even.

"There's been a change of plan" he said rather mysteriously and without looking directly at her.

"Really? That sounds rather intriguing" she said with an inquisitive smile on her face. She obviously didn't suspect that anything might be wrong.

He really didn't want to talk about it. It was embarrassing, humiliating, confusing.

"You'll find out soon enough" he added quietly.

He knew that he wouldn't be coming back here for a while, but he didn't want to make a scene, so he quickly picked up a few possessions from his desk that he didn't want to lose. He left photos of his family in place. No one else would want them. Most importantly he quickly looked up a contact number for the Fed' Rep', and left.

He focussed. The first step was to enlist the support of his Fed' Rep' as soon as possible. He needed to share this burden. He knew who that was. Roger Robertson. He had chatted to him several times over the past few years, when Roger had been a community officer in one of the rural towns that Pablo covered in his former role with drug addicts. He had found him rather drab and lacklustre, with the typical disdainful attitude towards addicts which hadn't been very helpful. Roger had fairly recently moved into the federation role, housed in private offices on a plush new business estate on the edge of the city. No doubt he wore a very smart civilian suit now. He was about the same age as Pablo, and was presumably looking forward to seeing out the last couple of years of his service doing a plush easy Monday to Friday job as a Fed' Rep'.

Pablo found a phone in an unoccupied office. He phoned Roger and was very relieved to get hold of him straight away.

"Rodge, I need to see you immediately, if not before."

"What's up Pablo?" he asked in a flat monotone manner. His voice had always struck Pablo as dull and emotionless.

"I've been served a form nine."

"What for?"

"You know my old role was working out in the field with drug addicts?"

"Yes, and you're on the POU now, right?"

"Yes, but one of my former clients has alleged harassment."

"Ok. That sounds fairly serious. I was busy this afternoon, but you'd better come straight over and give me that form nine, and we'll get the ball rolling."

Roger confirmed his office address and as Pablo was getting the train to work these days, he had to get a cab to Roger's place. When he got there he had to ring a buzzer to be allowed into the open-plan office. A young lady answered his call, and told him to wait for Robert to come to the door. This he did shortly. They shook hands. Roger's appearance surprised him. Pablo had only ever seen him in uniform, yet here he was wearing a smart dark blue suit, with clean highly polished shoes and an unobtrusive tie. He looked good in a suit because although he was not tall, he was lean, and a suit hung well on him. He looked quite dapper. He led him through the big open office to a private interview room somewhere in the background. For Pablo, it was something of a walk of shame. All the subtly prying eyes would know he was in some kind of trouble. He didn't look directly at anyone, but his peripheral vision informed him that he was walking down a corridor of desks attended by a mixture of men and women. Some would be officers, but most were civilian support staff. It seemed noticeably different to a normal police premises; much cleaner; a lot less clutter; the sound of a commercial radio station; the smell of strong, real coffee. He tried his best not to look furtive or execrable, deliberately holding his shoulders back, much as they felt like cowering forwards, holding his gaze directly ahead towards Roger in front of him. The interview room was sparsely furnished, apart from a few comfortable office chairs and a big modern desk. It felt like it was rarely used. They sat down.

"What's this all about Pablo?"

"It's malicious, but it's not Cassie. It's her boyfriend."

"What do you mean?"

"I worked with Cassie for almost the whole of the two years that I was the Harm Reduction Officer, and I got on with her great, and she did really well. She even got a job as a carer in the end. She was a high-calibre person compared to the rest of them, but towards the end, her partner, the bloke she lived with, got all arsey apparently. He didn't want her seeing me anymore because she got on too well with me. So he was going to put in a complaint about me to queer the pitch for me, but Cassie talked him out of it, but she had to agree not to see me anymore."

"When was that?"

"It must have been early last summer."

"Were you having a relationship with her Pablo?"

"Fuck off! She's a heroin addict. How stupid do you think I am? Anyway, even if she wasn't, I don't do that sort of thing. I've got a fabulous wife."

"Sorry, Pablo, I have to ask. Go on. Did you stop seeing her?"

"I told her that I wasn't going to be bullied by her boyfriend, and that it was her choice as to whether she wanted to carry on the contact or not. I was happy either way, but I wanted it to be her choice, not his."

"And?"

"She wanted to keep up the contact. She found my support and advice really helpful."

"So what happened with the boyfriend?"

"Nothing. She just made sure he didn't know that we were still meeting. By this time it wasn't very often anyway. She was off drugs, mostly, I think."

"Weren't you afraid he might find out and put in a complaint?"

"It was a distinct possibility, but what could he complain about? I was just doing my job."

Pablo paused and contemplated his feelings, then added

"Anyway, I wasn't going to allow him to dictate what I could or could not do."

"But he could have made all kinds of allegations."

"Yes, but they would have been malicious, without a leg to stand on. What I didn't envisage was that he could get Cassie onside with him."

At the thought of this, Pablo frowned deeply, the betrayal needling him painfully, and made him feel scared.

"And that's what you think this is all about?"

Roger looked at Pablo intently, looking for signs of lying.

"Undoubtedly. I've done nothing wrong Rodge. It's malicious, and Marlon put her up to it. Surely it won't go anywhere?"

He looked at Roger as if pleading with him to tell him that it will all be ok.

"You've not had a malicious complaint made against you before have you Pablo?"

He looked at Pablo as if to say 'you don't know how much shit they can throw at you just because some nasty piece of work wants to hurt you'.

"I've never had any complaints made against me Rodge, and that's not because I avoid work, like some people, it's because I do my job well, and I'm always fair. I' don't get people's backs up"

Roger maintained his even monotoned approach. He continued flatly.

"But you think he's behind this, not her?"

"Absolutely. Not that it matters. The complaint's been made, but she has no reason to complain about me. He's put her up to it. I'm a hundred percent sure of it. I sent her a Christmas card, and no doubt that is what sparked all this off. That must have annoyed him, and he's got her over a barrel. He pays the rent."

Roger looked at him with a little disbelief. Officers normally acted in a way to protect their backs. Sending a client a Christmas card when their partner believed that they didn't see you anymore was not a very sensible or cautious thing to do. His eyes spoke. His voice stayed quiet. Then he carried on. He read the form carefully.

"The complaint says you were trying to force her into an unwanted relationship."

"That's so fucking ridiculous. She agreed to see me right from the beginning. I've met her daughter, her mum and dad, her sisters, her partner, her drugs worker. How would I have met all of them if I was forcing her? That can all be verified with them."

"Did you keep records of your contact with her?"

"Of course. I kept records of all meetings with all clients. They're on my computer. Day, date, time , place. Anyone can see them. I couldn't have met her without her consent. Each meeting was arranged fairly randomly, at different places. For me to have met her without her consent I would have been the world's best clairvoyant. She was clearly compliant. Anyway, half the time she was calling me to arrange to see me. Her phone records will show that."

"Always business?"

"Of course."

"Always during job time?"

Of course."

"Always?"

"Absolutely always. I told you, I am a happily married man Rodge. I know that sounds corny, but it's true."

Roger recognised the sincerity in his voice and eyes. He believed him. He moved on to the second allegation.

"Unlawful use of police data?"

"No idea. Presumably it's the Internal Affairs department being completely anal and going for something which makes an interesting change from the usual dross they have to deal with, but it's just a technicality."

"What do you mean?"

"Mr Framlin explained that this one was about me looking at her criminal record after she was no longer my client. She wasn't POU."

Roger looked puzzled. "I can't see why they would throw that one in. We can access anyone's record. That's what it's there for."

He sat back in his chair, looking concerned.

"Have you been suspended?"

"No. The boss just said I couldn't do my normal duties. I'd have to be a glorified secretary or something like that until this all gets sorted."

"No Pablo. You can't carry on working with all of this crap hanging over your head. You'll have to go sick."

"Really? What with? I'm fine."

"Stress. Go and see your GP. Tell him what's going on and he'll sign you off until it's over."

Pablo sat silently for a moment. He wasn't used to throwing sickies. This idea didn't sit easily with him. Roger read his misgivings.

"Look Pablo. They're effectively laying you off. There's no point in going in just for the sake of it. Going off with stress is normal under these circumstances. Really. You'll be on full pay for the first six months, and then the second six months if it goes on any longer, are covered by the fed."

"What do you mean, six months? It can't take that long to sort out can it?"

"How long is a piece of string?"

Pablo looked at him as if to say that's not very helpful.

"Let's put it this way Pablo, nobody ever seems to be in a hurry when it comes to complaints. Things usually drag on for quite a long time, so just try to chill out in the meantime and enjoy the break."

"Great." he said sarcastically. "So I just go home and do nothing for six months?"

"Yes. You go home now Pablo and leave this with me. I'll take it to our solicitors' department tomorrow. Internal Affairs will liaise with us directly and we'll bring you in only when necessary for meetings and interviews. Ok?"

"I suppose so."

Roger tried to reassure him;

"I know it will be hard to put this all out of your mind Pablo, but that is what you need to do. Just leave it with us and don't worry."

Pablo was out of sorts. He'd never been in this situation before, and it was truly alarming, but he was good at keeping things in proportion.

"I'll try," he answered drily.

Roger had an afterthought;

"Have you got something you can be doing at home to keep your mind off this?"

"I'm part way through building a huge extension."

"That's ideal Pablo. Great. Try to focus on that, and as I say, we'll take care of your defence for you."

Defence? Had he done something wrong? He got up, they shook hands again, and he left. The worst of it was yet to come; having to explain to his dear sweet wife that he seemed to have fucked up, big time.

The train pulled into his station. He alighted, but with an uncharacteristic heaviness. Delilah would be waiting for him in their car. Now that he was working nine to five based in a city office, it was best for her to run him to the station in the mornings so she could keep their car for her own use during the day. They did have a car each, but Pablo allowed their daughter Sarah to borrow his car more or less permanently. He was wondering how he'd tell Delilah what had happened today. In fact he was terrified of telling her what had happened today. He had spent the last thirty years faithfully providing for her, and now something beyond his control was threatening their comfortable existence, and he felt bad. He went to the car and got in.

"Hello darl" she said breezily as usual, and he leaned across to kiss her briefly on the lips, as he always did. She looked lovely, her long blond hair tied up on top of her head in a stylish manner that complimented the attractive features of her face. She never spent ages making herself good. She was stylish, and could look good with the minimum of effort. She was wearing smart trousers with a pretty blouse and some kind of cardigan. He was more alert and attentive than usual. After supping briefly on her visage, he sank back onto his seat wondering what to do next as she negotiated her way out of the railway car park. He was unusually quiet, not knowing how to reveal his dilemma. He desperately didn't want anything to threaten his relationship with his wife, yet he himself had run a risk. He looked at her. She could see that something was wrong. She was presuming that another of his clients had overdosed, and that's why he was troubled. She didn't ask. He remained quiet and thoughtful for a short while, and then decided to bite the bullet sooner rather than later.

"I've had a complaint made against me" he announced bluntly.

She looked worried because she could see that he was worried. Her lips tightened. Her face looked taut. Her eyes seemed somehow to lose their warmth. He well recognised all these tells. She kept her eyes on the road.

"What sort of complaint"

"Oh the usual made-up kind of bullshit that's just plain vindictive and spiteful."

"Who by?"

"One of my old clients called Cassie."

"Why?"

"I don't really know. I think her boyfriend put her up to it because he doesn't like her being involved with me."

"Why doesn't he like her being involved with you?"

Straight away he could see she was suspicious of him. This concerned him. Throughout their entire marriage of almost twenty nine years, she had always been suspicious of him. She never actually said anything, but any interaction with any woman, anywhere, anyhow, always drew a scowl, a grimace, a special look reserved for her to display misgivings and disappointment. This wound him up, because he felt that he was being unfairly judged, and that it was an attempt to control him, to mould him according to her insecurities. He had unwisely failed to make any concessions on account of these insinuations simply because he knew in his heart that he was totally devoted to her, and he thought that should be enough. He didn't misbehave. He had no intentions of misbehaving, and it disappointed him that she didn't appreciate that. Conversely, he would never distrust her. For him, trusting was simply an integral aspect of loving. To love someone truly, you had to also trust them. Part of the problem in their particular case, was that he was naturally conversational, and he had more interesting conversations with females than men. He looked like a man's man yet the fact was that he got on better with women than men. It wasn't meant to be seen as a threat. He was just made that way, and it wasn't supposed to undermine their relationship. He continued trying to explain.

"I think he's jealous."

"Why?"

He knew that he had to explain what was going on to her, yet at the same time, he was afraid that her insecurities would blow it out of proportion.

28

"Just because she can talk to me, and she finds it hard to talk to him."

"How do you know that?"

"Because she told me."

She went quiet. She was a woman of very few words. She was driving. He was staring into the distance feeling very uncomfortable, but a quick glance towards her allowed him to see concern written all over her face. Over the many years they had spent together, he had expertly learned to read her body language, especially as she had never been free and easy with words. He was feeling guilty. He knew that by being in jeopardy at work, rightly or wrongly, he had let her down. He had taken risks without considering how the consequences might damage her. She was a sweet loyal hard-working person who had done nothing to deserve any worry or stress. The journey home was only about three minutes, but it was a long three minutes. She drove into the driveway, and they silently entered the house. Inside, Pablo tried to sound reassuring. He told her that he had been to see the Fed' Rep' already who would be handling the complaint for him. He wanted to make the compliant sound as frivolous and rubbishy as possible, but at the same time he needed to let her know that for the time being, he was out of a job! He quickly explained that he wasn't going to be allowed back onto the POU until the complaint had been dealt with and that the Fed' Rep', Roger, had advised him to go off with stress.

He studied her face to see how that all sat with her. She looked alarmed. He could tell that she was still suspicious of him. She thought he was hiding something. She started fishing.

"Why would they suspend you? What has she said you've done?"

"I don't know yet. All they've told me so far is that it's a complaint of harassment."

He looked at her appealingly, hoping for a more pragmatic acceptance that sometimes these things happen. He didn't see her alarm dissipating. He carried on bravely.

"And for good measure the complaints compartment are throwing in some data-protection stuff too. Presumably they're saying that since I was moved to the Prolific Offender Unit, I shouldn't have been looking at her record, but that's so ridiculous."

"Why is that ridiculous?"

He looked at her even more appealingly, as if to reiterate that he needed her on his side.

"The Prolific Offenders are almost all heroin addicts. Quite a few of them are my former clients. The list gets changed every month. They go on the list, come off the list, back on again. So of course I keep track of all of them, prolific or not. They're all linked."

He tried to sound like this would be a storm in a teacup, but she didn't look convinced, just like he wasn't. He felt uncomfortable being interrogated by her, but he knew he owed her all the explanations she wanted.

"So what are you going to do?"

"Well, Mr. Framlin wants me to go in and do some tedious, mind-numbing, soul-destroying, mundane, boring office admin job instead of my usual work, but Roger advises me to go sick with stress. He says that I can't be expected to function properly with all this hanging over my head. Also, If I'm off work until they sort it out, hopefully they'll get it done more quickly to get me back earning my money"

"So you're going off sick?"

"Looks like it."

She wandered round the kitchen busying herself, processing quietly. She didn't express her emotions verbally at the best of times, and it would seem, not at the worst of times too. He hoped that she was going to support him in this challenging time, but it didn't look like she was going to. He wanted them to stand together as a rock-solid couple. He went and got changed into his building clothes and went outside as he would normally do. His mind raced. He was searching for a solution which wasn't there. He felt quite distressed that his job might be on the line, and he had no idea as to how the process would pan out. Most of all though, he was worried about Delilah. He was truly terrified of losing her, yet he was wondering why he was even thinking that way. She had stood faithfully by his side since they were kids together. Why was he worried? She was his life. His rock. His childhood sweetheart. The mother of his four children. The woman he shared all of his adult memories with. All of them. He had worked his balls off for her and their beautiful family, and he would always do so, no matter what.

He occupied himself for about an hour moving thermal building blocks from the pallets in front of their house in many wheelbarrow loads, to a position round the back of the house, close to where he would require them when he next made up some muck. It was good hard physical work. And the view at the back of the house always warmed the cockles of his heart whatever else was happening. It was truly the most astonishingly beautiful location, and it's natural charm and serenity blessed him deeply. That helped. At about 7 o'clock as usual, Delilah called him in for dinner. There was little conversation over the meal, and at the end he, as always, did the clearing up and washing up. He then escaped to the lounge and slumped onto the sofa to watch some TV. He slouched, unconsciously trying to look smaller. Inside he was in the foetal position, in need of comfort which was not forthcoming. He needed escapism in more ways than one. He was under attack.

Chapter 4

The following days became indistinguishable for Pablo. He had been stripped of the framework of going to work Mondays to Fridays, and what he used to do during weekends he now did every other day too. Namely build, which thankfully, he loved doing. He liked being active and engaged in a project. During the day, Delilah would come and go, flitting between her care work, shopping, walking their two dogs, cleaning, cooking, etc. She was always busy. Always. She had only started doing paid care work about a year earlier. It had grown organically out of her kindly helping an elderly neighbour, then being engaged on a paid basis, and before long, through word of mouth, she was taking on new clients who were all old people still living in their own homes but in need of practical help. This helped fill the void left by her children growing up and leaving home.

Apart from building, Pablo liked to spend some time each day on his computer analysing the stock market. It fascinated him that a layman like him could use intricate sophisticated computer platforms on the internet, to engage in a form of trading, that just a few years earlier was the reserve of the esoteric in the city only.

Their daughter Sarah breezed into the kitchen one evening to show them a painting she had just finished.

"What do you think of this dad?" she enquired.

Pablo took the painting and inspected it. It was breathtakingly good.

"You did this from a photo?"

"Yes."

"It's amazing. It looks so lifelike. I can't believe it's an actual painting."

She smiled proudly.

"It's fantastic Sarah" her mum added.

"Is this the one for Mrs Powell?"

"Yes."

Pablo felt a little guilty. Delilah always seemed to know a little bit more than he did about what the kids were up to. She took the picture back and returned to her room. They didn't see much of Sarah, even though she still lived at home. She had just turned nineteen and worked in a local cafe, but her heart was in painting. One might ask why someone would pay a lot of money for a painting of a photo, but the painting was warmer, with added nuances and charm. Her evenings were taken up with socialising. Despite their splendid isolation far from the madding crowd, she had plenty of girlfriends nearby with whom she became very close. Her ambition was to become a professional artist. A tall order in a country with so many talented artists.

He and Delilah hadn't discussed the work and complaint situation any further. Pablo hadn't heard anything from Roger yet, so all they could do was sit tight. They tried to carry on life as normal. That wasn't hard. They'd been doing that for twenty nine years already, but there was a new tension in the air. They still had sex as regularly as ever, but their general level of intimacy had been robbed of some of its depth. Delilah was undoubtedly harbouring a degree of irritation with him, or more likely, distrust, and he felt it. She was apprehensive about the whole work situation, understandably, and carried a kind of ponderous, suspicious air about her. Pablo just wanted time to fly by to the point where the allegations were either dropped or found to be malicious, and he could return to work and normality. At least he had plenty of things to do to keep himself busy in the meantime. The not insignificant silver lining was that he was still being paid, and he could make good use of his time at home to make steady headway with the extension, and the build at home was coming on very nicely. They had a good relationship with the planning officer. They also had a big fat book on planning regulations for reference, which Pablo found most useful. Pablo's block-work was the neatest the officer had ever seen. It was good to impress him, because one day, his authority would be required to sign off the quality of the build and to issue a certificate of completion. Pablo could seriously see himself living out the rest of his days there in glorious, splendid, isolation, enjoying the fruits of his labour, never running out of little tinkering projects in the four acres outside, and never tiring of the heart-warming stunning views around the valley.

About a week after he'd been at home full time, he got a phone call from Mr Framlin. He wanted to come and visit him at home for a welfare visit. It was arranged for the next day, and when he turned up, he had a new sidekick with him, a freshly promoted young female sergeant. Apparently Caine had been moved sideways, and this young lady was now Pablo's new first-line supervisor, not that there was anything for her to supervise right now. Her name was Corinne. She was very pleasant, telling him that she would do whatever she could to help him. Despite her clear sincerity it was all rather hollow. What could she do? The due process had to be followed, and all any of them could do was wait, but it was a nice touch, them coming out to see him. Welfare was something he felt that the organisation only paid lip-service to, so in actual fact he was pleasantly surprised that they had made the effort. They stopped long enough for a cup of coffee and some general chit chat about the build. They even had a quick look outside to see how the work was coming on. Mr Framlin genuinely wanted to ensure that Pablo was coping emotionally. He was quickly satisfied and was probably ready to depart as soon as he had finished his drink. Pablo didn't try to keep them. Their duty was done. He walked them to the front of the house and bade them farewell. As they drove away from his idyllic domicile, he wondered what they had expected to find on their visit. A man broken and on the verge of self-harm? A man despondent and unmotivated? A man who had lost his purpose in life? No worries on that score. Pablo had every faith that the complaint would go nowhere, and even in the most unlikely event that it did somehow harm him, he would survive, no matter what. What was most important to him was his family, and no one could take that away from him. He suspected that the bosses were very mindful of a recent sad event in his district at work. It was only a few months earlier that one of the bosses had given in to despair after discovering that his wife was having an affair. He hung himself at home from the upstairs landing, leaving two young daughters fatherless and an errant wife a guilty widow.

As the days passed slowly by, there was still no news from Roger, so life carried on in this unfamiliar twilight zone. Delilah remained dutiful but wary. When he spoke to the kids, he played the whole thing down. When Delilah spoke to the kids, she played the whole thing up. For the past thirty years Pablo had always been so busy with work, and so devoted to his family, he had never developed a network of friends outside the extended family. Now he felt lonely, so he started to meet Henry from his local church for breakfasts or just coffee. He and Delilah had met Henry and Rosalyn when they had first moved into the area seven years earlier. They were almost parental figures, being that much older than them. It was as if they had trodden the same path as them, but previously, and as such, they had gained insight from the next level. They all had much in common, and had already socialised together occasionally.

Pablo arranged to meet Henry in a local cafe for a cooked breakfast. They met inside and shook hands in manly fashion.

"How are you getting on?" Henry enquired warmly.

Pablo shrugged a little. "Ok I suppose."

"Well you won't get bored with all that building work to do will you?"

He gave a little chortle. Henry was a practical man, and he understood the amount of work that goes into building a big extension.

"True. I won't get bored, and I am taking advantage of the situation."

"How's Delilah?"

"Not sure really. She's never very open with her feelings, but I think she's quite worried."

"Why? What's the worst that could happen?"

"Who knows? I've never been in this situation before Henry."

"You'll be alright. You're a good egg. They'll have it all sorted out soon, I'm sure."

Pablo appreciated his upbeat attitude, but he had to be realistic.

"You've never worked for a big organisation like this have you Henry?"

"No, thankfully" he mused.

"An attempt to get a speedy resolution is not a part of the process I'm afraid. They'll leave me hanging for as long as they want to. I honestly don't mind waiting too much. I mean it's great to be able to work on the extension full time, but I am worried about it affecting Delilah."

"How? You're still getting paid aren't you?"

"Yes, but she's a worrier. I can tell that she's not relaxed. Not her old self at the moment."

"Don't worry mate, she'll be alright. She's a tough cookie."

They enjoyed a well-cooked breakfast and chatted generally, and then they parted company. Pablo found Henry very reassuring and stable, and he liked that about him.

A few weeks later, in April, he finally heard from Roger. He was invited to a meeting at the federation offices. He duly attended. This time he didn't have to do the walk of shame through the main office. Roger came out and took him to a more private office upstairs. A smartly dressed podgy young man was already there. Roger introduced him.

"Pablo, this is Kevin. He will be your legal representative in this case."

Kevin stood up and they shook hands. He was very short. Pablo considered him young and inexperienced because he looked young and inexperienced. He had children older than this lad. It was difficult to have confidence in him. He could visualise mummy straightening his tie and making sure he'd packed his lunch box before he was allowed out of the house in the morning to go to his posh first post-graduate job. He was young, diminutive, and lacked presence. First impressions. They all sat down, spaced around a large conference desk. Roger continued.

"We just wanted you to come in and meet Kevin so he can explain a bit more of the process to you Pablo."

"Ok. Has anything happened yet?"

Kevin took up the reins.

"We're awaiting case papers from Internal Affairs Pablo. All we have so far is the form nine which you gave Roger. There's not much we can get our teeth into until we see their evidence."

"Fair enough. When might that happen?"

"That all depends on what investigations they need to carry out as a result of what Miss Woolridge alleges."

Pablo felt embarrassed. He still wasn't comfortable with the fact that someone was making allegations about him. It looked like the uncertainty was going to just drag on and on. He had a point to make.

"Cassie made her complaint on the second of January, and yet I wasn't informed about it until early March. Surely that can't be right? Why the delay?"

Kevin answered firmly and without sympathy.

"That doesn't make any difference Pablo. Internal affairs inform you, or us, when they feel ready to. Simple as that."

"Doesn't seem fair to me."

Kevin kept the conversation on track.

"They will want to interview you Pablo, in due course, but we don't want you to be interviewed. We'll offer them a full and comprehensive statement in lieu."

"Why?"

Roger interjected. "You're a great bloke Pablo, but you talk too much. If we submit a statement, we maintain control."

"Rodge, I don't mind being interviewed at all. I've got nothing to hide."

"Believe me Pablo, it's better if you're not interviewed."

Pablo was a little confused. He wondered why they didn't want him to be interviewed.

"Why?"

"To be honest, we think you might say the wrong things in interview."

Pablo didn't really know what wrong things he might say. He stayed quiet whilst he thought about it. Kevin picked up on his discomfort.

"Pablo, we just don't want you saying anything that might be unhelpful for our case. No disrespect, but Roger tells me you're quite a talker."

Pablo still felt perplexed. He had nothing to cover up. Why couldn't he be interviewed?

"So what if I'm a talker? I'd just be talking about my job, which incidentally, few people know about or understand."

Kevin advocated his position.

"If we prepare a statement in advance Pablo, we have absolute control over what we're giving them. In an interview you don't know what low-ballers they might throw in, and we don't want to risk anything."

Pablo was uncomfortable about this. He was a fighter. He keenly wanted to answer these spurious allegations. He wanted to justify his actions. He was well able to bat low-ballers. His face looked a little contorted and strained, reflecting the struggle his mind was having with the concept of going no-comment. Roger carried on the argument.

"Pablo, we know the system. It's what we do every day. We know what we're talking about."

Pablo gave him a quizzical stare, thinking to himself 'you've only been doing this role for a little while you pussy', but what he actually said was,

"But Roger. I've got nothing to hide. I have two years' worth of records of working with Cassie. It's going to be obvious that her complaint doesn't add up with reality. Not even close. So what the heck are we waiting for?"

"Well that's just it Pablo. We don't know, and we won't know until they serve their papers on us."

Pablo wanted to vent his frustrations.

"Look man, it's not right that they took over two months just to inform me that a complaint had been made. And now they're taking forever to deal with it, and in the meantime I'm being treated like some kind of low-life offender. How can that be right?"

Kevin piped up.

"We can understand your frustrations Pablo. Really, we can, but it's just the way it is. We can assure you that we'll deal with your case as expeditiously as we can. In the meantime, we all have to be patient and do what we can to be prepared. That's why I want you to make a statement before you're interviewed."

Pablo wasn't up for any more argument. He just wanted them to know he wanted this dealt with ASAP.

Roger interjected. Perhaps he thought Pablo was worried about money, so he reminded him of the arrangements.

"Whilst you're off work Pablo, the job gives you full pay for six months. If it goes on longer than that, the federation will pay you your full wage for another six months, so you'll be alright."

That wasn't Pablo's concern but he responded anyway.

"What a waste of fucking money. It's so stupid."

They both looked at him, not really knowing what to say next.

He realised that they were there to give him professional advice in a field which they knew better than him, and he ought to accept their advice, but his experience, and his gut-feeling shouted at him that anyone who refuses to give an interview is guilty of something, and that's what stuck in his gullet. He didn't want to make himself look guilty of anything. He didn't commit to anything. He'd heard their advice, but he still had to weigh up his instincts which to him, were more compelling. They wrapped the meeting up with a round of handshakes and reassurances. Pablo returned home in the knowledge that this nightmare was unlikely to be over any time soon. He felt a little empty-handed for Delilah. When he got home she was keen to know what had happened, and didn't seem convinced by the lack of substance in his report. She had a troubled look on her face and she quizzed him for a while, but he had no significant replies for her. She was suspicious of him, but that wasn't anything new.

The next week brought some lovely early spring sunshine. It was ideal building weather. Pablo continued with his building work every day. He was up to the first floor. One half of the extension was only going to be single storey, but the other section was going to be two stories. He had nursed an admiration for men who did self-builds for as long as he could remember, and he had always known that one day he would have to achieve something like that for himself, for his own self-esteem and sense of achievement. The project was far from over, but it was going surprisingly well. Delilah carried on with all the things she normally did, but nothing was really normal any more. There was too much uncertainty hanging over their heads.

Towards the end of April, he was apparently due another welfare visit from the boss. He was always in, so an appointment was made to suit the boss and his sidekick. They arrived one bright sunny warm morning. When they arrived, Pablo showed them into the kitchen as usual where they could sit at the kitchen table and have a hot drink. Delilah was out. Mr Framlin didn't seem as relaxed as before. He had a way about him that conveyed that something was on his mind. Maybe it was the way he stood, or the way he didn't look directly at Pablo, but it reminded him of that visit to his office back in early March. Shortly after being welcomed into the kitchen he spoke. His voice was strong and official.

"Pablo, I want to make you aware of another complaint."

Pablo stared at him in disbelief. How much trouble could he get in? He was only grateful that Delilah wasn't here to share his embarrassment. Mr Framlin picked up his briefcase and quickly fetched out another form nine.

"What do you mean another one?" Pablo asked lamely, as if wounded.

"It's from Marlon Smith, Cassie's partner."

"Now there's a surprise" he said sarcastically. Immediately, he felt better. Whatever it was, it was pure vindictiveness. He knew that Marlon had absolutely nothing on him.

"Go on" he said boldly.

Mr Framlin put on his spectacles, then said

"I'll read you the complaint Pablo and serve you a form nine."

There was a slight pause whilst he poised himself.

"That you on the twenty first day of February 2008 abused your authority in obtaining the mobile phone number of Marlon Smith and phoned him on it in furtherance of your alleged harassment of the complainant Cassie Woolridge. A breach of the police code of conduct in relation to use of force and abuse of authority." He then cautioned him with the official caution given to any suspected offender, and invited a reply.

"That's just bullshit. You know there is a paper trail and an electronic process to obtain phone numbers that has to be authorised by the inspector in charge of covert standards. Why didn't they just check that out first?"

"I can't comment on the investigation Pablo. I'm sorry. You know I'm just the messenger."

"Well I can assure you that it's just a total waste of everybody's time. I had his number because Cassie used to phone me on his phone when she was out of credit on hers."

Corrine sat there rather meekly and quietly, not giving anything away.

He looked sternly and somewhat incredulously at Mr Framlin's face across the kitchen table. He was annoyed because this was not going to go down well with Delilah. What was the point of pursuing a complaint which with one check of the appropriate records could be seen immediately to be false? He knew that he didn't have to justify himself to Mr Framlin, and he felt rather sorry for him. He knew that this was the last thing he wanted to be doing, heaping on more coals, but it was his job, and he was a professional.

"It's just more bullshit" he added determinedly.

"Make sure you inform Roger though" Mr Framlin advised. "I'm sorry Pablo."

Chapter 5

Pablo had been in town visiting the builder's yard. It was somewhere he visited often. He rather enjoyed looking at all the various fittings that were available for plumbing, or drainage, or constructing roofs, or whatever else he might need shortly. He felt like a child in a toy shop, checking out the airplane models. Often he felt the need to actually see the various fittings available, and to be able to pick them up to see how they fitted together in order to work out how he was going to do something. Whilst he was there he might lust after a sparkling new tool or two, but really, he had enough tools. He always bought the right tools for the job. Not to do so was a false economy. Buying nice tools was just about the only luxury he allowed himself in life. He was a strong believer in the saying that the best things in life are free. He left with just the essentials he had come for.

On his way home he stopped for petrol. Whilst he was quietly filling up the car, he watched a little mini pulled up on the other side of the pump to him. It was quite an old car, but was in good condition. A young lady probably in her late teens got out and prepared to fill up her car. A middle-aged woman sat in the front passenger seat of the mini. Just as he finished filling, the tannoy boomed.

"Would the person at pump six please report immediately to the cashier."

The voice was harsh and hegemonic and he found himself standing to attention. He searched rather desperately for his pump number. Relieved, he observed that he was at number five. The young lady next to him was six. She dutifully walked into the station. He was right behind her, as he had finished filling. There was one customer at the counter, and the young lady and he waited in line. Often there is a raised floor behind counters. Perhaps part of the reason for this is to make the cashier seem, or even be, more authoritative. The guy at the front moved away and the girl moved forward. The cashier, a stern plain-looking lady in her late thirties wearing a cashier's uniform, stared down at her.

"Proof of age please?" she barked tersely.

"I haven't got any" the girl replied meekly.

"Then I can't serve you."

The girl turned to leave.

"Hang on a minute" Pablo was not a little vexed by the manner of the cashier, and he intervened. He might be off-duty, but he wasn't going to just ignore this rudeness. He had a daughter about the same age as this young lady, and he would hate for her to be treated pejoratively like this. He was obliged to stand up for her.

"Why can't you serve her?"

"She hasn't got proof of ID."

"Neither have I."

"But you don't look younger than eighteen."

"That's just a matter of opinion" he answered cheekily.

The cashier more or less scowled at him, then hissed,

" I can't serve someone under eighteen without proof of ID"

"But she's just driven up in her own car."

"It might be stolen."

He couldn't believe what he was hearing.

"You can't presume a car is stolen just because it's got a young driver."

He was flabbergasted, and did his best to express that in his voice.

He sensed people behind him. He glanced around and saw that it was only a small queue beginning to form. Momentarily he felt the pressure not to make a scene, and just let everyone get on with paying for their petrol, but that didn't last. He was too angry to let this go.

He looked at the girl. She looked like she was having trouble fighting back tears. That only served to make him more keen to stand up for her. He was not going to let her be picked on like this. He questioned her softly.

"Whose car is it honey?"

"Mine."

"And who is the lady in the car with you?"

"My mum" she answered quietly.

He looked at the cashier appealingly. "It's her car and she's even got her mum in the car with her. Her mum's well over eighteen. You can serve her."

"I can't."

This cashier was very sure of herself, and it seemed that the more he argued with her, the more entrenched she was becoming.

"Why ever not?" He was biting his tongue now. People seem to think that swearing is vulgar and unnecessary, but to Pablo it was sometimes necessary to resort to expletives in order to express growing frustration, annoyance or anger. To that extent, swearing did have a purpose as far as he was concerned. It could be used like a warning signal. He felt like swearing right now in order to demonstrate his sense of outrage, but he knew that it would be counterproductive because he would lose the higher ground. So he restrained himself.

"Because I know she'd be buying it for her" the cashier answered cockily,

As she used the word 'her' she tossed a fleeting, dismissive, disapproving look at the girl. She grimaced as she looked at her. Pablo couldn't believe how rude and unpleasant she was, and he only felt more aggrieved for the girl.

"Why are you looking at her like that?"

"Like what?"

"You looked at her contemptuously."

"No I didn't."

He wasn't going to get into a childish argument. Some of the people in the queue behind him may have been growing impatient, but no one said anything.

A second cashier appeared and started serving them at a second till. That was good. It meant that he could see this argument through in the comfort of knowing he was not inconveniencing other customers particularly.

"That doesn't make sense. Surely her mum can pay for the fuel for her?"

"I told you. I can't serve her. It doesn't matter who's paying."

He looked at the girl, who was still on the verge of tears.

"Hun, please go out and fetch your mum."

She eagerly left the premises. He stood and watched her as she went to her car, got in and drove off. It appeared that she had had enough of this embarrassment and belittlement. He didn't think for a second that it was a stolen car. He looked at the cashier. She was looking a little triumphant barely suppressing a slight smirk.

"I want to speak to the manager please."

The cashier indicated the lady at the other till, who was currently serving other customers. He would wait.

"I'm number five" he told the hard-nosed, unfeeling, would-be despot in front of him. She took his card and processed the transaction. He waited for the manager to come free. When she did, he protested at the preceding interaction.

"It's company policy" she explained lamely.

"Really?" he said emphatically. "I would have thought that company policy would be to treat all customers with respect and decency, not to humiliate and embarrass and inconvenience them just because they appear to be seventeen or eighteen years old, or because you don't like the look of them, especially if they have a proper grown-up with them."

He waited for a response. All he got was a blank stare, so he carried on.

"Well, I think your treatment of that girl was outrageous, completely unjustified, and just plain nasty, and if that's the way you treat your customers, I certainly shan't be coming here again."

The manageress still just looked at him blankly. He got the distinct impression that she didn't give a fig if he remained a customer or not. In fact he was pretty sure that she and her assistant would prefer him not to come back again. Neither of them made any further comment. They stared passively into space.

"Next please."

He gave them the best disapproving stare he could manage before turning and leaving. He walked past the few people in the queue behind him. They averted their gaze, looking towards the floor or straight in front of them with glazed expressions. British reserve disguised their thoughts. They sensibly carried that opaque glassy look of 'it's none of my business.' And he was clearly alive, fired-up, intense, impacting, reactive, and that was rather scary.

He went home. Delilah was in the kitchen preparing one of her lovely meals. He told her about the little incident at the petrol station. She carried on stirring something in a pot, seriously, devotedly. She seemed disinterested in what he was relating. She didn't stop concentrating on her cooking. She didn't look up from the pot. She clearly wasn't in the mood to be regaled with stories of his chivalry, or any other small-talk for that matter.

He had already told her about the new charge against him, and she was more worried than ever. Of course he had poo-pooed it as the rubbish that it was, but she was unsettled by it all. She had no appetite for this kind of uncertainty. He didn't feel that she was on his side, and that saddened him.

More weeks slowly drifted by. Then he had a phone call from Roger. He had the prosecution case in his hands and wanted to come round and discuss it. Fantastic! Progress!. He arranged to come to Pablo's house the following morning. It was Wednesday. This was over two months since Pablo had been made aware of the allegation, and now finally, he was going to be allowed to see exactly what was being said. The following morning, Delilah ensured that she was present. Pablo was rather nervous about that, but he hadn't thought to query Roger about coming to his home. They could just as easily have met at the local police station. Too late now. If he changed the arrangement, Delilah would think he had something to hide. He just didn't want her seeing him as a suspected offender.

Roger duly arrived as planned, looking dapper as usual in his smart dark blue suit. Mr Framlin accompanied him. That was a bit of a surprise, but he made it clear that he was present in a supportive role. Pablo showed them onto the lounge. They all sat down, and Delilah fetched them all a hot drink. After a few pleasantries, Roger fished into his briefcase and produced a wad of papers.

"This is Cassie's statement Pablo."

He handed it over solemnly, giving it the due deference that a piece of paper acquires when it can rip a man's life apart. Pablo read it quickly. Cassie implied that on almost all the occasions that he had visited her over the past nine months, it had been without her permission. He knew that this was pure rubbish. It was her word against his, but the fact that the meetings were in a variety of places and times, the implication was surely that she had been involved in making arrangements with him. There was one particularly galling accusation, that he had visited her in hospital without her permission, just after she had given birth. He had indeed visited her, at her request, and he had felt rather honoured to be asked to see her at such a time. She had given birth in a special secure ward reserved for special cases, like heroin addicts. He only knew where she was because she had phoned him and told him. He could only gain entry to the ward with her permission. There were nurses present who would be able to testify that she happily authorised and accepted his visit. The whole statement was similarly ridiculous. There was no explanation as to how he found her in random public places against her wishes, or why she spent time with him, or how he managed to regularly liaise with her drugs counsellor about her, apparently without her permission, or why she texted him or phoned him on a regular basis. Or why she actually engaged in fairly lengthy phone calls with him. Her allegations were shot full of big holes. There was nothing of substance.

He gave the statement back to Roger contemptuously. Delilah asked to see it, and Roger passed it to her nonchalantly. Pablo didn't want to look worried about Delilah seeing this stuff, but he was worried. He knew how sensitive she was. Then Roger produced copies of four emails from Pablo to Cassie. He had previously admitted sending her emails, even though Roger insinuated that he should deny that they had come from him, as it couldn't be proved who they came from. But Pablo felt that that would be guilty behaviour, and he was willing to justify himself. He declined to read them. He knew what he had written.

"How can they use these?" he queried, aggrieved that they might be admissible.

"I sent these after she had gone quiet on me. After she had apparently made allegations against me. I was trying to find out what was going on. They've got nothing to do with the allegation she made in January."

Roger answered matter-of-factly. "They can use them if they want to Pablo, if Cassie has produced them as evidence, which she has."

Pablo felt that this was unfair. He felt like he had fallen into a trap. Delilah took the emails from Roger, placed them on her lap, and pored over them slowly and deliberately for what seemed like an age. In the meantime, the three men discussed the vagaries of the case. Pablo was giving Delilah sideways glances to monitor her expressions. It was as if a dark cloud was forming over her head. He watched the tell-tale signs rapidly take hold of her face. The taut lips. The cold wide eyes. Her complexion visibly paled. The longer she read, the darker the cloud over her. Pablo suspected a mixture of fear, hurt, concern, and pain. Pablo felt so sorry for her. He felt helpless. All the emails were much the same. Him reaching out to Cassie once a fortnight. She had ceased to answer her phone, and he had become genuinely worried about her. His emails expressed that worry, but also he verbalised an admiration of her as a person, an appreciation of her friendship, and a desire to maintain their friendship. He was trying to woo her out of hiding. He knew it was all a bit over the top, but so what? It was just between him and her. He trusted that it would stay between just the two of them. She knew that his intention had always to keep their friendship above board. It would always be based on his support for her through his profession. But he had blurred the lines. He had given her too much of his emotion, and now it was back-firing on him. He had dug himself a hole, and she had pushed him into it. He felt like an idiot. How could he be so stupid as to do anything that might even remotely damage his relationship with his devoted wife of nearly thirty years? That was all he really cared about, but it didn't look like it right now. Too late. The damage was being done right before his own eyes, real-time. Slowly, deeply, and with how much potency? He felt like he was in a slow-motion car crash, and it was very alarming.

Roger showed Pablo a statement from Marlon evidencing that on day date time place he had received a phone call from Pablo on his own personal mobile phone, complaining that the only way Pablo could have obtained his phone number was illegally. Nothing unknown there. Pablo read the brief statement and handed it back disdainfully. There wasn't much more for Roger and Mr Framlin to do. Pablo had seen the evidence against him, and as far as he was concerned it was frail to meaningless. The two visitors got up to go. They all shook hands and Pablo showed them to the door. Bizarrely Delilah gave Roger a very warm lingering hug just before he left, to the extent that he looked a little uncomfortable. This surprised Pablo because Delilah was not in the habit of giving out warm hugs. She was feeling hurt, let-down and vulnerable and she needed some comfort. The hug with the Fed' Rep' was the best reassurance she could find in the moment.

They left. She looked upset and vexed. Pablo instinctively knew that this may not be the best time to try to make reparations, but he couldn't just ignore the situation. He looked at her imploringly.

"Do you want to talk about it?"

"No" came the stark reply. She walked into the hallway, grabbed the dogs leads and walked out, two excited dogs bounding around her, totally oblivious to the convoluted complications of the human world. He watched her through the window as she strode out into the lane. He knew she would be grappling with lots of issues arising out of all of this. He felt so stupid. She was the sort of woman who got upset if her husband so much as looked at another lady in the street, or talked about a female colleague, and here he was sending nice emails to one of his clients. She would be livid. He went outside and got on with some building, his mind in some turmoil.

He was aware of Delilah returning a little later on, but then she went out in the car, without talking to him. She would usually tell him where she was going and say goodbye, but not this time. She was obviously very unsettled, and he felt useless. She didn't come home until it was time to prepare the evening meal. She did this as usual. Pablo came in, cleaned up and tried making small talk. She was clearly not in the mood. Her face was stony and she refused to engage in conversation. The dark clouds were still hanging over her pretty head. He had to give her time and space. They ate quietly together, and at the end of the meal she announced that she would be sleeping in one of the spare bedrooms. His heart sank. She was taking this too far. She was reading too much into it, but there was little he could say which he hadn't already said. He so regretted hurting her.

The following morning he awoke to find a letter by the bedroom door. He picked it up nervously and sat on the bed. He had made such a mess of things. He didn't want to read this letter. It would be just cold hard evidence of what a mess he'd made. But of course he had to read it.

"Dear Pablo. I lay in bed without you because I am having to come to face something that I have been trying to ignore for so many years. The fact that you don't really love me, and in fact in many ways, I am just an irritation. I am sure you are right about cause and effect, as I have already admitted and it is something I will have to live with for the rest of my life. I am deeply sorry for treating you this way. You deserve better. It is with great shame and deep regret that our relationship has come to this, just when in so many ways it seemed to be improving – more time for each other – prospects of new experiences to be had together, but now I see all this was just a pipe dream.

I am saddened that during the last thirty years I haven't been able to 'rock your boat'. Or you haven't had the strong feelings for me that you have had with

Cassie. It must have been amazing for you – a new lease of life. I do hope you may be able to experience this again. I'm sure you will as you have proved that you are very capable of loving someone and showing it, even when they are not really available to you, or seem to want it. Life has dealt you a bum deal. Well, maybe it is time for you to take the bull by the horns and turn your life into whatever you want it to be.

I am not sure that I fit into that life anymore. There are so many things that you wish for your future that as you know are not necessarily mine. You could go and start a new life abroad for instance. I would miss you terribly, as would all the family, but I wonder if it's just something you need to do. Maybe (and a rather small hopeful maybe) you will then be able to reflect on our life that we have had together and it might not appear quite so dire after all.

It's so easy to show your love when your guard is down and the soft Pablo shows through. It is a delight and brings me great pleasure to be able to lavish love upon you. Unfortunately the ground is up more than down.

I think the ball is in your court, or am I just passing the buck? I really don't know anymore. I'm sure you will fight your corner as you are so good at doing.

I wonder if the real reason you didn't want me to see the details was because the real truth about us was hidden there and you're not sure you can face it either? I left a message for Cassie telling her that her work was done, so maybe there is some hope for you there after all.

From a heavy heart that is struggling to see a future. All the things I have said to you recently still stand, if they mean anything to you.

Love, D x"

He felt a huge knot in his stomach. A sense of sheer desperation overwhelmed him. Yes, he had been somewhat cavalier in his dealings with Cassie, but how could Delilah be taking this so much to heart? He was desperate not to lose her. How could she think that he didn't love her deeply? He had to write back and try to reverse whatever damage he could. He went down the hall to get some photocopy paper. He realised that Delilah was out. The dogs were gone too. So was the car. He found some paper and wrote;

"My darling, how can you react in this way? I am so sorry that this has upset you, but please don't make it into something it isn't. I love you deeply. Cassie was part of my work. Yes I liked her and I got on well with her. I liked the way she used my name when she spoke to me. But she was a client. I only ever saw her as part of my job. I'm sorry I emailed her. Obviously I went over the top, but I was genuinely worried about her disappearance. Compared to you, she means nothing to me. Please accept that."

He was urgently trying to downplay the situation because he was facing consequences he couldn't imagine. He genuinely could not contemplate living without Delilah. She was so much a part of him. He did what he did for her. He couldn't understand how she couldn't see that.

A few hours later, after he had had breakfast and was outside working, he realised that she had returned home. He had never felt trepidation about approaching her before, but today he did. He downed tools and went indoors.

She was busying herself in the kitchen. He wanted to give her a hug, but she didn't look like that would go down well. Her face looked like she was in pain.

He began by stating the obvious.

"I got your letter hun. You're reading too much into this. Cassie was just a client."

"Do you send all your clients emails telling them how fond you are of them then?"

Ouch. That was a good point. He tried to disguise his embarrassment and guilt.

"Hun I'm so sorry. I shouldn't have said the things to her that I did."

"But you did."

What could he reply to that? Yes, he had, and he shouldn't have. He didn't really know what to say next. So he resorted to the obvious again.

"I have left you a letter too."

"Yes I've seen it."

Oh dear. That hadn't had a very beneficial effect then. She looked stony-faced and determined. She was moving around like he wasn't there. Most definitely she wasn't looking at him. He, by contrast, was looking at her very directly, his eyes appealing for some softness, a little concession maybe, but she wasn't engaging. He gave up and left her. He went back outside. This dissociation was horrible. Yes there had been lots of times during their very long marriage when they had fallen out over something, usually something pitifully trivial, and a painful disengagement had somehow wedged itself in place, sometimes for days, occasionally even for weeks, and it only really persisted because neither of them knew how to begin the process of overcoming it, but this time it felt different. It was truly scary because for the first time, he sensed that their very marriage was really under threat. It didn't feel like it would the usual fairly brief passing awkwardness whose existence persisted only because of poor communication skills. This time it went much deeper.

Later, she went out again. He guessed that she was off to see a friend, or maybe one of the sisters, in order to run things by them for a second opinion and advice. Pablo still felt so useless. He wanted to help her, but didn't know how to. All he could do was wait and see how the dice rolled. She returned in time to cook supper as usual, and they ate in a stony silence. He wanted to appeal to her but he didn't know where to start. At bedtime they retired to different bedrooms again. He had to give her that concession. He acknowledged that she needed time and space. To his surprise, he awoke to another letter. This was most unlike Delilah. She always kept her feelings to herself, yet here was another double-pager!

He sat to read it.

"My dearest Pablo. I write this letter with the saddest of hearts. To come to terms with the knowledge that all I have lived for has been dashed at the stroke of a pen. I have given my life to you – and I know I have made errors along the way (as we both have) which I am deeply sorry for.

The written word is so powerful, more powerful and carries so much more weight than the spoken word. The spoken word is said in a moment, sometimes with not much thought behind it, and then it's gone. We can hang onto it in our minds and it does have significance especially when said with sincere meaning. The written word is much more though. Thought-out carefully, written and re-read and then given with purpose. The recipient then can re-read it time and again. They can bathe in its joy or shrink in its sadness. It can be cherished or discarded. With the author though, it carries much weight.

It's quite bizarre in a way that it is not so much that you have declared your love for someone else but that you have at the same time then proclaimed that what we had was so much less and had never been so meaningful as what you have now felt. It has demeaned our love to a shadow which in turn has given you a life that you now realises is less of a life than you could have had, had you met her before.

How do I deal with such knowledge? It cuts me to the core. It is going to take me a long time. I'm obviously not as strong as Rosalyn. Different character I suppose. I am going to stay with Morag for the weekend. I'll take each day as it comes and try to work through this deep miry pit. The way I feel now, I won't be coming to your birthday weekend trip, but I'll bring the car back for you to take.

I feel so deeply for you. I long for the man I thought I had. To feel secure in your arms, but I fear that has gone. I am so sorry for being so weak. I thought and hoped that I could stay strong.

From a broken heart.

D. x"

He felt so bad about upsetting her so much. He was in torment. He was desperate to put things right, but he couldn't. Delilah was dealing with it in her own way. He was also frustrated because he considered all this a massive overreaction. He had never been any good at reassuring her, but now was a very good time to try. He wrote another note.

"Babe, you're reacting like I don't love you anymore, like I want to leave you for another woman. Nothing could be further from the truth. I do love you very deeply. I am horrified that you think otherwise. Haven't I always told you that I would never leave you? Please forgive my poetic licence with Cassie. I have stupidly given the wrong impression. Honestly, I have no interest in her romantically at all, and I wouldn't knowingly do anything to damage our relationship, but please don't be like Cassie and get the knives out for me too."

She was in the shower, so he left his note on her bed. They crossed paths in the kitchen after she had dressed, but he didn't know what to say. She looked upset and prickly, and he felt that whatever he said would be wrong. After breakfast, she politely told him that she was going out to see some friends but would be back later. He drew consolation from the fact that she told him that she would be back. There had been a hint of her leaving indefinitely over the past few days, so any reassurances were welcome.

Later on Delilah returned and cooked supper for them both as usual. She was still being supportive in a practical sense, but again, no real conversation. She was buried inside herself. He could tell that she had shut down, and any pathetic grovelling from him would probably only make matters worse. The following morning, a Friday, she was going off to stay with her oldest sister, Morag, for a long weekend. After breakfast he hung around indoors hoping she would say goodbye to him. She packed the car up with a bag or two, and the dogs. He went outside to say goodbye. She gave him another letter before leaving, and surprisingly gave him a brief hug. That was nice. He didn't know what to say about seeing her again. This was her home. He was her husband. It seemed stupid to make a comment which implied that her return was in the balance, yet he knew it might be. She drove off. He watched her go longingly, feeling wretched inside. He went back indoors and sat in his lonely kitchen proceeding to open the letter.

It read;

"I spoke to Rosalyn last night. She said writing letters was good and I need to spend time with God, letting him reassure me. Leaving you like this is not what I want and the promise I made to you on Tuesday that I will still love you – despite the disclosure - still stands. But my pain runs so deep. I've got no resources to pull from to show it to you. My emotional tank has run dry. Maybe some time away will restore me and we can start again from scratch. I'm sorry that you feel that I have the knives out for you or that you can bring me down to her level. I don't have the energy for knives or the inclination. Your note was lovely except for the 'but'. I'll try to ignore that bit and hang on to the rest - put it in my tank.

D x"

Chapter 6

Friday afternoon, he got a call from Kevin.

"Pablo, I've been through all the information Internal Affairs have in your case. I need you to provide me with that statement."

Pablo wasn't really in the mood for this. His mind was on Delilah.

"Ok." he managed.

"Can you do it on your computer and email it to me please?"

"Sure."

"I need as much information as you can remember. Don't wait till it's all done. Send it to me in chunks."

"Yeah."

"Great. Look forward to hearing from you."

Right now, Pablo wasn't motivated. It was strange and lonely not having Delilah at home. They had been living together for twenty nine years, and the only disruption to their sleeping together had been on account of his periods of shift work in the past. So her absence was sorely felt. A vital and essential part of him was missing. In addition to the disquiet caused by their estrangement, he found going cold turkey on sex was almost unbearable. He phoned Henry.

"Henry, fancy meeting up for cooked breakfast?"

"You bet. What time were you thinking?"

Henry was a self-employed businessman, and he was very flexible. They fixed a rendezvous at a local cafe. Henry had been married to Rosalyn for over forty years. They had four children, and what seemed like masses of grandchildren. They had even started having great grandchildren. They were solid, and possessed poise and aplomb. When Pablo arrived, Henry was already seated and sipping strong coffee.

"Sorry mate. I've already started. I didn't know how long you'd be."

"No that's fine Henry. It's good to see you man."

Henry stood up and they shook hands firmly. Pablo was already tearful just seeing Henry.

"Oh dear. What's happened mate?"

Pablo replied in low careful tones, as if he had no energy left.

"Work came round my house to disclose the allegations against me. Delilah wasn't very happy. She's taken it very badly."

"Taken what badly?" he enquired.

The waitress interrupted them. They both ordered a big breakfast, Henry with another coffee, Pablo with tea. He always had tea with food. Coffee was too overpowering with food. Then he carried on.

"She's reading too much into the fact that I emailed this girl."

"The girl who made the complaint?"

"Yes. Delilah thinks I wanted to have an affair with her."

"Did you?"

"Not in a million years. I liked her, but she was work, but Delilah just can't accept that. Women seem to think that if a man engages in a conversation with another woman, he automatically wants to rip her knickers off and do her from behind. "

Henry frowned at his coarse expression, but he didn't say anything. He was already in the picture. He told Pablo that Delilah had spent time with Rosalyn, pouring out her heart to her. Pablo was pleased to hear this because he knew Rosalyn would give her sound advice and was a big supporter of marriage. Henry was not a frivolous talker. He would say whatever he believed to be right with no beating about the bush. No whistles, bells or euphemisms. Simple down-to-earth honest language. He didn't say things to please people. He said what he thought was right, and Pablo admired his directness. He realised that Pablo had made a big error of judgement, but he didn't think that it was grounds for a marriage of almost thirty years to break up. He could tell that Pablo was still madly in love with his child-bride.

"We'll keep praying for you both, and trust that God will restore her faith in you, and him."

Henry was a very spiritual man and always included God's will in his desires and plans. He carried on.

"I haven't told many people this Pablo, but many years ago, Rosalyn and I wanted to break up."

"Really?" Pablo queried, very surprised but fascinated to know how they had clearly got over that.

"Yeah. What with one thing and another, we had both had enough, but we went to see a counsellor. I felt quite sorry for him actually. We had quite a lot of sessions with him, and he really did do his utmost to help us patch things up, but we were both resolute about breaking up, and we frustrated him enormously. He got nowhere with us." He chuckled at the memory of this poor man more or less pulling his hair out over them.

"Did you break up?"

"Miraculously no. This counsellor literally ran out of things to say. He got to the end of the road with us, and simply said that he had given us all the help he could give us and now it was all down to us making a decision. There was nothing else he could do. The only hope for us was if we simply made a decision to stay together for the sake of the marriage, and to simply work at it. It was totally down to us alone to make that choice or not. We got that close to walking away, but by God's grace, we somehow made that decision not to part, and the rest is history."

"Wow. I never would have expected that of you two. Thinking about breaking up I mean."

"It can happen to any couple Pablo. But as you can see, we are both very happy that we persevered. Interestingly enough, our relationship changed from that point on."

"Really? How?"

"It was less physical after that and more spiritual."

"What, you got closer, sort of personally, like, real love?"

"Yes, I suppose so. We grew into a new level we hadn't had before. It took a bit of time, but we both made the right decision."

"That's encouraging. Thanks for sharing that. It's so positive."

"Just keep praying. That's the best advice I can give you."

They finished their cooked breakfasts, and Pablo returned to his empty home encouraged but still fearful.

Monday morning, Delilah returned home. He welcomed her as she came in but she was no more than polite. Still struggling then, he thought. Of course he was very relieved that she had returned. He tried to be reassuring.

"I'm glad you're home. I miss you so much when you're gone."

She made no comment. Her face carried a look of scepticism. The dogs bounded up to him wagging, licking, barely restraining themselves from jumping up.

He checked them anyway.

"Get down!" he hissed as he happily fussed them.

Delilah busied herself moving bags around, then putting the kettle on. She didn't look at him directly, or comment. He was used to that. When she was upset, she always withdrew inside herself. He didn't understand how someone can go so silent when there is so much to talk about. But, even at her very best, she gave little away verbally. Everyone is different, and that was just the way she had been made. It was unfortunate that it clashed with his style so directly. He decided to leave her to her hidden thoughts.

"If you want to talk about anything, you know where to find me."

He felt that the best thing for now was to give her space to settle back in. After all, he so wanted her to settle back in. The weekend without her had been scary. The following weekend they and all the kids were planning a camping weekend away in the country near the seaside to celebrate his fiftieth birthday.

"I don't want to spoil your birthday weekend" she announced, "But I don't think I will be able to come."

He was horrified. He didn't want this situation robbing them of precious time with the family together. He wanted her to be there with him.

"Babe, don't let this spoil a rare weekend of us all being together. You've gotta come."

"I'd love to go, but I don't think I will be up to it emotionally."

She really did look tired, exhausted even.

"Hun, you can't not come" he said ruefully, desperate for her not to feel this way.

She went quiet. She had stated her case, and he made his protestations. He looked at her sadly, and appealingly, then left to go outside to work.

The whole week passed in much the same vein. She carried on sleeping in a different bedroom. He respected that although he didn't think it was very helpful. She was in and out. Sometimes walking the dogs. Sometimes shopping, sometimes working, sometimes visiting a friend. Sometimes she told him where she was off to, and sometimes she didn't. She was making him feel that he had no right to know anything about her movements because he had been friendly with another woman. She was still dutiful though, cooking, cleaning, washing the laundry etc.

She left him another letter;

"My dearest Pablo, your first letter felt hard and cold, your second much warmer and I thank you for that. I felt like a smashed vase that may have been precious once upon a time, but, with age and use, has become dull and uninteresting. I'm not sure if I can collect all the pieces together. Maybe I have to forge a new vase altogether. Some of the pieces have been flung so far. Can God heal the broken-hearted? Can I captivate your heart again? It is so full of resentments towards me and you wanting such different things. I am full of despair. I like the thought of the dawn coming after the darkest hour. You have such a way with words when you want to, both for building up, and sometimes to undo. I am waiting for the dawn, whatever that will be. I don't seem to be making much sense right now so I'll come back to this some other time. Maybe things will become clearer as the days go by. Do you want to love me more than anything? Again, I have so many questions. Did you choose me because along with me comes so much more? The package includes the house, the build, the family. If you could keep all of those and have someone else, that might have been your choice. I am so confused. Things are so unclear and not straightforward. Can I find it in my heart to forgive? Please help me.

Love D xx"

His heart bled for her. He realised above all that she needed reassurance. He sought her out. She was in the kitchen. He went up to her and hugged her. She stood straight, not resisting but also not responding. She was in no-man's land.

"Babe, I do love you more than anything. I don't love Cassie or anyone else but you. Please don't underestimate my love for you."

He pulled back a little to look into her eyes. He wanted her to see his utmost sincerity, but her gaze was to one side. She was frozen. He waited for a short while, hoping that she would say something, but she didn't. She just stood still continuing to stare to one side, looking so sad, and avoiding his gaze. He didn't want to pressurise her. He had made his point, and he left her to carry on whilst he went outside to work.

The days passed slowly and painfully. She kept her distance. Apart from the letters she had already given him, she said nothing. Occasionally he would try to enter into communication with her, but after he had said his piece, she remained silent. It was like she was deeply wounded and there was no way of healing her. On the Thursday prior to the weekend they were due to go camping with the family for his birthday weekend, she relented and said she would go. He was so relieved. He didn't want to go without her. She didn't particularly want to be with him, but she did want to spend time with the kids. The following morning, they packed up all the things that they would need. Over the years they had done a lot of camping with the family, and they still had all the gear. She was still distant from him, but they were doing something together, and that was good.

After they had arrived at their weekend campsite, and the children started to arrive, she was much more herself. She was fairly jolly with them. They were both busy just mixing with the family as they walked, dined and talked. Pablo turned fifty. In fact the weekend got cut short by the weather. By noon on Sunday they had to all break camp, as a gale had arrived, and as its ferocity increased, it became more and more obvious that the camping was over. As they took down their tents, they witnessed all the other tents on the site get reduced to flapping rags by the enormous gusts of wind. Delilah and Pablo returned home with little conversation. She had made a big effort to overcome her pain and withdrawal whilst she was with the kids, but now she seemed drained.

The next day he visited his local police station. He felt uncomfortable going in there. The staff there all knew him. They would also know he was under investigation, and that he was off sick, and nobody consorted with someone who was under investigation. It was as if whatever had tainted him could somehow contaminate anyone he came into contact with, and nobody wanted any insinuations or contamination coming their way. For the time being, he was like a modern-day leper. He hoped to minimise the awkwardness by getting everything he needed on this one visit. It was only a very small station, and support staff and officers shared the large ground floor office. Upstairs were the CID and local inspector's office. He wouldn't need to go up there. There was a lady support staff member on the front counter with a female traffic warden. They both looked at him with surprised expressions on their faces as he entered. He grunted an acknowledgement as he nodded to them and walked past. There was no one else around at that time, and for that he was grateful. He found a spare desk and computer, and logged in. His access to police intelligence was now restricted, but he could still access his own computer files. He printed off all the records he had made of interactions with Cassie, and all the monthly reports on her progress. It covered the previous two years, but it didn't take long to print them off. Then he quickly left, glad to have avoided any awkward meeting with colleagues. He took the print-outs home to use as a basis for his statement for Kevin. He started this work that evening.

He spent the week building by day, and statement writing during the evenings. By the end of the week he had completed the first ten pages. He emailed them to Kevin on Friday lunchtime, so that he could start going through it at his earliest opportunity. There was still much to write. It would end up being a ridiculously long statement. He couldn't help feeling that he would not have been so much at risk had he simply agreed to be interviewed. At the end of the day it would probably just have been a few basic questions about his role, with a few more poignant questions about his particular relationship with Cassie, asked by an interviewer who in all likelihood was not particularly stimulated by or interested in the case. He was still so unsure about this no-interview decision.

All week Delilah kept herself to herself. The lack of closeness was so awkward, strained and alien. Anything he said to her seemed to have no impact whatsoever. She was still going out without saying anything. It seemed so unfriendly. Sarah was at that stage of life where home was little more than a hotel room, so he saw little of her to distract himself. Friday was a long lonely day. Delilah had been out all day, and when she returned at tea time, she obviously was preparing to go off somewhere. He dutifully awaited her announcement. When she was ready and the car was all packed up apart from the dogs she told him in a business-like manner that she was off to Morag's for the weekend, again. At least she was letting him know what she was doing. That was something to be grateful for. He didn't really know what to say. He didn't want her going away without him, but he wanted to sound upbeat if possible.

"Ok darling. I'll miss you" was all he managed. He gave her a letter. He had thought she might go away again this weekend, and he wanted her to take something of his heart with her. She took the letter with an expressionless face. Then she called the dogs to her and strode out with them bounding excitedly around her. He walked into the lounge where he could watch her longingly as she shut the eager dogs into the boot of the car, and drove off. The uncertainty of it all was evil. Hope kept him together. Hope that her love for him would prove to be sufficient to overcome whatever it was that she was struggling with right now.

His letter to her read:

'To my darling wife. I love you so much. I am so sorry if I have been useless at showing you that. Maybe you feel that I have taken you for granted, and all the hard work you have put into our relationship and our home over so many years. I probably haven't shown you enough gratitude and appreciation, and for that, I am truly sorry. You have been particularly wonderful over the past few months when times have been so challenging. I have failed to show you sufficient support and encouragement and for that too, I am sorry. I suppose I have been somewhat preoccupied with the allegations against me and the work situation. Please be patient with me. I have been arrogant. I was so wrong to jeopardise my relationship with you by becoming overly familiar with Cassie. I was a fool. You have been so good to me over the years. I do appreciate it. I love you and only you. Yes, I was concerned about Cassie, and I did like her, but at the end of the day, she was just my work. Part of my job, not someone I was trying to have a relationship with. Please forgive my stupidity. I know we can achieve a blissful union if we both want to, and that my attitude needs to be right. Help me learn better to show you my love, understanding and appreciation.

All my love.

Pablo xx'

Again it was a long weekend without her. Monday morning, he was outside, building as usual, when he heard their car return. He went apprehensively into the house to greet Delilah. To his surprise she walked up to him and hugged him. His hope sprang up into a bold beast within him.

"My place is here with you. I am your wife and you are my husband."

Succinct as ever, but this was more than enough. This was so wonderful to hear. He felt so relieved. He was used to her being committed to him, just as he was to her, and whilst she appeared to be questioning that commitment, his world was falling apart. Now his faith in her was being rewarded with certainty and loyalty. A great weight left his shoulders. He hugged her some more. Maybe it would have been nice for her if he could have cried, but he felt no tears, even though he felt a sense of relief bigger than he had ever known in his entire life. They didn't stumble into the bedroom clumsily tearing at each other's clothes. This was real life, not Hollywood. He helped carry her cases indoors. He didn't want to cramp her or seem to want to take advantage of her. She started to busy herself in the kitchen. He was a quiet, stable, confident, and unexcitable type. Getting ecstatic was not something he did. This was probably as good an opportunity as he had ever had for being ecstatic, but he had never understood ecstasy. Equanimity was his thing. In that sense he was very like Delilah, except that he was so much more talkative. They quietly got on with their lives, simply grateful and reassured that they were both there for each other. That night she returned to the matrimonial bed, and they did what they had done over six thousand times before. This was beautifully normal, and for Pablo in particular, this was his rock. He knew that he truly loved her so much.

The following week was so much more pleasant. He felt sure of Delilah. He knew that she was a woman of her word, and when she had restated that she was his wife, he knew that her heart was secure with him. He completed his statement during the week, and dealt with several phone calls from Kevin who sought clarification over various parts of it. Kevin was playing devil's advocate. He was very thorough. He picked up on any parts of it which could be misconstrued or lead to awkward questions. Pablo was not that bothered. As far as he was concerned he had been doing his job, and as it was a pilot role, it was up to his discretion as to how he executed it. Part of his brief had been to build rapport and relationship by whatever means possible. Isn't that what he had done? The allegations were malicious, and the stuff about misuse of data was just some office-waller being overly clever and overly zealous to draw blood from what he saw as low-hanging fruit. He knew that his heart was in the right place and he shouldn't have anything to fear.

One evening when they were back sitting in the lounge together, Delilah said she had something she had to ask his forgiveness for. He was surprised and very curious. She was the sweetest most reliable person he had ever known. He couldn't imagine what she was about to confess. He felt awkward. He was the one who should be asking for forgiveness for getting himself in such a mess with his job, the ramifications of which, although he didn't like to think about them, could become pretty disastrous in a worst-case scenario. He looked at her searchingly. She looked upset. Clearly this was going to be hard for her. But he could see that she was steeling herself to get this out. He was beginning to feel nervous. He waited quietly whilst she forced the words out purposefully.

"I have to ask you for your forgiveness because I have always tried to undermine you."

He felt puzzled, but didn't want to interrupt the flow. He waited with bated breath for her to go on.

"I have always been afraid that I wasn't good enough for you and that one day you would leave me for someone else. So I have never said anything to affirm you or make you feel better about yourself. I was afraid that if you felt any better about yourself, you would definitely feel that you should be with someone better than me. I'm so sorry."

This was dynamite because he'd suspected for most of their marriage that she felt something like this. She had always hidden her feelings, and he had suspected that it was something to do with vulnerability. He had occasionally tried to talk about it with her, but she had always denied any issues. Now he felt such a sense of relief. His gut-feelings had been right, and now that she had admitted it, he felt that they could take their relationship to a new higher level. He was deeply grateful.

"Babe, you shouldn't be apologising to me. I should be apologising to you. I'm the one who's fucked up."

Then as a bit of a cheeky afterthought, he added

"Is that why you refuse to use my name?"

She looked painfully guilty as she quietly answered "Yes."

He didn't know how long she had refused to use his name when addressing him. The penny had dropped three or four years earlier. Perhaps it had been going on longer than that, and he simply hadn't registered it. What had switched him onto it was one day it just suddenly dawned on him that when she spoke to the dogs, she almost always used their names, but when she didn't, he was confused as to whether she was addressing him or them. He suddenly realised that whereas she often used their names, she never used his. Never. All of a sudden he felt less important than their dogs. He had pointed this out to her and asked her to please use his name when talking to him. He didn't think it would be a problem, but it was. She had looked pained when he made his point as if this was not something she could rectify. He was disappointed. Was it so much to ask? She didn't have a name for him, of any description. Not his real name, nor any kind of nick name or term of endearment. Just occasionally she might call him darl', but that was rare. This rankled, but he knew Delilah's character too well to argue about it. She was very prone to being contrary and silently resolute. Every now and then he would bring the subject up in frustration, knowing full well that he was not doing his cause any good at all by actually making a request of her, but he couldn't help himself.

But now, however, he was just so happy that she had finally owned up to this holding-back thing. He felt that it was such an incredibly positive thing for her to do. Something very good was coming out of this dilemma they found themselves in. He was very grateful.

"Babe, thank you for sharing that. It is so relevant. I always knew something like that was going on, but you should have known that I would never leave you, not for anyone. Never. When I married you it was for life. I am proud of you."

He took her hand and squeezed it gently. She looked upset. It had been really hard for her to admit what she had just told him. She knew that in that area of support and affirmation, she had let him down. Her soul-searching of late had led to a very positive outcome.

Even though he was still off work, life was normalising. The most important thing to both of them was their relationship, and that was now healing. He was keen to maximise the recovery, and so he made two proposals. Firstly that they take up a hobby together, and secondly that they attend counselling. They had spent all their years together tied to the house during their evenings because of young children, and even as the children grew up and left home, the habit remained. Now was definitely a good time to spread their wings. As for the counsellor, he was afraid that Delilah's emotional state was still fragile, and he wanted to do whatever he could to help strengthen their relationship. He knew that his job sponsored counselling sessions for a period of time. He just needed to find out what the protocol was.

Chapter 7

They pulled up outside a big mature detached house in a salubrious isolated hamlet deep in the countryside. It was a beautiful warm summer afternoon. They had driven down a maze of narrow country lanes with grassy verges to find it. They would have struggled to find it without the benefit of a sat-nav. The house had plenty of character. It nestled behind a red brick wall which wasn't so big, that it didn't look artistic and pleasant. The house itself was also made of red brick, and was half tile-hung, with established climbers adorning most of the walls. The front garden was not particularly deep, but it was a lovely wide spacious plot with lots of space on either side of the house. Conveniently, it was only a fifteen minute drive from their own house. It was where the counsellor appointed for them lived and worked. *Very nice!* they both thought. Delilah had rather reluctantly agreed to see her with him, and she was feeling nervous. They had been to see counsellors before in the past, and she had never felt that it had worked well for her. Pablo by contrast was feeling optimistic. On those occasions they had visited a counsellor in the past, he felt that he came out of it well. It wasn't supposed to be a battle where one party scored points over the other, but in reality, one would seem to be more right than the other, and it usually seemed to be him.

Just before they exited the car, he took her hand and gently asked her if she was ok.

She nodded and said quietly "What have we got to lose?"

"Rather a lot" he replied, slightly puzzled.

They walked through the wrought iron gate up to the front door. Pablo rang the bell and waited. A smart well-presented, middle-class and middle-aged lady answered the door and politely introduced herself as Sylvia, whom Pablo had already spoken to on the phone. She had a nice smile. She was dressed conservatively in a knee length skirt, blouse and light cardigan. She invited them in and she showed them to her nearby counselling room. It was a big house, and this would have been a second lounge or a dining room. It was decorated quite brightly, and was furnished as a lounge. It had big windows and a patio door leading out into the garden. They could now see that the rear garden was very large indeed, with mature trees all around it. Pablo felt he would like to have a look around her garden. There was a man in his fifties out there pottering, and Pablo presumed that he would be Sylvia's partner or husband. Sylvia invited them to sit on the sofa whilst she sat on a harder lounge chair opposite them. Pablo noticed that she wasn't wearing a wedding ring. The seating arrangement was to induce them to relax. Her harder chair reflected that she was there to stay alert, and work. There was a small coffee table between them with a box of tissues on which he seriously hoped they wouldn't need.

"Well," she said as she smiled at them both, "what can I help you with?"

Pablo took the reins first. "Well, I've been effectively suspended from my job, and it's put a strain on our marriage. We think we've sorted it out, but we just want to make sure we've dug out the issues properly."

"I see" she answered pensively, then added "I don't counsel couples. I deal with clients as individuals."

"Oh." Pablo was a little taken aback. At this point, if he'd had any common sense as a married man in the modern world, he would have stood up, thanked her for seeing them, and quickly ushered Delilah protectively and deftly out the door, but instead, he was polite and deferential, feeling that he'd made a faux-pas.

"Does that mean we can't see you as a couple?"

"Not at all, so long as you understand that I am here to do the best for each of you as individuals."

"Ok" he pondered, wondering why she had been so emphatic about this. He decided that as she was actually seeing them both together, it should be fine. He wanted it to be ok. He looked at Delilah and she nodded with a slight shrug of the shoulders. So he said that was fine, although inside he was muffling little alarm bells. Really, he wanted to know that anyone counselling them as a couple had their best interests at heart as a married couple. Now he had reservations, but he had that awkward feeling that as they had made a start, they ought to get on with it, even if it was only for one session. He placated himself by remembering that this was really about getting Delilah to open up and make sure any issues she was still harbouring were dealt with. Surely that could happen.

Delilah entered the conversation very directly.

"Pablo's had an allegation made about him by a female client. It seems he has overstepped the mark in his professional relationship with her, and it's jeopardised his job."

She sounded hurt. Pablo felt embarrassed. That felt like something of an attack. Sylvia picked up on Delilah's hurt immediately.

"How has that made you feel Delilah?"

"Betrayed."

Pablo was feeling a little more keenly now that this was not necessarily a good idea. He'd only been in the room for a minute or two, and he already felt under attack. He felt particularly awkward because whenever he had tried to discuss issues with Delilah, she would always accuse him of being defensive, as if making a defence of any sort showed that he was incapable of accepting any fault or responsibility. She seemed to think that he was always in the wrong, and he shouldn't try to defend himself. So he was loathe to start defending himself from the very word go. That would definitely not win him any brownie points. So he waited to see what would happen next. Sylvia looked at him sort of dispassionately, yet he couldn't help feeling that he detected a hint of judgement. She asked him a question.

"Pablo, did you know that you had made Delilah feel betrayed?"

Ouch! That was rather direct. He parried.

"It was my work. She was a client who I only saw by appointment, and I was effectively supervising her in her battle against heroin addiction. Why would Delilah feel betrayed by that?"

Sylvia looked inquiringly and sweetly at Delilah. That was enough to stimulate Delilah's response.

"He sent her emails telling her how much he liked her."

Sylvia looked at Pablo with thinly veiled disgust, challenging him with her hard stare.

"That's true" he replied pleadingly, "but I was only trying to flush her out. She had gone dark on me."

He hoped that was sufficiently opaque so as to buy him a few moments to gather his thoughts whilst Sylvia worked out how best to twist the knife next.

"What were you trying to achieve by telling her how much you liked her?"

Good lord, she was really putting him on the spot. Pablo stumbled around for his defence.

"She was always unpredictable, and I know that she wanted to know that I actually cared about her as opposed to her being just a job, so I reassured her that I did care about her, hoping that might help flush her out."

"What do you mean by flush her out?"

"She had disappeared. Gone off the radar, and I was genuinely concerned about her."

"Didn't she have a right to go off the radar if she wanted to?"

They were discussing Cassie, and he wanted to be discussing him and Delilah, but then he considered that the subject of Cassie had to be aired, so they might as well get it out of the way early on.

"Yes, but that doesn't mean that I should have just ignored her."

"Should? Was it your job to flush her out?"

Before he had a chance to answer that Delilah interjected.

"Part of the problem with work is that he had been moved into a different department. He wasn't supposed to be seeing her anymore."

Sylvia looked at him very sternly, her disgust less thinly disguised now. Her eyes narrowed considerably. He thought that counsellors were supposed to be impartial, but he didn't think she was very good at being impartial, and Delilah seemed to be relishing putting him on the spot. He felt let down by her.

"Can you explain that Pablo?" Sylvia asked him pointedly with a fixed demanding gaze.

He was being interrogated, and he was beginning to wonder why he was having to justify himself to this strange woman. He was already having to justify himself to his wife, and his job, and now this smug counsellor too. It was getting tedious. He wanted to keep this brief.

"It was a sideways move. I was dealing with the same client group almost, except officially, after they moved me during a cost-cutting exercise, I was only responsible for the ones with the actual 'prolific offender' label, and Cassie wasn't a prolific offender."

"So why did you continue to try to stay in touch with her?"

"Duty of care." He hoped this would be a strong argument to a woman in her role. And it sounded professional and trendy.

"But it sounds like you didn't have a duty of care towards her after they moved you."

She wasn't going to give in, and neither was he.

"That's the antithesis of duty of care, just dropping people you've set up to need you. That's what my organisation does, but I don't. I remain true to people I am involved with. I stayed in touch with about half a dozen of my former clients who weren't on the prolific list at the time."

Oh dear. Here he was again, fighting his corner. Justifying himself instead of blindly pleading his guilt, but he thought that the inclusion of other ex-clients was such a strong point to make, and it wasn't a lie. Delilah would not be impressed. She seemed to want him to go down with a sinking ship, not seeming to realise that if he went down, she went down with him. Sylvia responded to his argument.

"How many of this half a dozen were women?"

She was clever. This seemed like a fairly innocuous question, but it veiled an insinuation that he had an inclination towards female clients. Fortunately he could honestly refute the insinuation.

"Cassie was the only female . The others were all male."

"Why did you carry on seeing them?"

"I told you. A duty of care. I would have felt guilty just dropping out of their lives so suddenly. I still wanted to encourage the positive behaviours I had helped them adopt and give them moral support. Plus, they were a great source of information for me regarding my prolific client group, and some of them were very likely to get the prolific offender label in time anyway."

"That was good of you" she said as if innocently, but he detected her sarcasm.

She then spoke to Delilah for a while, finding out more about her life, her achievements, her goals, and her current role in life. She seemed concerned that Delilah had sacrificed her life for the wellbeing of the family. He wondered if that was such an unusual thing these days.

She then focussed back on him.

"It seems to me that Delilah has devoted herself to you and the children whilst you go out and pursue your own career."

She said this as if pursuing a career was a selfish thing to do.

"That's true, she has, and I have devoted myself to work my butt off for the past thirty years to support us all."

He looked at her a little aggressively. He was definitely having to fight his corner.

She mused on that for a moment then baited him with another question.

"Maybe she now needs to pursue a career for herself. Would you support her if she did?"

He felt she was toying with him.

"Of course. I've done nothing but totally support her through her first career of bringing up our four children, and that was her choice, and she has been very happy with that choice."

He thought that was a clever deflecting answer, but tried not to look smug himself. There was a battle of wits going on. He didn't want to ask what career Delilah might pursue, as that would demean her, but he was thinking that she left school aged fifteen with no qualifications, and no ambitions other than to get married and raise a family, and was therefore quite limited on the career front. Quite like her three older sisters really, who between all four of them barely had two GCEs to rub together.

"You control the purse strings?"

This sounded like an accusation. He was feeling got at.

"I earn the money. I pay the bills. Delilah doesn't have to worry about money. I look after everything."

He thought that this sounded generous, but Sylvia was a little horrified.

"She doesn't need you to look after her. She is a grown woman, not a child."

If she was trying to make him feel small, it wasn't working. He didn't feel the need to justify their lifestyle to her. It had worked very well for three decades. Who was she to try to undermine them? He was surprised at her discomfort about the way they ran their life together, and he felt like she was chiding him like an errant child. His instinct was to defend himself again, but he was growing weary of this and he decided to say nothing in response but to see where she was going with it. He was ready to state the other side of the equation; that he had been the one who had worked earlies, lates, and nights, decade after decade. He was the one who finished work at ten pm some nights only to be expected to be bright and punctual for work the next morning at six am. He was the one who had to commute long journeys to and from work each day. He was the one who was locked into a strict timetable of when he had to be at work five or six days a week. He was the one whose lifestyle was dictated by a big faceless corporation to whom he was just a faceless number. He was the one who didn't see the children as often as he would have liked to. He was the one who had the worry of making sure there was enough money for the mortgage, the rates, food, clothing, insurance, petrol, the kids, etc, and he did this single-handedly whilst Delilah managed her time each day exactly as she wished to. Was that really so abusive?

"Don't you think she deserves to be treated like an adult?"

"Of course. I didn't mean that I don't treat her as an adult."

Delilah wasn't coming to his aid, and he rather hoped she would.

Sylvia then asked Delilah a few more general questions. Delilah seemed happy to answer. Things were going her way it appeared. Sylvia was asking her all the general questions as if she didn't trust John. At least, that's how it was beginning to feel to him. Thankfully their hour drew to a close, and Sylvia announced that they would have to end there for this session, but she hoped they could make another appointment in a week's time. Pablo resisted the temptation to shout out a loud 'Hallelujah!' as he made for the door and relief.

The police service would foot the bill for six sessions, so it looked like they might be returning. They all bade farewell politely when they reached the front door, and Pablo and Delilah retreated to the car, he a little more purposefully than her. When in the car he asked her if she thought that had been useful.

"Yes, I think so." She had a rather self-satisfied look on her face.

"Don't you think she was rather harsh with me?"

"No. She was just doing her job."

He looked at her a little pained, but left it at that. He didn't want to dig a bigger hole for himself than Sylvia had already dug for him. The fact was that on their own, they were getting along really well. Delilah seemed to be making more of an effort to make things work out well between them, and for that he was eternally grateful.

At home, he prioritised completing the statement for Kevin. By the end of the week he had completed it. He emailed it to Kevin who in due course would occasionally phone him to discuss certain bits of it, and to advise clarification or amendments. This fine-tuning process went on for about another two weeks, until Kevin was relatively happy. It was now nearing the end of June. Pablo couldn't believe how long it was all taking. He had to attend the offices again, just to sign the finalised printed copies, but he was happy because, surely they must be getting towards the end of this nightmarish process.

Meanwhile, with Delilah, he had suggested taking up a new hobby, together. Initially they had no idea what that might be, but she spotted an advert for something called modern-jive dancing. Lessons were held once a week in a local hotel. Neither of them knew what modern-jive dancing was. They had never even heard of it before, but Delilah fancied giving it a go, and Pablo was happy to be involved in anything with her.

Chapter 8

The following Wednesday evening, they turned up at their local jive class at a dancehall in a large hotel. They were very warmly greeted by the lady on the door, who took their entrance fee, and happily explained to them the nature of the evening's events. There was only a small group of about thirty people, and as Pablo and Delilah walked slowly and curiously into the hall, other participants came up to them to welcome them and chat. It seemed refreshingly friendly and open. When the lesson began, the lady from the door was partnering the teacher, who was her boyfriend. All the dancers on the floor mirrored the teacher and his partner who stood on the stage, facing each other. They talked through some simple moves as they demonstrated them in very slow motion. This was the beginners class, and later on, there would be an intermediate class along the same lines, but involving more challenging moves. It seemed very unusual to Pablo, because participants were getting physically close to people who either were, or had been, complete strangers. They seemed happy to accept this breaching of personal space as the price to pay to learn a beautiful skill. For some of course, the closeness was something that they craved in their lonely lives. Every few minutes, the ladies moved down the line one or two places. This was standard practice at all classes. It enabled each member the opportunity to experience every other lead or follow, and it broadened everyone's experience. Pablo was wooden, stiff and mechanical. Beginners always were. He was focusing more on remembering than performing. His body was tense and forced, not free and flowing. His movements were slow and unsure. It was alien trying to copy someone else's precise movements, and it was hard work. The lady partners, who were all far more experienced than him, were generous and encouraging.

"We were all beginners once dear" they would reassure him. "You'll soon get it."

At the end of lesson one, a selection of music was played, and everyone got the chance to practice if they wanted to. At this point Pablo stood back and observed how different everyone was. Some of the couples seemed very accomplished and flowed in a beautiful syncopated manner in time with the music. Others seemed more intent on having a bit of a laugh. Still others were clearly struggling with either the music, the moves, or their partner, or maybe even all three. He watched Delilah. She was proving popular. The male leads all seemed very keen to take her on the floor and impress her with their prowess. She looked beautiful and seemed full of life and fun. She had clearly really warmed to this.

He chatted to another male dancer standing nearby to learn more about this pastime. Apparently there were lots of different moves that could be learned, and they could be strung together in whatever way the lead chose to lead them. The follower's skill was different to that of the lead. It was the leader's job to learn the moves, and the follower's skill was to learn to follow seamlessly, as if without effort. She wouldn't know in advance what moves would be led. None of this was choreographed. She would pick up on all kinds of small signals, mostly from his fingers and arm movements, but sometimes from the movement of his chest. It all seemed incredibly clever. He wondered if he was too old to get the hang of it. Apparently musicality was the most important thing. That meant doing things with style and panache, to suit the mood of the music. It might mean going quicker or slower as the music dictated, or throwing in sudden stops or drops, or certain foot or leg movements to emulate the beat. Both he and Delilah sat out for the intermediate lesson. It was interesting to just watch, and when that lesson came to an end, they had another opportunity to just practice with the others.

By the end of the evening, they both felt enthused. It had been a real boost to do something different, but particularly this, where there was so much human interaction. Learning to move to music was something of a revelation to them both, as neither of them had been involved in any kind of dancing before. For Pablo it was the birth of a new and fresh appreciation of music itself. In the car on the way home, they eagerly exchanged little anecdotes from their activity on the floor. They were both impressed by the genuine warmth and friendship of the fellow dancers, and were both very keen to carry on with this new hobby.

The next day brought their second counselling encounter. Pablo was feeling cocky. Even though he felt that the first session had gone seriously against him, he was wallowing in something of a renaissance between him and Delilah. Her confessing to him about deliberately not encouraging him or building him up during their entire marriage had been the breaking of a glass ceiling, and he was now excited about taking their relationship to new heights. He had always known that she was holding back, but whenever he had tried to talk about it, she had denied it, and accused him of imagining it. Finally she had been honest with him and he felt gratified and hopeful. Not that she had suddenly changed into a loquacious, verbally-supportive, and appreciative type. He hadn't expected any sudden changes in her attitude, partly because he knew she was currently rather preoccupied with his work situation, and partly because he knew that her nature didn't well dispose her to being effusive in any way. Changes would be gradual and incremental. He was just happy that they seemed to have overcome what had been the biggest threat to their marriage in thirty years. She was at least beginning to use his name, and he cherished that. She had always been keen to please him in the bedroom, and now even more so, which was quite something, because he already felt very lucky to have such a willing and able sexual partner. Their sex life had never waned in thirty years. So, as for Sylvia, he was not unduly worried. Surely she wouldn't want to harm their relationship? Why would she? She didn't even know them. She was just some random counsellor earning her keep. So this week, as they entered the lion's den, he felt safe. His wife had been making him feel very loved in her own way, and he felt secure. And surely she knew how much he loved her.

"How have things been this week?" Sylvia politely enquired.

Pablo answered in upbeat fashion. "Really good. We seem to be getting on really well, and we've started dancing together too."

He seemed pleased with himself. She looked at Delilah.

"And Delilah, how have you been feeling?"

"Yeah, pretty good. Obviously I'm still really worried about Pablo's work situation, but apart from that, things are pretty good."

"And has there been any progress on that front?"

She was looking at Delilah. As usual she seemed more interested in how Delilah felt than Pablo. Delilah answered with some uncertainty.

"No change, as far as I know. Things are still under investigation, as far as I know."

She seemed to emphasise the 'as far as I know' bit, as if to imply that she didn't trust that Pablo was keeping her fully informed.

"It must be very worrying, not knowing what the outcome might be."

"Yes it is."

"And for you too Pablo."

He thought that she was just being polite to bring him in on this subject. He didn't get the impression that she was concerned about him at all, only Delilah.

"I am sure that in the fullness of time it will prove to be just a storm in a teacup" he asserted.

She had a way of looking at him that made him feel that she didn't approve of his attitude. She gave him that look. He decided that he would like to air the subject of Delilah's lack of emotional support over the decades. He thought it would be good to show her their progress, but also that Delilah was not quite so fawning and sweet as she seemed to be.

"I think we've overcome a massive hurdle."

"Really? That sounds impressive. Can you share it?"

"Yes. Delilah made a confession to me that throughout the course of our marriage she has deliberately held back any praise or encouragement to me because she felt insecure and she didn't want to big me up. She believed that if I had even more confidence in myself, she wouldn't be good enough for me. Now she has finally admitted to it, and asked for me to forgive her, which naturally I have done."

Of course this was going to backfire on him. Sylvia didn't want the emphasis shifting from him onto Delilah. She looked at Delilah with an expression of mild pity.

"Have you always felt insecure in your marriage Delilah?"

"Yes." she replied simply. "I never thought he would stay with me."

"Why is that?"

"Pablo has always been popular with women, and I thought that it was only a matter of time before he met someone he would prefer over me. That's why I always held back."

Pablo was biting his tongue. He was fighting the urge to jump in and defend himself too quickly.

"What do you mean, 'popular with the women'?"

"He has always worked with women, and he seems to get really close to them."

"In what way?"

"He'll talk about them like he's really fond of them. I always got the impression that he was too friendly with them. It just made me feel like I was living on borrowed time."

Pablo was chafing at the bit. Under attack again, and so unfairly he thought. It would look bad if he charged in with his defence like a bull in a china shop, so he bided his time. He waited uncomfortably like a coiled spring. Sylvia continued to address Delilah.

"Did his interest in the women he worked with make you feel inferior?"

"Yes" she replied sadly.

"You stayed at home looking after the kids, cooking, cleaning, doing all the housework whilst he went off to work having a gay old time with his female work colleagues? Is that how you felt"

"Yes."

This kind of questioning reminded him of a police interview where the defence counsel would jump in at this stage claiming that the officer was making unfair assertions or unsupported assumptions. Here, he was his own defence counsel, and he jumped in with his oppressive imperious opinions. The spring had sprung.

"That's not fair. I've never had an affair, I've never tried to have an affair. I've never even fantasised about having an affair, but at the same time, I don't think that because you're married, you're not allowed to talk to the opposite sex. This is not Afghanistan you know."

Sylvia looked at him with quiet defiance.

"Don't you think you had an emotional affair with Cassie?" she challenged bluntly.

"That's not fair either. You're using terminology that makes it sound like something wrong. Who's to define what an emotional affair is?"

"Your wife?"

"I can't be ruled by her insecurities. I know my heart is in the right place. Nobody else is in a position to judge my heart. She only knew anything about the people I worked with because I talked to her about them. Surely if I had something to hide, I wouldn't have mentioned them would I?"

This was getting heavy, he thought, and he didn't like being on the back foot again, feeling the need to defend himself as usual.

"Did you talk to her about Cassie?"

"Yes." He said this with only a little conviction, because he knew that he hadn't spoken about her much.

"Not much" Delilah added. "I didn't know half of what was going on."

Pablo was embarrassed. That was true. He looked directly at Delilah sitting right next to him on the couch.

"I've admitted overstepping the mark with Cassie, and I've asked you for your forgiveness."

She made no response. She probably sensed that Sylvia would pick up the gauntlet for her. She did.

"Pablo, did you overstep the mark with other women you've worked with?"

"No, I don't think so." He emphasised the 'I' and carried on.

"As far as I'm concerned, I've always been faithful and devoted to Delilah no matter who I met or got on with. I've always loved her very much, and I cherish my family. I would never do anything to threaten our marriage or family."

Sylvia looked at him with steely-eyed composure and quietly added "But you did."

"How?"

"Why are you here, suspended from your work?"

"That was a malicious allegation."

"Your organisation doesn't think so."

"My organisation is an ass."

"Really?" she said, with an air of disbelief.

He looked at his wife, wondering what she was thinking. He couldn't help feeling that this counsellor had it in for their marriage, as if it was an anachronism, a throwback to a bygone age, a historic wrong, and poor downtrodden Delilah needed a gallant noble maiden on a white steed to charge into their lives and rescue her. Was she going to buy into this modern bunkum that marriage was little more than a restriction, a stricture, an obstruction to future independent life, a paternalistic artifice to deny her the best life possible? She was giving nothing away.

Sylvia pulled back from the attack for a bit. Perhaps she sensed she was getting a little too intrusive for Pablo, and she started to broach another subject.

"Communication is the key to a healthy relationship, and it's important for you both as individuals to feel that your partner is hearing you. Pablo, how is communication between you and Delilah?"

"Good enough I think. I mean, we're very different. I wear my heart on my sleeve, and she hides her feelings. It seems to me that she always knows what's going on in my heart but I have to decipher her through a series of minuscule clues. But I'm used to that. I've been doing it for thirty years. It's her nature, and I'm never going to change it. The important thing is that we share similar values and goals, which makes it easier to understand each other."

"And you Delilah?"

"It's true. I'm not very good at communicating. I do tend to keep my thoughts to myself."

"Do you feel free to share your thoughts generally with Pablo?"

"Not really."

"And why is that?"

"I'm afraid of his reaction."

Pablo winced. Sylvia firmly pursued the topic. She smelled blood.

"In what way?"

"Sometimes he gets angry, and I don't like that."

"How does he show his anger?"

"He gets loud and insistent."

Time to go on the defence again, Pablo decided.

"Wait a minute." He looked at Delilah, not Sylvia. "If you decide to keep your thoughts to yourself, that's your choice. You can't blame me for you not talking. You know I'm always trying to find out what you think, and it's hard work."

His voice conveyed forcefully his exasperation, but he did his best not get loud and insistent.

Sylvia interjected, saving Delilah from having to talk.

"Pablo, you are a big strong confident man. I'm sure that in the police service, you have learned to speak to all sorts of people in all sorts of circumstances, and you are a good communicator. But communication is about listening as much as speaking. If we use a simple analogy to help us understand the differences between people, we could liken you to a rhinoceros, and Delilah to a hedgehog. The first sign of danger, and you will be charging around like a rhinoceros, making sure everyone knows how big and strong and confident you are, but Delilah will stay still and curl up into a tight ball."

"Yeah. I know that."

That was not the first time he had heard that analogy applied to them by a counsellor.

"Which makes communication between the two of you difficult. What do you think you can do to make it more effective?"

He felt like he was being pushed into a corner, the obvious answer being teased out of him.

"I suppose you're implying that I need to be more sensitive. More quiet. Allow Delilah to come out of her shell more safely."

"Yes, and maybe resist the urge to state your case. Allow her more space. "

She took a little pause allowing him to process what she was saying.

"Pablo, you're a quick thinker. You put your thoughts into words instantly. I suspect that Delilah takes more time to process her thoughts, and to find the words and idioms she needs to effectively express herself."

Delilah sat there quietly, processing her thoughts slowly. She had a self-satisfied look on her face. She seemed to be enjoying watching him being made to back down.

Sylvia looked sympathetically at Delilah and asked her,

"Delilah, are you confident that you can openly express your feelings to Pablo?"

"Not really."

"But you've been together for over thirty years. Have you been hiding your thoughts and feelings for all of that time?"

"I suppose so, to a large extent."

Pablo sank back in his seat a little. He didn't think that it was his fault if his wife was reticent by nature, and he had always done his best to understand her.

"Would you like to work on some skills to help you express yourself more confidently?"

"Yes. That would be very useful."

Pablo was the bogey man. The rest of the session went along in a similar vein. As matters were raised, such as decision-making, projects, activities, home improvements etc, it seemed that he was too strong, too opinionated, too dominant, too cock-sure of himself. Of course to contradict these points in any way was to virtually prove them at the same time. It was something of a catch 22 for him. Thankfully the session came to an end, and he was released from this slow-burn purgatory. He eagerly drove home, Delilah sitting by his side, looking a little smug again.

Come the middle of July, Pablo got a call from Roger. He had begun to think that Roger had forgotten all about him. He hadn't heard from him in what seemed like ages. He was not the type to phone up regularly just to see how things were going, or to touch base, and Pablo had become accustomed to the neglect.

"Yes Roger, what is going on?"

"Pablo, they're ready to interview you."

"Thank God. It's taken long enough. They've had my statement for over a month, and Cassie's for what, six, seven months?"

"Yes I know Pablo. These things take time. You need to go to police headquarters on the 22nd of this month at 10:00 am. I'll meet you in the reception of the Internal Affairs department. Ok?"

"You bet. I can't wait to get this crap over and done with."

"Don't forget. We've served them your statement. You must answer 'no comment' to all of their questions. That's all you've got to do."

"I still don't feel comfortable with that Roger. It makes it look like I've got something to hide."

"Believe me Pablo, it's the safest way to deal with them. With that comprehensive statement you've provided, they won't even expect you to answer their questions."

"Really?"

"Really. Don't worry about it."

"Well, obviously I'm taking legal advice on this, from Kevin and you, but it really doesn't feel right."

"You'll be fine. I'll see you on the 22nd. I'll be in the interview with you."

"Ok. See you there."

The conversation was curt and minimal, as always, but at least he had been in touch.

He sought Delilah out to tell her the news. She seemed fairly nonchalant, as if this was a mere tiny step. It wasn't an outcome, and she was right, of course. She said little, and was undoubtedly much more worried about all of this than he was. He had hoped that she would be more pleased about this small step forward. It would bring this nightmare closer to an end. They desperately needed this horrible episode to close as soon as possible. He was confident that nothing would eventually come of it. He had done nothing wrong. He had just over a week to prepare himself, but what was there to prepare, if all he was expected to do was say, 'no comment.' For him, the interview would be just a waste of time. A mere formality.

On the day in question, he met Roger in the reception area of Internal Affairs department. It was a formal chilly atmosphere. He wore a suit specially for the occasion. There wasn't much for them to discuss. Roger assured him again that he would be fine. He reminded him that he could acknowledge his name and role, and his statement, but nothing more. Then, a burly, overweight and rather dishevelled detective constable called Jim appeared. He was relaxed and seemed a little disinterested. He told Pablo that he would be interviewed by Detective Inspector Mooney and himself, and then led him and Roger down a corridor to an interview room. As he did so, he turned slightly towards Pablo and said

"I take it you're going to go no comment what with this lot?"

He waved a wad of A4 pages which Pablo presumed was his statement.

"Yes" he replied rather ashamedly.

"Good" he replied. It seemed that he just wanted an easy life.

Pablo was shown to a seat in the interview room across a table. Roger sat way behind him by the wall. DC Jim sat opposite him, with a second seat next to him that was shortly taken up by the DI who formally introduced himself and then told Pablo that the interview would be recorded. He then cautioned him. That always cut him to the quick. Was he really a criminal? The DI held a few papers in front of him. He had prepared the questions he wanted to ask. He started off by getting Pablo to confirm a few basic details such as name and occupation, and that the twenty one pages the DC held were in fact his submitted statement. Pablo was allowed to actually say yes to these questions.

"Do you accept that the chief constable expects absolute integrity and honesty from his officers at all times?"

"No comment." That hurt. He so wanted to say 'yes, of course' but if he didn't say 'no comment' to all questions, there would be implications about the questions he did go no comment on.

" Do you understand that it was incumbent upon you to carry out your duties with utmost professionalism?"

"No comment." Ouch. That hurt too.

"In regard to one of your charges, named Cassie Woolridge, do you accept that you used undue influence over her to force her to meet you?"

"No comment."

This was such a bad idea. Inside he was screaming out his defence.

"Do you accept that you used your authority to pursue a personal agenda with this woman?"

No comment."

Now he was really squirming inside. He was being painted in the wrong colours and he so wanted to protest and state his side of the argument. But apparently, that had been deemed to be a bad idea.

"Was it your intention to develop a sexual relationship with this woman?"

"No comment."

He sounded guilty by refusing to stand up for himself. This was insanity. He could hold his own in a discussion with anyone.

And so it went on. Lots of sensible questions, that merited sensible answers, which he was well capable of giving, but he had agreed to say nothing but 'no comment.' Eventually, thank God, the questions dried up. It seemed a lot longer to him than it had been, only about ten minutes. He was asked if he had any questions.

"No comment" like a robot.

The interview was over. The tape machine was turned off, the tapes removed, signed, and put into an evidence bag. The DI left promptly. The DC led them out to reception. Strangely, and surprisingly, he shook Pablo's hand, very sincerely, as if to say 'I'm sorry this is happening to you buddy. It's a bum deal.'

Roger congratulated Pablo on doing a fine job during the interview. Pablo himself was not convinced at all. He had felt really uncomfortable and was now absolutely certain that he should have gone with his gut instincts, and sod this official bullshit about going no comment. But it was too late now. The damage had been done. He went home feeling very stupid indeed. He should have trusted his own instincts, not Roger's.

Delilah was out. He got on with his building work, burying his mind in anything other than how the interview had gone. The weather was reasonable, and he still had an entire afternoon to be getting on with something. Delilah returned about tea time. He went in to see her.

"How did the interview go?"

"Crap."

"Why?"

"It just felt so wrong going no comment."

"Isn't that what you were supposed to do?"

"Yes, but I think that was bad advice. In police circles, if someone goes no-comment, it means that they've got something to hide, and I've got nothing to hide. I should have gone with my instincts and just answered their questions."

She looked at him as if in two minds.

"You were advised by professionals to go no-comment weren't you?"

"Yeah, but I think they were wrong."

"And you're right?"

"Yes."

She gave him a slightly contemptuous look but made no further observations. Later, they had dinner together as usual, and later, he made love to her with gusto. She liked it when the animal in him came out.

Chapter 9

Life had settled into a comfortable pattern. Pablo spent most of his time building. He had been off work for five months now, and the summer had been quite a good one. Delilah was building up her care work and was getting busier and busier. They seemed to be getting along fine as a couple, with the dancing as a new added bonus. The black cloud of the work issues loomed menacingly in the background, but after the interview, any activity or progress seemed to have dried up. Roger had gone very quiet. Pablo was good at being patient, Delilah less so, not that she would say much, but Pablo knew she would be constantly concerned in her own quiet way.

Their new dance friends proved to be very sociable. They had been invited to barbecues and parties. This was of course in addition to the weekly classes which they attended and the monthly freestyles. There had not been any noticeable development in their relationship following Delilah's disclosure about deliberately not bigging him up and withholding compliments etc. Pablo still hoped it would lead to her being more appreciative, more encouraging, and more emotionally open in the future, which would be great for their relationship, but for the time being, he was sure that she was being hampered by the investigation hanging over their heads. In the bedroom, however, she seemed to have more appetite, and was more experimental. Obviously that pleased Pablo, yet it seemed strange that there should be a noticeable change in her sexual behaviour for the first time in about thirty years. He mentioned it one night, saying that he appreciated it of course, but he was just curious. She didn't say anything. It was dark and he couldn't see her face to read it. Perhaps he had just embarrassed her a little. If one ignored the work situation, life was sweet.

The series of six counselling sessions with Sylvia had come to an end, thankfully. The tone had never changed. Pablo felt that she was always fishing for reasons why Delilah could be offended or let down by his behaviour or attitude. It riled him no end, as he actually believed that he had been a model husband and father. Not perfect of course, but way above average, and he based that opinion on all the other fathers and husbands that he had met over the years, especially his work colleagues, a lot of whom were prone to having affairs or shirking family responsibilities. It was almost as if Sylvia had a contempt for marriage itself, and sought to undermine what they believed in, like it was illusory, and only really served the man, and not the woman. To him, she had come across as quietly smug, subtly arrogant, and with her own agenda which opposed his own. He was glad that he didn't have to go and see her anymore, but her influence wasn't over. She had become like a stain you couldn't wash out. She had invited Delilah to continue seeing her, alone, as she deemed her in need of further counselling to help her learn to express herself and to be better equipped for effective communication. Pablo was uncomfortable with this, but he could hardly deny the provision for his dear wife to continue her counselling if both she and the counsellor considered it beneficial for her. That would make him seem like the dictatorial, hegemonic, paternalistic, demagogue that he had just spent six weeks arguing that he was not. So Delilah carried on seeing Sylvia weekly, at Pablo's expense of course. The job sponsorship had been all used up. He could only hope and pray that deep down, Delilah's faith in her marriage was strong enough to withstand any cleverly disguised subversive ideology, and the attrition of Sylvia's corrosive, subtle, insinuations.

Finally, at the end of August, he got a call from Roger. Purely business of course. He never just phoned for a casual catch-up chat or a welfare check.

"Pablo, Im sending you some forms to sign and return to me. It's to do with your pay. Six months will soon be up since you first went off work, and the job will stop paying you, but the Fed' will pick up the tab. They farm it out to their insurers, but you will have to sign consents and acceptance of conditions etcetera, and oh, provide bank details of course."

His voice was dull. His attitude, dull. He seemed to be such a dull, tedious person, which was unusual for a copper. Most coppers had plenty of character, and were emotionally strong, which is why they gravitated towards such a challenging career, with difficult people and demanding situations, that benefitted from exceptional levels of initiative and personality.

"No problem" Pablo answered brightly.

"Everything else ok?"

"Yep. Keeping myself busy."

"That's good Pablo. That's really the most important thing."

"No news on my case then?" He presumed there wouldn't be.

"Not yet Pablo, but it shouldn't be long now. I'll let you know something as soon as I know anything myself."

"Ok."

Short and sweet as usual. Pablo went back to his building work. As he worked quietly outside in the warm summer air, he wondered about Delilah. He was concerned about her. He knew very well that she was not an emotional person, yet over the past few days he had observed obviously, and increasingly, that she was deeply unsettled. He hadn't confronted her initially because he didn't want to make matters worse. It might be hormonal, or it might just be the worry about his work situation. Either way there was nothing he could do to help, so he had decided to overlook it and just be his usual self with her. Yet she was particularly quiet, and that was saying something. She was becoming more upset by the day. She looked strained, her face drawn by some unspoken burden. Sometimes she appeared to be on the verge of tears. She avoided any eye contact with him. There came a point where he felt it was time to confront her. Late one afternoon in the kitchen he stood in front of her.

"Babe, you're obviously upset about something. You've been this way for several days. I think you need to tell me what it is."

She crossed her arms and turned away from him. She said nothing. He stood behind her and wrapped his strong arms around her waist, as he often did. He loved to hug her.

"Is it to do with you looking for work?"

He enquired softly and kindly. No reply. he continued. He needed to coax this demon out of her.

"Only really, you don't need to worry about that. If you want a job, fine. But you don't need to go out and work if it's just about money. You know I'll always provide for you, don't you?"

Again. No response. She pulled gently away from him and moved a few paces to stand at the sink looking out the window over the building site at the magnificent view beyond. Her eyes weren't focusing on anything in particular. She was lost in thought and pain.

"Look Delilah, I know you don't like talking about your feelings, but this can't go on. You really need to tell me what's wrong. You're obviously in a bad place, and I need to know why, and if there's anything I can do to help. I'm worried about you."

He was actually being quite forceful now. He really needed to know what was going on. He had never seen her like this before. She turned around, arms still crossed, as if to face him but without looking directly at him. She said quietly;

"I don't want to be with you anymore."

He died.

He couldn't believe what she had just said, yet instantly, he knew he was done for. He stood still. Shocked. Looking into her lovely face which was turned away. That short pithy phrase repeated in his head over and over, like he was being repeatedly stabbed to death but he was able to relive the moment, like a nightmare. He absolutely knew that she wouldn't have said that if she didn't totally mean it. He didn't know what to say. He just stood there fighting back tears, looking so torn, his brow deeply furrowed. She knew she had just dropped a bomb. She knew that she had as good as killed him. Time stood still. He was trying to process this, but he didn't know how to. His insides felt weird. He felt weird, suddenly lost, destroyed. She was his life. He had devoted his entire adult life to her for thirty three years. And she, him. In an instant, he had become totally defeated, obsolete, discarded. He knew in that moment that there was nothing he could do. If all that he had done over the past three decades weren't enough to hold her, nothing was. He grappled in his confused mind for something to say. He had to find something to say.

All he could come up with was,

"Is it me?"

"Partly."

"Is it the house?"

"Partly."

And that was it. He didn't know what else to say, and she didn't volunteer any explanation whatsoever. His mind was whirling too much to conduct a thoughtful focussed enquiry. She was clearly upset and was fighting back tears too. They stood there awkwardly for a few moments. What are you supposed to do when you have just told your husband of thirty years that you don't want to be with him anymore? What are you supposed to do when your wife of thirty years, whom you believed would love you until the day you died, announces that she doesn't want to be with you anymore?

Neither of them knew what to do. He walked away. His heart was beating a lot faster than normal. It felt like a life-threatening fight or flight scenario. Yet it was nothing physical. A lot of the discussion with Sylvia had been about Delilah needing space. So he went to the bedroom and removed some clothing. He got what he needed to be able to sleep in one of the spare bedrooms and transferred his stuff there. He would give her space.

There was no further contact that day. He was shell-shocked. The misgivings, confusion and desperation were not diminishing as the hours slowly ticked by. There was no point in arguing with her. If he tried to, she would just clam up, and more to the point, he just couldn't argue with her. He felt completely deflated. He realised that she had to do what she had to do. He didn't understand what was going on, but a change of heart could only come from her. He could only hope that she would see the folly of what she was doing, in time. When he went to bed on his own, in the spare room, he wept deeply, like a child in great pain or fear. He cried, but he didn't know what to think. Just two nights earlier they had made passionate love in their bedroom as they so regularly did, and now their lifelong relationship had come to an end. He simply couldn't comprehend this. He had thought that they were getting along fine. In fact, he thought that things were improving between them. They seemed to have overcome the initial disruption caused by Cassie and her complaint. How could this happen so suddenly, out of the blue? Why had she given him no warnings? Could this still be something to do with his emails to Cassie? But hadn't they got over that six months ago? And if it was to do with that, why had it blown up in his face now? He wrote her a letter. It was easier to put his thoughts down on paper compared to trying to actually talk to her.

'My darling, you seem to have given up hope. You've pulled down the shutters. You want to protect yourself. I am in the wrong and so you have shut me out completely. But babe, you can get your hope back. I have learnt so much recently about me and you. It's clear to me that I have hurt and damaged you. It is also clear to me how much and how deeply I love and need you. I want to replace any bad attitude with care and sensitivity. We have an amazing depth of love together. I have never not loved you. I have just been useless at showing it. When I look over your old cards to me, I realise how deep your love has been too. Come back to me. I want to cherish, nurture and care for you. My love has been tested, and I find that it is so deep, that I want to sacrifice my life to you, properly, entirely. I know that there is hope because I have never been in this place before, and I find that all I want to do is mend, keep, grow and enjoy your love for me, and my love for you. I don't want anything else. Have hope. Help me, forgive me, have me. You are not my possession. I am yours.

Love Pablo.'

The next day he left the letter out for her. It disappeared, but between them personally, it was very awkward. They both carried on doing what they would normally do in terms of eating and preparing for the day ahead, but she was understandably avoiding him. If they passed, there was no small talk. Neither knew how to deal with the situation. After a quick breakfast, she went out. He got on with his building. He wondered if she would return. How could they live together if she really didn't want to be with him? It would be so traumatic for them both. Later on however, she returned and walked the dogs. After that she actually cooked dinner for them both. It was as if she had decided to find a new life, but didn't know how to start it. Maybe she still respected the one she had. Maybe she wasn't sure. They sat down at the same table. He wondered what she would say to the children. And when.

"What are you planning to do?" he enquired, as unobtrusively as possible.

"Move out."

This seemed crazy to him. She had no money of her own, and had only recently started working part-time. And here she had a fabulous home with him.

"Are you going to get a full-time job?"

He was reminding her indirectly of the practicalities of life.

"If I have to. I don't know how I'll manage. It scares the shit out of me, but I'll have to get by somehow."

She was clearly determined, yet confused.

"Why are you going?" he asked so deeply sadly.

"I need space." This was going to become her stock answer, but it was one he really didn't understand, but this was not the right time to push the subject. She seemed too vulnerable, and he didn't want to upset her more. This needing space lark smacked very strongly of Sylvia.

"Have you spoken to the kids about this?"

"Not yet."

He knew that she would find that very difficult. The last thing she would want to do was somehow damage her family.

"When will you?"

"As soon as I can I suppose."

That was the extent of their conversation that night. After dinner he cleared up as usual, and then watched telly, but she went to her room. They were living separate lives now, and there was nothing he could do about it. Was this really going to be the new normal after thirty years of togetherness?

His thoughts and feelings soon found their way onto paper again. It was the only way he felt comfortable reaching out to her. Each time he wrote her a letter he would type it out on the computer, then fine tune it, re-read, and fine tune it some more. He wanted it to be as effective and focussed as possible. When he was finally happy with the way it sounded, he would write it out long-hand for Delilah to read at her leisure. It was a long-winded but thorough process. That was his nature. How could it not be when he was so immersed in his thoughts and feelings. In essence, he wanted her to know that whatever she was not happy about, he wanted to put it right.

'To my dear Delilah. I love you with all my heart. Always have done. Always will. It breaks my heart that you can no longer bear to be with me. I hate myself for turning your love into contempt. Please forgive me. Your love has always been precious to me. I don't know how I have been so stupid not to have convinced you of that. I'm sorry that I've made my need for your love and affection such a difficulty for you. Please forgive me. I suppose I haven't coped well with losing your love and my job. I am so grateful to you for the past thirty years. You have been a wonderful wife, and I think you are more gorgeous now than I did thirty years ago. We have been through so much together. You have been incredibly supportive of me over all those years, and I am so grateful to you for that. You misunderstand me and I misunderstand you. I don't want anyone else. Only you. I will always be there for you. I only think of you fondly and with love. No recriminations. I will miss you forever if you go. I don't want to live without your love.

All my love, Pablo."

It was hard for him. He was constantly fighting back the tears. He was desperate to reach out to her and to reassure her of his undying love, yet he knew that appearing too needy would seem pathetic, weak and unattractive. There had to be a balance between his care, concern and love and his own dignity. He also realised that she had to do what she had to do, but it would be very hard for him to juggle this situation despite his best efforts. As usual, he left the letter out for her in the kitchen, and again, it disappeared. When they ate together, she never made any reference to it.

The next day he had arranged to meet Henry for breakfast in town. He started crying as soon as he sat at the table with Henry. There were a few other diners around, but Pablo was more or less oblivious to them. He just couldn't hold back his emotions. It was a release.

"Oh no Pablo, what's happened?" Henry's genuine facial expression revealed his empathy for Pablo's pain.

Through the suppressed sobs, Pablo managed a subdued

"She wants to leave me Henry."

"Oh no. I can't believe that Pablo. She's so family-orientated. I really can't believe that. What has she said?"

Pablo spoke quietly, finding it really hard to talk and cry at the same time.

"She just announced that she doesn't want to be with me anymore Henry" He paused, lost in thought, bathed in deep pain, then added

"I don't know why. She didn't explain anything. I suppose it's still to do with the complaint at work, and me sending Cassie emails. She just hasn't got over it."

"That doesn't explain why she would want to leave you Pablo. Have you asked her anything?"

"I've tried, but all she says is that she needs space."

"What does that mean for goodness sake?"

"I don't know. I suspect that it's got something to do with that counsellor we were seeing. Delilah's been seeing her by herself. I don't trust what she's trying to do."

"Oh." He hesitated and thought carefully.

"We saw one of our daughters turned against her husband by a counsellor. You can't trust some of them at all you know."

"Tell me about it."

Henry paused to consider things carefully, then he asked very directly;

"Do you think someone else is involved?"

Pablo didn't need time to think about that. He answered quickly and quietly

"No. No question of that Henry. I just think this job thing, and the house taking so long to do up as well. I think it's all got to her."

"Well Pablo, I know you're a bit of a rough diamond, but you're a great guy. I'm sure your love will survive this. I mean for both of you." He took Pablo's hand and gave it a firm squeeze. He looked pretty vexed himself.

"I hope you're right Henry. I honestly can't imagine life without her."

Henry took both of his hands in his over the table.

"Rosalyn and I will pray for you both, every day."

"Thanks Henry. I appreciate that."

Breakfast arrived. They ate. It was just nice for Pablo to be with him. He really appreciated having Henry to talk to. Henry had no answers, and Pablo didn't expect him to. He made no apology for crying most of the time. He had never been distraught like this during his entire life. It was simply impossible not to cry when thinking or talking about losing Delilah. He was truly heart-broken. Devastated even. He felt absolutely no compunction to apologise for that. Whenever he had seen someone break down in tears on the telly or less frequently, in real life, they always apologised, and he always wondered why. It wasn't wrong to be upset, or to display emotion. It simply wasn't. He wouldn't apologise. If he needed to cry, then he needed to cry, and he hoped that Henry wasn't too embarrassed by it, and if anyone else around was embarrassed, well, that was their problem, not his. He didn't know them, and they didn't know him, and he didn't need to make any excuses to anyone.

He returned home feeling a tiny little bit better having shared his problem. He pondered the feeling that he hadn't really had the words to communicate realistically with Henry. Eskimos apparently have over fifty words to describe snow, yet how many words does the English language have to describe the various depths of heartbreak? He couldn't think of many. Sad? Sorrowful? Upset? They're all so underwhelming. So tame. Distraught? Maybe that starts to tap some depth, but it still sounds manageable, temporal. What's the word for a kind of loss that leaves you searing with emotional pain, that numbs all other thoughts and feelings, that shatters your motivation, that obliterates your sense of purpose in life, that renders your future agenda meaningless? Maybe devastation comes close.

He set his mind to working out what positive steps he could take to maybe help the situation. Then he got a phone call. It was boy solicitor Kevin.

"Hello Pablo. How are you?"

"Fine" he lied. He wasn't going to discuss his marital problems with this lad.

"Just to let you know that Internal Affairs have submitted a file to the CPS."

"Do we know what for?"

"Yes all the original allegations and the data protection allegation too." Pablo felt like saying 'am I bovvered?', but he couldn't expect other people to put effort into protecting him if he didn't seem to be taking the matter seriously himself. But really, he wasn't that bothered anymore. The only questions on his mind were about Delilah. Ultimately, she was the only thing that truly mattered to him, and his kids of course.

"Well, that didn't take them long then, did it?" he added sarcastically, "Only nine months."

Then, thinking about time scales he added

"Any idea how long CPS will sit on it?"

"They should be able to make a decision in the next couple of weeks."

"Ok. Thanks for letting me know."

He didn't want to talk any more, and he politely terminated the call and went back to thinking endlessly about Delilah.

Chapter 10

The next evening Sarah arrived home from work. Pablo was in his office at his computer. She sought him out and immediately hugged him. Thankfully she was only a little tearful. Pablo spoke;

"I take it mum's spoken to you?"

Delilah had obviously found an opportunity to explain to her what was going on.

"I'm so sorry dad." She hugged him. She knew instinctively that he was crushed and in despair. But she felt helpless and hurt too.

"I think she's gone crazy Sarah. What do you think?"

"I think she's gone crazy" she answered with equal astonishment and a little anger in her voice.

They hugged for a while, then he did his fatherly bit and assured her that everything would be ok in the end.

"She needs to have some time out, but that doesn't mean that a new life will work out for her in the long term. I think she'll come back."

"I hope so dad."

She was sincere and confused. He was so sorry that she was going to be living in the thick of this dreadful mess. He really was. She deserved better. Her three older brothers had all long-since left home, and to that extent were more protected from the pain of a parental split-up. Over the next few days Delilah spoke to all the kids on the phone. Pablo left that to her. She had to suffer the discomfort of informing them that she was going to walk away from their dad and her marriage. Pablo made follow-up calls once he knew that Delilah had spoken to them. It is fair to say that they were all shocked, and didn't really understand what was going on with their mum. She was acting so much out of character. But they all realised that there was nothing that they could do to change things. They questioned her wisdom, but were wise enough not to try to interfere. They all reassured both parents of their love and devotion no matter what might happen in the future.

The days passed painfully slowly by. She was effectively hiding from him. Not literally, but emotionally, personally, and physically to an extent. She had nothing to say to him. She was sort of starting a new life as best she could whilst still living in the family home with her husband. She wasn't telling him where she was going when she went out. She had detached herself emotionally. Yet she did still cook for him in the evening, just as he was carrying on with the building work to improve the house. He hated to think where this was leading. Would they have to sell the house? This house that he had put so much of himself into, and loved so much?

Over the next few days there was still a modicum of decency; occasional hellos and goodbyes, but overall, she had withdrawn from the relationship in quite a harsh way. Not only did they not sleep together anymore, which was obviously a major thing, but she was also refraining from the little things like saying where she was going, or what she was doing, or where she had been. Her life had suddenly become private to the person who was supposed to be her soul-mate, her confidant, her lover, her other half. The corollary was that she would show no interest in whatever was going on in his life too, not that he was doing much, except working on their house. He could do no more than accept what was happening, and simply hope and pray that one day, and it would take just one day, she would get up one glorious morning with a revised attitude to life. But, as a man, it was hard for him to resist the urge to fix things.

One evening as they ate dinner quietly together, he asked her to write him a list of all the issues that needed addressing. He wanted to know exactly what he needed to focus on. He stressed his commitment to her and his determination to get things right for her. She didn't seem keen on the idea. She wasn't looking for any solutions. She had made her mind up, but as he persisted that she should at least give him a chance to put things right, she reluctantly agreed. He suspected that she would cooperate just because that looked good. Her heart however was not in it.

As he was being strategic, and as he suspected that he was doing the build too slowly for her, he took this opportunity to let her know that as they had maxed out their mortgage already, Daniel and Mia, his brother and sister, who were joint powers-of-attorney with him for their mother, who was no longer compos mentis, had agreed to let him borrow some of her money to do whatever he needed to help get the work finished more speedily. He would still do all the actual building work and carpentry himself. One day he wanted to be able to look at a wonderful extension, and say 'I built that!'. But he also needed to be able to pay tradesmen to get on expeditiously with the second fix, namely the plumbing, electrics and plastering. His mother was in a care home. Her own home had been sold to pay for her care, but there was still quite a big chunk sitting in the bank waiting to seep out slowly but surely into the coffers of the caring establishment.

Finally, he asked her boldly

"Babe, is there anything I can do to help the situation?"

This she responded to keenly and quickly.

"Yes, you could move out."

That was not the answer he had expected or hoped for. She was so cold and calculating. He considered it for a moment. That would reduce the tension, and it might make her miss him. He surprised himself.

"Ok. I could go and stay with Mia for a while."

Mia was a little older than him. She and her husband Marvin were always welcoming, and he always felt at ease and able to really relax at their place. It was a two and a half hour journey, but it was always worth the effort.

Delilah fixed him with a steely look and said coldly

"Go on then, go."

That was not very nice, but the next morning, he went. He had phoned Mia to make the arrangement. On the phone he had said that it would be only him, and when asked why, he declined to answer there and then because it was too complicated. He said he'd fill them in when he got there. When he arrived, it felt very strange with no Delilah by his side. Mia was not slow in coming forward with her questions. He was very teary as he tried to explain what was happening. She hugged him tightly. She felt desperately sorry for him. Their younger brother Daniel had suffered a marital breakdown about fifteen years earlier, and he had become almost suicidal. It took him several years to be able to start putting his life back together again. So she knew first-hand how devastating these things could be. Marvin simply made him feel very welcome and pampered, but he did seem gutted and astonished by what was going on. However, they weren't acting like it was the end of the world, because it might not be. Nobody knew what Delilah might do next.

During the weekend, they had lovely meals together. Both Mia and Marvin were excellent cooks and hosts. The weather was fine, so they spent lots of time lounging in the garden and taking the dogs for country walks. He visited his mother, who lived in a nearby care home. He could say absolutely whatever he wanted to her, because within seconds, she would have forgotten what he just said. So he told her all about what was going on with Delilah; his hurt, his uncertainty, the strangeness of it all. She was always in surprisingly good spirits, and despite having no short-term memory whatsoever, she still exercised a keen sense of humour. He wondered how the human brain could be so mixed, unable to retain any basic fresh information, yet was able to decipher the complexities of wit and humour. She always laughed a lot when he was with her, and that pleased him. He enjoyed making her laugh. He missed having Delilah with him. She was so good with his mum. He wished that he could do a lot more for her. It was always very hard when she would get to the point where she begged him to take her home. This happened on every visit at some point, and it seemed so cruel that he couldn't, but she was paralysed from a stroke years earlier, and she needed twenty four hour care. She couldn't understand this. She talked as if she could still walk and care for herself.

At the end of the weekend, Mia and Marvin assured him that he could stay with them for as long as he wanted to. That was so kind of them. He was truly touched by their love. He knew they were being genuine, and not just polite. He thanked them and told them that it would not be necessary. The two and a half days he had been there without Delilah had felt long, because of her absence. He wanted to get back to her. Being away denied him any potential opportunity, and he couldn't afford to miss out on any opportunities. Anyway, what would he do here day in day out? Yes, he could do his stocks and shares trading, but what about the extension? He couldn't just leave it three-quarters done. It was his main purpose in life at the moment. It was lovely to know that he was welcome to stay at Mia's for as long as he wanted, but he really had to get back to his 'work'.

He returned home late Monday morning. As he made the final approach to his home in the car and he slowly descended the steep windy lane into the hidden valley, surrounded only by fields and trees, the beauty of the surrounding countryside struck powerfully, as it always did when he had been away. He felt welcomed by it. He belonged here. This place had been an amazing find. He had hoped to spend the rest of his days here, but maybe that was in the balance now. He pulled up in the driveway. Delilah was clearly out, so he prepared to continue his building work. It was early September, and after a rather cool start to the day, it rapidly warmed up as the sun's strength still seared through the air. Delilah returned late afternoon. He was nervous about seeing her. How could that be after three decades together as man and wife? He went indoors to see her. She was in the kitchen putting food away. He so hoped that she would be pleased to see him. What folly.

"Hi" he said tentatively.

She looked at him with thinly veiled mild disgust.

"I thought you were going away" she said sharply and rather fiercely.

"I did."

She gave a short mocking laugh.

"One weekend. Is that all you can do for me?"

He reacted.

"Look, you're the one who wants to leave, so you fucking leave. I don't want to leave. This is my home, and in case you hadn't noticed, I've got a lot of work to do here."

A little anger was unintentionally unleashed.

"I intend to," she replied coldly, and walked away.

The starkness of her resolve was shocking, He had to get used to shocking. He observed her inner strength. He stood for a moment, wondering if there was any point in following her and trying to pursue a conversation. He decided foolishly that he had nothing to lose by trying. He followed her into the hallway.

"Why?" He called after her. He was so confused.

"I already told you. I need space."

"What does that mean?"

"It means that I need space."

She was really telling him that the matter was not up for discussion. She was not happy about being constantly challenged. She got the dogs together and left the house to walk them. He wrote her a letter.

'My dear Delilah. I am sorry for coming back home so soon. I just can't give up on you that easily. I know that you have lost your hope, vision and purpose for the moment, but I want to be here, close to you to help you restore it. I accept that I am the problem, so please let me be close and help me work through the things you want changed. I still want you to make a list for me of all the things you are unhappy about, and I promise to do my best to resolve those issues. I want you to evaluate my progress weekly to help me remain focussed and determined.

I can't leave you. You are the most important person in the world to me, and I will do whatever is necessary to win you back my love. I have never wanted to be with anyone else. I have been stupid to alienate you over what I thought were trivial things. Please forgive me. My job is insignificant alongside you. So is the house. I know you have become frustrated at the slow pace I've been developing it. I'm sorry. I've been doing it in my own time without considering the discomfort that you're in. Please forgive me, and let's work on putting things right, please.

Your ever-loving husband.'

The next day when he saw Delilah, he gave her a sad pathetic imploring look. Had his letter achieved anything he wondered? Clearly not. Since announcing that she was going to be his wife no longer, she simply oozed distance, a coldness, a detachment. There was an emotional veil around her that made him feel like her defences were unreachable. His hopes had very little to be pinned on.

Chapter 11

It was Wednesday. They would still both go to the midweek dance class. It was the only thing they did together, and Pablo cherished it, even though whilst there, they would have minimal contact. He would have her in the car with him for each of the five minute journeys, and that was an opportunity to talk. He was grateful for small mercies. There was very little talk though, if any. As far as she was concerned, nothing was up for negotiation. Fortunately they both loved the dancing, and Delilah in particular seemed to be relishing making new friends. The women were much better and more at ease with socialising amongst each other than the men were. The ladies did all the groundwork, and the men would gratefully tag along to any resultant functions. She bloomed at the class, smiling, fun, personable, but as soon as they left, the veil came down and her personality got put back into the 'off-limits' box. It was lovely for him to see her when she was out dancing. It reminded him of who she really was. The rest of the time he was only seeing a facade, a very faint photocopy of the original. The real person was being increasingly hidden behind a growing battle-mask. There was no yielding, only defending.

Every day, at some point, and often more than once, he cried. Strangely, it occurred mostly when he was eating. He supposed that this was because eating was an autonomous process rather than a thoughtful one, and as the mind slid into some opaque subconsciousness where emotions were given free rein to surface unencumbered. This was most often when the surge of sadness overwhelmed him. It was as if his soul was cleansing itself of the hurt and pain, like a function of his immune system. He was often close to tears at home where he was now living such a quiet life, working alone all day long, but if he was with anyone, and they got talking about his situation, he would cry without exception. He simply couldn't talk about Delilah without tears flowing freely. It might be someone he bumped into at the supermarket, or a friendly cashier at the petrol station. It didn't matter. He was so fragile, though strangely not hopeless. He instinctively knew that both the crying and the talking were cathartic. He was releasing the pain and the anguish, bit by bit, in tiny doses, but he always had hope.

When Delilah was around, he might try talking to her, but she would barely reply. She repeatedly resorted to the same worn-out stinted mantras; 'Everybody says so'; 'You're the only one who can't see it'; 'I need space'. Nevertheless, he still considered it vitally important to try to talk with her. Their marriage depended on it. For him it was about ministering love to her, his precious unrequited love, but for her, he was invading her personal space; he was not respecting her wishes. For him, he was offering her forgiveness and hope. For her, he was violating her. Whilst he had breath in his lungs and blood in his veins, he would reach out to her, whether she responded or not. She was completely shut to him. It was like an alien had taken over her body. Maybe it was this frustration that led him to write copiously. It was two days since his last letter, and time for another.

'My darling Delilah. I am desperate to win your heart back. That is why I have apologised sincerely and declared my undying love. I am here for you twenty-four hours a day. I am a broken, contrite man, offering to rectify my faults. I assert my appreciation and support for you and my unfailing commitment. I am working ceaselessly to provide a wonderful home for you, for us, for the family. But you want to leave because you don't want to be with me anymore. Deep down though, I know that you still love me. I think you just can't forgive me, but I do want to be the best husband for you that I can be. I want to make whatever changes I need to make to keep you happy. But nothing can be achieved whilst you harbour life-long resentments in your heart for what you consider a catalogue of my wrongs. I understand your hurt and that you want to punish me for it. You have the power to hurt me, even to destroy me, but would that free you from your pain? Your anger? Your resentment? I doubt it. I think it would just add to the misery and bitterness. Your heart is hard, your eyes are cold, your face is dead. You need the love of your husband to get back your life, you love, your joy. Please, stop shutting me out. Forgive me instead. Let's both choose to move into a new and deeper love together."

He finished with one of his favourite bible passages, from 1 Corinthians 13. He couldn't remember if this passage had been quoted during their wedding service almost thirty years earlier, but the probability that it had been, was high.

'Love is patient. Love is kind
It is not jealous or boastful or proud or rude.
It does not demand its own way.
It is not irritable, and it keeps no record of being wronged.
It does not rejoice in injustice, but rejoices whenever the truth wins out.
Love never gives up, never loses faith, is always hopeful.
It endures through every circumstance.'

At the end he added a few words of his own;

'Wow, you have all this in your heart. So do I. Please, let's make this work.
All my love, Pablo.'

Nothing he said seemed to have any impact. She was still making searches on their computer for housing. Each week the local paper had asterisks alongside some of the rental properties. He presumed she had been out viewing some of them. She was full of purpose, but that purpose excluded him. There seemed to be nothing he could do or say to distract her from that purpose. She had become a different person, but to him, that didn't feel real.

Delilah was out. The house phone rang. This was in the early days of mobile phones when people were reluctant to use them because of the exorbitant fees.

They would still phone for conversations on land lines when possible because they were very cheap. Pablo answered. It was Morag, Delilah's oldest sister, asking for Delilah.

"She's out."

"Oh."

There was a cool silence, then she politely added

"How are you?" He could hear the reluctance in her voice. She didn't really want to know how he was. She just felt she ought to be polite. He knew that. He had never had any meaningful conversations with her in all the time he'd known her. She looked down her nose at him, for reasons quite unbeknown to him. He presumed that she didn't know that Delilah was planning to leave him, so he thought he ought to mention it.

"Not too good really. Delilah is thinking of leaving me."

He expected this to be a shock to her, but it wasn't. She casually replied.

"Oh well, it's for the best."

He was taken aback.

"What did you say?"

"I said it's for the best"

"How can you say that? She's breaking up a wonderful family. We've been married for thirty years"

"She'll be better off away from you"

This was harsh and cruel. He already knew that she was an opinionated, tactless, pessimistic, and rather bitter woman who was hard to get on with, but he'd always made a big effort to be nice to her, and to accept her, because she was family. He had always got on really well with her husband James, so as a foursome, and with their families, they had socialised together a great deal. The surprising callousness of her remarks stunned him momentarily. He was shocked that she was obviously supporting Delilah without even bothering to have one conversation with him. Really shocked. He would have expected her to express deep remorse about the situation and offer him hope and encouragement, not bland, cruel condemnation.

"How can you say that? You have no idea what is going on."

"She wants to be away from you, and I think she should be."

"Why?" He was horrified.

"You're controlling and manipulative."

This was offensive and so unfair. Everyone knew that her husband, James, was a control freak, and that's what she was used to in her life, but for her to paint him with the same brush, especially in the circumstances, was outrageous, and cruel. He had no time for this.

"Well you can fuck off then."

He was angry. She hung up, probably because he had used the 'F' word. Now he was even more alarmed. Over the years he had observed how much Delilah put all of her older sisters on a pedestal. He had never understood why. She was a much better person than all three of them put together as far as he was concerned, but now he realised that the battle was more complicated than he had realised. Delilah had Morag behind her pushing her in the wrong direction. He felt so betrayed.

This new alarm set off the urgent need to write again. Morag's betrayal made him feel extra desperate. His letter was nothing more than a verbose, desperate, five-page rambling, snivelling apology where he begged for her forgiveness, stating that he was so disappointed in himself for bringing her to this place where she found herself so disillusioned. He offered unending promises of being a better person, of having and showing more love, and how their future together could be so wonderful. He wanted her to feel his depth of emotion, and his hurt. He did his best to engage with her heart. He peppered his ramblings with pictorial references of mighty rivers flowing down mountains; about rusty dull tools being cleaned up and sharpened anew. Overall, it was repetitive, predictable and smacked of panic. He left the letter out for her to find as usual. When she returned later he didn't mention the call from Morag. He didn't feel the need to remind her that she had reinforcements.

At least at the moment she was still living under the same roof as him, and he had dinner with her each evening, albeit in a rather strained and subdued atmosphere. But she was of course still planning to move out. He had no idea how her plans were going or if indeed she really would ultimately leave. He was the confident optimistic type who hoped that if and when she did leave, she would miss him and realise her mistake, and before too long.

Just a couple of days later, he answered the phone, again on Delilah's behalf. This time it was middle sister Lilith. If Morag knew what was going on, Lilith would definitely know. She hadn't phoned to speak to him, but as Delilah was out, she engaged him. She wasn't reluctant. She always liked a good conversation. He knew that she would be sympathetic towards him because although they often didn't see eye to eye, they both liked each other. They always had sparky spunky conversations together.

"How are you?" She sounded a little bit concerned.

"I think you can imagine Lilith. Devastated. Heartbroken."

"But Pablo, you've driven her to this."

Good lord. Not more accusations?

"Really? How"

"You've been unfaithful to her too many times"

She sounded like she was enjoying putting him on the spot.

His prickles were fully erect at this insidious attack.

"I've always been faithful to her. Over thirty years. What are you talking about?"

"Oh come on Pablo" she said as if everyone in the whole wide world knew it. What about all the girls at the garden centre?"

She was referring to an era many years ago, when he and Delilah had owned and run a small retail garden centre business in a small rural town, and had employed a few female staff.

"What about the girls in the garden centre?"

"Oh come on Pablo. We all knew you were messing around with the girls there."

"What, by employing them, talking to them? Treating them like human beings?"

"There was more to it than that."

His stomach was churning. How could he defend himself? How could he prove a negative? He knew this woman was a trouble-maker and a stirrer. He had seen it many times over the three decades that he had known her. She could be very charming and conversational, but she was also something of a sociopath. She didn't care who she trod all over to achieve her goals, and her goals often appeared to be spiteful. He had observed many times how she derived a perverse satisfaction from bringing people down, and members of her own family seemed to be the easiest targets.

"Really? And how would you know that? Were you there? Did you ever speak to those women?"

There was a very brief silence before she moved on.

"Pablo, why have you been suspended?"

Another knife. He hadn't been suspended actually, but he didn't care to digress on that point. "Because the organisation I work for is so completely anal."

"I see. Not because you've been having an affair with one of your clients then?"

"Definitely not, but you seem to have made your mind up nevertheless. What do you base your evidence on?"

"Delilah told me."

"Delilah believes what she wants to believe. I've done nothing to let her down. I've always been faithful to her no matter what stories you want to make up."

She became more conciliatory in tone. Perhaps she didn't want to drive him quickly to the point where he would tell her to just fuck off, like he had done with Morag. She wanted this conversation to continue so that she could carry on casually twisting the knife in the wound whilst she was smiling at him with her crocodile smile.

"I'm really sorry it's come to this Pablo. You're a nice guy, but you can't go on abusing Delilah like this."

"Like what? Loving her? Working my bollocks off to give her a great home and a great life? Being faithful to her constantly, no matter what the opportunities out there?"

"Pablo, you need to be honest with yourself."

She sounded so smug, like she knew all the answers, like she was so obviously right, like she knew more about his behaviour than he did. She was just making trouble as usual. It reminded him of the period just a few years earlier when her parents had become old and weak, and she would regularly visit them to make them feel bad about the way they had neglected, starved and abused her as a child. Nobody else in the family was aware of any substance to her allegations. Certainly not her parents, and each of her sisters only remembered happy loving childhoods for them all. Her upsetting accusations and heartless treatment of her old frail diminishing parents puzzled and upset her sisters, but no one, apart from him, could stretch their imaginations enough to believe that she was just tormenting them for her own twisted pleasure.

He realised that his battle was much bigger than he initially thought. His stomach was churning again, with fear. Fear of how Delilah was gradually slipping away. Fear of how other people had their hooks in her and were dragging her away from him. He had naively thought that she was having some kind of mid-life crisis. Now he was beginning to see that there was something of a concerted conspiracy against them as a couple. He was starting to feel like the whole world was against him and his marriage. It was time to pull up the drawbridge.

"I haven't got the time or energy for this bullshit Lilith. Go and bait some other hapless victim."

He put the phone down. He was feeling alarmed, betrayed, attacked, and not a little horrified at the turn of events. His Pavlovian response was to reach out to Delilah. This was his default every time he felt more threatened. He wrote another letter. It was a whole month since she had announced her intention to leave him. It was only a two page letter this time, but it was just more of the same, telling her how devastated he was by her rejection, how terribly sorry he was for offending her, how frustrated he was by her resoluteness etc. The only thing in it which was new was that he agreed that she needed to go away to find out what it would be like without him. Obviously he hoped that she would miss him and want to return to the fold. He reiterated his love and commitment to her, yet again. Perhaps he was afraid that she didn't really believe how much he loved her, and so he thought that constantly repeating his message might achieve something. But it didn't. Her resolve was immutable.

The days were becoming a blur. Each day was the same. He would do a lot of building and a little trading online, or if the weather was bad, very little building and a lot of trading. He was very self-disciplined about being busy with something, and making constructive use of his time, but in reality, his life had become just a waiting game. Waiting to see how the complaint at work would resolve itself. Waiting to be allowed to go back to work. Waiting for his wife to actually move out, or not move out, or maybe, waiting for her to come back, or not come back. What he really struggled to understand was the depth of her coldness. She wasn't blaming him for anything. When he asked for explanations, all she would ever say was that stuff about space, and what everybody else wanted. None of this made any sense to him. She wasn't giving him anything to get his teeth into. His frustrations poured out into another letter.

'To my dear wife.

Whenever I ask you to explain what's going on, you say that surely I wouldn't want your affection if it's not borne out of genuine love. You make it sound like someone can only show love if they feel overwhelming exhilaration or romantic infatuation with someone. Surely that's not true? If we rely on that to happen all the time, where would true love be? What about commitment? You seem to have decided not to display any compassion or humanity towards me for fear that I would interpret any such fleeting kindness as a decision on your part to put the troubles behind us and make up, which is something you don't want. Why is being cold and distant your highest priority? Why not kindness, humanity, compassion or love? That might feel sacrificial for you at the moment, but surely it would be a sacrifice worth making? You have said that to show me any affection or consideration would be because you're being a robot, and nothing more, and surely I wouldn't want that. Well, I think that if you made that decision in your head to be loving, your heart would surely follow in time. It's a bit of a chicken and egg scenario. I could more than justify withholding my love for you, but I choose to persevere because of my commitment to you and because you and I together are responsible for a beautiful family, that has a future. I don't always feel blindly infatuated with you, but it's not just about feelings, sometimes it's about decisions. I decide to love you, support you, and be patient with you because deep down, I do love you, and I am committed to our marriage, and our family, and I want to push through any challenges to maintain a wonderful relationship with you. This isn't achievable through fairy-tale magic. Sometimes it takes a bit of work, and making tough decisions. You're going ahead with your plans to move out, for emotional space, you say. Well I can only hope that the separation will serve to focus your mind on fond memories, and the positive aspects of marriage, such as love, support, company, physical affection, conversation, familiarity, purpose, security, family, hope, financial provision, commitment, etc. I hope you will make a decision to recommit. Yes, I know you want romance and for me to woo you and win you afresh. I want that too, with all of my heart. I want to relearn how to grow your love, to make impressive sacrifices for you, to demonstrate my love and devotion to you. I beg you to love me again. Your heart will follow your decision, I'm sure of it. It's happened before in the past. We've been married for nearly thirty years and there have been other challenges during that time, and we have both always chosen to love, to commit, and love has always flourished. Why is it different this time? Why have you decided to walk away instead? We can rekindle our love, and it could be better because I want to be the perfect husband for you. We have more time for each other now. We could make big life-changing decisions to benefit our marriage, but I need you to let me back in.'

He finished by quoting a scripture from Ephesians chapter 5 which he considered to be very wise words;

'Husbands, love your wives as Christ loved the church. He gave up his life for her, to make her holy and clean, washed by the cleansing of God's word. Husbands ought to love their wives as they love their own bodies. For a man who loves his wife actually shows love for himself. No one hates his own body but feeds and cares for it, just as Christ cares for the church. And we are members of his body. A man leaves his father and mother and is joined to his wife and the two are united into one. This is a great mystery, but it is an illustration of the way Christ and the church are one. So I say again, every man must love his wife as he loves himself, and the wife must respect her husband.'

'Babe, I want to be that husband to you. We are one flesh, and cannot be wrought apart. Our roots have grown completely entangled over the decades. Please choose to come back to me.

All my love. Pablo."

He was still desperate of course, but at least this letter was more focussed and objective; a lot better than other recent ones, which had been not much more than whining about his pain and shock, and begging for empathy and understanding. Now he was appealing to her core inner values and her family values. He was appealing to her reason and common sense. He was doing his utmost to convince her that she ought to stay with him, her husband.

The next day at dinner, she opened up to him, a little.

"You need to know that your letters are pushing me away"

"How?" he asked, genuinely confused, and so disappointed.

"You're trying to pressurise me, and that only pushes me away."

"Babe, I'm sorry, but I feel like I am fighting for my life here."

"You just need to let me go."

"But that's what I am struggling with. It's not right. I don't want you to go. I can't imagine a life without you."

She was not in the habit of talking about her feelings. She always played her cards close to her chest, so this was something a little special, and he was careful not to spoil the occasion and this opportunity for dialogue. She said nothing more, so he encouraged her.

"How can I change if you don't tell me what's wrong? I so want to put this right."

"You don't listen to me."

This was a hard one. If he argued, he'd be accused of not listening to her needs of course, but he struggled with this because he actually considered himself a good listener. He felt that when she told him he wasn't listening, she was really telling him that he didn't agree with her.

"I think I do listen. You don't say much about your feelings though."

"And why do you think that is?"

"It's your nature?"

"No. You don't let me have my say."

"Do you think it's fair to say that?"

"Yep."

"Why?"

"You don't let me finish. You interrupt me. You're loud. You always have your own ideas anyway."

He fell silent. He didn't know how to answer these accusations. He was sad that she felt so strongly.

"Why don't you help me learn to listen better then?" he added hopefully.

"It's too late for that now. I've had enough."

"Of what."

"Of you. Of this house. Of the mess. Of not knowing what to do with my life."

He felt the weight on her shoulders. He felt sorry for her. He knew that now that they were experiencing empty-nest syndrome to a large and almost complete degree, she had lost one of her main functions in life, and maybe she was struggling with the notion of going into paid work.

"You can get a job if you want to. You certainly don't have to. This house will be fabulous when it's all done. I don't get why you think you have to leave."

"I need emotional space. I need time-out to learn to communicate."

He was fairly sure that her sessions with Sylvia had pushed her to this point. Sylvia's counselling had undermined her faith in her current life, and was dangling new, unknown, but better prospects in front of her, and she'd fallen for it. The best he could do was to not push her away further. He just looked at her sorrowfully. He didn't know what else to say. He realised that she had to do what she had to do, but he hoped she would miss him and their home, and their future together.

The next day he wrote her another letter. It wasn't another appeal which apparently repulsed. It was simply an expression of gratitude. He wanted her to know how much he appreciated her effort to communicate with him. It slid into an elongated expression of love and hope as usual, but at least he had a little something to be grateful for.

Chapter 12

The break in the secrecy clouds, where the sun of openness shone through, didn't last long. He didn't write to her anymore for the time being as she had told him directly that his letters were pushing her away. He couldn't ignore that. Every now and then he would try to talk to her directly, but she had gone back into her dark hole. The best he could get out of her was a terse and harsh 'there is no other way'. This was one of her regular monotonous mantras. He would protest at her mantras with something simple like 'of course there was another way', but she was not listening, and any such protestations were inept and fruitless. She was no longer a person to him. She had transmogrified into a sterile machine. A heart still beat inside this apparently cold machine, but it was completely shielded from him.

It wasn't long before he answered the phone to Sirenna, the next sister up in age. Like when the others had called, she was after Delilah, who was out. He had no reason to expect this conversation to go any better than the ones with Morag and Lilith. Sirenna was the quiet one, even quieter than Delilah. She never felt the need to say much, but she was astute.

"How are you?" she enquired, with a little genuine empathy in her voice.

"I don't know Sirenna. Fearful mostly, although Delilah has said some fairly positive things lately."

"I know it's hard for you both, but it's not good to stay together when you're both hurting."

"I don't get why she has to leave. We've been happily married for thirty years. Why?"

"She's not happy anymore. You can't expect her to stay if she's not happy."

"But we're married. We have an amazing family."

"Not many marriages last Pablo. You can't just carry on for the sake of it."

"What about working through whatever she's unhappy about?"

"But she doesn't want to work through anything. She wants to leave. It'll work out in the long term. You'll both find new partners. You'll both be alright."

It was nice for her to try to be reassuring, and unlike the other two, she wasn't being judgemental, but her flippancy, the blandness of her approach and the disregard for their marriage deeply saddened him. Was he really the only one who cared about their marriage? He was sure the kids did too, but it wasn't their place to intervene, and he certainly didn't want to drag them into this mess. He knew that Delilah would be drawing a great deal of support from her sisters right now, but in his opinion, it was not healthy balanced principled support. It was skewed towards breaking up. Why? He was really unsettled by everyone's attitude. Both Lilith and Sirenna had broken marriages behind them, and they had both remarried new partners in time, so to an extent, they were defending their own choices in life. Morag was still married to her original husband. She was just being a bitch.

Pablo desperately wanted to counter this insipid indifference, but he couldn't find the dynamic words he hoped for.

"I don't want another partner. I want my wife. How is that too much to ask?"

"Staying together is bad for both of you. All this upset is not doing either of you any good."

"I don't get how you all feel qualified to encourage her to leave me. Do you really know what's going on?"

"I know that Delilah is really upset and troubled at the moment. If she needs to get away, you shouldn't try to stop her."

He stayed quiet for a moment. He wondered if Sirenna knew more than she was letting on, but he knew she wouldn't divulge any confidences. The witchsters were as thick as thieves. The fact was clear that she was firmly on her sister's side, just like the other two were, and she seemed to be firmly behind that dreadful decision to leave him. That's all he needed to know.

"Ok. Whatever. See ya."

He terminated the call. He didn't have the energy to try to convince anyone else what a bad idea Delilah's leaving was.

From then on, it seemed that the sisters managed only to phone Delilah when she was in, and she would scurry off to her bedroom with the cordless handset and keep their conversations completely private. He suspected that she was using her mobile a lot more too, to keep things private. A big part of his life was being cut out and withdrawn. He had lost his relationship with his wife, and by extension, her side of the family were also cutting him off. That was a lot of loss in one hit. Even Morag's husband James had cut him off, and he had considered him to be his best friend.

Wednesday evening, they still went to the dance class together, but when there, she more or less avoided him. He felt like a little lost puppy. She was enjoying the sessions much more than he was because she was revelling in mixing with new people whereas all he really wanted to do was mix with her, his wife. That would have been novel. It was a horrible experience, being so close to someone, yet so far away at the same time.

It was about mid-October when she made the next big announcement to him. She informed him in a business-like way that she had found a place to move to and would be moving there at the end of the month. The guilty expression on her face betrayed that she knew this was very painful for him, but she tried to make it sound routine, mundane, innocent. She also tried to look unflustered, but she couldn't look him in the eye. However, she was strong, and did what she had to do. She was full of steely purpose. He had been dreading this moment. Hopeless defeat. He had hoped that when it came to the crunch, she would deflect from actually walking out on him, but it looked like she was really going to do it.

She also informed him that she had taken five thousand pounds out of their bank account to pay for a six-month rental.

He was alarmed on two counts; One, that she had taken money out of their joint account, which was earmarked and specifically obtained for the build, and secondly and more importantly, six months? He had been hoping that if indeed she did leave at all, it would be for weeks, not months. He expressed that concern first.

"Six months? Surely you won't be away that long?"

He had a look of shock and despondency on his face. He was really hurt and worried. She tried to reassure him a little;

"I don't have to stay away for six months. I can cancel at any time and get my money back. I just have to book initially for six months. I've found a place that really suits me."

She was doing her best to downplay this terrible blow, but there was far too much uncertainty for him. He wondered if she would find it hard to return simply because she would have to swallow her pride? Might she actually prefer living on her own? It all still seemed much too potentially permanent for him. He quietly mulled over the shock of this announcement. He felt so impotent. Then he considered the money issue.

"That money was set aside for windows." He said this quietly, but poignantly. She made no comment. He had wondered how she was going to organise herself financially. Now he knew. She was going to just help herself to the money he was borrowing to build the extension. Or maybe she would just put everything on the joint credit card. He felt his mettle firming. He made a decision there and then.

"You can have that money for this rental that you've already arranged. And as your husband, I will carry on providing finances for your food and vehicle expenses and other everyday expenses, just as I have always done, but this is your home. We are mortgaged to the hilt on this place, and I won't pay towards any more rentals elsewhere. If you want to carry on living somewhere else you will have to finance it yourself."

He wasn't trying to blackmail her. He just wanted to let her know that despite his fawning love for her, he wasn't going to be taken for a ride. He wouldn't let her bleed him dry. She looked at him defiantly and contemptuously. Her eyes flashed with angry bitterness. She didn't like relying on him for her financial security, and now it was her who felt alarmed. Finding that sort of money herself would be very hard indeed. She had only relatively recently started part-time work. She said nothing more and went to her room. He sat down and wept like a baby. His hope was being crushed, step by step. It was tortuous. He felt like the life-source in him was seeping slowly away.

The next day he went to their bank first thing in the morning. It was an open-plan bank where to see an advisor one sat at a desk in full view of the public, possibly with a queue of people a little way behind you. He joined that queue for a few minutes until an advisor came free. As he waited, he could feel himself becoming emotional. Everything swirling through his mind was upsetting him.

An old gentleman sitting with the advisor just finished his business. He slowly shuffled some papers together like he had all the time in the world, then stiffly and cautiously rose from the chair and scuffled away. He smiled at Pablo as he carefully walked past him. Pablo briskly took his place in the chair. He sat in front of a nice-looking smart middle-aged lady who was bright and cheerful. She introduced herself as Anne and asked him what she could do for him. He sat forward and lowered his head. He was trying to be inconspicuous. He found unsurprisingly that he couldn't speak. He was struggling to fight back tears, and to keep them suppressed, he couldn't try to talk. He had always taken such pride in providing for his wife and family, and now here he was having to take some of that away. It broke his heart. He was feeling terrible. The advisor was quickly on the ball. She stood up briskly and asked him to follow her. She walked to a nearby office door, got a key out, and unlocked the door. She showed him in. He was concentrating hard on trying to keep himself composed, yet he still had the presence of mind to admire her level-headedness. He was thankful that she had minimised his embarrassment in public.

The office had glass walls, but with opaque stripes on them, so the adviser wasn't completely isolated, and no one could see them very well, and they certainly wouldn't be overheard. She got him to sit at the desk opposite her. He sat, crumpled up. Now his emotions released, and he cried deeply.

"It's ok" she said kindly. "You take your time. I'll do whatever I can to help."

She had no idea what was going on, but her heart was open and warm. She looked at him thoughtfully and with patient compassion. He was touched by her empathy, humanity, and thoughtfulness. He cried for about a minute, which must have seemed like a long time for her. It seemed like quite a long time to him. When he got some composure back, he spoke in short quiet squeaky sentences, with big pauses between them, as he fought off the sobs.

"My wife and I have joint accounts here. She's taken money out for something she shouldn't have. She's leaving me. We have joint credit cards. I'm worried she will start using my credit for all sorts of things she shouldn't and that could go up to my credit limit which is over seven grand."

"Oh dear. I'm so sorry." She emphasised the 'so'. She looked genuinely concerned for him.

" How long have you been married?"

"Thirty years."

"Oh that's terrible." She looked genuinely surprised and sad. She leaned forward and rubbed the top of his arm reassuringly.

"I'm afraid that we get this sort of thing regularly, and there are certain things we have to do. I take it you don't want the accounts and credit cards in joint names anymore?"

" Correct" he whimpered.

"Ok, but there is nothing that we can do without your wife's signature. Your accounts will be frozen from now until we get you both to sign consent forms. It's what we automatically do when there is what we call distress on the account."

"Ok."

"Do you think you can get your wife to sign a form for us? Everything will stay frozen until you both sign those consent forms. Do you understand that?"

It was as though she wondered if he could understand what she was saying when he was clearly so upset, but his mind was clear and focussed.

"Yes. I'll explain it to her."

"Well, tell her that neither of you will be able to access any money at all until we get these forms back. I'm sorry, but that's just the way it has to be, now that you've disclosed this issue. I have to do this, you understand?"

"Yes, of course."

He spoke quietly, and was beginning to wonder how Delilah was going to react to this. He didn't want to annoy her.

"Wait here. I'll go and get them."

He sat there alone with his thoughts flitting between the sadness of having to take this action, and the starkness of the breakup starting to be solidified in practical ways. He considered that this was probably the first of many unforeseen difficulties that this new situation would bring about. Anne returned shortly and gave him the forms. She also gave him her card.

"Pablo, if there's anything else you need help with, please contact me directly, or just pop in. I'm here most days. Oh, and if your wife needs to discuss this first, please get her to come and see me. Ok?"

He got the impression that if Delilah visited her, she would definitely not get the same dose of empathy that he had received. Sometimes a woman will take the man's side because she understands the shortcomings of other women so well. He would have liked to express a meaningful appreciation for her courtesy and understanding, but as he was still choked up, all he could manage was a quiet, subdued, squeaky 'thank you'.

"Are you ok to leave now, or do you need a little more time?"

"I'm ok. Thank you so much."

She owed him nothing, but she had shown such kindness and understanding. It was the so-called small things like this that give people faith in humanity. They stood up. She took his hand in both of hers and said very sincerely

"I really hope it works out for you." Her kindness was making him want to cry more.

"Stop being so nice to me . You're making me cry."

This startled her for a brief moment, then she laughed.

"Well, at least you still have your sense of humour" she said brightly, and then she showed him out, looking at him with genuine compassion in her eyes.

He returned home. Delilah hadn't gone out yet, so he was able to immediately explain the situation to her. She was cross.

"You didn't have to freeze our account!" She was blaming him immediately.

"I didn't freeze it. I just wanted to put our account in single names. I don't want you raiding the building money again."

"You said it's frozen now."

"Yes, but that's what they do automatically if joint account holders start falling out over money. I didn't know that, did I?"

She looked worried. Maybe she hadn't really thought this money aspect through. She looked at him defiantly, which was beginning to become her stock look for him. He looked back at with a look of resignation. What was done was done. He justified his cause;

"I can't just let you take whatever money you want out of my account to do whatever you want behind my back. Get real."

She was angry. Her eyes were piercing, her mouth taut. He got the impression that she wanted to hurt him. The last thing he wanted was to offend her even more, and somehow make a bad situation worse, but he had. He tried to placate her.

"Babe, no matter whether you think this is fair or not, you'll have to sign this form, or our account stays frozen, and I need it to be unfrozen to be able to pay the mortgage, and don't forget, I have promised to continue to support you financially. I won't be able to do that if you don't sign this form."

How could she argue with that? She snatched the form from him, and stared at it. She looked thoughtful. She was weighing up her options. She pondered for a few more moments, then capitulated and reluctantly signed the form. He did so too, but happily, and grateful that she hadn't put up too much of a fight. He drove straight back into town and returned to see Anne at the bank. She was pleased that he had managed to get Delilah to sign the forms, and so quickly. It made sorting this out straight forward. In a day or two they would have their own single bank accounts, and Delilah would no longer have a credit card linked to his account. If she wanted a credit card now, she would have to get her own, and the limit on it would be a lot lower than he had on his. He returned home very relieved. Delilah had gone out.

Understandably the next couple of weeks were rather strange with them both knowing that she would be gone soon, properly. She had told him that she didn't want him to know where she was going because she didn't want him turning up and making a scene. He thought that her keeping him in the dark was par for the course, in the sense of her getting away from him, and creating 'space' but the excuse of not wanting him to make a scene didn't ring true. He wasn't the kind of person to make a scene and never had been. That perplexed him, but he didn't argue the point. He wondered what she would say to the kids. If she was going away for up to six months, she would want them to know where she was so that they could visit her. She would have to tell them that her location was a secret to him. What would they think of that? What excuse would she give them? That she was afraid that he would come round and beat her up? Or abduct her? Or smash the place up? He had no idea, but whatever it was, it was unfair, and the kids wouldn't believe it because they knew him better than that, and it would put them in an awkward position. They wouldn't want to be keeping secrets from their own father. He made it easy for them. He never asked.

The day of her departure arrived. It was a cool, sunny, early autumn day. Coincidentally, Troy, their youngest son had already come down to stay with them for a few days. He was going to help Pablo fix the roof A-frames in place on the two-storey part of the extension. Delilah busied herself to-ing and fro-ing to the car with her things. They had a family car and a small run-about which Pablo shared with Sarah. Delilah had not discussed the car at all. It seemed to be a presumption that she would take it away for her sole use. Pablo didn't question this. He would manage fine sharing with Sarah. He didn't want to be petty or merely obstructive. The last things to go into the car were the dogs. Then she was ready to go. Troy and Pablo walked out into the driveway where she stood near the car, expectantly. Troy hugged her, but he really wasn't sure what to say, apart from a simple goodbye. He looked perplexed. Then he backed off and made room for his dad. Pablo hugged her. She barely responded.

"Come back soon" he said, obviously.

"It'll probably only be a couple of weeks" she said in a strangely yielding way. Then she got in the car, and was gone.

Partly because of his work, and partly from reading, Pablo was aware of a surprising phenomenon concerning people who commit suicide. Their loved ones often express astonishment at the timing, because the dearly departed seemed to have improved in their outlook and mood in the days leading up to their death. The theory was that when they have finally made up their minds to carry out the act, a kind of peace and an allusive sense of purpose comes over them. They have decided to cease the struggle with life and they therefore appear much less troubled and are content with their purpose. Pablo could associate with that phenomena to some extent now. Nothing to do with suicide, but with the end of a big uncertainty. The unsettling wait to see if Delilah really would leave or not was now over. She had. Disappeared. Gone. And he didn't even know where to. The constant battle to influence her thinking and perhaps the outcome was all over now, and a kind of peace came over him. There was nothing more he could do except pray and hope. He was confident that she would return. She had never let him down in all the thirty three years they had been together, and he didn't expect her to let him down now. He was in strangely good spirits as he and Troy got on with moving the roof frames. As a father, he reassured his son

"Don't worry Troy, She'll be back" he said with a smile, and he meant it.

That day they fixed the roof frame up and completed the gulley troughs. The next day they did the felting and started on the tiling. It was lovely for Pablo to have one of his sons with him at this time. It helped him to feel that they were still a family when quite clearly the family was falling apart. Then Troy had to go back to university, and Pablo was left more or less alone. Yes, Sarah slept there, but he saw very little of her, although when he did see her, she was lovely towards him.

Pablo respected Delilah's need for space. He wanted her to miss him. He didn't phone or text, or write. He just looked forward to seeing her when she was ready. Delilah was not communicating with him, her husband, in any way shape or form, but she was communicating with herself. She started to keep a diary after she moved out. Her first entry was the day after she had moved into her new abode.

'Why do I feel so low when you leave? It's such a roller-coaster ride – the anticipation of your visit is filled with excitement. Your presence and passion is euphoric. Then comes the time for you to leave. Till when? That is the big question. My mind is filled with so many questions. What am I doing? Why am I doing it? What good is it? What future does it have? Is this what I really want? Can I handle the frailty, but also the depth of feeling? What is it? Filling a need with what? Nothing lasting. Nothing that will give me lasting satisfaction. A moment's escape from reality, to then feel such deep loss all over again as the door closes. Do I have the strength to keep picking myself up, shaking myself down and getting on with life? You go back to your life. I feel I am left hanging by a thread to be picked up at some time. Why can't I just go with the one who so desperately wants me? Why do I feel like a person bound from head to toe when I am with him? And if I go back to that, what will it be like? Or is it all in my mind? Do I sit here getting things all out of proportion? Do I need to just 'get on with it girl'? Who am I? What do I want? I want a soulmate, someone to love me as I am, someone who cares about me and the little things in my life. Someone to laugh with, enjoy life with, walk through the troubles with, with understanding and empathy. I thought I had all that, but now I am not sure. I feel so let down. So much was put at risk – our love, our livelihood, our marriage, our house, for what? It makes me angry that so much was risked, that we might be left with nothing. How can I put my trust in that man again? Can I make myself that vulnerable again? Should I walk away? Can I walk away? Why the tears? Have I sold my soul, my innermost being? For what? Flattery? Personal challenge? Weakness of character? Lack of self-esteem? Novelty? Such an aching deep inside of me, that is what I am left with. Tomorrow I will feel a little better as a new day dawns. I can leave the pain with the day that has closed.'

Pablo eagerly awaited the next Wednesday evening dance class. He hoped that she would be there. She was. He was so pleased to see her. It was weird though, like she was supposed to be a stranger, but really, she was a part of him, through and through. It still felt like that for him, but as usual, she more or less pretended not to know him. At the end of the evening, he walked her to her car. She accepted that he would want to talk to her, but it was all very brief. He told her that it was lovely to see her, and he hoped she was sorting out her issues. He kissed her on the cheek, gave her a little card which he had prepared, and she left. He went home sad and confused. He cried. He was still crying every day. He was lonely.

The message inside the card was:

'Thinking about you. Missing you. Hoping you're ok. Crying over the hopelessness. Nursing unrequited love. Wondering what was real and what was not. Wondering how we got here. So sorry you had to leave. xxx'

A few days later, she popped home late afternoon, unannounced. She wanted to use the computer and to see Sarah who normally paid home a flying visit for some tea. That was nice. Pablo was there to welcome her. He gave her a hug. She told him that he shouldn't hug her anymore. His unwanted hugs were an invasion of her personal space. He was violating her. Ouch! That hurt. He still wanted to demonstrate his love for her. He couldn't write to her anymore because she said that had the opposite effect of what he wanted. He couldn't talk to her because she was absent. And now, if he did see her, he wasn't allowed to hug her or kiss her on the cheek, just as a warm greeting? Life was a bitch. He asked her when she was coming home, with puppy-dog eyes.

"Not yet" she said quietly. She did her computer stuff for about an hour then briskly left. Pablo had never felt so lonely. She went home to the seclusion and quietness of her hideaway sanctuary. Somewhere.

It was early November when he got a call. The sisters didn't call his home number anymore. They knew that Delilah was no longer there. He had such a quiet life now, he wondered who it might be calling. It was Roger. Roger! He hadn't heard from him for a couple of months. He was surprised to hear from him, but presumably there was news on his case.

"Hello, Pablo?"

"Roger?" He recognised his dull voice.

"Yes. We've had a decision from the CPS."

"Go on" he said, his stomach beginning to churn.

Well, there's good news and bad news."

"Go on" still churning.

"The allegations made by Cassie and Marlon are not going to be proceeded with. They have decided that there is no evidence to support their claims."

He wanted to make sure he'd heard that right.

They're not proceeding with any of their claims?"

"Correct."

"That's great news, but quite right too." He felt finally vindicated after eight months of uncertainty and suspicion. Then he added

And the bad news?"

"They've decided to charge you with the breach of data protection offence."

"Why? That doesn't make any sense."

"I don't know Pablo. You'll get a chance to discuss that with Kevin in due course."

He was not so elated now. This was still worrying.

"So what happens now?"

"You'll get a summons through the post to appear at court. It won't be a local court. Police officers are never tried in their home territory. It will be in an adjacent county. We'll have a meeting beforehand at my office. Ok?"

"Yes, I suppose so, but doing me for data protection is such a waste of time. What do they think they're going to achieve? I'm a police officer. I look at police records. Err?"

"I don't know Pablo. I have to say, this is highly unusual."

There was an awkward pause. They had nothing else to discuss. Pablo finished off.

"Ok. Thanks for letting me know. I'll wait to hear from you about a meeting."

"Yes. It's mainly good news Pablo. They've dropped all of the original complaints. Shame they're pursuing the data charge."

"Yes. It's crazy. Ok, I'll see you soon."

It was pouring with rain outside. He busied himself for the rest of the day with his computer and the stock market, but his thoughts were on the case, and on Delilah.

She had gotten into the habit of popping back home for something about twice per week, always unannounced. The next time she dropped by, he eagerly informed her that the charges against him were being dropped, well, apart from just the data protection one. Maybe this could have been a catalyst to kiss and make up, but she didn't look impressed. He expected her to show some joy, some relief, but nothing. Hoping for a bit of support and encouragement from her was obviously hoping for far too much. He was surprised that she wasn't more pleased that all the original accusations were being thrown out given that she had been so apparently disturbed by events in the first place. Wasn't that mainly why she was absent now? He looked at her quizzically. He really was confused by her.

"You've still got a charge against you" she said sombrely.

"But that one hasn't got a leg to stand on. What? I'm a police officer who's not allowed to look at police intelligence? They make me look at intel. Everyday. It's the first stuff that comes up after I log on the computer. Get real"

"So why are they doing you for it?"

"I don't know. It's ridiculous, but what I do know is that no magistrate in the land is going to find me guilty of anything. Of that I am certain. I was just doing my job to the best of my ability."

She was not so certain.

"We'll see."

"Are you ready to come home yet?"

"No."

He looked at her in disbelief, his confusion and disappointment obvious. She collected whatever she had come for, and left. He wouldn't see her again until the Wednesday dance class. The idea of following her home after the dance did cross his mind, but he considered it a pointless exercise. There was nothing he could do whether he knew her address or not. It was her choice to stay away, and only she could change her own mind.

A few days later, he spotted a fabulous card. It was the picture of a rather fine naked male leaning over a wooden beam the picture was taken from behind him, so it looked a bit like a cross, his body being the upright, with the stout wooden beam at right-angles. He bought it. He felt that he had to give it to Delilah. He composed a brief message for the inside;

'Delilah, I am bearing my cross patiently for you, bearing your pain with you deeply. I am forlorn in spirit without you because you are my better half. I am forlorn in soul without you because you are my true soulmate. I am forlorn in body because we are supposed to be one flesh, and you are absent. I am waiting for you because I believe in you and love you with all of my heart. Pablo xxx'

He put it in its envelope and addressed it to Delilah. He gave it to her after the next dance class as he stood by her in the car park afterwards, so desperately hoping to hear her say that she was sorry. He just couldn't stop hoping and trying.

104

He told her that he thought it was very unfair to him not being allowed to give her a little hug when he saw her. She was still his wife, and he thought he should be allowed a little concession to express his love for her on the rare occasions that he did see her. She looked at him sternly. She had told him about not violating her personal space. She wanted to be in charge, but a little humanity, or was it pity, crept through.

"Ok" she agreed. "But only when you greet me, and don't expect me to respond."

"You don't anyway" he corrected her. He was pleased that he had permission to hug her when greeting, even though she would stand stiff as a poker, arms firmly held against her sides.

She went to her home. He went to their home. The next evening she wrote in her diary.

'Why is it so beautiful when you are here? I feel so relaxed when I am close to you, resting in your arms, leaning on your body. How can I capture that feeling and keep it? What is it? The feeling of being loved or loving? I just never want to leave that place – stay there forever! Can I ever have that feeling with anyone else again? How do I make the choice to give it up? Can I? Should I? Why? Do I let it run its course, see where it goes? Oh how I want to be in that place forever!'

Chapter 13

Middle of November 2008, Delilah's forty-ninth birthday. He hoped to see her that day, but she didn't come round for anything. That made him feel forlorn, a nobody. He had bought her a very poignant card. It was a colour drawing of two scruffy young people hugging. Their heads were cowed over each other's shoulders. The arms were holding each other tightly. It was a blur of arms, wild hair and baggy shirts, but it spoke of the priority of passion, love and devotion. He didn't need to write much inside the card. The picture spoke for itself. Apart from wishing her a happy birthday, all he said was that he wished her a fulfilled life and hoped that he would become a part of it again.

He had settled into a new lonely normal. He was more or less living alone. He spent his days working on the extension. On weekends he would spend at least one day away, visiting one of the kids, or one of his siblings. His own family was clearly his rock-solid support network. His brother had experienced a divorce about fifteen years earlier, where his wife had deserted him for another man, so he was particularly understanding and wise. The highlight of his week was Wednesday evening, when he would still see his beloved wife at the dance class. It was lovely for him just to see her, and it provided an opportunity for communication, an opportunity which she never exploited. Occasionally she would still pop home for something. He would always give her a quick hug and tell her that he still loved her and was waiting for her. She always froze and said nothing. He would also ask a simple straight-forward question like 'how are your communication skills coming on?' or 'have you had enough space yet?' or just a plain 'are you ready to come home yet?' Her responses were always blunt and negative. She had become an unfathomable enigma, and his mind was constantly engaged in the challenge of solving this enigma. But it was always good to see her. She never made any comment on his building work. She knew he was conscientious and would finish the job no matter what she did or didn't do. Each day alone, without her, and without company, communication, or any certainty, seemed like an age. He channelled his energies into the build, but his thoughts never strayed far from Delilah. He wrote her a poem;

'To Delilah, my love.
When we meet I want so much
To feel your love, to feel in-touch.
But every time, your hackles out,
I feel your barriers, I feel your doubt
That your reservations will ever go,

That I will ever cease to be your foe.
Forlorn are all my desperate tries
To breach your wall, your heart the prize.
For it is locked behind a wall of pain,
Impenetrable behind cold words, so sane,
And yet denying something true,
My undying love for you.
What I offer is really precious,
But you see it as something atrocious,
An invasion of your private space.
No room for soothing healing embrace.
So we set the scene for more erosion,
Start each episode on a path of ruction.
We can't go on, it's just so mad
To waste each rare opportunity had.
The only hope that I can see
Is give you space, wait graciously,
For you to feel you want affection,
Not treat it as unwanted invasion.
Then we'll both feel positive and feel like building,
Rekindling and nurturing, yielding.
Am I mad to still have hope?
Only you know if I'm being a dope.
I'm so sad without you and long for reunion.
Like you said, 'phoenix', then communion.
You hoped a few weeks, but it's taking so long.
Don't give up. We will be strong.
One day you'll think I'm not so bad,
And then you won't feel so hurt and sad.
I want to be there into your old age,
To help and love you in our dotage.
 For the best thirty years, I owe you so much.
I won't be robbed of my devotion for such.
I will be there to have and to hold.
When you need me most, I'll be like gold.
So, what does a kiss mean? What does it say?
Commitment, devotion, it should say.
Despite the rejection, the loss, and the troubles.
It says that my love is redoubled.
I'm still there, whatever you do,
Waiting, hoping, for my dreams to come true.
You live in my heart. You will forever.
I give you your space, but give up? Never!'

He left it with her mail as usual. In his post he got a summons to appear in court in a few weeks' time. The next time he saw Delilah, he told her about the court date in the middle of December.

"I'll come with you" she said determinedly.

"Really? Why? It's a long way to go. All I will do is enter a plea of not guilty, and the hearing will be adjourned."

"I want to go."

"Ok."

He was surprised that she wanted to go all that way with him. Did she just want to see him humiliated in the dock? Or was she genuinely supporting him? He couldn't tell. She left him a note, asking him to read these two extracts from a book she had been reading because she hoped it would help him to understand the place she was at. This was good. She was trying to help him understand her. He read them voraciously.

'Mirroring or reflective listening is primary proof that someone else is out there, attentively listening to you, understanding you, validating you. On a deep fundamental level you begin to sense that yes, you are separate from your partner, but you are not alone. The mirroring exercise gives you the confidence that you can survive as a separate entity at the same time that it reassures you that your partner cares about you. These seemingly contradictory insights result in a highly evolved state of mind called differentiation; the sense that I am separate from you but still able to connect. A person who is differentiated fears neither abandonment nor engulfment. I know I can still be me and still be in a relationship with you. Paradoxically, this feeling of independence allows me to bond with you all the more deeply, because I am no longer terrified of being left alone or being engulfed. I don't have to put up so many defences. It's not fear that binds me to you but conscious choice. I am a distinct and separate individual who chooses to be in a relationship with you. Understanding the limitations of others - they simply ask for your compassion. They do not say that you are bad, ugly or despicable. They say only that you are asking for something they cannot give and that they need to get some distance from you to survive emotionally. The sadness is that you perceive their necessary withdrawal as a rejection of you instead of a call to return home and discover there your true belovedness'.

He wasn't at all sure what the message was. She seemed to be justifying her need of space, but he still couldn't see why it meant her moving out indefinitely, him not knowing where she was, her refusing to have proper conversations with him, or him not being allowed to show her affection, or express his love for her. She was always so evasive. She was however expressing herself openly and honestly in her secret diary. A lot later that evening at her home she wrote:

'It was better this time when you left. Why? I am not sure. Was it because you gave me time to talk about where and what is happening to me? Is it just my state of mind at the moment? Did I feel less used, and more thought of? Probably. The loss is still there though. Still want more but I know I can't have it. Why do I pursue such a futile situation? For a moment's satisfaction, and then, the desperate longing that follows. Is it about having a choice and a voice? Have I got to make a choice? A huge choice for once in my life. A choice that could cause me pain and regret, but if I don't make that choice, that could also cause me pain and regret! If only I had a crystal ball. I need to be rational – think!- use my head. But part of me wants to follow my heart and throw caution to the wind. Take a risk! Or is it just fantasy? A dream? - bring me back to reality – a husband, a home, a family. Why doesn't that inspire me? Is it that I have tasted candy? But candy doesn't sustain – it makes you sick after a while. Then one craves the solid and sustainable. Why is this choice so hard to make? And yet I made my choice the day I got married. Why can't I just learn to fend for myself - Oh help me God -I almost feel too past it. The dreams of family life have all gone. It looks like a new life dawns, one that is uncharted, and unplanned, and I feel totally unprepared for.

But I made a choice in 1979!'

Slowly, the court date came around. Delilah arrived at their home early. She was the one with the car after all. He had to be in court by 10:00 am at the latest. Neither Kevin nor Roger would be there as he would simply be confirming his identity, hearing the charge, and entering a plea of not guilty. He was pleased to be in the car with Delilah. This was the most time he had spent with her since she had moved out almost two months earlier. He tried talking to her, to understand where she was at, what she was still needing to do, and maybe what she planned to do in the future, but she was as evasive as ever. She obviously found it awkward and uncomfortable being questioned by him. She made him feel guilty for trying to talk to her. He was not honouring her need for space. He had no respect for her. His attempts to converse with her withered away. It was a long quiet journey. When they got into court, they were both searched on entry, and then they waited outside the courtroom until his case was called. He looked around the waiting area. It wasn't particularly busy; it seemed that most of the accused this morning were scruffy men of late teens to mid-thirties, of a certain ilk, bedecked with tattoos, accompanied by the rather loud young ladies, one or two of whom were trying to keep young children in check in the strict confines of the court house. When he was called, a sombre ancient usher adorned in a wrinkled and worn faded black gown showed him into the dock. Delilah deftly entered the public gallery and sat bolt upright, very alert and attentive. The court was empty apart from essential staff. He stood in the dock looking smart and middle class in his dark suit and closely-cropped hair. He deliberately stood proudly. He refused to be cowed by the situation. He confirmed his name. The clerk read out the one charge about data protection, and asked him how he pleaded. He said in a loud confident manner

"Not guilty."

The stipendiary magistrate peered at him over his reading glasses as if to quickly size him up, then had a quiet mutter with the clerk below and in front of him. He announced a new court date in the new year, and released Pablo on bail, reminding him that should he fail to appear as ordered, he would be arrested and brought before the next available court.

"Do you understand that Mr Pinkerton?"

"Yes, of course."

"Very well. Then you may go."

He left the court thinking that this whole case was just a charade. It was pointless. He had done nothing wrong. It was just a game that someone inside the system wanted to play, and he was just a pawn. Delilah walked out behind him and they walked back to the car in silence. This small part of the ordeal was over, for now. The journey home was a lot quieter than the one to court. He had got nowhere trying to talk to her before, and he realised that the journey home would be no different. Now they had to wait for another hearing in the middle of January, a whole year after Cassie had made her complaint, and now that complaint wasn't even involved in the process. It had morphed into something else. Like cancer.

The next day Pablo had another breakfast with Henry at a local cafe.

"How are you holding up buddy?" Henry asked affectionately.

"What choice do I have mate except to hang on in there. I have to be strong for both of us."

"That's a good way of looking at it Pablo. I like that. She's really gone off course. I would have never expected that from her, but yes, you've got to hold steady, for her."

"Yeah" he replied thoughtfully.

"How was court?"

"Just a waste of time. They already knew I was going to plead not guilty, but I had to drive an hour and a half away just to say it in person, then an hour and a half back. Such a waste of time."

"It does seem like a crazy system. How was Delilah?"

"Her usual self, I mean usual as in what she's like these days, not like how she was for the first thirty odd years."

Henry groaned a little, sharing Pablo's disappointment.

"You know Henry, what I find really galling is that her sisters all seem to be right behind her. I've considered them my family and friends for the past thirty years. I thought I was close to them, but now all of a sudden, I'm the enemy. Shut out. Cut out. I don't suppose they know any more about what's going on than I do. So why are they like this? Why haven't they talked to me, or to both of us?"

"People act strangely in these circumstances mate. It's probably jealousy. You and Delilah have a truly wonderful family. Your kids are great. Sometimes people can't cope with other people doing better than them, and they want to see them fail, and they're more keen to help them fail than succeed."

"Bastards."

Henry looked at him with a frown of distaste for his language. Pablo mused, feeling none the wiser or any better about the situation. Henry asked him a very blunt question.

"Pablo, do you think she's involved with someone else?"

Pablo gave a short laugh to demonstrate how ridiculous that was.

"Oh, Henry, come on. She's the most pure, trustworthy person you could ever hope to meet. You know that. She thinks that to even talk to someone of the opposite sex is wrong. That's why I'm in so much trouble. I talk to people of the opposite sex when I'm at work! I've been in trouble with her for my whole life because of that. Even now, when we go dancing, I can feel her daggers when I'm talking to one of the ladies, and that's now, when she's having nothing to do with me. No, this hasn't got anything to do with anyone else. It's all to do with me and my behaviour. She feels so let down by me."

"Ok mate. I just find it puzzling that she's moved out and won't tell you where she's gone."

Pablo brightened up a little, feeling a little pleased with himself.

"Actually Henry, I do know where she's gone."

"I thought it was a secret."

"It's meant to be, but before she left, I made a note of the adverts she had circled. Then more recently, I noted which direction she goes off in when she leaves dancing on a Wednesday. Then I narrowed it down by knowing the kind of property she likes. When I went out on my first recce, bingo! her car was outside the very first one I looked at. It's a small converted farm building down a private track about seven miles north of town. She's there on her own."

Henry laughed.

"I suppose that's the copper in you."

"Yeah maybe, but it just felt right to know where she is. She's still my wife y'know! I won't go there again though."

"Afraid of what you might find?"

"Absolutely not. I trust her with my life. No, to be honest I'm a bit worried about her. She's gone to live on her own in a very isolated, converted farm building in the middle of nowhere, and she's quite naive. I could imagine her being attacked out there all by herself. If she phoned me up in the middle of the night and only got as far as screaming down the phone, I'd know where to go."

"Now that's the copper in you! Thinking like that."

"Probably. I don't like her being so vulnerable. She's not very worldly-wise."

"Well Pablo, it's not your fault if something happens to her. She's put herself in that position."

"Oh I realise that Henry, but that doesn't stop me worrying about her. I still love her and care about her."

"I think we all know that Pablo" he said with a laugh.

They finished up, and Pablo went home feeling much better for a little human contact.

Back to the build. The shell was complete now. He had started making enquiries of window-fitters, plasterers, electricians, and plumbers. They could all do the second fit leaving him to concentrate on renovating the original building, tiling the floors, decorating, and one day eventually, making a beautiful patio outside to fully take advantage of the wonderful southerly aspect. He started with the lounge where he wanted to brick up one of two doorways and introduce more electrics, suitable for what would become the master bedroom. The place had been built in the sixties when one, or maybe two electric sockets per room were deemed sufficient. Not any more of course. He wanted two sockets in each wall. The bookcase was chock full of books. There were books on top of books, books behind books. Every nook and cranny was stuffed with books. A lifetime's collection. He decided to get rid of about half of them to a charity shop. He contemplated running this by Delilah, but he didn't know when he'd see her again. Anyway, she'd deserted him, and the house, so would she really care?

Christmas arrived. Pablo busied himself visiting all the children in turn, and staying with each one for a day or two. He also visited his siblings, but he didn't get to see Delilah. She by contrast spent very little time with the family. She had a brief visit from them all at her hideaway, but her window even for them, was a brief one. For Pablo, this all felt so wrong. It wasn't a proper Christmas. It was supposed to be a particularly special time for families to get together, not to start new separate lives apart. He was grateful for the time he spent with his kids, but it was so piecemeal. He felt robbed. He loved to see his wife interacting with their family. Christmas came and went without a single interaction between him and his wife. That saddened him deeply.

Afterwards she wrote in her diary:

'He gave Christmas cards to the kids signed just him and Sarah. I was gutted. It feels like he is making a point. I feel for the children. How must they feel when receiving a card like that? It is so unnecessary. We could still send them a card from us both. Why does he want to make such an issue of it? - need to challenge him on this.'

After his first Christmas without her, he felt compelled to reach out again. Apart from a couple of cards and a short poem, he hadn't written her a letter from his aching heart since before she had left. The space that he had given her didn't seem to him to have achieved anything. He felt that he had nothing to lose by writing again. He started off quoting some advice that he had read in a daily help series:

'There is no painless, fool-proof guarantee. Healing a relationship involves shared effort and risk. I have to trust that ultimately you'll forgive me and put the offence behind you, and you have to believe that I'm sincere about changing. Healing wounded relationships is a two-person job. Your job is to work at trusting me again, and mine is to provide you with evidence that I'm trustworthy. When we do that, we invite one another's cooperation, encourage each other and shorten the distance that separates us. Making a relationship work means deciding you have real and positive options, and both committing to them.'

For the rest of the letter, over two more pages, he droned on and on about how he was changing for her, how he was going to be a better listener, more respectful, more loving, more supportive. He apologised for having regarded her departure as a negative event. Now he could see that it was a good and necessary thing for her to develop her sense of self-worth and independence from him, and to give him space to sort out his issues for her. He threw in the occasional loaded metaphor to add impact to his pleading - his love had emerged from the furnace like toughened steel - and he finished as always with a great deal of hope:

'I want for us to fall deeply in love, deeper than ever before. To both feel blissful in union, intimacy, eroticism, mutual understanding and support. I truly believe that we can get there my love. We can deal with the skeletons, face the demons, learn new strategies, and all of this will enable us to find and relish a deeper more meaningful love.

Yours always, Pablo'

She only wrote in her diary:

'I do feel so desperate - I hate the feeling of being alone, fending for myself - I remember that feeling of oneness we once had - but it's all gone. He goes on about me getting what I want, craving to get away and live my life separately. He doesn't understand the desperation I feel about the prospect. He thinks I'm so strong, but I feel so weak, so helpless, so trapped. Please help me God to keep me going, for what, I don't know. I feel like a totally different person when with him - it's not really me - he feels it too of course. It must be so hard for him to see me like this. Am I just sick? Having a breakdown - a shadow of my former self, fun, happy, relaxed conversational. I am just so shut down to him, it is quite incredible. I loathe myself for it.'

Chapter 14

A week or so later she popped into the matrimonial home to use the computer. She noticed how much work Pablo had done since she had last been there, but she didn't comment to him on anything, not about the house, nor about how Christmas had gone for her, nor her plans for the future. She just kept her distance, physically and emotionally, as usual. He fawned around her as much as he thought she would tolerate, which wasn't very much, and then she left. Later on at her home, she unbottled her emotions in her diary.

'I feel like I am now losing control over the one thing maybe I had – the house and how it's arranged inside. It's all being changed around and sorted out. I feel out of control and panicky and I don't feel like going back. It's very unsettling. I don't know where anything is. It's not my home anymore? I wonder if there's an element of spite going on - I can't control you so I'll control something that was yours. You've left, so hard luck! Why don't I feel like he cares for me? He says so many nice things - why don't I feel it? What's the matter with me? I must be living in a delusion, or someone else's, like he says I am. Am I being too sensitive? Please help me God to keep things in perspective. I can't see any alternative but to go back and bite the bullet. I felt so desperate over the weekend, thinking about the children - them having to choose who to see - whether to use us to babysit or which one to ask, or not bothering at all because it's so awkward. Not being around for Sarah as she comes and goes. Troy coming down and me not being there. Christmas wasn't the same. I feel like I'm destroying the thing I hold so dear to me, so important to my life and my children and grandchildren - the nuclear family - It is such an integral part of my life. It is my life. Do I then carry on, once again, for the sake of the family? Is that a good enough basis to return? I want to return because I want to be with him, the man - Is that ever going to happen?'

Time dragged by for Pablo, all lonely and desperate, but it raced by for Delilah who by the end of January was halfway through her paid-for rental, and she knew that she would not be able to afford to renew it. She faced an unavoidable dilemma. Then it was nearly Valentine's day. He selected a special card for this one. It was a drawing of two old people sitting on picnic chairs on a beach facing out to sea. The caption over the picture read 'Love does not consist of gazing at each other but in looking outward together in the same direction.'

Inside the card he wrote:

'My dearest Delilah, because I love you I care about you, I want to grow old with you side by side, loving, supporting and nurturing. I am so sorry I have lost my way with you, but because I love you so much, I will make the right changes so we can find our unique path again, and grow old together, happy, fulfilled, and deeply in love. Love Pablo xx'

Delilah wrote in her diary.

'Where are you now? After the passion and heart-pouring of last weekend you have pulled back or that is what it feels like. Is it only when you are in trouble that you feel anything, when you are low. Then reason and responsibility come back and you step back from me - why? Are you fearful of your feelings? I miss you so much. But then I question the situation again. Why am I setting myself up for this roller-coaster ride of feelings and emotions? What am I afraid of if I pull out? - Feelings of utter loss and loneliness? Afraid it will force me back to a situation I don't really want? But will it? Can I be strong enough to see? Try? Text? I so wish we were both free to feel, to love, to test the waters, but we are not. Does patience play a part in this, is that just fantasy, hope? Talk to me. Wherever I am, whoever I am with, I find myself wishing you are there with me, loving, laughing, living – together!'

At the end of February, around midmorning, with the weather relatively mild and dry, Pablo sat quietly in a local cafe awaiting Henry. It was busy. He casually observed the clientele whilst he waited. Most customers appeared to be with friends, engaging in coffee, cakes and conversation whilst relaxing in the café ambience. It was a rather modern café with a mixture of traditional tables and chairs with leather sofas and armchairs for those seeking a little extra comfort. The better part of the trendy comfy area had been taken over by a noisy assembly of young mothers with babies. They were cackling away in between sipping coffee and feeding their young, some from the breast. Their outer garments were strewn over the settees. Their rather cumbersome pushchairs more or less blocked that area off to passers-by. Pablo made sure he didn't stare. The clientele seemed mostly bright and cheerful, unlike Pablo who was feeling dour and rather pitiful.

Henry strode in looking cheerful and dapper. He had the confidence of the older man who had seen it all, done it all.

"Hello mate, how are you?"

"Yeah not too bad old fruit."

They had a quick catch-up about life in general. Henry was busy with his latest business adventure involving property. Pablo felt rather envious of the progress Henry was making in his life.

"How's the build coming on?" Henry enquired chirpily.

"Really well actually."

Pablo immediately perked up.

"I've chopped through the old kitchen floor and broken into the new stairwell. Just making that all good, then I'll get a staircase made up for it. I'm chuffed that it all lines up perfectly. Plasterers have started."

"Sounds great. I suppose that is the one saving grace of all this; you've been able to stay at home and get on with it."

"True, but funny you should say that. I had a call from my Fed' Rep' last week. In a couple of weeks' time I will have used up my allowance of one year's sick leave. I'm going to have to go back to work or I won't get any more money."

"Oh dear. I can't believe this has all dragged on so long. What a waste of public money."

As a hard-working self-employed member of the public, he was truly astonished at the lackadaisical manner of this public-office affair.

"I totally agree with that Henry. I also cannot believe how long all this is taking. It's not what I want."

"Oh Pablo, it must be so rough for you, constantly not knowing what's going on. So what will they get you to do? You've still got the court case outstanding haven't you?"

"Yep. They're talking about putting me in an office called logistics."

"To do what?"

"Update computer systems and crap like that."

"Just admin then?"

"Yep."

"You won't like that will you?"

"Not at all, but I don't have any other choice. I still need to get paid. They've got me over a barrel. It will be boring, mundane, frustrating, and way below my pay grade in fact, but it will pay the bills."

He looked discomforted just thinking about being stuck in an office for the foreseeable future. He carried on.

"I won't be using any of the people skills I've built up over the years, so I expect I'll feel pretty wasted."

"Well, I suppose you just have to focus on the money."

He hesitated before he brought up the main topic.

"How's Delilah?"

"Terrible. Just can't get close to her. Still see her once a week at the dance class, and just occasionally she pops back home for something, but her defences are always up. It's so horrible."

Tears trickled down his cheeks. He still couldn't talk about Delilah without becoming visibly upset. Henry didn't flinch. He expected this.

"Any talk of her coming back?"

"Nope."

"What happens when her six months rental runs out?"

"Your guess is as good as mine. I really don't know what she's planning Henry."

"Are you still writing to her?"

"Of course. What else can I do?"

"Do you think that helps?"

"I hope so."

"Well mate, I think you need to be careful. Women are funny creatures. If you chase them too much, they run away."

He gave a little chortle. Pablo already knew that he was pathetic, feeble and grovelling, but he couldn't help himself.

"My fear Henry, is that if I don't carry on writing , she'll think that I've given up on her. I think most guys would have given up by now, but I want her to be assured that I am still there for her. I did stop writing to her before Christmas, but since then, I'm writing to her at least once a week"

A smart waitress interrupted them to take an order for two large all-day breakfasts with coffee. Henry carried on.

"Maybe it wouldn't be a bad thing if she was left to wonder?"

"Maybe, but I'm just following my heart Henry."

"I know mate. I know."

"She acts like I shouldn't be trying to save our relationship, that any effort I make to show her love is worse than me beating her up or something like that. It's not just that she's gone emotionally, which is hard enough, but she makes me feel like the worst person on the planet, just for trying."

The tears rolled down his cheeks. His face contorted with real pain. Henry thought it was best to change the subject.

"So what's happened to the court case?"

He took a few moments to compose himself, then spoke quietly and slowly.

"They just keep putting it off. You know I appeared again at the end of January, pleaded not guilty, again, and the CPS asked for an adjournment till the beginning of May to have enough time to prepare their case."

"More delay! Unbelievable. Did Delilah go with you again?"

"Yes, but it's a nightmare going all that way in the car with her. She just says nothing. It's so foul. I think she just likes to see me in the dock. Truly I do."

More tears, then he quietly carried on.

"And she gets so angry about me pleading not guilty. She says that I'm not taking responsibility for my actions. I tell her that as far as I'm concerned I've done absolutely nothing to breach the data protection act, so why should I plead guilty? It would be crazy. I mean, I'd definitely lose my job because that would be a criminal conviction, and for what?"

"And what does she say to that?"

"She insists that If I had one iota of integrity, I'd plead and go down. She doesn't seem to understand that she'd be losing her bread and butter too."

"She's really not thinking straight mate."

He leaned across the table and put a hand on Pablo's shoulder as a sign of reassurance. "Don't worry mate. I'm sure it'll all work out in the end, somehow. Remember, you have to love someone the most when they deserve it the least."

"Yeah that's a good one Henry. I'll remember that. Thanks."

Henry looked at him with real compassion in his old grey eyes.

"To be honest, I'm not too worried about the job. I can always get other work. Sometimes I just feel like telling them to fuck off. I just don't want to lose Delilah. I don't think I could face a life without her. She is irreplaceable."

Henry looked at him as if he didn't really know what the best thing to say was, but as always, Pablo benefitted from just sharing his woes with such a good reliable friend. They chatted some more as they ate, then, breakfast finished, they departed.

Later that day, after work, ensconced in her secret hideaway, Delilah wrote in her diary:

'I felt so low today - hormonal - but it makes me question so many things. I find myself thinking how much I miss my home, my familiar surroundings, my things, children and their things and their comings and goings, but not the man. How very sad is that? Can I ever love him again? Is it really a decision to? I've done that in the past and so many times. I have found myself questioning it time and again. Is that what life is though? I feel so lonely. I hate this life of solitude - no one to share the beautiful sunshine, countryside etc with. No one to laugh with, smile with, chat to, lean on, to love, to hold hands with, to hug, to kiss, to share life with. Don't know I could live a life like this - I need somebody. I could just go home and have all that but feel it would all be false, or would it? I feel this loneliness so deeply today, I just want to cry the whole time.'

The weeks dragged by. Fortunately for Pablo, with the weather outside often windy and wet, he was able to work on alterations inside the house. He was chuffed that the extension roofs that he had built were completely watertight, and all the alterations he had made at the meeting of old and new were sound too. He was proud of his accomplishments. Not many guys could do the range of practical things that he did. He wondered why Delilah didn't appreciate those things.

It was the middle of March, Delilah made one of her occasional visits to the house. Pablo was outside. She went outside and found him. He wondered if she had some proposal for their imminent thirtieth wedding anniversary, because whatever challenges they were going through, this was still going to be a milestone. Thirty years! He downed tools and looked at her. He could tell straight away that it was not going to be good news. Her face was already angry-looking, and she hadn't even spoken yet. She stood directly opposite him, upright, proud, confrontational. Close up he could see that her eyes were almost on fire, as if they were discharging her contempt directly at him like evil lasers. His spirit shrivelled inside of him. He was already battling disappointment and fear, but he tried hard to maintain his equanimity.

"My tenancy runs out next month. I can't afford to renew it, so I'll be coming home, but I want to make it absolutely crystal clear that I will be returning purely for financial reasons, and definitely not because I want to be with you. Is that clear?"

He got the feeling that she had rehearsed this quite a lot. She was forthright and authoritative. He thought carefully before he spoke. He wondered why she was making such a big announcement about it. He guessed that she wanted to know that he would accept her terms first. He would just be happy to have her back home, so he had nothing to argue about. He simply hoped that one day she would wake up with a small crack in the ice encasing her heart and the opportunity to encourage her down a different path would present itself. He didn't need to say much, just that he'd heard her.

"Fine" he said evenly.

"Obviously I'll have my own bedroom, and I won't want anything to do with you. Can you respect that?"

The last bit she asked in a mocking tone that reflected disbelief that he could actually achieve such a thing.

"Yes" he replied meekly, like a broken, belittled man, meekly accepting the orders of a superior.

"I don't want you trying to talk to me all the time, or touching me, or anything like that. Can you honour me enough to do that?"

She was asking him to show his love for her by not showing her any love. She wanted to be treated like a stranger.

"Ok."

His acquiescence didn't seem to appease her one little bit. She was still visibly angry, not so much at him directly, but at the defeat she was going to suffer by having to return to the matrimonial home. She was on the verge of tears, but she was able to resist them because she was in fight mode. Her body was taut and slightly trembling with anger at the situation. She stared at him fiercely. She was a little stunned by his failure to argue. She wondered what to say next, but couldn't think of anything. He had nothing to say. He was there to receive her instructions and to comply. Nothing more. He looked at her rather lamely. She turned around, and left, job done.

He felt terrible. The love of his life, his childhood sweetheart, the mother of his children couldn't bear the thought of having to return home. She clearly wanted to stay away. He wept. He wondered where this would lead. So far, she had only talked about needing space, but not of proper separation or divorce. For that, he was grateful. But if she really wanted to stay away indefinitely, what did that imply? His discomfort about her being so upset didn't leave him over the next few days, so he decided to give her an option. He placed an advert in the local paper offering rooms to rent. Within a week, he had three reasonable potential tenants in the pipeline. They were prepared to put up with the alterations going on around them, as they could appreciate that before too long this house would be like a palace. The next time he saw Delilah was at a Wednesday evening dance class. At the end of the evening, he walked her into the carpark outside, as he always did. They stopped by her car, and rather pleased with himself he made an announcement.

"Babe, when you came round to let me know that you would be coming home, you were obviously deeply distraught at the thought. I don't want to put you through that, so I've arranged for lodgers to come and stay. They can use the three spare bedrooms. That will provide ample income for you to carry on renting the place that you want."

He looked at her in the poor light of the car park to gauge her reaction. He hoped that his understanding and kindness would melt her a little, just for once. That would be so nice. Maybe she would give him a hug. A kiss was probably a step too far. He was surely demonstrating real love for her. She determined her response very quickly.

"I don't want strangers living in my house!"

She was cross at the thought of lodgers. He was taken aback. He thought that she would have bitten his hand off at his offer. It would have meant that she could stay away. Returning home seemed to horrify her. He expressed his surprise.

"But you seemed so upset at coming home. This provides a way for you to be able to afford to stay wherever you are now, and without me sponsoring you."

She repeated herself sternly.

"I don't want strangers living in my house."

She gave him one of those glares that says that she means business, and that there was nothing more to discuss.

He was confused, but he was fine with that. He simply said "Ok."

He kissed her quickly on the cheek, and she deftly got into her car and drove off.

It was a little embarrassing to stand the potential lodgers down, but he did so. He would prefer to have his wife living with him anyway.

She expressed herself in her diary:

'Why do I feel so dead towards him? Sometimes there is a glimmer of sympathy but I even struggle with that, and whether or how to show it, for fear that I am giving the wrong message - give an inch and he'll take a mile. He says he needs to be able to show me his affection because he loves me. It makes me want to recoil. It means nothing to me if he kisses me - I can hardly even look at him! Can the love in me ever be rekindled? I hate the thought of being on my own - nobody to love and no one to love me - to be held in another's arms. How do I cope with this feeling of loss on so many levels? I do feel intensely lonely and unhappy but is that any reason to return to him? Will that change anything? Can I bring myself to give a little without him taking a mile? It feels like I will just slip back into that place of being manipulated. Can I let that happen? I need to recognise my feelings - acknowledge them -feelings that are not necessarily right or wrong, they are just feelings. Act on them and trust them. Take control of the situation rather than sitting back and letting things happen to me - Compromise - willing to do this just for the moment. I feel anxious about the whole thing. If I start to let my defences down will I be taken advantage of? Why have I got to this most terrible place? Why is he so angry? Have I really destroyed him so much? I can do this when feeling strong but he can wear me down so easily with his verbal torrent. I want to go back because I am pulled by the positives, not pushed by the negatives.'

A few days later Pablo had to go back to work. He drove to the railway station, and got a train into the city. Sarah had just a few days earlier embarked on a three-month-long vacation to the far east, so he had the use of his own car back. His new office was located in the local area headquarters where Mr Framlin was based. Roger had told him to report to an Inspector Brown, who would be his new boss. He was in charge of admin stuff. Pablo knew him quite well from having served under him when they were both on the same operational squad some years earlier. He found Mr Brown's office, and stood in the doorway. Mr

Brown unwittingly looked at him as if he was someone to be pitied, someone very fragile, someone who had the equivalent of a terminal illness, but he welcomed Pablo to his team very warmly. He assured him that he would be treated just like anyone else, and the outstanding case against him would not prejudice him in any way. Pablo thought it was very kind of him to be so inclusive and welcoming. He could tell that the man was being genuine. The system however was against him. That is why he was only being allowed to work as a clerk. Mr Brown personally took him along to his new office and introduced him to his two new work colleagues. One was a long-in-service fellow constable who had a severe mobility disability, and as such was no longer fit for normal police duties, and the other was a middle-aged woman who had recently returned to work after her children had left home. They seemed nice enough, and they readily introduced him to his workload. He missed being free to work on his house full time. He had been spoiled. Now he would have to rely purely on weekends.

The next time Delilah popped home to use the computer, he told her about his new position. Of course he enquired as to where she was emotionally, and expressed hope that when she returned they would be able to work on their differences. She didn't say anything about that. As usual it was just business for her, and then she returned to her secret home having avoided any meaningful conversations. She wrote in her diary.

'I feel so low today - the aching of a heart that has loved but may not be able to show love to that special person again. You've stolen a part of my heart - it is like grief, such a deep loss, such a heavy heart. How could I have let this happen to me? Oh, to be held in your arms again - will that ever be? Should I just let it all go, and walk through this pain and leave it behind? Will I ever be able to pick myself up? Please give me strength to work this through. The loss is so deep. You love a lot and risk being hurt a lot. How do I live with myself? May the day come when I am free of all this turmoil and devastation - it is exhausting. I wish you well my love. You have taught me a lot about myself, life and love. I pray that I will embrace the lessons and be able to use them for good. Will I be able to stop looking for that elusive text? Will the expectation begin to fade?'

A few slow weeks later, towards the end of April, Delilah returned home. It was a Saturday, so they were both able to be at home all day. Pablo was working on plastering an internal doorway which he had bricked up. She was terribly upset by the fact that she had returned, and spent most of the day in tears as she went about resettling her things. He was also in tears quite a lot too, just from seeing her so upset. It tore him apart. But he had made an alternative option available to her, and she had chosen not to take it. That was his saving grace.

He gave her a few days to settle down, then he approached her to discuss a way forward.

"Delilah, I know you said that your return had nothing to do with me, but as you're here now, I want to try to improve things between us."

He paused and looked at her quizzically, to see if she had any comment to make. It seemed not, so he carried on.

"I want to use this opportunity to put right anything I can put right for you."

Still no response. She stood still, stony faced.

"I want you to make a list of all the things you'd like to see changed in me, so I know what I can be working on. I have asked you before."

She didn't look keen, but as far as he was concerned, she still hadn't explained to him why she had left him, and he needed to know why. Whatever it was, he wanted to put it right.

"Please?" he implored her.

She dismissed him with a reluctant "ok."

A few days later she gave him her list;

'Find other ways to deal with anger and frustration without shouting or swearing.

Listen to me. Use my language, not your slant or interpretation.

Resist from always having the answer. Telling me what I should or need to do, unless I ask for it.

Think about what you say. Mean what you say, say what you mean.

Be consistent in the above.

Respect where I am at re: the physical relationship. No hugging, kissing, touching, sexual or romantic touching that makes me feel awkward.

Respect my need for my own room

Talk about issues at an agreed time and not after 9:00 pm.

Discuss finances. How they are arranged and what money is spent on.

Please let me be me, not what I think you want or expect me to be, the way I sit, what I say.

Resist from pressuring. Digging up the flower to see if it is growing. Let it bloom in its own time.'

He poured over it, rapacious for things he could work on in himself for his beloved. But it didn't seem much like a recipe for repair, just a tool kit for keeping him at bay. Some of it actually confused him. Hadn't he always been straightforward in the way that he spoke? Yes he would use the 'f' word when he was cross. That was his way of demonstrating that he was cross, but shouting? He couldn't remember ever shouting. Where did that come from? Respecting her need for no contact, that was hard for a rejected husband. She had already removed herself from the matrimonial bed. She had coldly denied him sexual intimacy and any kind of affection. That had been so hard for him, but he'd had no option other than to get used to it. All he had asked for was to be allowed common social courtesies like a hug on hello or goodbye, or a kiss on the cheek. Was that really too much to ask of a wife? Respect for her own room. Hadn't she had that since September? If she demanded an appointment for him to talk to her, he could do that. Discuss finances? He was more than happy to do that as it was her who was threatening their financial stability, not him. Let her be herself? How could he not? She had boldly taken charge of her destiny. He had been just left starkly on the side-lines wondering what the hell was going on. Was he really not allowed to protest? Resist from pressurising. That was the most difficult one.

He so wanted to win her back. He just had no idea how to. In fact everything he was doing was making matters worse.

He digested the list very carefully. In the end, he couldn't shake off the feeling that it was a bit of a smokescreen, and that she was still hiding her innermost thoughts and feelings, but this was what she had given him to work on, and he would work on it to the best of his ability. Over the following days and weeks, he did whatever he could to comply with her demands. He occasionally breached the no-touching order though. Every now and again, he would put his arm across her shoulders briefly as he told her that he still loved her very much. He felt that he ought to be allowed at least that little bit of expression.

They were living separate lives under one roof. He was back to work. She was doing more and more care work. His spare time was spent working on the house and organising plumbers, electricians and plasterers. She would cook for them both each evening, but the only thing they did together was attend their weekly dance class. Everything else about her was private. He respected her wish for him not to try to talk to her, but to help him achieve that, he did leave her a short note each day telling her in a different way each time of his unending love for her. He would leave the note out on the kitchen worktop. It always disappeared. He hoped she was reading them. Maybe they were going straight into the bin. He checked. They weren't.

Once a week, he would ask for a meeting to discuss his progress. She would report no progress. He was trying so hard, but it was as though she didn't want him to improve. She only made it very clear that he was getting nowhere with her. It was one big, bad, ugly stalemate.

Chapter 15

Early May and Roger invited him to a meeting at the Federation offices again. He was informed that the case had been adjourned yet again, and he was introduced to a barrister, Nigel Caruthers, who would be representing him when the case eventually came to court. Apparently it was really good news that the Federation had agreed to finance his defence with a full-blown barrister. Roger hadn't been sure that they would go that far for him. Nigel was quite a large man in his mid-thirties. He exuded an air of confidence befitting a man of his profession, and Pablo was immediately far much more confident in him than young Kevin. Rather alarmingly though, Nigel asked him what his line of defence should be.

"Isn't that for you to work out?" Pablo replied rather surprised at being asked.

"Well we can't just pluck any old thing out of the air. We need to focus on something realistic."

Pablo felt obliged to offer something.

"I think they're making a big deal out of the fact that I still monitored my old clients after I moved to the POU. I think we just have to emphasise the close connection with the druggies I was dealing with for two years as the harm reduction officer, and the motley mob I inherited on the POU. There was a lot of crossover, and besides that, when is a police officer not allowed to interrogate police intelligence?"

"I see" Nigel said rather unconvincingly. Roger and Kevin were both present too, but they were quietly deferring to the big man. Pablo was beginning to feel rather exposed and unsupported. Nigel carried on.

"They're saying that you were monitoring subjects not within your jurisdiction."

"In that case the whole police intelligence dissemination machinery is illegal."

"Explain."

"The first thing every officer does when coming on duty is to familiarise himself with the latest intel. The system constantly spews out blanket information concerning all and sundry. There is no sifting of any kind. It could be to do with absolutely anyone, but it is cascaded to each and every officer. That is the intelligence environment. It's huge, and it's not officer or role specific. The more you know, the better prepared you are. That's the theory. So how could it possibly be wrong for me to be interrogating intel on drug addicts in my area, who are either on the POU list, or who are their associates?"

"I see" he added in a muted pondering voice.

Pablo's initial confidence in the man was wavering fast. He had been involved in so many cases where the defence had got their client off on a technicality, or some spurious argument, yet all he was asking for was a reasonable interpretation of the use of comprehensively disseminated police intel. Was that so hard? Nigel continued.

"I think they are going to challenge your motivation. Specifically, Why did you carry on checking the records of people not on the POU and in particular, one Cassie Woolridge?"

"Professional interest. Human interest. I had been working closely with some of these people for two years, and I was still interested in their progress, or lack of it. I was still able to get good quality intel from some of them, and that is always a part of a police officer's role."

"But that wasn't your job."

"Really? Who says so?"

"They say so."

"Then they are out of touch with reality."

This was going nowhere fast. Nigel seemed to lack even basic knowledge of how police intelligence is gathered and disseminated. Roger could have backed him up as a fellow former operational officer, but he declined to wade in. Pablo felt let down by him. Nothing new there. Really, he was next to useless. He drew solace from his rock-solid conviction that no magistrate in the whole land would find him guilty of an offence simply for looking at police intelligence. He came to his own defence.

"I thought data protection act misuse was to do with actually misusing information, like trying to influence a witness, or a suspect, or bribe or blackmail people, or sell intel to people, or use it somehow for some other financial advantage. Something substantial, none of which I have done. I have looked at intel to be best able to do my job. How could that possibly be wrong?"

Kevin was being very quiet. Pablo presumed that he dare not speak in the presence of a full-blown barrister. Nigel looked at him quizzically on this last point, and Kevin piped up in response to the non-verbal question.

"That's true. I've not heard of anyone being charged with any data protection offence who hadn't clearly benefited in some illegal way too. This case is most unusual."

"I see" mused Nigel. He seemed to have heard enough for now, and after a few routine pleasantries, Pablo was released, leaving the three of them to talk about him behind his back.

When he got home later, Delilah wanted to know how the meeting had gone. He summed it up as an introduction between him and the barrister, and a preliminary exploration of his defence.

"So you're still pleading not guilty then?"

He looked at her in disbelief, wondering why she was so fixated with him pleading guilty.

"Of course I am." He refrained from adding a phrase about having done nothing wrong, because he knew that would simply rile her. She thought he was guilty of something. She wanted him to be guilty. She gave him her strongest dirty look and then carried on preparing some food in the kitchen.

Since her return in April, life had been a disjointed and perplexing mess of limbo, deceit and awkwardness, and it looked like it was just going to carry on that way. Pablo however was the unquenchable optimist. Every day he left her a short love note. Sometimes he would remind her to her face that he still loved her very much. He refused to become her opponent. He remained her devoted husband, no matter what. He was convinced that one day she would wake up and realise that actually, she didn't want to jeopardise her family relationships, and give up her home, and her financial support, and the devotion of a husband who had stood by her rock-solid for thirty years. He just had to be kind and patient.

Later, in the privacy of her locked bedroom, she wrote in her diary.

'Beginning to wonder if I am going crazy! Can't seem to get the message across about demands and threats if they're not met. Am I imagining it? It may be that's not what they are. It's just his way of telling me what his needs are and where the boundaries lay for him. He still wants to put his arm around me sometimes. He needs to temper his language; not 'I'm going to do this or that' (resign from job) but 'I feel like that is what I want to do.' Allow room for discussion – exploring the consequences, reasons, options. Am I being unrealistic in my expectations? I'm finding it increasingly depressing when we keep going round in circles. I can't see things are going to change and I can't imagine a life without anyone to love and be loved by. So where do I go from here? Nothing's changed.'

One day at the end of June she seemed quite pensive. He knew that something was on her mind, and he waited dutifully for her to let it out. He didn't push because he was afraid it could only be bad news for him. She waited until after dinner when he was clearing up the dishes.

"I want a separation" she announced curtly. She didn't beat around the bush, and she didn't look him in the eye, but she was very assertive. He wasn't too surprised. It was after all ten months since she had first told him that she wanted to leave him, and in reality, wasn't she effectively separated from him already? She had already made it amply clear that if she had the money, she would be living elsewhere without him. So it wasn't really news, but he did wonder where she was going with this. He enquired.

"What does that mean?"

"It means we sell the house and go our separate ways."

Of course he was gutted, but he already knew this is where she was aiming. He loved this house, and had put so much of himself into it. He would be happy to live there for the rest of his life. It was the epitome of his life's work; all the other houses he had done up and sold over the years made it possible for them to be able to live somewhere like this. All the monthly mortgage payments he had struggled to pay over three decades was so that he could live in splendid isolation here in the depths of the countryside with his beloved wife. He wanted to make their marriage work, but the stark reality was that she clearly didn't. He asked the question he dreaded to ask.

"Does that mean you're divorcing me?"

At this, she looked pained. It clearly caused friction within her.

"I struggle with that" she answered in all honesty.

That was some consolation for him. She appeared strong and resolute, but inside, there was at least some turmoil, maybe even some doubt about her actions. He decided to be direct.

"When are you leaving then?"

"When the house is sold."

Well that certainly took the sting out of it. There was still loads of work to do before the property would be ready for market. At least six months. And then there would be the actual marketing process. He wondered if they could live like this for another whole year. Would she really want to?

"Why?" he poignantly asked.

"There is no other way."

This was one of her regular mantras, but its meaning still eluded him. He didn't understand it for one moment, but he wasn't going to argue with her. There would be no point in doing that. He shrugged his shoulders as a sign that he felt that he simply had to accept what she was dishing out, as usual.

He continued to have a time of weeping each day. Every single day. It was simply something his soul needed to do to maintain its equilibrium. He felt that it was somehow cleansing his soul, and allowing the pain to seep out and not poison him. He didn't want to internalise all this hurt and confusion. In fact after the separation announcement, the only change was that she ordered him to stop going to their local dance. She wanted to go alone, without him. He could have been awkward and carried on going anyway, but he didn't want to fight her. He stopped going. She kindly told him that he could go to the next city along, half an hour away, and dance there. He didn't want to go without her, so he just stopped dancing. She carried on, without him, but with her new friends. He was likewise barred from any social events arising out of the dance scene. That hurt. It made him feel like an outcast, as if nobody liked him. He had long since been barred from any social events with her family, but now the dance scene too. It was rather humiliating, but he knew that he had to rise above it. He was only really concerned about her, his true love.

His mind was constantly preoccupied with ideas of how to salvage the situation, mostly about what was wrong with him, and what he could change in himself, but he had exhausted all the possibilities. The only area where he could still give ground was his plea. He had been adamant about pleading his innocence. She was adamant about him accepting responsibility and pleading guilty. He was at a crossroads. He could choose to honour his marriage over keeping his career and his own honour. He asked himself what was more important, his work, or his marriage. It was a no-brainer. The allegations from Cassie and Marlon were gone. The only sticking point now was this blessed data protection charge. The next time he had an opportunity to talk to Delilah he told her.

"Babe, you've made it very clear over the past year that you think I'm in the wrong to plead not guilty to this data protection charge. I've obviously offended you somehow by declaring my innocence. Quite why you think you know more about my work than I do, I'll never know, but as you're so adamant, and for the sake of our relationship, I've decided to change my plea. It does mean that I will lose my job though. You do realise that don't you?"

"Don't put that on me."

"But it's what you want."

"Don't put that one on me" she repeated fiercely.

He said no more. He had made a decision, and he would stick by it. The next day he phoned Kevin to inform him.

"What made you change your mind after all this time John?" he queried.

"Delilah. I'm doing it for her."

"You know it won't go down well at your disciplinary hearing don't you. They will have a convicted man in front of them."

"I know, but I don't feel that I have any choice. Right now, I'm not feeling too mad about the job anyway, and it's the last thing I can do to maybe save my marriage."

Of course, he didn't expect Kevin to understand what he was talking about. He doubted that he had ever even had a girlfriend yet.

"Are you sure?"

"Yep."

"Ok. I'll inform the CPS."

He wanted something in return from Delilah. That evening, at dinner, he told her.

"Del, I think that period of counselling we did with Sylvia was not helpful."

Delilah cut in very quickly.

"What, because it didn't go your way? Because she didn't agree with you?"

"In all honesty, I think she had it in for our marriage."

Delilah laughed.

"You can't take responsibility for anything can you" she said mockingly.

He just looked at her and bit his tongue.

"I'd like us to go to Relate."

A troubled look swept across her face. She clearly didn't like the idea, and she didn't respond. She was thinking. He suspected that she wouldn't want the kids to hear that she had refused such a basic step to try to resolve their differences. He knew the way she thought some of the time.

"Is there any point?"

"I think so. I, at least, would like to take advantage of their experience and knowledge."

"I'll think about it" she said flatly.

She clearly wasn't keen. A few days passed before he brought the subject up again. He wasn't going to let this matter just slip by because generally they weren't communicating. She felt she couldn't refuse and reluctantly agreed. Pablo fixed up an appointment at the earliest possible opportunity. He knew that he was clutching at straws, but that's what a drowning man does. Never say never.

Their first appointment was within two weeks. Their counsellor, Jane, was a plump middle-aged woman who was confident, personable and caring. Because of their respective jobs, they journeyed independently into the city to see her, Pablo straight after work in the same city. They didn't go out in the car together anymore anyway. The first session with Jane went very similarly to the first one with Sylvia, except that Jane was not judgemental. Delilah waded in with her usual story of how abused a wife she had been over the years because her husband had had so many extra marital relationships. This time Pablo put a bit more effort into defending himself. After all, what did he have to lose? He countered that he had never had an affair, and that these so-called relationships were simply women he worked with, with nothing underhand happening whatsoever. He stated that he had never strayed from his wife. He had always been faithful to her, no matter what crazy ideas she had about him, and he was very proud of both himself and her. Jane quickly discerned that there was a deep trust issue here. The first session established the background.

During the second session they looked at where they were now, and Pablo didn't feel like he was in the dock any more. In fact, he felt like some of the positives about him were being highlighted. His devotion, commitment, provision, lack of obvious flaws. She was looking at the dynamics of their relationship, and what they had achieved over the years, and how they had overcome their challenges previously. In the third session, she sought to find common ground and reasons to persist through the current challenges. Obviously there were the four children, one grandchild, more grandchildren in the future hopefully, and all that time and experience together - over thirty years. But what impressed Jane failed to impress Delilah. She was unmovable.

In the fourth session, Jane really pulled the stops out in encouraging them. She realised that Pablo was still devoted to his wife, so her efforts were directed at Delilah as she was clearly the driver of this breakup. As she gently and deftly delivered her wisdom, Pablo couldn't hold back the tears. What she was saying was so apposite, and so powerful. It was exactly what he wanted Delilah to hear from someone other than him. He was so grateful, and hopeful. He was overcome with emotion. As Jane talked, he sat forward, face cupped in his hands, feebly unsuccessful in fighting back the tears. It was such an emotional release for him. It felt so powerful to hear someone else stating precisely the kind of things he had been stating to Delilah for the past ten months.

"The past holds hurt and disappointment. The future holds separation. Live in the present. Enjoy the moment. Let go of the past. Let go of the hurt and unforgiveness. Give the marriage a real chance, so that if love doesn't return having given it a real chance, you can go for separation knowing that you had given recovery a real go. Thoughts lead to emotions. Have loving thoughts. Be loving. Being loving means wanting what's best for your partner emotionally, physically, spiritually. Letting go of the past, the hurt, the unforgiveness is a hard thing to do. Deciding to be loving is a hard thing to do. But it is the only way to really explore if a reconciliation can be achieved. One can easily hold on to the hurt and unforgiveness for the rest of one's life, but it blocks out chances of repair. Let go of the thoughts of the past and the future and allow yourself to enjoy the moment, freely. Why can't you show your partner love? Is it because you're hanging onto hurt or anger? Is it because you're living in the past? Try to release that hurt and anger. Move on from the past and live in the moment. Accept love, happiness, enjoyment. Every day in every relationship, there is a risk. A risk that you might be hurt or let down. There can be no relationship without a willingness to take risks, a willingness to let go of fears and to venture forth, because nobody is perfect."

For Pablo, Jane had verbalised such beautiful and powerful truths. How could Delilah not be affected? As they left the meeting, he felt so pleased. Jane's words were lovely and meaningful. Delilah didn't look impressed or obviously affected, as always. They went home separately, Pablo hoping that those words would be ringing around Delilah's head as she drove the half hour home, worming their way into her very soul. He was so grateful for Jane's input. She had really tried her best to help them, and she had been so good, so accurate, so insightful. That evening, he didn't try to engage with Delilah. He didn't want to disturb her thoughts, which were hopefully mulling over today's session. The next day however, ever hopeful, he asked Delilah what she had thought about Jane's encouragement. She stiffened up.

"What she said was good, but all that is much too late for us."

He was so disappointed. Nothing seemed capable of penetrating her steely resolve.

"So you still want to separate? You don't want to give us a chance?"

She responded with her most common mantra. "There is no other way."

Later, she wrote to her diary:

'What a ride coming home in April. So many mixed emotions, ups and downs. Arguments and pestering's. Visiting Relate. She won't change him. I feel unable to give myself over to him. Traveling in circles the whole time. Life can seem surreal at times. Wonder if I can make this work only to come up against something that reminds me of how I can't. It's so sad. He's pleading guilty - too much evidence against him. Says he is pleading guilty for me - bull shit! Shouldn't be for me anyway - should be for him. He gives me lectures about how I am unforgiving, bitter, angry, full of hate - makes me feel like shit the way he goes on - I'm such a terrible person. I want to crawl into a hole and die. I want to die or get my life back. It makes me cringe when he touches me. Why can't he understand that? I do feel so desperate - I hate the idea of being alone, fending for myself. I remember that feeling of oneness we once had - but it's all gone. He goes on about me getting what I want, craving to get away and live my life separately. He doesn't understand the desperation I feel about the prospect - He thinks I'm so strong, but I feel weak and so helpless, so trapped. Please help me God to keep going, for what, I don't know.'

A week later they attended Relate again. Jane fished for signs of improvement since her epic speech of the week before. After a few minutes, she realised that all her efforts over the past few weeks had made no impact on Delilah at all. She seemed genuinely disappointed and dispirited. To Pablo's horror, she announced that there was nothing else she could do or say, and that her job now was simply to help mediate the separation. A look of satisfaction came over Delilah's face in complete contrast to the look of horror and consternation on Pablo's. He literally didn't know what to say. He was shocked. They couldn't give up so easily. The session was used to discuss practical matters, which didn't interest Pablo at all. He wasn't giving in. As they parted for the last time he sincerely thanked her for her efforts. She had done a sterling job, and he wanted her to know how deeply he appreciated her input. He and Delilah returned home separately. Very separately. Another counselling series had ended in failure as far as Pablo was concerned, and in victory for Delilah. It was the beginning of August, a beautiful time of the year. The weather was glorious, the house improvements were coming on apace, and Pablo was feeling a deep sense of impending doom.

A couple of days later he was informed of his new court appearance date, towards the end of the month. He informed Delilah. Of course she would want to go too. This would be the first and final hearing as he had entered a guilty plea. A full twenty months after Cassie had made her original complaint. Pablo needed another catch-up with Henry. It had to be a Saturday morning. They met for a delicious cooked breakfast as usual. Pablo had told him some time ago on the phone about Delilah wanting to separate, and about their going to relate. Now he wanted his wise friend's opinion on the outcome.

"Henry, the Relate counsellor was so good. She gave us such meaningful advice about basically persevering through the tough times to let the love grow stronger still."

"How did Delilah take it?"

"She was as hard as stone. She wasn't having any of it. Totally closed."

"That's so sad. I'm sorry mate. Still, no one can say you haven't tried."

"True, but I don't care about what people think, and I don't want to just try. I want to win her back"

"I know mate. I know."

He could see that Pablo was particularly low and perhaps even fatalistic.

"Maybe you should just let her go now mate. You know the story of the prodigal son don't you."

"Yes" he replied quietly.

Henry decided to drive his point home.

"The son had no right to his inheritance at that time. His dad was still alive and in good health, but the kid wanted to leave home with his inheritance just when he felt like it. His dad didn't argue or fight. He would have had to sell half of his property to be able to give him what he wanted. But he did that for him, and then let him go. You well know the story. Eventually, the kid ran out of money and realised that he had thrown away the most precious things in life for short-term gain. He learned his lesson and returned home where good old loving dad was patiently waiting for him. Maybe there's a lesson in there for you."

"Maybe Henry, but I'm so useless at letting go. I can't seem to overcome the urge to struggle for her and our family."

Henry changed the subject. He had made his point, and he never laboured anything.

"Any news on the court case?"

"Yep, at the end of the month, and I'm changing my plea."

He confessed this with some embarrassment. He knew it would sound crazy.

"But you don't think you've done anything wrong do you?"

"Correct. I don't, but it's become such a huge bone of contention with Delilah. I'm changing my plea because she wants me to."

"Isn't that tantamount to professional suicide?"

"Yes Henry, but sometimes what seems bizarre to onlookers, is perfectly sensible to the person concerned."

"Explain."

"An extreme example would be somebody committing suicide. They do the exact opposite of what any normal person would do, but at the time it makes sense to them. It's what seems right to them, but not to anyone else."

"That doesn't make sense and it doesn't make it right."

"No of course not. But consider people who voluntarily disappear. They tire of a certain life and decide to escape by simply disappearing without saying a word. They're probably giving up a lot, everything they own and everyone they know in fact, but at the time, it makes sense to them. It's a bit like that for me. It looks stupid for me to plead guilty to something I haven't done, but to me it makes sense to me because it might help me with Delilah. I don't expect anyone outside the situation to understand me."

"But Pablo. I think she's made up her mind no matter what you do."

"Maybe my good man, but it's still something I have to do, just in case."

He looked at Pablo with a little smile. He thought Pablo was a little crazy, and very stubborn, but he loved him like a son. It wasn't his place to try to dissuade him. He had made his point. They carried on chatting, and not just about him and Delilah. It was a nice time together. Pablo really valued the dependability of Henry. He was always there for him. A true friend. When some people prove to be so unreliable, the reliable ones feel like treasures.

Chapter 16

The court day at the end of August finally arrived. It just so happened that Troy was visiting them for a few days, and Delilah wanted him to go too, to keep her company. Pablo didn't particularly relish the idea of his son seeing him in the dock, a guilty man, but he had to let it happen. This was real life, and sometimes real life was unpalatable. He had never tried to wrap his kids up in cotton wool. They had to learn to deal with the real world, just like he did. The journey to court was more pleasant than usual, because Troy gave them an opportunity for normal conversation. It was a warm sunny summer's day, but Pablo was wearing a full suit and tie. He wanted to appear respectable and professional although he was never remotely comfortable in a suit and tie, but court is one of those places where appearances count. On arrival they each had to walk through a security scanner like the ones that are ubiquitous at airports. They were further frisked having passed through by blasé uniformed security officers. It made Pablo feel like a common criminal. He considered how he would have to get used to that epithet. He went straight to the case list posted on a nearby notice board to find his court number. Court number six. As he stood perusing the list of miscreants and offences, one of the old ushers came up to him, clipboard in hand.

"Which case are you involved in sir?"

Pablo looked at the man and found himself choking back the urge to shed a tear or two as he admitted to be one of the accused. He realised that his emotions were likely to swing wildly over the next few hours.

"I see" he responded without changing his tone or attitude as he scrolled down his list.

"Name please sir" he enquired directly.

"Pablo Pinkerton."

"Ah yes" he drawled as he peered through his bifocals at the list. He found the name and put a line through it.

"Court number six sir. Please wait outside until you are called."

"Of course" Pablo responded respectfully.

He led Delilah and Troy to the court entrance and they all sat in the large communal area outside. It was 9:30 am, and the first case would not be heard until 10.am. It was already busy in the waiting area, with quite a few small groups lounging around in the seated area. The building had a rather austere feeling about it. It seemed dark and somewhat foreboding, yet most of the people waiting around seemed perfectly at ease, oozing a familiarity with the place. Not an unusual event for them maybe. He wondered if this is what his dog felt like when it arrived at the vets. An uneasy sense of foreboding. The security officers were milling around the entrance. The court ushers by contrast meandered around constantly in a seemingly endless quest to locate the accused, and witnesses, their ancient faded gowns and greying thin hair adding to the anachronistic atmosphere. A modern touch though, was the small perfunctory cafe at the end of the waiting area furthest away from the entrance. Hot drinks and snacks were available. Pablo fancied a coffee. Some normality. Troy was up for one too, and Pablo fetched one for each of them. As he returned to his seat, Roger appeared, looking as dour and dapper as ever. Pablo greeted him politely and carefully so as not to spill his coffee.

He turned to his family sitting next to him.

"You remember Delilah?"

"Yes, of course." Roger briefly shook her hand with barely a glance.

"And this is Troy, our son."

Troy politely stood up to greet Roger, which was a little shocking because Troy was so tall and broad. As he stood he unfurled and towered over Roger by at least seven inches, menacing in an unintended way. Roger was quite diminutive by comparison, and he recoiled slightly, instinctively, as the huge Troy expanded in front of him. They shook hands, and Troy sat down, and Roger looked a little relieved. Then he led Pablo off to meet the court defence solicitor, explaining that as he was pleading guilty, the prosecution would deal with the case, finally, today, and that there was no need for Kevin to be there. The court defence solicitor would deal with any enquiries regarding the accused, i.e. him. He still hated being on the opposite side of the equation and being referred to as the accused. They found the solicitor sitting in his office with a rather large stack of case papers in front of him on his desk. They knocked, entered, and sat. He seemed like a pleasant enough chap. He was dressed in a rather bland shabby suit, and was very matter-of-fact about everything. He introduced himself as Brian and explained his role. He told Pablo that he would answer most questions on his behalf. He then dug out Pablo 's case papers from the pile in front of him, and took a few moments to quickly peruse them. Pablo sipped his coffee, trying so hard to be nonchalant.

"Ok" he continued. "You're pleading guilty still I take it?"

"Yes sir" Pablo answered , rather subdued at the admission.

"Ok. then all I really need are antecedents, you know, a bit about your role, how long you've been a police officer etc. Did you bring a payslip with you?"

"Yes." Roger had told him to bring details of his pay and monthly household expenses. He was about to be laid bare in public. Pablo gave him as much information as he seemed to need at this time. Obviously, they would both be in court, and if there was anything they'd missed, they could cover in when he was in the dock. Business was conducted in less than ten minutes, and Pablo returned to his seat by Delilah and Troy. Roger made himself scarce, saying he would return when the case was called.

"You ok dad?" Troy enquired. He felt sorry for his dear old dad being hauled over the coals like this, being made an example of.

"Yes son, I'm fine. It will be just so good to get this nightmare over and done with, at last."

Even as he said that, he realised that the nightmare would not be over. Today he would leave the court a criminal. That would have huge repercussions for a man like him, not least of which would be his future employability. Then he would also have to await the internal discipline tribunal, which would only be heard after the result of this court case. Deep joy. More waiting. More uncertainty. He focussed again on the present. He looked at Delilah. She appeared a little uncomfortable even though this is what she wanted. She was quiet and thoughtful. Perhaps she did have some buried reservations about seeing her husband accused in the dock, admitting to a misdemeanour which might cost him his job.

"Pablo Pinkerton" a voice boomed. These old ushers had learned to project their voices when making the ominous summons to court. Pablo was surprised. He was expecting to be waiting in line for hours, and here he was going straight into court, first case. Butterflies time. The usher showed him into the dock as Delilah and Troy swept in behind him and entered the public gallery to one side of the entrance. Roger followed shortly afterwards and joined them in the public gallery. The court house was as empty as it could be. For that he was thankful. The usher moved away, adding to Pablo's sense of isolation. He stood erect, facing the bench. A stipendiary magistrate sat high up, alone. His clerk sat beneath him and slightly to one side. They both looked down on him. They looked suitably professional and serious. The clerk asked Pablo to confirm his name, which he did. Then he read out the charge.

"The charge against you, Pablo Pinkerton, is that between the 22nd of March 2007 and the 9th of March 2008, you accessed police intelligence for an unlawful purpose contrary to section two of the Data Protection Act 1998. How do you plead?"

Pablo swallowed his pride, steeled himself, and announced very reluctantly, "Guilty."

The clerk looked towards the CPS solicitor at the bench to his left, who, with some degree of kudos, slowly stood up. He offered a summary of the offence, explaining to the court how Mr Pinkerton had become obsessed with one Cassie Woolridge and had been accessing her records for personal reasons. Pablo froze in the dock. He knew he wouldn't be allowed to speak or challenge the prosecution, because he had pleaded guilty, but this was so wrong. He had agreed to plead guilty to the anal, hair-splitting, jobsworth allegation that he was accessing intel on former clients who were not on the POU, as if that was actually some kind of abuse of the system. He wasn't pleading guilty to any of the notions involving Cassie. The CPS itself had thrown out her allegations as unsubstantiated, and those of her boyfriend. Why try to use them here to fabricate a salacious untrue story to justify this charge? This was so embarrassing and offensive, but there was nothing he could do now to change it. Inside he was squirming. He just had to swallow it. Of course there was a member of the press present who devoured this bone and embellished it in his report in the local paper.

Whilst the prosecutor spoke, Pablo felt like a bound man being repeatedly slapped across the face. He was helpless. He hadn't anticipated this. He wouldn't have pleaded guilty to this. Finally, after what felt like an age, the man shut up and left the magistrate and clerk to whisper amongst themselves for half a minute. Pablo focussed on the bench but he was wondering what Delilah was making of all this.

The magistrate then asked the court defence solicitor for antecedents and personal circumstances for the accused. He stood and recounted all the relevant information. More whisperings, then the magistrate handed down a fine of nine hundred pounds and asked Pablo if he could pay that today. Pablo quickly said no. He knew that they wouldn't really expect to pay all that up front. He was asked for a suggestion.

"One hundred pounds a month?" he queried.

"Agreed. You are hereby fined nine hundred pounds to be paid at one hundred pounds a month. You are dismissed."

The usher approached him to indicate the way out of court, and he walked out, relieved, annoyed, and afraid. Afraid of what obstacles the future would hold for him as a branded criminal. Annoyed about the story the prosecution had made up, and also afraid that Delilah's antagonism towards him would now be fortified. She walked out behind him. No word, or touch or consolation, but she did look highly embarrassed. She must have felt so disappointed. Troy walked next to him silently, but with his arm around him. Solidarity from his son. Roger joined them in the hall. He spoke efficiently to Pablo about the practicalities of paying the fine. Pablo half expected a senior officer to turn up now, and suspend him there and then, but no one else appeared. It was the lull after the storm.

"What happens now?" he asked Roger.

"You go back to work in the morning, and we wait for the internal hearing."

"You think they'll let me carry on working?"

"I don't see why not. I've not heard anything different."

Pablo was a little surprised at this. In all honesty, at this stage, he'd rather be actually suspended.

Roger seemed to read his thoughts.

"Pablo, it's better for you to go before the disciplinary panel as a working officer rather than someone who's been suspended."

Pablo wasn't convinced.

"How long do you think?"

"A month or two. Hopefully not more."

"And you don't think they'll suspend me?"

"I don't think so."

He didn't sound certain. Pablo wondered what would happen when he reported to logistics in the morning. Would they really carry on employing him now he had a criminal conviction? In his own mind, this was a really big deal. He wouldn't mind being suspended. Then he could carry on with the building work full time. The journey home was quiet. Delilah had nothing to say, and Pablo felt like a complete idiot.

At home, nothing changed. He had done as she had asked, but it accomplished nothing between them. The next day he went to work as usual. His colleagues were surprised to see him. Maybe everyone expected him to be suspended now that he had a criminal record, but that didn't happen. Roger was right, nothing else would happen until the disciplinary hearing occurred. He had no idea when that would be. Just more waiting. So he carried on doing his dull, menial, logistics job, week in, week out, waiting for the next step to occur. Still allowing life to dish out what it had to dish out to him. Then he would regroup.

At home Delilah was still focusing on separation. He was still leaving her little love notes every day, and most of the time, he had no idea about her new life. The extension was structurally complete, and tradesmen were coming in to help finish the project off. The electrics had been done, and the new walls and altered internal walls had all been plastered. The plumbers had made a start, and were currently installing underfloor heating in the new ground floor areas. When they were finished there, Pablo would tile those floors. The only thing he and Delilah did together was to plan the new kitchen, with visits to showrooms and a couple of site meetings at home. They also chose floor tiles together. They hoped to have the house ready for Christmas when all the children and their wives would stay with them. This was equally important to both of them. When they did things like this, together, they were amicable and efficient.

Early September. The anniversary of her decision not to be with him anymore. He had to write on this sad anniversary.

'To my dearest wife,

Today is an anniversary - one whole year since you announced that you wanted to leave me. We have endured a year-long separation of sorts. It is with great pain and sadness that I ponder the lessons and harshness of the past year. I have pretty much resolved not to write to you or text you anymore, as you seem totally unmoved by my outpourings. Today I feel like I am visiting the grave of a loved one. Instead of bringing flowers, I bring words and thoughts. You have demonstrated great resolve over the past year. I respect you for your strength, but I still love you and want you back. I still believe in you, in us. I still hope that one day you will throw the switch as you have said so often that you could do if you wanted to. I don't know the answer. I do know how much I miss you, your touch, your friendship, your acceptance, your support, you being a part of me, me being a part of you, common interests, shared activities, shared goals, the comfort of love, the purpose of caring, serving, helping. I'm not touching you because that's what you insist on, yet eighty percent of communication is through non-verbal touch and signals. I feel like you have closed me down. I have been gagged. I can only hope that one day you will again appreciate my love and affection. I hope you will find a new hope, a new ambition to overcome, a new strength, a new vision to rebuild our broken life together. I don't want a life without you my love.

Pablo.'

He never, ever got any replies.

Come late September, he had to go to hospital for an operation on one of his knees. This was due to complications arising out of a very old injury he had incurred during a motorcycle almost thirty years earlier. He needed Delilah to take him in. She was reluctant to take him, but really, he had nobody else to lean on. She walked up to the ward with him. He asked for a hug. She refused.

"I'm going under general anaesthetic. This might be the last thing I do."

"You'll be fine."

She refused to hug him goodbye and walked away. He had hoped she might make an exception under these circumstances, but no, she was so resolute. She hadn't bought into his implication that he might die, that this might be the last time they saw each other, ever. Of course he survived the operation. He was kept in overnight then released the following morning on crutches. His leg had been broken and a bone wedge and a metal plate had been inserted just below the knee. He wouldn't be weight-bearing on that leg for quite some time. Delilah fetched him. She wasn't at all happy about being his taxi, but she also knew he had no one else to call on, and she was still his wife. There was a tiny fragment of duty left in her. She showed no sympathy for his plight. Within days, he was finding ways of doing DIY on one leg. He even managed to demolish an internal wall in an old bathroom whilst on only one leg, but moving the rubble was difficult, and painful, but he had no one to help him.

The following Sunday he got Sarah to drop him off at a local Methodist church. He had only been there a few times before, and for no particular reason, he just fancied attending on this day. He was on crutches, and sitting in traditional pews, having to keep his leg straight, was not easy. It was awkward. The church was not well attended, and most of the congregation were elderly. The ladies mostly fell into the category of 'blue-rinse-brigade'. The minister was lovely and most sincere, but overall, Pablo was a little disappointed, not by the minister, just the sadness of a church that felt like it was on its last legs. At the end of the service he asked someone if tea or coffee was being served which happens in most churches. The response was negative and leaning on his crutches became a little theatrical.

"What no coffee?" he said rather loudly, putting on his rather astonished face.

At that, a nearby man in his late forties interjected.

"Bruv, you can come to mine for coffee if you're desperate. I'm only just over the road."

Pablo didn't know this man. He appeared not to be with anyone in particular. Pablo looked at him quizzically, wondering what kind of a guy takes strangers back to his house for coffee.

"You sure?"

"Yeah. I'm literally just across the street."

Pablo was feeling a little embarrassed now. He hadn't meant to make anyone feel like they had put themselves out for him, and he really wasn't sure about going back to a stranger's house.

"As you can see, I can't really walk too far."

"It's ok mate, it's not far. Come on. I'll do you a bacon butty."

Pablo felt that he had put himself in this position and that he ought to take up this kind stranger's offer. He seemed like an okay guy, so he went with him feeling slightly apprehensive that this could become socially awkward. The chap introduced himself as Tim. He was easy to talk to. He was very confident and relaxed, and he laughed readily. He lived in a small old cottage down a tiny side street just off the main road opposite the church. He was five years younger than Pablo, but at their age, the age gap seemed completely insignificant. They were both middle-aged men tackling similar issues in life. They were overweight, but Tim more so. He showed Pablo into the small kitchen where there was a simple picnic bench on one side, with minimal equipment elsewhere. It was definitely a man's kitchen. As Tim prepared tea and butties, they chatted freely, getting to know each other through very open honest conversation. Tim was clearly a generous person. He kept offering Pablo more food, more bread, more biscuits – 'please, have the whole packet'. He opened a bottle of wine and repeatedly invited Pablo to help himself to anything he fancied from the fridge. Pablo found himself having to be quite forceful to fend off all this kindness. He was thinking about his waistline, although he did indulge in the wine. He could see why Tim was quite overweight, and in that regard, he didn't want to join him. Tim had been married for over twenty years. He had three daughters, but whilst they were still very young, his wife left him for another man taking the girls with her. As a result Tim had suffered some kind of mental or emotional breakdown, which in turn led to a life-changing spiritual experience which gave him the inner strength and purpose to carry on. He was very open and honest about everything, and he spoke with great passion and feeling. But all this was now ancient history. It had occurred ten years earlier, and he enjoyed telling Pablo how many girlfriends he'd had since then. Nothing seemed to embarrass him. He wore his heart on his sleeve. Perhaps that was why they got on so well, because Pablo was like that too.

"Pablo , I live for my kids. Everything I do is for them."

"That's nice Tim. Do you see them much?"

"As often as I can mate. I usually go down there once a fortnight, but their mum can be such a pain in the arse. She doesn't really help much. It's always a bit of a battle with her."

"Mate, the important thing is that you keep doing it for the sake of the girls. My bro suffered a very similar fate, and his ex-wife made it so difficult for him to see his girls, he eventually gave up trying. That was so tragic, for all of them. It was a terrible failure and loss."

"Oh, I'm sorry mate. That must have been so hard for him."

"You're not kidding. It nearly killed him. Is your ex still with her new fella?"

"Nah. That didn't last, and she's never admitted to having an affair. She still denies it to this day. She's been on her own now for years. Pablo, I think she's actually quite lonely."

"She probably is mate. People often don't appreciate what they've got until it's gone. We're all aware of that aren't we?"

"Yeah, that's true mate. So tell me, what happened to you?"

Pablo eagerly divulged his plight over Delilah, and Tim truly understood what he was going through, because he had gone through exactly the same trauma himself so many years earlier. A significant bond between them was born this day. Deep, quick, and thick.

Pablo stayed for about two hours, and at no point did Tim make him feel like it was time to leave. He finally left because he was beginning to feel emotionally exhausted. The conversation caused him to cry quite a lot, and that was always strangely tiring. Tim had been so understanding and supportive. When Pablo went to leave, Tim gave him a big hug. They exchanged phone numbers, and Tim promised to stay in touch. Pablo phoned Sarah and asked her to pick him up. Tim waited in the street with him, and briefly met Sarah when she arrived. He was genuinely interested in Pablo and his family. He was very much a man of his word.

He phoned Pablo the very next day to enquire how he was. They would chat for about half an hour. This was a new experience for Pablo, having a close male friend, and he really appreciated it. He had been really grateful for the support that Henry had given him, but this bloke was on another level. It was like there was a spiritual connection. Henry's time was understandably limited, whereas it seemed that Tim was available whenever and for as long as Pablo needed. He was like a guardian angel. As the days grew into weeks, they chatted every single day, and occasionally went down a pub together to chat and play snooker. It wasn't long before they felt like brothers.

At home, he still occasionally tried to reach out to Delilah. She wasn't impressed. She wrote in her diary.

'I feel like killing myself. I'm so angry. I can't cope with his demands, the constant bullying, engulfment, manipulation, and all the pressure he puts me under. He says he cares for me, but does he really? Would he be so demanding if he cared about my feelings, and what I want? Maybe I should just kill him instead. I wish he would just bugger off and never come back. I wish I could throw him out of the house, but really, what can I say to all this. I can't point the finger can I? When I am in the place I am in. I find myself caught between the devil and the deep blue sea. How shit life is. How on earth do I get out of or through this one? I get the feeling I'm going to come off worse here - I will be left with nothing and he'll go swanning off with who he likes, where he likes - living it up. The big question is... do I care, or why should I care? I find his kisses cringe factor nine. I can barely bring myself to look at him. Sylvia once asked me who I felt really cared about me. I told her that I only felt that from my mother. How sad is that? He says that he is trying so hard to change for me, but why can't I see it? Am I now just so prejudiced and blind? I always feel in such a muddle after I have spoken to him. I struggle with his anger, lack of respect, domineering attitude, intensity, inconsistency, not accepting responsibility, not accepting me as I am, or my decisions. How can I live with all of that? I need to feel empathy from him.'

Chapter 17

The largest room in the old part of the house was now Delilah's bedroom. Originally it had been the lounge. Pablo had converted what had been a spacious adjacent hallway into an en-suite shower room for her, so she had plenty of space in her bedroom for all the furniture she needed to make her privacy comfortable. The end of a balmy summer was turning into a cool autumn as September gave way to October.

She made another entry to her diary.

'I felt so low again today when I had to leave you, knowing I won't see you again for a while. Very aware of the life you go back to and I'm left with an emptiness. I know you are aware of that too and feel bad for me because you can't give me what I want. You have probably learnt to deal with those sorts of emotions because you have had to handle so much loss, loneliness and hurt over the years. I think you care. You say you do, but are stuck with circumstances. Didn't feel this way last time. Is that because I knew I would see you again so soon? I think so. You said you would be in touch as soon as you get back, I hope so. Am I grasping for attachment and connection with someone who is unable to give that? The answer is always yes. Why do I want it so much? It's better if I have something to go on to do when you leave - people to be with. I do feel so deeply for you. Following my heart. You told me I was a fool. You're probably right.'

With Christmas looming, they both worked as hard as they could on the house in their free time. Delilah was excellent at decorating, and readily decorated when an area was finally ready for finishing touches. A professional kitchen-fitter started kitting out their new kitchen in the extension, and Pablo started tiling the floor in the adjacent dining room. It was all starting to come together very nicely.

By the middle of November he was free of crutches. The operation had been a great success, and he felt no pain in the troubling knee. It also brought about Delilah's fiftieth birthday. Pablo was always in reconciliation mode. He bought another card of two people hugging. Unlike the previous year, where the card was quite an artistic masterpiece, this one was very simple, just two plain plasticine figures hugging each other. It represented the simplicity of his hopes, but with the same message. Inside the card he wrote;

'My darling, it is your birthday, and I must give

To show my love, but what with?

Something shiny? Something smart?

Something pricey? To show my heart?
Not enough! I hear myself say.
You can get those things any day.
I want to give you everything,
Not just something bling.
My heart, my love, my all, is supplied.
Any less, and it would not be implied
That you are everything to me.
Please let me give you all of me,
Now and forever!'

He also bought her a rather nice laptop because he knew that she wanted one. When he gave it to her, she barely said thank you. She always seemed so angry with him, even on her birthday. There was no let up. She was as remote as ever, week to week, month to month. He was disheartened. She went out for her birthday, but not with him. He was always banned. At least there was Christmas to look forward to and quality time with all of their family.

He carried on going into his office job every day, knowing full well that it was no more than an illusion. An axe was hanging over his head, yet he still had been given no notice of the disciplinary hearing three months after the court hearing. He only hung on because surely there was a possibility of him keeping his job. Yes, he now had a criminal conviction, but he had done nothing wrong.

Each lunch time he took himself out for some brief exercise and fresh air, walking ten minutes to a nearby bakery. It was an independent family business and their made-up rolls were delicious. Food prepared by somebody else always seems to taste better than when you do it for yourself. One particular day, after the short walk, he stood in the queue behind a couple of other customers, hungrily surveying the goodies behind the glass counter. There were trays of all kinds of sandwich fillings, and they would make you up the roll of your choice. He usually preferred ham and salad, but he could be tempted by the tuna or coronation chicken, but always in a crusty half-baguette. Three middle-aged women in homely aprons and hairnets were serving. They were busy ladies, As soon as they had made up one roll, they were onto the next one. When it was his turn, he politely requested the usual half a white crusty baguette with ham and salad.

"We're out of half-baguettes." he was informed listlessly.

This was a blow. He didn't care much at all for their soft rolls. He much preferred crusty rolls. There was something much more satisfying about biting into a crunchy crusty roll. They were so much more substantial. He looked to the shelves behind the sales assistant, and saw plenty of full size baguettes.

"That's ok." he said helpfully.

"I'll have a whole baguette, and can you make up your normal half-baguette with it, with ham and salad please."

The woman held her arms down in front of her plump tummy and clasped her hands tightly together.

"We can't make up customer's rolls" she said matter-of-factly.

He looked at her to search for clues. Was she joking? Had he misunderstood her? Had she misunderstood him? He was rather lost for words feeling genuinely perplexed.

"Excuse me?" he queried, needing further explanation.

She folded her arms against her copious girth. This was not a good sign.

"We are not allowed to make up customer's rolls." she repeated, obviously feeling that this was self-explanatory. She was not so much listless now as defensive.

He thought for a moment. He was losing his wife. She was going to make him sell their home, and before long, he would probably lose his job, and this lady was refusing him his favourite lunch-time roll? No, this was too much. He was going to fight this one.

"I don't want you to make up my roll." he explained. " I want you to make up one of your rolls for me. It's what you do here."

"But we have run out of half-baguettes."

He was vaguely conscious of a few other customers behind him, and the notion of not making a fuss, and not holding up other customers began to envelop him. He quickly shrugged that notion off. He wanted his lunch. He was in the front of the queue. It was his turn to be served, and it was this obnoxious so-called assistant who was holding things up, not him.

"There's a whole shelf of baguettes behind you."

"We don't make up whole baguettes."

She was terse and determined. Quite why she was being obtuse with him, he had no idea, but that wasn't his problem. He had spent ten years of his life running a retail business, and he was offended not only for himself as a would-be customer, but also for whoever owned the business.

"I think you misunderstand me. I am happy to pay for a whole baguette, and for you to use part of it to make me up a crusty roll with ham and salad, and I'll pay for the roll and the baguette."

He really thought that would clarify the situation. But no.

"I've already explained to you that we are not allowed to make up customers' rolls ."

"But it's not my roll. I didn't bring it in. It's sitting on the shelf behind you. It's your roll."

"Not if you pay for it."

"But I haven't paid for it yet."

Was he going to allow himself to be defeated by this obfuscation? No. This was too silly for words. He felt the need to explain a few things to her, from a business perspective of course. He glanced towards the other sales lady. She didn't appear interested in the micro battle that was going on. She was burying herself in sawing up a roll for someone else, staring intently down at her work.

"Whoever owns this business wants you to sell your products to the customer, and relieve the customer of their money. That is what you are here for. That's what they pay you for. To make money for the business. I want to give you my money for your product. I'm sure that if the boss was here, they would instruct you to do as I ask."

"I've already told you, we are not allowed to make up customers' rolls."

Not that again.

"You're being ridiculous. It's obviously not my roll. I haven't touched it. All I want is for you to make me up one of your rolls. Please, use one of your baguettes, which I will pay for after you have made up my roll. It's not mine until I have paid for it, right"

He looked at her with steely eyes. He was going to stand his ground. The next step would be to demand to see the manager, who he had no doubt was not present, in which case he would demand to speak to them on the phone. This proved not to be necessary. Her chubby arms reluctantly unfurled, she gave him a dirty look, and she slowly turned around. He watched with bated breath. Was she going to reach for something to throw at him? No she reached to the shelf behind her and took hold of a full-size baguette. Victory! She used a knife menacingly on it, glancing at him maliciously. He looked sideways at some of the other waiting customers. One lady quickly looked at the floor as soon as he looked her way, like he was scary. A tall thin man in his thirties smiled towards him. He smiled back. Maybe this was a small victory for modern-day down-trodden male-kind. The sales lady finished his roll, and laid it heavily and unlovingly on the glass countertop.

"Three pounds seventy pence" she announced rather harshly, with no apology for her awkwardness. He handed over a fiver, and duly took his change. He didn't want to be smug, but his 'thank you' did come out with a slightly sarcastic tone, which he didn't really intend. He walked out, relieved that something had gone right for him. The roll was especially tasty.

Later that day, he wrote to Delilah. He knew that it was against the rules, but sticking to the rules was getting him nowhere. She was as cold and distant as ever. The last time he had communicated with her was a month earlier with the birthday card. Again, he needed to reach out, to try.

'To my darling Delilah. I am proud of you, proud of our family, proud of what we have achieved together. I don't want to see our wonderful family pulled apart. I am truly sorry for risking it the way that I did. I have comprehensively repented. Please, forgive me. The consequences of unforgiveness are dire. Time heals, but not if time stands still. You're in a place where you were almost two years ago. Your emotions are fresh and raw. You're locked in the past. You're still feeling hurt, rejection, disappointment, grief, resentment, etc. If you hang onto those things, our love will surely die. Recovery is confession and apology on my part, and forgiveness and healing on your part. You can't forgive me whilst you're hanging onto the hurt and anger of the past. I implore you to let them go. Let's move forward. Your bitterness is eroding your relationship with your own children. Please speak to them and listen to how they are being affected by your attitude. They love us both very much. They have seen my tears and contrition. They know my heart. They share my hope. Choose to move forward with love, not without it. It hurts me so much when you reject me each day. I am empty inside without your love. I crave your presence, your acceptance, our melting into one another. Your counsellors are wrong. Separation is not the answer. It would simply add misery on top of misery. Love Pablo.'

As usual he left the letter out for her in the kitchen, and in due course, it disappeared, but there was no acknowledgment. A couple of days later he had to go to a meeting with Roger and Kevin. They brought him up to speed about the disciplinary case. He would be charged with bringing the force into disrepute by getting a criminal conviction. They didn't know when the case would be heard, but they did need to let him know that he wouldn't be automatically represented by a barrister or solicitor. The Federation would consider his case on its merits, and would make a decision in due course as to whether they could justify spending more of their limited resources on his defence. Roger reassured him that if the Federation were unwilling to pay for legal representation, then it would be down to him, Roger, to represent him. Pablo left the meeting with that thought troubling him. A couple of days later after mulling it over he emailed Roger.

'Roger, if I have to be represented by a police Federation Rep', then it needs to be someone other than you. Over the past twenty one months, whilst this matter has been dragging relentlessly on, I have never felt that you were particularly engaged in my case. This is not personal, I just don't feel that you have been interested in me or my plight. I have always felt that something was missing, and I frankly would not be confident with you representing me at such an important hearing.'

He kept it short and blunt. There was no point in beating around the bush. He didn't want to seem rude, but overall, he was very disappointed with Roger's performance. He felt that his support had been extremely minimal and he was just letting him know the consequences of that. The following morning he received a reply from Roger.

'Dear Pablo, I am very sorry that you feel this way. I have put one hundred percent into your case and have always acted with the utmost integrity. In fact I feel quite offended by your comments as I feel that I have represented your interests both conscientiously and professionally. However, if this is how you feel, I will ensure that your case is taken over by another Fed' Rep'.'

Pablo was relieved. As far as he was concerned anyone else would do a better job than Roger.

That evening whilst Delilah was downstairs in the kitchen cooking dinner, he noticed her mobile sitting on a shelf in the lobby. He picked it up guiltily. He knew it was ethically wrong to spy on someone, but whenever he got the chance to glean any information about what she was up to, he would seize the opportunity. Sometimes he would look carefully around her bedroom for clues. He didn't even know what he was looking for. It was simply a compunction because deep down, he knew she was hiding something. He was very careful not to leave any clues for her that he had been in there snooping. Mostly she kept her phone safely on her person or in her bedroom, but occasionally she let her precautions slip and she absent-mindedly left it out somewhere he could see it. Each time he'd had a chance to interrogate it he had simply found that it was locked, and he had no idea what the code might be. This time was different. He flipped open the lid and the screen lit up. His heart beat faster. This was an amazing opportunity. He scurried off to his bedroom, phone in hand, and shut the door. He sat on his bed. He was almost panicking. He felt that she was bound to find out within minutes that her phone was missing and would have a premonition that he had found it, and she would be bursting into his room at any moment. He had to rush. His mind was racing and he was losing his concentration. What should he look at first? Texts! Fortunately, he had the same model of mobile phone, so he was familiar with the controls, and even in this befuddled state he quickly found what he was looking for. He scrolled down the list of conversations, hoping that his instincts would guide him. They did. He alighted on Mon Ami. Mon Ami! That was not very subtle. He clicked on that conversation. Earlier that day, to Mon Ami:

'Don't take any notice of Pablo. He's so arrogant. He doesn't deserve your help. Let him go and let him rot. You're too good for him. He doesn't appreciate what you've done for him. He's got his head in the clouds all the time. Don't let him upset you xx'

Pablo was stunned. He immediately realised what this implied. He eagerly read the previous message of the previous day, from mon Ami:

'Yes I hope so. I'll text you in the morning about when and where.'

The one previous to that:

'Will I be able to see you on Friday my love? I do hope so.'

And prior to that:

'It was so lovely to see you again today. You are such a lovely man. I'm so lucky to have you in my life. Can't wait for next time. Xx'

He couldn't focus anymore. His mind was a whirl. He rapidly looked through the list of contacts again. Nothing else caught his eye. He needed pen and paper. He had to write these messages down, and the phone number. It was hard to think of where he could get writing materials without drawing attention to himself. He rummaged through drawers in his bedside cabinets until he found something. As he wrote, he found that his hand was shaking. Too much adrenaline was surging through him. This discovery was a huge strategic victory. He was alarmed and excited at the same time. He hid the paper and went directly downstairs into the kitchen. She was standing at the work-surface looking away from him. He needed her to look at him.

"Look what I've got" he announced dryly.

She turned around and looked. At first she looked at his face with exaggerated disinterest. Then he slowly held out one arm to reveal her phone in his hand. The colour visibly drained from her face. The look of disinterest on her face rapidly changed to one of alarm, almost terror. She stayed still, calm and silent. She said nothing. She slowly turned her head away from him, looking into the distance. She must have known that this day would eventually come, and here it was, finally, the evening before Christmas eve. She made no attempt to take the phone, or even ask for it. She said nothing. He knew that she knew that he knew.

"Who is Mon Ami?"

He knew who he was, but he wanted to hear her say it.

"Roger."

He paused. He had to ask certain questions, but he didn't want to hear the answers. Asking was a sign of bravery.

"Are you having an affair with him?"

"Yes."

He admired her honesty. She looked so incredibly embarrassed, and even a little ashamed, just a little. She stood perfectly still, maintaining her composure in what must have been the most awkward moment of her entire life. Pablo didn't want to hear that she had been having an affair. He hoped it hadn't been too serious, at least not serious enough to have sex.

"Are you having sex with him?"

He also maintained his composure. He just wanted facts, at last, solid, hard, lurid facts, At last, the truth!

"Yes."

She didn't flinch. Neither did he, even though he was truly shocked. The only thing he could hope for now was that she didn't love him.

"Do you love him?"

"Yes" she replied with no hesitation whatsoever.

He had no other questions for her. He knew from her behaviour over the past eighteen months exactly how long it had been going on.

He thought momentarily as he looked at her. He almost felt sorry for her. She was in such an awkward situation. He stepped forward and put her phone on the worktop next to her. Then he took her in his arms. She stood rigid and unyielding like she always did when he came near her.

"Babe, I forgive you. Can we can get our life back now?"

He looked into her face, hoping for some signs of contrition. There were none. Her stony expression was defiant. He really thought that now that her secret love affair was out in the open, it would be all over, and pave the way for them to repair their broken marriage. He turned around and walked away. He had never imagined he would find himself in a situation like this, so he had never wondered what it would feel like. In fact, he was surprised that he felt no anger. He had been deceived and betrayed by the woman he loved so much, and over such a long period of time, but instead of feeling anger or a desire for vengeance, all he really felt was relief. He had spent all that time trying to fathom out what was going on with her and himself. He had been so confused and frustrated, but now it was crystal clear. She loved another man. He had been blaming himself the whole time, and now he was relieved of that guilt. She had chosen to give her love to someone else. That was her choice. She was responsible for that choice, not him. He went back upstairs to his bedroom. He got that piece of paper out and tapped the number into his phone, and he stored it under Mon Ami.

Chapter 18

Just moments after leaving Delilah downstairs in a shocked quandary, he dialled Mon Ami from his bedroom. He couldn't wait. He didn't know if Delilah could hear him or not. He didn't care.

"Hello?" a voice enquired, which he instantly recognised, and expected.

"Roger, I want to know why you have been screwing my wife?"

There was a moment of stunned silence.

"Pablo, I'm so sorry. It shouldn't have happened."

There was no denial. Pablo presumed that Roger worked out pretty quickly that Delilah must have confessed.

"You're damn right it shouldn't have happened. I want to know why it did."

"I'm so sorry mate, it just happened."

"How did it just happen?"

"Pablo, it's hard to explain. I didn't intend for it to happen."

"How long have you been shagging my wife?"

"It hasn't happened that many times."

"How many times."

"I don't know Pablo."

Pablo wasn't happy about this obfuscation. He wanted answers.

"Roger, this isn't really a matter to discuss on the phone. I'm coming round to your house right now. I'm going to have it out with you, man to man."

He actually had no idea where Roger lived, but Roger didn't know that. He wanted to make him squirm and put the fear of God into him.

"No Pablo, you can't come to my house."

There was more than a note of panic in Roger's voice.

"Just watch me. I'll be there in less than half an hour."

"No Pablo, you can't. My daughter's here."

"And?"

"I don't want her seeing this."

"You should have thought about that before you started shagging my wife you bastard. What's done is done."

"No Pablo, please, don't come to my house."

"I have to. I need to know exactly what has been going on, and one way or the other, you're going to tell me to my face."

Roger was desperate for Pablo not to attend his home and make a scene.

"Come to my office tomorrow, and I'll tell you everything you want to know, but please Pablo, don't come here."

This was a good outcome for Pablo, seeing as he didn't actually know where Roger lived, and he accepted it.

"What time?"

"Eight o'clock. No one else gets here before nine."

"I'll be there at eight. If you're not there, on the dot, you fucker, I will go straight to your home, and I won't leave until I've seen you."

He rightly presumed that Roger would do everything to stop Pablo seeing his own wife.

"It's ok Pablo, I'll be there at eight, I promise."

Pablo could barely wait to see him the next day, but he would have to. It was going to be a long night. His thoughts turned back to Delilah. He knew how awkward and guilty she would be feeling, and he wanted to use this opportunity to reassure her of his deep unending love. He had some spare blank cards in his room, and after revising a few drafts on scraps of paper, he wrote in one of the cards.

'My darling, this revelation breaks my heart. I never thought you could be unfaithful to me. I have always loved you and that love incorporates total trust too. I am deeply hurt and disappointed, but as you know, I love you deeply, and love forgives, and I forgive you. I want you to focus on me and our marriage again. Your future is not with Roger, it is with me and our family. Please, come back now. All my love, Pablo.'

He took the card down to the kitchen. Delilah wasn't there. She must have gone to her bedroom. She had left his dinner on the aga. He went back upstairs and posted his card under her door without a word, then went downstairs to eat. Later, he sat on his bed and contemplated. He was shocked that Delilah had been having an affair. He was shocked that she was so devoted to her lover. Of course he was upset, and he was drifting in and out of tears, but he had cried a lot harder on other occasions. What took the sting out of this revelation was the hope that came with it. The hope that she would now want to do the right thing, to move on from this affair now that it was out in the open. Wasn't Roger a married man after all? And the release he felt from his own guilt that it had been all his own fault, all to do with his own shortcomings. It answered lots of little puzzles; why on occasions she had been out for four hours when she had allegedly been just taking the dogs for a walk. Why she had been so secretive the whole time. Why she had been so impervious to the steering of the Relate counsellor. Why she had been so receptive to the leanings of Sylvia. Why she had so suddenly and comprehensively cut herself off from him. Why, for the few months prior to that, she seemed different in bed, more alive, more experimental.

He presumed that she had managed to satisfy her husband and her lover for a while, but in time, the duplicity of it bothered her too much to be able to carry on that way, and she realised that she had to choose between them for her own sanity, and sadly for him, she chose her lover. That would explain the deep turmoil he sensed that she was in in the few days before her big announcement.

Then he thought about Roger. What a two-faced piece of shit! He had emailed Pablo that very morning to declare his integrity, and that he had always acted with professionalism and probity, with Pablo's interests as his priority. How is shagging his wife behind his back for eighteen months acting with integrity? He was angry and oozing contempt for the man. He had never had any good vibes about him, even before he had truly shown his real character, or lack of it. Now, he absolutely despised the man, and he was incredulous that Delilah could be drawn to such a spineless, immoral low-life. Pablo couldn't see what any woman would see in him. He didn't want Roger and Delilah comparing notes, and making strategies before he had the chance to interrogate him, so he disconnected the landline phone and hid it. Delilah's mobile had no signal at home in the valley. She could go out and call him from elsewhere, but that was a chance he had to take.

The following morning he was up bright and early. He was on a mission. He arrived at Roger's office in good time and Roger was already there. He demurely let Pablo in and led him to the privacy of his office. As he had stated the day before, there was no one else on the premises yet. He looked dour, as always, and sullen, and worried. They sat opposite each other, no barriers between them. Pablo was simply feeling upset. Just the thought of having to ask this obnoxious man about his intimate relations with his wife. He was barely managing to hold back the tears.

"Tell me about it" he started quietly.

Roger looked awkward. He knew that his job was on the line here, and he needed to keep Pablo sweet if at all possible.

"Well, that day I came to your house to give you the disclosure file, I left you my card. Delilah picked it up and called me a few days later. She asked to see me because she thought you were keeping her in the dark about the case. We arranged to meet at a pub. She was very upset, Pablo."

"Go on."

"Well, we discussed your case that day, but she asked to see me again as a friend. I agreed, and the next time she asked me to make love to her."

Pablo found it hard to believe that she had been that bold, but then, there were a lot of things hard to believe about her at the moment.

"And did you?"

"What would you have done Pablo?"

He was implying that Pablo would have done the same thing in the circumstances. In fact, Pablo would not have taken advantage of her. He was proud of the fact that he had only ever made love to Delilah, his wife. He had never exploited another woman, but he wasn't going to be drawn into a discussion of his own morals.

"She's a very attractive woman Pablo" he continued, trying to justify himself.

"The wife of your client" Pablo stated bluntly to remind him of the gravity of his situation. He wanted details.

"Where did you make love to her?"

He was not being prurient. He wanted to understand exactly what had been going on: how, why, where, when?

150

"The first time was in a field near the sea."

"And other times?"

"Sometimes in my car. Never yours Pablo."

A pause. Pablo waited silently.

"Sometimes at my house in my daughter's bed."

"How often?"

Pablo's voice was getting quieter every time he asked a question as he dwelled on the significance of what he was hearing.

"Not every time we met Pablo."

"How often?"

"About once a week."

Roger looked guilty and trapped.

"I'm sorry Pablo. I know I was wrong. Sometimes, I tried to break it off, but she was very persistent."

"She says that she loves you. Do you love her Roger?"

"No Pablo of course not. It was just a fling. I love my wife. Pablo, I promise you, it was only a fling."

"If you love your own wife, why are you shagging mine too?"

He didn't answer. He just looked guilty, and embarrassed.

Pablo seemed to have run out of questions, so Roger asked him one.

"What are you going to do Pablo?"

Pablo knew that he was referring to the very strong possibility that he would make a complaint against him of professional misconduct, for which he could easily lose his job. This was gross professional misconduct.

It was Christmas Eve, and Pablo wanted to make him stew, fret and worry over Christmas. The very least he could do was spoil his Christmas.

"I don't know yet. I'm going to think about it over Christmas, and I'll let you know afterwards."

There was silence. Roger wondered if the questioning was going to continue. Pablo was simply considering if there was anything else he needed to ask. No, he'd heard enough.

"Ok. I'll contact you again after Christmas, and we'll have another meeting."

"I suppose you'll want to hit me now."

Pablo was surprised that he said this even if it was what he expected, but he felt no violence towards this man, just contempt.

"No Roger, but you'll excuse me if I don't shake your hand."

With that he got up and left. Back in his car he wondered what to do next. It was Christmas Eve, but he didn't want to go home. He phoned Henry. By the time Henry answered the phone he was in floods of tears.

"Oh no Pablo" Henry stated, concerned for his deeply upset friend.

"What's happened?"

It was hard for Pablo to talk. He had been forcing himself to be brave in front of Delilah and Roger, but now he was relaxing, and the emotions were running riot.

"She's been having an affair Henry" he sobbed.

151

"Oh no Pablo. I'm so sorry. I can't say I'm surprised though given what she's been like. What are you going to do?"

"I don't know Henry. I've just been to see the bloke concerned, and now I don't feel like going home."

"Is he still alive?"

"Yeah. I didn't hurt him Henry."

"Oh well, you'd better come and stay here for a while Pablo."

"Are you sure that's ok Henry? It's Christmas after all, and you've got family coming."

"We can always squeeze a little one in. Come over."

"Thanks Henry. I will. I really appreciate this."

"Don't mention it mate. You're family too."

Pablo spent Christmas Eve with them and their family. He felt a bit guilty because he was not much fun. He was in a very subdued, pensive mood, but they all seemed happy to make allowances for him. Henry's home was actually a guest house with lots of lovely bedrooms, and they had about ten of their family staying with them. They were all wonderfully hospitable to him.

The next day was Christmas Day. Troy and Sarah would already be at their home, and Reuben and Lucien and their families would be arriving during the morning. Pablo presumed that Delilah would explain to Troy and Sarah why he was absent. Mid-morning, he phoned each of them in turn to make sure they were ok. He was cross. Delilah hadn't said anything to them, and he had wanted her to face that awkwardness. So he briefly divulged his news to them. They were both predictably shocked. He then phoned Reuben and Lucien to warn them that Christmas was going to be a strange one because of what he had just found out, and was about to divulge to them.

Mid-afternoon he returned home to see his kids. They were all there and they all wanted to make sure he was alright. He was grateful for their concern and compassion, but he wanted to play it all down. It was Christmas Day after all, and they had all got together to have a great time. Delilah was putting on a very brave face. It must have been so hard for her to try to behave normally, knowing that her guilty secret was out after so long. She buried herself in getting the Christmas dinner ready for nine adults and one toddler. She was a fabulous cook, and loved playing hostess with the mostess. Everyone tried to behave as normally as possible. Great food, games and lots of chatting. They would all be sleeping there for at least two nights, but come mid evening, Pablo excused himself and returned to Henry's place. By excusing himself, he was expressing his protest to Delilah about her affair. He would return the next day, but before he did so, in the morning, he had a call from her asking for a meeting with just him, somewhere neutral. They met and went for a country walk.

She was trying to smooth things over for the sake of the family, but there was no contrition, no thawing. Pablo was so disappointed. He hoped that this would be an opportunity for a new start, but she was being as distant and repulsive as she had been for the past year and a quarter. There was no change, and he vented his frustrations to her about the disappointment he felt that she couldn't relent her decision to leave him. He just didn't understand why she still wanted to leave him. They both returned to their home to be with their wonderful family. They tried to keep things as normal as possible, but they had no good news for them. Again, Pablo returned to Henry's for the night. Staying in his own home just wouldn't have felt right. He returned home for Boxing day. More food, drinks, games, walks, talks, and the troubles between Pablo and Delilah were the elephant in the room which no one mentioned. That evening Delilah wrote to her diary:

'He stayed away at H&R over Christmas. He stayed calm while confronting me - offered me his forgiveness -desperately wants me - I don't feel I can come back from this road I have travelled. Met up with him on Boxing day for a walk - he talked at me - I feel such an emotional wreck - got too loud in cafe and had to leave - walked and talked. Came home totally and utterly exhausted by it all - he just can't listen to me - I said 'I can't give you what you want' he heard 'I can't give you what you want, so fuck off.' How do I get him to listen to me? Why don't I feel grateful that he has offered me his forgiveness?'

The day after Boxing Day would be their last day all together. They happily did the usual things they always did during relaxed family time together. There was a lovely afternoon walk with the dogs to clear the lungs and a few calories. The elephant in the room continued to be ignored until after the evening meal. Some of them would be staying another night, but some of them would be going home that evening, and Lucian felt that they ought all to discuss what had been going on before they all broke up. They were all sitting around an enormous dining room table, the remnants of a fabulous meal strewn out across the table. Bravely, he spoke up.

"I know that this is a very awkward subject to bring up, and I know we've all been avoiding it for the past three days, but I think we should talk about it before we all go home."

There were murmurs of approval from all around the table. Pablo stayed quiet. He knew that this was going to be between his children and Delilah. He was at the opposite end of the table to Delilah. He watched her face go ashen. She didn't know where to look. This was going to be extremely difficult for her, but she was trying to look brave too. Lucian continued.

"Mum, I think we're all stunned to hear from dad that you've been having an affair. We'd like to know what you have to say about it."

There was an expectant silence around the table. Delilah spoke up, looking embarrassed, but accepting that she owed them all an explanation.

"I'm sorry. I feel that I've let you all down. But it's what happens when you don't feel loved at home."

She was trying to appear pragmatic. Beatrice, Lucien's wife took up the mantle.

"Pablo says that Roger is a married man."

Delilah was seriously cornered now. The Daughters-in-law would not take kindly to her having an affair with a married man. They would be able to relate to the cheated wife. Him being married did make matters worse. Delilah looked incredibly sheepish.

"He told me that they were getting divorced."

Beatrice carried on.

"Are they getting divorce?"

"I don't know."

"I find it hard to believe that you had an affair with a married man."

Delilah stayed silent. She had no answer to this. She just looked incredibly guilty. Then Troy spoke up.

"Mum, why did you have an affair in the first place?"

"What do you do when you find the grass is greener on the other side of the fence?"

This made Pablo wince. As far as he was concerned, he had been a good father, a good provider, a loving and reliable husband. How could a two-faced cheating selfish reprobate like Roger be more attractive than him? But he said nothing. This was the kids' time. They didn't look impressed with her logic. There was just silence, then Troy continued.

"Is that it mum, the grass is greener?"

"I found a deep love like I've never experienced before."

Pablo mused over the words Roger had given him - 'It's just a fling - I don't love her'

More silence whilst they all cogitated. Troy's wife Dahlia broke the silence.

"We feel like you've been lying to us for the past year."

Pablo was surprised at the strength of feeling that was coming out. Dahlia sounded quite cross. Delilah wasn't going to argue.

"Yes, I know. I'm so sorry. I got myself into an awkward situation where I had to hide things from you all. I didn't mean to deceive any of you."

She was upset, tears beginning to drip slowly down her cheeks. Pablo felt sorry for her, as usual, but he was also pleased that her own children were challenging her. This was their family too that was being broken up, and they clearly weren't very happy about it. There were a few more questions, a few more platitudinous answers, some allusions to all the relationships Pablo had allegedly had in the past, but he avoided getting drawn into any bickering. The atmosphere was heavy and emotional. The challenging seemed to have dried up, and it really was time for some of them to go. They had long journeys ahead of them, and they had left this airing until the last possible opportunity. Everyone except Pablo got up. Then in turn, they took it in turns to hug Delilah, to express their sadness and love for her. Pablo bade farewell to them all and returned very thoughtfully to Henry's. Later, Delilah entered her emotions into her diary:

'Oh what a Christmas. The truth is out about you my love. What a terrible shock and so much pain caused to my children and daughters-in-law. The deception is the hardest thing for me to bear. I think about how some kids reject their parents who've had an affair. I wonder if my children will feel the same. It would be less painful if I was no longer around. If I was braver I think I would have tried to take my own life. The emotional upheaval, the questions about what

I do or don't do. What I should do, what I feel, where do I stand with God? I can't answer them. How I have let my family down. And then there is my dear Belinda. The last thing I would have ever wanted for my beautiful Belinda is to have a divided family...

A very emotional meal with the children. Lucian took the chair and started family discussion on it all. So proud of him. All spoke except Reuben and Sarah, poor Sarah. What have I done to her? Please God protect her if I dare ask. I love them all so much, but have let them down so terribly. Much sorrow expressed by all. I told them all of dad's previous friendships and how it made me feel.'

Chapter 19

Pablo couldn't stay indefinitely at Henry's house. He was so grateful that they had hosted and comforted him during one of the most hurtful and distressing periods in his life. They were true friends, but he needed to sort his life out, at home. The next day he returned late in the morning. Reuben and his wife Sharon were still there. They hadn't wanted to go home because they were worried about Pablo and Delilah. Emotions and tensions were running so high. They were scared of what might happen. Sarah had had enough. She had moved out to live with her best friend and her family in the big house next door. Pablo felt so sorry for her. She was a victim in this through absolutely no fault of her own. He was glad she'd moved next door. They were a lovely family, and they would look after her a lot better than Delilah and he could at the moment. He was so jealous of joined-up families. They all found themselves standing in the kitchen, and a mini-conference ensued. Sharon attempted to establish some ground rules between the warring parents-in-law. She addressed them both.

"You can't carry on living together like this. You're tearing each other apart emotionally. It's damaging you both. There has to be a change. What can you both do to improve the situation?"

Sharon came from a family of counsellors. Clearly. Delilah piped up callously;

"What about Pablo stays here during the week so he can carry on working on the house, and I'll stay elsewhere, then at the weekends, I'll stay here, and Pablo can stay elsewhere."

"That sounds reasonable. Pablo?" Sharon enquired hopefully.

Pablo replied in his best derisive tone.

"You really think that I'm working my bollocks off to turn this place into a palace so that she can swan around here at weekends with her lover?"

"Yeah, I see your point." Sharon stated, rather deflated.

It quickly became clear that there was no easy solution. Delilah was deeply angry at Pablo's obstinacy because he wouldn't move out and let her just carry on her own sweet life as she saw fit. However, she realised that the situation was untenable as it was, so she capitulated.

"Ok. I'll go and stay with one of my sisters for the time being whilst we think about it."

With that, she went off and started packing. Within the hour, she bade them all farewell, taking the dogs with her, of course. Reuben and Sharon still looked worried and fairly exhausted. They commiserated with Pablo and offered him as much comfort as they could, but now that they were happy that the volatility had been taken out of the situation, for the time being at least, they felt comfortable about going home themselves, and they too left. Pablo was left all alone. He thought to himself, 'what a fucking Christmas!' The next step was to think about that creep Roger. It would be nice to see him pay the price for his skulduggery, but he knew that any retribution that he could inflict on him would be returned ten-fold upon his own head by his dear wife. He was going to have to resist the temptation for any kind of revenge. He phoned Roger and made that second appointment to visit him again at his office in a couple of days' time. He kept the call as brief as possible. He didn't want to give anything away. He wanted him to worry and fret for as long as possible.

Two days later, he arrived at Roger's office, but to his surprise and disappointment, he was greeted by Roger's supervisor instead, one Sergeant Toffee. He didn't know him personally, but he'd heard that he was a straight-talking, honest, reliable guy, and he was happy just to be called Toffee. Toffee got straight to the point. He spoke quickly and assertively.

"Come in Pablo. I know you were expecting to see Roger, but he won't be here. He's told me all about it and he wants me to deal with it for him."

Pablo was deflated. He had wanted to make Roger squirm again. He politely followed Toffee to his office. They sat down, either side of Toffee's desk. Toffee was quite a bit younger than Pablo, being in his late thirties, but he had rank, and he spoke with authority. He started.

"Pablo, he's been shitting himself all over Christmas. He's in a right state. He's not been sleeping. He's at the end of his tether. He couldn't face you again, which is why he's confided in me."

Pablo was very pleased to hear about Roger's discomfort. Toffee continued.

"You know as well as I do that coppers shag."

He said this as if that was ok. It just happens. It's to be expected.

"Really?" queried Pablo. "Who's shagging your wife then?"

"You know what I mean Pablo. It's no big deal. If a guy gets the opportunity, he fills his boots."

Pablo appreciated that Toffee was trying to play down Roger's infraction, but he wasn't buying it.

"Toffee, he has abused his position. He came to my home, my fucking home, as my official representative, in a professional capacity, representing my interests. The last thing he should have done was use that to take advantage of my wife. It's not even as though it was a one off. He's made a proper habit of it. A year and a half!"

"I know Pablo. I'm not saying that he wasn't out of order, but he's a good officer. I don't want to lose him."

"Is that what you call a good officer? One who shags his clients wives behind everyone's back? You know he was doing her in job time don't you?"

"Look Pablo, he's really sorry. He's assured me that he won't come anywhere near your wife again. I just don't want to see matters getting any worse. They don't have to."

Pablo knew that as far as Delilah was concerned, it was in his interests not to make Roger lose his job. Against his deeper instincts for revenge, he knew he had to let this go.

"I don't owe him any favours at all Toffee. In fact, I think him shagging my wife has actually distracted him from my case and my interests. It's been doubly bad for me."

"I don't know about that Pablo, but of course, you are bound to be really angry with him. I understand all that, of course I do, but you don't have to dob him in the shit."

Pablo took his time, then asked

"Can you promise me that he won't go near Delilah again?"

"Pablo, I've already made him promise me that, and I've made him delete all records of her. I can assure you that it's over."

"Toffee, I haven't touched him this time, but if it happens again, I will rip his friggin' balls off and make him eat them. I promise."

"Pablo, I can assure you, it won't happen again. I'll be keeping a close eye on him."

"Ok. I won't put in a complaint, but it's only because I don't want to make my situation with Delilah any worse. I have nothing but utter contempt for him. He's a complete cunt."

"I understand Pablo. So are we agreed then, no complaint?"

"Yes."

"And this conversation never happened, ok?"

"Ok."

Pablo returned to his silent empty home, unsure if he'd made the right decision. It didn't seem fair that Roger would get away with this. Here he was, being hauled over the coals because he'd been concerned about one of his clients, and had sent her some emails just to establish that she was still alive, God forbid! Yet Roger, who had been screwing a client's wife for a year and a half in job time, was going to walk away scot-free.

Towards the end of the first week of January, Delilah returned home. It was fully two years since Cassie had made her original complaint, and the dire consequences of it still hung over their heads like a very dark lightning cloud, and Pablo never knew when the latest lightning bolt was going to strike. He remembered the time when Delilah had returned home from a weekend away with one of the witchsters, and she had restated her devotion to him. How he longed for that to happen again, but it wasn't to be. As soon as he saw her, he could tell from her body language that she was in warrior mood. As soon as she stepped into the house she nailed her colours to the post.

"I'm coming home. This is my home, and I won't be pushed out of it, but let me make it quite clear, the marriage is over. Do you understand? The marriage is over."

She spoke loudly and with steely purpose. He just looked at her, perplexed and deeply saddened by her renewed defiance. She continued sternly.

"No more letters, or cards, or flowers, or chocolates, or anything. Is that clear?"

Again, he stood there silently like a naughty little boy being chastised. He was so deflated. It was wrong for him to love her.

"I don't want you talking to me, or trying to change my mind, and if you touch me again, I'm going to call the police and have you arrested for assault. Do you understand?"

He looked at her with great pain in his heart. He had only ever touched her lovingly. He was a very tactile person. Not touching her was going to be very hard for him. He had been hoping daily for the past year and a half for reconciliation, but all she was giving him was a slow-motion train crash, which just got messier and more injurious by the week. There was no pretence anymore that maybe he could do things to improve. It was simply all over, except that they were still living under the same roof of course. Tricky. She had said her well-rehearsed set piece. No doubt the witchsters had helped her to prepare the steely delivery of her demands whilst she had been staying with them. Now she stomped off to her bedroom to unpack. He had never seen her so determined and defiant. He felt useless. He had no more weapons left for this fight. There was still a glimmer of hope; she still hadn't mentioned the 'd' word.

The next day he was back at work, in that dreary mundane office. It could be worse of course. At least he was still being paid his full salary. He had a call from Steven, his replacement Fed' Rep' who informed him that his disciplinary case would be heard in a couple of weeks' time, and that he would be represented by the barrister whom he had met previously. This would be five long months after the court case had been finalised. He couldn't believe that it had all taken so long. He looked forward to the situation reaching a climax one way or another. Later he told Delilah about the date of the hearing. He knew that he wasn't supposed to be talking to her, but he thought she would want to know this. She just looked at him contemptuously like he had let her down so badly. Err, wasn't it her who'd had the affair? She still cooked for both of them each evening. They just sat in silence whilst they ate. At least they had some music on. After dinner, he tried to talk to her. He felt she owed him an explanation.

"Deli, why are you so aggressive still? I finally know what motivated you for the past year and a half; your love of Roger. But now he's off the scene, and he's run back to his wifey, so why can't we make up?"

He was so frustrated.

"You have fucked my life up. You had to interfere, didn't you?"

"What am I supposed to do? Give you two my blessing?"

She said no more but stomped off up the stairs. He followed her. He wanted an answer. She got to her bedroom and was about to slam the door in his face. He put his foot in the doorway and prevented her from shutting it. He knew that this was not going to go well for him, but he was so frustrated and desperate for an explanation that he could understand.

"If you don't move your foot, I'll call the police."

"I just want to know why we can't try to put things right between us."

"Just fuck off!"

He looked at her longingly, then removed his foot. She slammed the door shut.

The next day she was on the phone to the police domestic violence officer. She made an entry into her diary.

'Spent the week with Morag, then Sirena. Came home with my decision. I told him the marriage was over and that I didn't want his letters, cards, flowers, notes etc. No persuasion, talking about us, and touching is 'out'. Of course he can't accept this - I phoned DVO about his persistent trying to question me. This has upset me so much - that I have had to make a call about my husband who I don't know anymore - I don't really think of him as my husband - all that conjures up in my mind has gone. He has become a familiar stranger. I looked at wedding photos yesterday and they left me cold. How sad is that? Will I ever find that place of peace and rest with someone again. Not sure if I ever had it - so many things have got so muddled.'

The next two weeks passed with them having virtually no contact, apart from the shared silent evening meals. Her announcement that the marriage was over added an extra tough skin to their emotional separation. Her threat to have him arrested added a lot more fragility to the ice he walked on daily. Despite her ban on him giving her cards or messages, he left her a card. He still felt compelled to reach out to her, his love. On the front was a drawing of a beautiful woman that reminded him of her. Inside the printed message was;

'When two people join together and bond their lives forever because they are certain they have something special that will make their marriage last... This is the first act of faith. Upon this act of faith, these two people will build a life, and as long as their determination stays with them, this life will always be their hope, their dream, their truth, their being, their inspiration, and their source of strength. Through their life together, they will hurt and laugh. Together they will learn and grow through trial and error. The lessons will show them the meaning of true love that lasts and one that just gives up. These two people will face each failure together and discover the strength to go on. They will encourage each other's dreams and forgive each other's faults. Through a labour of love, these two will become as one - fighting against the odds and ultimately creating a marriage that will grow into an infinite love.'

As usual all blank spaces on the card were festooned with his own handwritten messages of love. This really made him look wretched and pathetic.

One evening after their meal, she coldly made the announcement he had dreaded for eighteen months.

"I'm divorcing you."

Icy, splintering words that froze him all over.

"Why?"

"Everyone says I should."

"Fuck everyone."

"No. It's our marriage that is fucked. Get used to it."

"I agree. Our marriage is fucked, but only because you've been out there shagging all and sundry."

She was past arguing with him. She left the table and retired to her room. He quietly wept, his head cradled on his collapsed arms over the table. He didn't know what to do. Later on, he phoned Tim, who he always referred to as 'Fatboy'. They both referred to each other as 'Fatboy'. He shared his woes for the next hour.

Two days later was the day of the internal hearing. The 19th of January. He was up early, dressed in his best suit. He left the house before Delilah was up. He fantasised about her getting up in time to give him a hug and wish him well. That wasn't going to happen. She genuinely seemed to want him disgraced, and found guilty, and she didn't seem to give a shit. Admittedly, she had asked him if she was allowed to attend the hearing, and he had said no, which wasn't true. She could have attended, but he didn't want her there gloating over his misfortune once again. He attended police headquarters alone, where he met Steven for the first time. He was just a young lad, but nice enough. He led Pablo to the courtroom like a lamb to the slaughter. It was set up like a real magistrates court, with the bench for three people set up high and pews to either side of it, with seats opposite for a public gallery. It was strangely dimly lit, which gave it a slightly archaic feel, even though it was not an old building. Nobody else was there yet, apart from his barrister, and that gave them a chance to briefly discuss his case. Of course, he had no defence. He had pleaded guilty at magistrates court five months earlier, and he had been convicted of a criminal offence. Today's hearing was simply his opportunity to offer mitigation before the panel dished out punishment number two. Slowly other participants arrived. The prosecuting counsel from the original court case arrived next. Apparently, he had summoned Cassie and Marlon as witnesses, and he was hoping to drag their original complaints into the proceedings, even though the CPS had dropped their case as spurious long ago. He seemed to really have the knives out for Pablo. Thankfully, he had been instructed by the Internal Affairs department, that unless Cassie and Marlon actually showed up to give evidence in person, their allegations could not be used as part of the evidence in this case. Pablo was relieved to hear this. He knew that they wouldn't show up. Why would they? They had achieved more than they could have hoped for already.

Several representatives from the Internal Affairs turned up next, shuffling papers behind the pews opposite Pablo. One of them would lead the proceedings just like a court clerk would do in a Magistrates Court. Finally the panel marched in through a private door behind the bench. There were two superintendents, and an assistant chief constable, all in full regalia. Everybody stood up, then sat after the panel had sat, except Pablo of course, who was standing in the dock, trying to be brave. A female detective inspector who was acting as the clerk stood opposite him. She outlined the case against him and invited the solicitor for the prosecution to present his case. It didn't take him long. He was able to confirm that the accused had pleaded guilty at court on day, date, time, place, to misuse of police data contrary to the Data Protection Act 1998. He then proceeded to give his slant on it, suggesting that Pablo had acted out of a desire to exploit a former female drug-addict client for personal gratification. Pablo winced. It had been nothing like that, and he thought that he had been told he could not bring Cassie into it if she hadn't turned up to give evidence directly. He resented this man making whatever insinuation his dirty little mind chose to throw into the mix. When he had finished casting all the aspersions he thought he could get away with, it was then the turn of Pablo's barrister.

In all honesty, he was rather weak. By the end of his presentation Pablo wished that he had presented his own mitigation. Of course, he wouldn't have been able to, he was too distressed by the whole thing. He wouldn't have kept his composure. He was always on the point of tears. The barrister focussed on what Pablo had not done, such as he hadn't exploited his position for any pecuniary advantage, or to influence anyone or anything. There had been no deceit of any kind, and his track record up to this point had been exemplary. But he failed to challenge the prosecutors story about Pablo exploiting a female client, and that looked bad. He could have emphasised that Pablo had stayed in touch with several clients, all of whom were male other than Cassie, and that he did so for the same reasons as he tried to keep in touch with Cassie. For intelligence reasons and as a duty of care. He failed to emphasise the nature of Pablo's role as the Harm Reduction Officer, where he had been required to form as close liaisons with the drug-taking fraternity as possible, and that when his role changed slightly to working within the narrower confines of the POU, these associations were still very useful. The problem was that the barrister knew very little of Pablo's role and how he operated. Effectively he was woefully underprepared to present a decent defence. And of course there was no mention of the fact that Pablo had only pleaded guilty because his aberrant wife insisted that he should, and he put her desires before anything else, including his reputation, his career, and his very livelihood, because he was desperately trying to save his marriage. Who would have believed that?

A character witness was called. It was no less than the head of the probation service for the area, who was overall in charge of the POU. He was amazing. He testified to the court that Pablo had been an exceptional member of the unit, that Pablo had always acted professionally and with integrity, and he went on at length to assure the court that Pablo's contribution to the work of the unit was remarkable; he possessed exceptional abilities at securing rapport and cooperation from a very challenging client group.

Pablo was so grateful for his genuine and heartfelt support. The man only attended to testify because he wanted to, and because he felt that Pablo deserved his support and backing. No other reason.

The panel then withdrew to discuss their options privately. The next ten minutes were very tense for Pablo. His life was in the balance. He hoped he would be fined. Again! He saw no reason for them to relieve him of his role. But the timing wasn't good. Forces nationally were under fresh pressure to shed staff, ten thousand in all apparently, and Pablo was giving his force a very easy opportunity to help achieve a small part of their number reduction target. The panel marched back in and sat. None of them looked directly at him. That was a bad sign. The chair read out their decision;

"Pablo Pinkerton, you have been found guilty in a court of law of breaching the data protection act. Your actions have fallen below the standards expected by the chief constable, and by receiving a criminal conviction, you have brought the force into disrepute. It is out decision today therefore to dismiss you from the force with immediate effect."

With that, he stood. The superintendents stood. Then they all walked solemnly out. The court remained quiet. This was a solemn moment. An honourable man had just been stripped of his identity, his professional standing, his future and his income. Smalltalk would only have added to the insult. Twenty one years of exemplary conduct and exceptional ability didn't apparently count for anything.

Chapter 20

Later, on the phone.

"Fatboy, how's it going mate?"

"Could be better bro."

"What's the latest calamity?"

"Funny you should say that. I've been sacked."

"On no bruv, I don't believe it. That's terrible what are you going to do?"

Pablo cried, then quietly carried on.

"Gonna have to put the house on the market."

"Mate, you've only just finished it, more or less."

"I know. I'm gutted."

"You'll hardly have time to enjoy it."

"I know. It's a real pisser. Stop going on about it!"

He was being humorous. Tim knew that.

"What are you going to do for money bro?"

He sounded so worried. It was in his nature to worry readily and excessively.

"Now, there I'm lucky. I can dip into my mum's money to keep us going until the house is sold, then I'll pay it all back to her out of my half of the equity."

"Ok mate. That sounds good. The house must be worth a mil."

He sounded relieved.

"Well, not quite that much, but it's going to fetch a pretty penny, but Tim, I don't want to have to sell it. It's my dream home"

"I'm so sorry mate. That's horrible. How is Delilah?"

He replied slowly, deliberately, thoughtfully.

"Horrible. Callous. Distant. Militant. Totally alien. I'm so disappointed. I honestly thought that with Roger out of the picture, she'd start to thaw, but the opposite has happened. She's really got the knives out for me. She says that I've fucked her life up, and she's oozing resentment the whole time. Hence the divorce I suppose."

"Oh mate. That's so sad. What did she say about you being sacked?"

"We haven't discussed it. She knew I was going to the hearing, but she didn't ask me how it went, so I didn't say anything. She doesn't talk to me Tim."

He cried some more, then managed to carry on.

"Anyway, it will be obvious. I'm not going in to work anymore. Funny, because when I was under investigation, she knew more about what was going on than I did. Roger was keeping her informed much more than me, and that's a fact!"

"And the rest!" Tim added. He thought for a while, then he asked

"Are you going to contest the divorce?"

"I don't think realistically that you can these days bud. If someone wants a divorce, they can have one. Simple as. That's what a lawyer once told me. I'm not going to try to make it hard for her. I'm just going to pray that she has a change of heart one day. That's the best I can hope for. You know I said she doesn't talk to me anymore?"

"Yeah bro, you just said that."

"Well there was one morning last week she did say something. She was proper disconcerted and volunteered to me that she was off to see the witchsters that day, and she was going to tell them about the affair. She was genuinely worried about them condemning her, or falling out with her over it, but she felt that she had to come clean with them and face the music now the cat's out of the bag."

"Do you really think they didn't know?"

"Oh yes. I could see that she was genuinely worried to bits. She must have felt desperate to actually talk to me. I felt quite sorry for her. Do you realise that for over a year and a half she was keeping a secret like that from everyone. She was living a double life, and managed to hide it for so long. She managed to keep it from me, obviously, and the kids, but even her own sisters. I thought that was incredible. It must have been so hard for her to act so secretively for that length of time. I don't think many people could keep a big secret like that to themselves for that long. It goes to show how strong she is, emotionally. She's incredible."

"Yeah, I suppose you're right. And how did they react?"

"Quite the opposite of what she expected. She came home all cocky, saying that she didn't know what she had been worried about. All three of them gave her their full support and blessing."

"That's rich."

"Yeah, I stupidly expected one or two of them to frown upon her actions from a moral perspective. But apparently not. I half expected apologies from them for backing her up so blindly, now that they knew what had really been going on, but no. No apologies. I thought that was sad, and disappointing. People take sides no matter what their so-called principles are."

"It's what is called two-faced Pablo."

"Yep. I get hung drawn and quartered because someone thinks I looked at a woman the wrong way, yet she can go off shagging someone else's husband in a full-blown squelchy, cummy, clothes-ripping, never-ending, iron-clad passion-fest, and everyone's fine with that."

"Listen mate you can't stay there with Delilah the way she is. It's too horrible. Come and stay with me."

"That's really kind of you Tim, but I can't give up on her. I need to be here. Time is running out."

"Ok bro, but remember, you can stay here whenever you want, for however long you want. You know that don't you?"

"Yes bro. You're such a brick. I appreciate it."

"I love you bro."

He really did. They carried on talking for another ten minutes. Tim had a gift for just being present, and lending his emotional support. He had come into Pablo's life at such an auspicious time. He was like a chubby human angel sent to support him in his worst hour, whenever he needed him.

The way that he and Delilah were bizarrely living separate lives under one roof had become the new normal, yet, after thirty years of one-ness, it felt totally perverse to Pablo. He busied himself making a very large wrap-around patio alongside the finished extension. This was the final construction job of the house renovation, and it exploited the fantastic views there.

He was complying with her orders about no letters, notes, conversations, and touching. Well, apart from one card. She had a far more aggressive air about her, and he was genuinely afraid of the consequences of transgressing against her wishes. He had started dancing again in the next town along. He had her permission for that. So he was out two nights a week dancing, which was so refreshing for him. Otherwise he was at home pretty much alone all the time. No work to go to of course, and there was no point in trying to get another job if she was divorcing him. If he was unemployed he couldn't be made to pay her alimony. Every cloud has a silver lining. He felt that her still cooking for him was her one concession, because he was still paying all the bills for her. She was fiercely repulsive if he tried to talk to her, but surely he had some right of expression? Towards the end of January he found another lovely card with a very appropriate printed message inside. On the front it simply said: 'Forgive me ....' On the inside it read appositely:

'Forgive me for my faults that seem to follow my life. Forgive me for my insecurities that have caused you hurt and pain. Forgive me for my dependence on you; it can be hard to bear. I love you and I'm sorry for any mistakes I have made. But remember that my heart needs your smiles and laughter. My soul needs your friendship and love. And I need you.'

He was always at home when the post arrived, and a few days later a large envelope arrived for her with a stamp on it from the family court division. He wept, as he did every day, but this was today's trigger. He couldn't fight this attack. He left the letter out for her. She removed it later without comment. The next day when she was out, he entered her bedroom and saw the papers in the opened envelope on her mantle piece. Nothing had been filled in. Each day from then on, he checked to see if the forms had been filled in, or indeed removed and presumably sent off. Each day, nothing had been done. Each day he felt so relieved. She was definitely struggling with the concept of divorce, and he was facing such devastating loss in his life. The sense of impending and unavoidable doom hung heavily over his head constantly, yet it couldn't crush his hopes completely. Weeks passed by and nothing happened. Occasionally as he crouched outside her bedroom door, straining to hear a secret phone conversation going on behind closed doors, he got the impression that she discussed the divorce with the witchsters regularly, and they seemed to be encouraging her. He heard her thanking them for their offer of help with the form-filling.

Then it was Valentine's day. The rule he was least worried about was the one about no cards or letters. He was after all abiding by all the others. He'd already given her two cards, and the sky hadn't fallen in. He had to get her another one. He still loved her very much, and she was still his wife, sort of, and it was Valentine's day! How could he not leave her a card on Valentine's day? He sought out an appropriate printed card. It read:

'The day we were married I pledged to you that I'd love you forever and that's what I will do. I'll always be here to depend on each day, and close by your side is where I will stay. Some things may change in our lifetime together, but I promise I'll love you forever and ever.'

Again, so apposite, and of course he embellished it all over with copious childlike declarations of his undying love, as if repeating himself would somehow add credence. As if.

A few days later his son Lucian and Beatrice had another baby daughter. They called her Acacia. This was cause for celebration, but there was no celebration between him and Delilah. That felt so wrong. During the next week, they both visited Lucian to see the new baby, but on separate days. Pablo wanted them to both go together, but Delilah wasn't going to fall for this 'trick'. When seeing his family, the joy was tinged with sadness. He missed seeing Delilah's joy at meeting her second granddaughter.

With her contrived aberration of separation, she never commented on the building work, or the loss of his job, or the cards, and not even Acacia. The separation was total. About a month after Valentine's it was time for another letter. The need to reach out to her welled up over time, to the point where he just had to write something. It was his hope that was keeping him going. He quoted 1 Corinthians chapter 13 again. It was the best description of love he had ever come across, and he wanted to remind her of the meaning of his love. Then he added:

'Delilah, I know it is very hard for you at the moment. You found a deep love with another man who you described as so lovely, and you described me as arrogant. You declared that you had committed yourself to him and that you couldn't give yourself back to me. I understand that you don't want to settle for second-best, but remember, you only had great secret times with him. Has he stood by you like I have? Has his love proved steadfast and true like mine has? Has he promised to love honour and cherish you until his dying day? for better or worse, for richer or poorer, in sickness and in health? Soon, you will be alone or with someone else. All I can ask is that you remember my true love and devotion. When the dust settles you might find that my love and commitment cease to be an irritation to you. Maybe you will begin to see the value of them. They will still be there for you until the day I die. I love you with every fibre of my body, soul, and spirit. Xxx'

The following morning he entered her room after she had gone out as usual, and stared at the blank wall over the mantle-piece. The starkness of the space where the application papers had been shocked him. He stood transfixed, allowing the realisation to sink in that he had lost yet another battle. They had sat there poignantly for over five weeks. That was some measure of the dilemma Delilah found herself in, but that morning, she had gone to a love-in with the witchsters, the meeting he always referred to as a coven, and they were going to help her complete the task. There was no doubt in his mind that they had pressurised her, and that they wanted to get this job done more than she did.

A few days later in her usual subdued business-like fashion, she informed him that she had applied for the divorce. He already knew that, but he declined to mention that he knew it from snooping around her bedroom looking for clues. He just looked at her with a look of despair and disbelief. She said nothing more. The very next day was their thirty first wedding anniversary. Of course he commemorated it with a card. Naturally, she ignored it. It was completely irrelevant to her. Since her affair with Roger had ended and having made her mind up about divorcing him anyway, she no longer made any entries to her diary. She was not questioning herself anymore. No more struggling with the issues and questions. She had made up her mind and was not countenancing any internal scrutiny or dialogue. She was being entirely single-minded and resolute, or was that mindless, like a machine?

His anniversary card had a picture of two people dancing together. On the front it read:

'I love to kiss you. I love to hold you. I love to love you ...'

Inside he wrote:

'When you are kind and when you are cruel, I still love you.

When you are loving and when you are cold, I still love you.

When you are happy and when you are sad, I still love you.

When you are close, and when you are far away, I still love you.

When you are happy and when you are sad, I still love you.

When you are young and when you are old, I still love you.

When you are well and when you are ill, I still love you.

When you are mine and when you are not, I still love you.

I loved you then, and I love you now.

I'll love you always, with all of my heart, no matter what. Xxx'

His letters never elicited a response from her. He was in darkness. The next day a big envelope arrived addressed to him. It had that big crest on it from the family court division. He left it on the doormat where it had fallen. It stayed there for a few days. He didn't want to touch it. It was unclean. It was a travesty. He checked online to learn what would happen if he didn't acknowledge it; He would be sent another copy. If he failed to acknowledge that one too, a court officer would attend in person and serve the notice on him. That would delay the process by several weeks and incur an additional fee. He wasn't trying to deliberately delay anything, he just didn't want to be a part of it. Three days later the envelope still lay on the doormat. Delilah tackled him over it. She couldn't ignore it any longer.

"I knew you would be a pain in the arse. Why can't you just fill in the form and send it back. Are you going to make every step of this process awkward for me?"

"I'm not trying to be awkward. I just don't want to read what nasty things you have made up as grounds for divorce. That will break my heart just a little bit more. I am protecting my heart."

She stared at him fiercely. When she was really mad, he sensed that she could hurt him. Good job they didn't live in America, with guns readily available for the weak. He got the impression that her thoughts then drifted to her allegations, and she suddenly looked a little guilty.

"Please don't make my life harder. You've already fucked it up enough" she stated emotionally, and walked away.

He felt sorry for her as he often did. He still cared about her. She was in emotional pain, and he didn't want to make her life harder. He picked up the envelope and took it to his room. He didn't open it because he had nothing but contempt for the contents, and he really didn't want to read them. He already knew why she was divorcing him. It was because of Roger. She had discovered that real love existed elsewhere. Whatever was in the envelope was bullshit, because he was pretty sure that she wasn't citing her love for Roger. The next day he asked a friend in the legal business to recommend the very best local divorce lawyer to him, which he did. A few days later, with the unopened correspondence accompanying him in as undignified a manner as possible, in a flimsy supermarket plastic bag, he arrived to see her at her office in an adjacent town. He was tearful, just like when he had gone to the bank to change their joint account. The solicitor, Sue, was about the same age as him. She was wearing a matching dark skirt and jacket, and looked every inch the professional. He noticed immediately that she wore a wedding ring on her finger. She had a reputation as being a very experienced and effective in divorce issues and for getting things done her way. As they sat either side of her big desk, they had an introductory conversation which helped to settle him down. He then explained the situation between him and Delilah, including the bit about Roger, of course. There were a few tearful moments, but all in all, he managed to keep himself together admirably.

"I've brought the divorce papers which have been sent to me, but I haven't opened them. I don't want to see them. I want you to handle it all for me please. I want to be involved as little as possible."

She took the big envelope routinely but stated certainly

"You will have to read them because I need to know what your response is."

"Really?" he pleaded. "I have to read through all this pack of lies?"

"Yes I'm afraid so. I need to know if you agree with her grounds or not."

He was not happy. He didn't want to rub his nose in this dross. She opened the envelope, put on her reading spectacles and quickly perused the papers. She was very familiar with the general contents.

"Shall I tell you the gist of her grounds and you can tell me how you feel about them?"

"Ok. If I have to."

"I'm afraid you do. At this stage all we are doing is replying to her allegations to the court."

"Her overall grounds are unreasonable behaviour."

She said that routinely as if that was obviously to be expected. It was after all Delilah who had been engaged in an affair, not him. She was the adulterer and she had been caught out. Sue then read out each ground in order.

"She refers to an obsessive and emotional relationship at work which resulted in a complaint of harassment and misuse of data resulting in a conviction under the data protection act. This left her feeling betrayed and upset."

She waited quietly for a response without moving her gaze off the document.

"That's based on truth, except that it was not an obsessive relationship. It was my work, and that relationship worked very well for two years before the client's partner got her to make a spurious complaint about me. In fact, for good measure he made a complaint too, but both complaints were dismissed after an investigation found them to be malicious and unfounded. I went off work whilst the investigation was being carried on. The data protection thing was what Internal Affairs decided to throw at me separately. They were just being anal. I only got a conviction because I pleaded guilty to please Delilah."

"Why?"

"I felt that I had to choose between my career and her. She was adamant about me pleading guilty and taking responsibility as she put it, and I put her wishes first."

She made no judgment, but carried on.

"She says that as a result of your conviction you were dismissed from your job and that you are not looking for another job. This is causing her financial insecurity and much stress."

He thought that was rich.

"She's choosing to leave me. She wanted me to plead guilty. I told her that if I did, I'd lose my job. It was what she wanted. She didn't think through the consequences, even though I tried to explain them to her, so I hardly think it's fair to complain now."

"She says that throughout your marriage you have formed close relationships with other women, giving her feelings of low self-worth, and lack of trust in you."

This kind of thing always frustrated him so much. He answered with some exasperation in his voice.

"I've always been totally faithful to her. Because of her own insecurities, she has always felt that I shouldn't converse with women at work, but I have never been prepared to live like that. She needed to trust me, and that was something she just couldn't do. No reason for it on my part. I never have strayed, and never would. It's been her choice not to trust me."

"She says that throughout the marriage you have been very controlling towards her, verbally arguing your point over and over again, and that you use your physique to intimidate her."

"We were very happily married for twenty eight years. Our relationship has only become contentious since she announced that she didn't want to be with me anymore. It's true that I have been trying to talk her out of leaving me for the past year and a half, and there was one incident where I followed her to her bedroom, pleading with her to talk to me. I was so frustrated. That has only happened once. She was on the phone to Domestic Violence the next day."

"She says that during 2008 your behaviour became so intense and threatening that she left the matrimonial home for six months, and only returned due to financial constraints and in an attempt to repair the relationship, but it didn't work."

"That's really rich. She left because she set up a little love nest with her lover. I didn't know that at the time. I only found out over a year later. She was only away for six months because I only sponsored her for six months. When she returned, she stated very clearly that it was purely for financial reasons, and emphasised that the relationship with me was still well and truly over. There was no attempt on her part to reconcile. In fact, her affair carried on for another ten months until I finally found out about it again, so basically, she's lying."

"She says that over the past eighteen months you have been obsessively writing her letters and texting her as a result of which she feels like she is going out of her mind."

"It's true. I have been messaging her lots. I've lost her, and I'm fighting my corner to win her back. She's not going out of her mind. She is very resolute and emotionally strong. I'm the one who's in tears every day."

"Well those are her grounds, and on balance you don't seem to agree with her contentions."

"They're all seriously twisted. Is there anything in there about her having a real affair for a year and a half?"

"No."

Sue seemed to be convinced by him. Over the years she had probably developed a good nose for cleverly disguised lies and embellishments. Like him, she seemed to carry an air of disdain for these allegations. She focussed on the plan ahead.

"We'll state that we don't accept the grounds for divorce but are willing to comply with the request for one. We'll go for a clean break. Fifty-fifty split on the house. She's entitled to half of your pension by law. No ongoing support of any other kind. Ok?"

"Sounds good to me. I'm happy for her to have fifty percent of everything, but I don't want to be supporting her in the future. She's walking away from me after all. If she wants to be with someone else, then he can jolly well pay for her, not me."

"Is there any chance of you getting a job?"

"Not at this point in time. I'm a criminal now, remember?"

"Do you have any dependents living at home?"

"No."

"Have you put the house on the market yet?"

"No."

"You will need to do that. The divorce can't be settled until all the finances are agreed."

"Ok. Just one thing. If the divorce can be avoided, that would be my biggest hope, but if it can't, I just want to be treated fairly, and I want minimal involvement. Ok?"

"Ok Mr Pinkerton. Leave it with me."

Chapter 21

Conversation between them now was only by solicitor's letters. On a practical level they might talk about something of a shared interest, such as which estate agent to use, but that was rare. He would still leave her a letter, just once a month, stating the usual snivelling apology for not being good enough for her, and declaring yet again his undying love, and of course his never-ending hope, but hope seemed to be running out. Shortly after putting the house on the market, they had accepted a good offer on the house from the second couple to view it. The solicitors were making progress both on the house sale and the divorce. The patio got finished and Pablo spent more time on his computer, dancing, and visiting family. But things were not going Delilah's way. Pablo's solicitor was getting her way for a clean-cut divorce, and he was sure that Delilah had absolutely expected some kind of alimony settlement. As that meant no ongoing support for her, she was pushing for the major portion of the proceeds of the house sale. She believed that she was entitled to this because he would no longer be supporting her after the divorce. She had spent a lot of time online looking at houses to buy, and she realised that half the proceeds would not go nearly far enough for her in terms of buying an acceptable home, but his solicitor was sticking to her guns for a fifty-fifty split. Facing such a disaster, Delilah tackled him head on, belligerently, as usual in the kitchen, their only common ground.

"A fifty-fifty split is not fair. You've been the one out working for the past thirty years. You've got the experience and qualifications, so you can get another well-paid job. I've got nothing to market myself with. I've sacrificed any career I might have had to have a family, therefore I should have much more of the capital."

She looked at him as if she made sense.

He looked at her with irritated disbelief.

"You wanted me to get a criminal conviction. What kind of job do you think I can get now with that on my record?"

He waited for a response. It was time for her to get real and stop living in cloud cuckoo land. She cogitated quietly. He continued.

"Am I not equal to you? Has my contribution been less than yours? Who's been paying the fecking mortgage every month for thirty years? Who was the one who did all the renovation work on all the houses we've done up over the years?"

Again he looked at her as if to say: 'wake up and smell the coffee'. She looked in pain. He softened.

"Delilah, I am happy for you to have fifty percent. I want to be fair, but if you fight me for just one percent more, I'll use all my resources if necessary to fight you, even if I end up with nothing. It's a matter of principle. I will not be treated as inferior."

She was a slow thinker, but she must have been seeing the sense in what he was saying, because she tried negotiating.

"I'm only asking for a sixty-forty split."

There had been talk of a seventy-thirty split.

"Maybe you should have thought all this through before you decided to divorce me and fuck off with someone who is already married."

He had always provided for her, totally, and now for her, the thought of providing for herself was beginning to feel positively scary.

"You're so fucking arrogant!" she hissed angrily.

She stormed off. He didn't feel clever. He never wanted to fight or upset her, but this was a matter of principle that he was absolutely determined to stick with. He didn't like the contentious atmosphere at home. It was so disheartening, so he arranged to stay with Tim for a while to see if the break would be beneficial. It was the end of May. He loved spending time with Tim, because he was so upbeat and jolly, and Pablo had complete faith in him as his confidant. He found Tim's place rather claustrophobic. He had to sleep in the lounge. The kitchen was small. The garden was tiny. There were no views. But it was peaceful, and some evenings they went out for a pint and a game of pool, which was fun.

Pablo wondered if he could add to any second thoughts Delilah might be having by asking her for a contribution to the household bills. After all, she was divorcing him, and he was unemployed, and he did want to make the challenge of finding money more real to her. His solicitor thought that this was a very reasonable request under the circumstances, and agreed to moot the subject with Delilah's solicitor. A few days later he got a text from Delilah, saying that she had left him a letter, and asked him to pick it up from their home. Curious. This wasn't like her at all. The last time she had left him a letter had been more than two years earlier at the very beginning of their troubles. He popped home to collect his mail and in particular, her letter. He took it back to Tim's house to read it.

'Pablo, as things are panning out and I very stupidly once again took you at your word, when you emphatically promised over and over again that you would pay for the house until it was sold. Borrowing money from your mum and paying it back from your half. You assured me time and again that it was your responsibility, that you had lost your job and you would honour those payments come what may. So where is fairness now? I am not delaying the house sale in any way so I am not having a free ride as you say. Just trusting you to honour your agreement. How stupid of me. I was advised to get it in writing but I said 'oh no, he's promised. I trust him.'

How wrong of me to trust you again. Where is the fairness now?

I'm thinking that you will always get the better of me, as you always do, in some way. Never mind the fairness. Unfortunately I know what you are like.

You will delay getting a job as you have been doing. Finishing the house has just been an excuse. If you do get a job, you will ensure I don't benefit in any way. 'Work the system' - that's obviously one of your mottos. Where is the fairness now? So, I'm contemplating dropping the divorce suit and not signing contracts for the sale of the house. Then you can get back in control and do whatever you want with me, the house, a job, your money or lack of it. Never mind fairness.

Maybe in the future if I can get myself into a more financially secure place I can reconsider things, but at the moment, with the lack of earnings and you going back on your word, and you working the system, I'm going to have to pull out of the fray and let you do what you want. So, well done you. When I hear from my solicitor, I'll inform her of developments. I'm sure the children will be delighted and you will delight in telling them whatever you feel like telling them as you have done throughout this sorry business. So to you... congratulations.

Delilah.'

He was stunned. He hadn't expected her to capitulate like this. It was so bitter and resentful. He had hoped for something more conciliatory or contrite, or even a little loving. He felt that he couldn't respond positively to it, although he was very excited about the possibility of a change. At the same time, he felt frustrated, because in all honesty, this offered no more than a temporary postponement of the divorce, and only because it didn't suit her at the moment, now that the financial details were being thrashed out in a manner not to her liking. He was afraid that any response he made directly would end up being disastrous. He believed that using a trusted go-between was far more likely to secure a positive outcome, so he phoned Henry.

"Hi Henry. Can we meet for a coffee today at all?"

"Something happened mate?"

"Sort of. I need your opinion on something if you can help me mate."

"Is it urgent?"

"Yes, I suppose so."

"Ok Pablo. 3:00 pm ok?"

"Great. Thanks Henry."

They arranged to meet at a coffee shop in town. Pablo took the letter with him and handed it to Henry as soon as he arrived and sat down. Whilst Henry read it curiously, Pablo went up to the counter and bought his friend a large cappuccino. When he came back to the table, Henry discarded the letter on to the table and exhaled disdainfully.

"You're not taking this seriously, I hope?"

"I'm not sure what to make of it Henry."

"You're not going to want her back if she's just gritting her teeth for the time being, only to go through all this again at a future time when she thinks she can get more out of you?"

He gave a little contemptuous laugh.

"Of course not. I just wanted to know how it comes across to someone else. I don't think I can trust my emotions at the moment, but you've interpreted it the same way as I did."

"What's all this resentment about fairness?"

"I've suggested that she starts paying towards the household bills. After all, she's working part time, and I'm unemployed."

"And she's all uppity about that?"

"Seems so."

"It can't be just that. That wouldn't make her decide not to proceed with a divorce."

"I suspect that her solicitor has told her that she's not going to get anywhere with her crazy idea of getting most of the house equity. That's what's really pissed her off. Seriously, she was expecting sixty or seventy percent of the proceeds."

Henry snorted out a laugh.

"Why should she?" he asked incredulously.

"I think the witchsters have built up her expectations unrealistically."

"So now that she realises that she can't get enough money out of you, she's going to just let you do what you want with her, like a plaything, until she's ready to go again? Surely you don't want her on that basis Pablo?"

"No, of course I don't."

He contemplated the situation sadly, then added

"I can't accept her back on these terms Henry, but it could be the start of something more positive. Would it be ok if I asked her to contact you and Rosalyn to discuss a way forward, using you two as a go-between?"

"Of course mate. We'd be only too happy to help."

"Oh that's great. I think you'd get a lot further forward with her than I would. She doesn't listen to anything I say."

After another ten minutes chatting, they parted company. Henry was a busy man and he had already been very kind to fit in a meeting with Pablo at such short notice. Pablo texted his wife.

'Delilah. Thanks so much for your letter. I appreciate it. However, I don't want to just control you, or do what I want with you because you feel trapped. I don't want to take advantage of you. I've asked Henry and Rosalyn to act as go-betweens. Please arrange to meet them at your convenience. I am sure that they can help us find a more acceptable way forward. I still love you completely. Pablo.'

He was ever hopeful, and he knew that wise old Henry and Rosalyn would be ideal arbitrators. However, a few days went by, and he hadn't heard anything from anybody. He phoned Henry to ask if Delilah had been in touch. No. Henry assured him that he would let him know immediately something happened. Pablo waited patiently. More days passed by. No news. He began to fear that this had been just an angry flash in the pan. He was still at Tim's but was popping home regularly to check his mail. Eventually there was a letter from his solicitor. Apparently, it was business as usual. Divorce was firmly back on. He wondered if he should have done more. Maybe he should have returned home to speak with Delilah directly after all. He was sure that Henry and Rosalyn could have achieved something positive, but she needed to contact them, and she hadn't.

Pablo was so disappointed, his hopes dashed again. He decided to return home. He missed his spacious fresh clean home and the magnificent views. When he was home, it was straight back to the impassive alienation he had left nearly two weeks earlier. Strangely, neither of them mentioned her aberration.

A few weeks later towards the end of June, the decree nisi came through. Delilah's application on the grounds of unreasonable behaviour had been accepted and approved. There was no surprise there, but it was nevertheless very sad. It meant that there was just one more step to go. She would be able to apply for the 'absolute' next, but the law insisted on a six-week cooling off period first. Pablo's reaction was to be upbeat. He already had a few cards on standby for when an occasion justified one. He selected the one with a picture of a beautiful young lady walking down a country lane. The sky was grey and black and looked stormy. The picture was in black and white, apart from the lady's bright clothing and the balloon which she had on a string, trailing in the air behind her. It was bright red and heart shaped. It just all looked so meaningful.

Inside he wrote:

'Delilah, you went out today a married woman. You return divorced, free of love. My love for you remains steadfast and true, never giving up or losing faith. It will endure through this circumstance too. True love lasts forever. You have truly loved me Delilah, but your love had been buried under a burden of ill-feeling. One day, God will heal your heart, and your cherished love will flow again, like a new spring of life. Pablo xxx.'

As usual, the days turned into weeks with no change in their relationship, apart from the end coming closer into sight. He felt that he had nothing to lose by sending her letters more regularly. She had achieved the decree nisi. It was only a matter of time before she could seal the deal, so in his alarm and terror he felt he had to keep reaching out. She avoided any conversation with him, but in mid-July, an opportunity occurred, all their kids were having a weekend away surfing at the seaside. Both Pablo and Delilah wanted to spend a day visiting them, but for various reasons both of them could only be available on the Sunday. Pablo suggested that they actually travel together. Delilah was not happy about that. She suggested that he took a train instead of going in their car with her. Pablo felt that was ridiculous and wasted no time in telling her so. She felt that she had to reluctantly agree. Making him go on the train was too unreasonable. He had after all bought the car, insured it, and paid all its running costs. He was excited. It would be a two hour journey. Surely that would give them a great opportunity to talk. When the journey began, he started a little chit chat. Nothing about them or their situation, but she failed to make any response. She was driving, and kept her attention fixed resolutely on the road ahead. Her lips remained tightly sealed like they really had been zipped together. It didn't take him long to realise that she had made a decision not to get drawn into any conversation whatsoever. So the journey continued in complete silence, apart from the saving grace of the radio. They both had a lovely day with the kids. On the return journey he hoped that the day's events might have softened her, and she might be willing to talk about the kids etc, but just as earlier, her lips were tightly sealed. They had just spent the day with their four children, three daughters-in-law, and two grandchildren, and she was not willing to share some thoughts on the day. He gave up to the stony eerie silence. When they got home and got out of the car she looked angry, and finally spoke.

"Thanks for spoiling my day. I feel like you hijacked it from me."

He looked at her, hurt and so disappointed.

"They're my kids too y'know."

The journeys had been painful, uncomfortable and humiliating for him, and he was sure that it must have been just as bad for Delilah. He made up his mind never to share a journey with her again, no matter what.

He spoke to Tim on the phone most days. The guy was amazing. Devoted and caring in a way Pablo had never experienced before. And he was so down to earth. He challenged Pablo about his letters and cards.

"Why do you keep writing to her, you plonker? It's got you nowhere. It might be doing more harm than good."

"Didn't you keep writing to your wife when she left you?"

"No mate. I knew she was with someone else, although she never admitted that, not even to this day."

"Well, it's different for me Tim. I'm still living with her. I still have hope. She hasn't actually gone yet."

"Yeah, but she's only waiting for the money to come through."

"Whatever. Anyway, there are three good reasons to write."

"Go on."

"Firstly it's to complain."

"About what?"

"The way I'm being treated. The coldness, the betrayal, the robbing us both of our future together."

"Buddy, complaining about it won't change anything."

"I know, but it has to happen for a little while. That was mostly an early phase thing."

"What else?"

"To ask why? Why throw everything away for a crappy affair? Why give up after thirty years together. What have I done wrong? Why can't we put it right ? Seriously, there are so many answers I need."

"Ok, but if she doesn't answer, there's no point in going on and on is there mate? She won't answer. She's got too much to hide."

"That's probably true, but it doesn't stop me asking. I have a right to know. Thirdly, and this is the really important one, it's to offer the olive branch."

"Yeah bruv, but she already knows how you feel. Why keep going on?"

"Look, people judge you according to their own standards, right?"

"I suppose so."

"Ok, so I need to make sure that she knows that her standards are not my standards. She probably expects me to get all bitter and twisted like she is, and I don't want her thinking that, because it's not true. I want her to know that despite

178

everything, I am still here for her. I forgive her, and I still want to put things right between us. I don't want her thinking that I've given up."

"When will you give up?"

"When will she stop being the mother of my children?"

"Mate, that makes sense, but I think you've got to be careful not to annoy her. You don't want to alienate her even more."

"How can I alienate her even more? She's given her heart and all her other bits to another man. She's actually divorcing me and forcing me to sell our home. I don't see how I can make matters any worse."

"Be careful mate, you might be underestimating her."

Early August and the decree-absolute came through the post. A piece of paper telling him that thirty solid years of relationship had evaporated. He left her a card telling her how much he loved her.

'Delilah my darling, today is absolute, and I cannot believe it! What else can I say except to ask you to remember in the future that I do love you very much. I could never love anyone as much as I love you. I may form new friendships, but they will seem shallow. You wrote of Roger saying that wherever you were, you only wanted to be with him forever. That is how I feel about you my love. You have made a deeper spiritual, emotional and sexual union with another man, and you have vowed to me that you cannot break that bond. I believe that in time that bond will be broken, and you will realise that our love was real and special, and that it can still grow and mature. I hope that your new dreams of solitude or new lovers will prove to be built on sand, and that I will prove to be your rock. I hope that your new experiences will eventually cause you to value my love, devotion and support. You are my life, the mother and creator of my children. You are my history, the song in my heart, and the pulse in my veins. Only you are the apple of my eye. You're forcing me to move on alone, lost, half-dead, but no matter where I go or whatever I do, I will be waiting for you because you are truly the only love in my life. You always have been, you always will be. All my love, Pablo.'

She had yet to send off one more form simply asking for the decree absolute to be finalised. At that point a certificate of divorce would be issued, and they would be officially divorced. She could do that any time she wanted to now, except the house would need to be sold first and the proceeds legally divided up, and that hadn't been done yet. Also her solicitor would also have to arrange for his police pension to be split, and as far as he knew, that hadn't been done yet either.

Chapter 22

The house sale could be just weeks away. Delilah was as distant and resolute as ever, and Pablo started making plans. He would have plenty of money in the bank from the sale, so there was no pressure just to get a job just for the sake of it. He was more concerned with finding a new direction in life. He felt that some time abroad, distancing himself from the situation would be healthy, so he enrolled in a four-week course in the south of France to qualify to teach English as a foreign language. He had no idea what the opportunities to get a job were like, but the possibility of working abroad, somewhere hot, teaching what he already knew well, was appealing, and the course with new people would provide him with a much-needed distraction after the trauma of the past two years. As soon as the solicitor confirmed the date of completion, he organised somewhere to stay convenient for the course in France, and he paid the course fee. He would drive there in his little car, which he would be taking back from Sarah, and he would be taking with him only whatever worldly goods he could squeeze into a small hatchback, Photos, clothes, shoes and not much else.

He had already told Delilah that she could have all the contents of their house. He was not attached to things. They were not the important bits in life. He considered it wise to move on unencumbered by needless possessions. She was only too happy to have everything. She wanted to make a home from home. He arranged for his precious tools to go into storage only because he couldn't possibly get them in his tiny car. He hoped that one day, he might need them again. One day. They were a part of his identity. They were the things that he needed in normal circumstances. As far as he could tell, Delilah was still looking for a house to buy or rent, but she wasn't saying anything to him about it.

During these weeks of a beautiful late hot August, the end was clearly nigh, and they both knew it. The atmosphere between them was chilly. Communication was virtually nil. One day, she coldly and boldly informed him that she would be driving their daughter to university at the beginning of October. Fait accompli. The matter obviously wasn't up for discussion, but he didn't mind. After the debacle where they both shared the trip to see the kids at the coast the previous month, driving Sarah to uni' had to be done by just one of them, and certainly, not both together. He was resigned to the breakup actually occurring now. They were too far down the road, but he still wrote to her copiously. He was a desperate broken man, appealing for some kindness, or some other miracle. He tried to make each missive original, sometimes veering into the abstract.

'Delilah, you started walking down a strange path two years ago. That path became a gully with close sides, then it became a tunnel-like chasm. The sides are now much higher than you, as it goes on getting deeper and darker and narrower. You can't turn around now. It's easier just to carry on walking downhill. There are people behind you, pushing you, blocking your escape. They promise you that there is light at the end of the tunnel. They lie. It just gets longer, deeper, and darker. I stay alongside you, but high up above the tunnel. I can still hear your lovely voice, but it's getting harder and harder to see you properly. I call down to you every day: 'Delilah, my lovely wife, I am reaching down to you. Take my hand. I am strong enough to pull you out. I can still reach you. Join me up here on the flat ground, in the light. We can go anywhere you want, together again. Please my love, take my hand. We could be touching, joining, sharing, supporting, believing, hoping, planning , caressing, loving, dancing, living, enjoying .... Why not? Are you still listening to 'everybody'?'

He was talking to a person, who in regard to him, was deaf and blind.

At the end of August he learned from one of the kids that she was planning to rent the stone and thatched cottage that was literally their next door neighbour. It was down a long concrete track through a field. You could see it clearly from their house. It was at the bottom of the valley, about two hundred yards away. It had been empty for two years and was apparently in a state of disrepair, and she had arranged to rent it cheaply because of that. Work would have to be carried out on it whilst she was there, especially on the thatched roof which was leaking. He admired her tenacity to stay in their beautiful valley. A little while later, she announced that she would be moving out the weekend after next, and that their sons would be helping her to make the move. He was glad that family were helping her with the practical arrangements, but of course he was sad to see the finality looming towards him very darkly and surely over the horizon.

Maybe because her plan was almost completed, she got sloppy with her phone. One evening she left it out in the hallway whilst she went into her bedroom. He noticed it immediately as he walked by it because it was normally hidden away. He naughtily picked it up and flipped it open. It wasn't locked. He flicked through the text messages. What he saw made him feel like he was about to convulse. The adrenalin raced through his veins. His heart pumped harder and faster. The enormity of it. The offence of it. The temerity! His heart was racing, yet at the same time it seemed to become so heavy. One moment it was sagging in the pit of his stomach, then it felt like it wanted to escape his body, racing, seeking more space than his body could provide. Mon Ami! Again! Messages about clandestine meetings. Once or twice a week. Regular. Ongoing. Not much text, but lots of 'love you' and kisses. He couldn't believe it. He suddenly realised that all his efforts during the past nine months had been completely thwarted again by that loathsome, reprehensible, shameless, piece of shit. Still! How could she? They promised!

She was in her bedroom. He walked in, phone in hand. She turned to fiercely order him immediately out, but then she saw his outstretched arm, mobile in hand. That stopped her dead. Her body softened. He examined her face. This would tell him a lot. Her features all seemed to narrow A look of determination and defiance seeped visibly across her face, yet the way she looked away from him betrayed a hint of shame and embarrassment. As before, her face seemed to drain of blood, but not nearly to the same extent as last time. Getting caught out for the second time was not nearly so bad. He didn't say anything. He just looked at her incredulously, as if lost for words. She spoke quietly.

"We did stop. I didn't intend to try to see him again. You won't believe this, I know, but I had to contact him. I'd enquired about a job, and an interview was arranged with a lady called Evita. That's such an unusual name, I had to check with Roger that it wasn't his wife. It was, and so I didn't go for the interview."

He waited. No further explanation.

"So because you made a phone call about something innocuous, obviously you just had to start fucking him again?"

No reply. She had no other excuses. She had been caught out, and she knew it.

He left the room momentarily, then returned with a very powerful weapon in his hand; The cordless landline phone. She stood there, frozen to the spot, wondering what he would do this time. He tapped Mon Ami's number into it and chucked her mobile onto her bed contemptuously. The last time he confronted Roger was in person, eight months earlier, and Delilah had not been privy to their conversation. This time he wanted her to hear every word. He put the phone on loudspeaker. She could hear it ringing.

"Hello" Roger answered.

"Roger, you just couldn't stop could you?"

There was the briefest of pauses.

"Pablo, it's not what you think" he protested feebly.

"You've got your own wife , but you still had to screw mine too, even after you promised me to my face that you'd stop. And I believed that you'd have at least a modicum of decency and stop screwing her behind my back, but no, you're much too big a cunt."

"Pablo, I'm really sorry. She got back in touch with me."

"You spineless, immoral, loathsome, maggot. I don't want to hear your feeble, pathetic excuses."

"Pablo, please, I can assure you it won't happen again."

"I've heard that bullshit before you disgusting, nauseous lowlife. It won't wash. Well you've got what you wanted Roger, My wife. She's divorcing me so she can be with you, her true love. She's giving up everything with me and my family because she loves you so much and wants to start a fantastic new life with you."

"That ain't going to happen Pablo."

"Oh yes it is you weedy fucker. It's time for you to take responsibility for your actions, you pathetic cunt. In just a few days' time she's moving out of here into a beautiful little chocolate-box cottage just down the field, and you're going to join her, you obnoxious, contemptible, piece of shit, for a wonderful new life together. You have my blessing."

"That ain't going to happen Pablo" he repeated lamely.

Pablo answered forcefully.

"Oh yes it is Roger. She's giving everything up so she can be with you. So now, you come on down with your little pink suitcase, and your overactive dick, and you look after her properly. You pay her bills. You make sure she's clothed and fed. You pay for her car. You make sure she's happy because obviously I can't do it. You don't just fuck her in the backseat of your car, you take responsibility for everything else too. I don't suppose you know what I mean when I use the word responsibility do you, you cheating fucker?"

"Pablo, I've got my own wife to look after, and it's her that I love."

"No, no, no, Rodge, you don't love her. If you did you wouldn't have been screwing my wife for the past two and a half years. Obviously. Get real. It's time for you to do the right thing you shirking devious bastard. You leave your wife as you have been promising Delilah for the past two years that you would do, and you come down here and you look after her, properly. You'll make a great couple. You both get a kick out of fucking other people's spouses behind your own spouse's back. You're ideally suited to each other."

Even as he was scolding Roger he was surprised that he hadn't put the phone down on him yet. He sounded weak and alarmed, but he kept taking the verbal punishment and abuse. Pablo presumed that he hoped that there was a tiny chance that he would get it all out of his system, and leave it at that. Not a chance. He looked at Delilah standing just a few feet away, still frozen to the spot. He actually felt sorry for her. Perhaps finally she was realising what a complete fuck-up she had made. She looked almost tearful. What she was hearing must have been so painful for her. Her dream was evaporating before her very ears. Pablo just couldn't believe that she had actually believed in this weedy feeble excuse of a man. He continued hauling Roger over the coals. He was enjoying this.

"Do you know what she said to the kids last Christmas Roger? That she had found a deep love with you, much deeper than anything she'd ever had with me. I've got no chance of getting her back Rodge, and it's because of you. She's actually told me to my face that she can't go back on her commitment to you, you despicable dog. Her commitment!"

"I've got my own wife Pablo."

"I know that you dick, but you seem to have forgotten that once or twice a week at least for the past two and a half years. You must love my wife very much."

"No Pablo, I don't love her. I told you before, it was just a fling."

"But Roger, if it was just a fling, you would never have risked carrying on the affair after you were found out, you snivelling, deplorable, lying creep. You've made her think that you love her. She really believes it."

"No Pablo, I don't love her."

Pablo looked defiantly at Delilah. She looked like she was grinding her teeth slightly. She was looking steadfastly at the floor. He had said enough.

"Just get your pathetic arse down here on Saturday. That is when she'll be expecting you, and if you don't show up of your own accord, I'll come and get you and drag you down here where you belong, you sick fucker!"

He terminated the call before that worm started begging for mercy or trying to find out what he intended to do next. He wanted him to sweat again. He gave Delilah one last shocked, incredulous look, then walked away. In the morning he would phone Evita. Many months earlier whilst rummaging around Delilah's bedroom, he had found a landline number on a scrap of paper. He knew where the area code related to, and he was pretty sure that Roger lived in that area. He had made a note of it just in case it might come in handy one day. Tomorrow morning he would find out if his hunch was right. If not, he would somehow find some way of getting hold of her.

He didn't sleep well. His mind and emotions churned constantly. In the morning he waited for Delilah to go out. Then he phoned that number. A woman's voice answered in an even tone.

"Hello?"

"Hello. Is that Evita?"

"Yes."

Bingo. He felt rather joyous.

"Evita, you don't know me. I work with your husband. My name is Pablo Pilkington."

He paused to let her query him.

"I've heard of you" she said quietly.

"Look Evita, I've got something I think you should know about, but it's going to be upsetting for you. Do you want to hear what I have to say?"

He didn't know if she would treat this as a hoax call or something like that, but her instincts led her to trust him. Perhaps she had been here before.

"Go on" she said quietly. She already sounded resigned.

"Roger is dealing with a complaint that was made against me over two and a half years ago. For most of that time, he's been shagging my wife behind my back. I'm sorry."

He listened for her reaction. All he could hear was quiet sobbing. After a short while she asked him to go on.

"I initially found out about it at Christmas last year. I found her mobile phone and discovered texts between them about their trysts. I immediately confronted her, and she readily admitted it. She told me that she loved him and that he was divorcing you. The next morning I visited Roger at his office. He also admitted it, but he promised to stop, and I left it at that because I was hoping to win her back. Last night I got hold of her phone again. Found the same thing. Loads more texts about meetings and how much they love each other. They've both admitted it again, but this time it's different. She's divorcing me. There's nothing I can do, Evita. I've lost her, and I have to accept that, but you might want a say in what happens next for you."

She cried some more and then composed herself in commendable fashion, and spoke with surprising aplomb.

184

"'I'll talk to Roger before I decide what I'm going to do. I'll call you back in a couple of days."

"Fine. Thank you. I'm sorry to be the bearer of bad news. By the way, have you two ever contemplated divorce?"

She answered flatly but certainly.

"No, never. I'm grateful that you decided to tell me. Thank you. I'll let you know what I decide."

When Delilah returned, he didn't tell her about the call to Evita. He wanted her to sweat it out too. She offered him no further explanation about her behaviour. Everything was in place for her to actually move into her new home a week later, and the emotional wall was getting even bigger and bigger. The completion of the house sale was scheduled for a month's time. Then there would be no going back. Yet she looked perturbed. Perhaps she really had been actually relying on Roger in some way. She wouldn't want to be on her own, but presumably her future was now in the balance depending on Evita's decision.

As promised, Evita phoned him back a couple of days later.

"I have discussed all this with Roger, and we have decided to try and mend our marriage. He won't be in contact with your wife ever again. He has deleted all contact details for her. He told me that she threw herself at him and it was nothing serious for him. Anyway, I don't want to hear from either of you ever again. This is the last contact we will have, Ok?"

"Sounds all good to me. Thank you."

Well, that was short and sweet and to the point. Later when Delilah came home, he told her that he'd heard from Evita, and that she had reined Roger in, completely and absolutely. He got a great deal of satisfaction telling her that. She looked embarrassed and hurt, but she said nothing. A steely look came over her face. He added rather sarcastically

"I think it's nice how some couples make a real effort to overcome their difficulties. He's got a good wife there."

He was genuinely jealous. Delilah made no comment. Her mind was made up no matter what. She wasn't going to lose face at this late stage.

During the second week of September, she moved out. It was a Saturday. She left quite early to go get her new place sorted. All their sons came down to execute the move. Both Pablo and Delilah appreciated seeing them and a few of their friends who were helping with the move. Pablo himself was present during the proceedings, but as a matter of pride did not engage in assisting her move. He was technically opposed to it and felt it would have been wrong to help to facilitate it, but he didn't mind his sons helping out their mother. She had left him a card. His heart pounded faster as he wondered what she had written. It had a picture of a poppy field on the front. Inside it said;

'Dear Pablo, like the poppies on this card - used for remembering - I do remember the good times we had together, and will be eternally thankful for the wonderful children we have. I understand that the agony for you is huge. I have betrayed you for which I am truly sorry. I do forgive you and don't feel that you owe me anything. It is with much sadness that our relationship has taken this course - the loss of the dream. I want to say thank you and wish you all the best. Delilah.'

That was sweet. He felt like a little of the old, real Delilah was showing through, but if she was truly sorry, why not make up? Why stick to the vendetta?

By the end of the day, he was all alone. Sarah was still next door the other way. The boys had all gone home. The house was almost empty of things. She had left him enough things to sleep on and cook with. The last few things would also go down to her new place when he moved out on completion. That would be three weeks later. Then he would be off to France for a while, totally unsure of what he would actually do when the course was completed. One day at a time. Strangely, Delilah would still pop round occasionally, and without notice, mostly to use the computer, and sometimes to collect vegetables from the vegetable garden.

On one of these occasions she told Pablo that she had changed her mind about driving Sarah to university. It was too far away, and she didn't like driving long distances.

"I'd like you to come with us and share the driving" she announced.

He was surprised at her request because of the way she had behaved the last time they drove together. He also remembered very well the vow he had made to himself as a result, and he was going to stick by it. That's what vows are for. Sticking to.

"You told me that you wanted to do it on your own."

"Well, I've changed my mind. It's too far."

"I'm happy to drive her myself, or for you to drive her yourself, but after last time when you refused to talk to me for the entire journey, there and back, I vowed never to do that again."

He knew that this would displease her but he was also making sure she knew that he was only being awkward because of her unreasonable behaviour. She was not pleased.

"Can't you think of someone else for a change apart from yourself. What about Sarah?"

"Like I said, I am more than happy to drive her if she wants me to. It's simply that I'm not going in a car with you again. Last time you made me feel terrible, and I'm not going to subject myself to that kind of abuse once more."

He looked at her defiantly. She looked at him contemptuously.

"You're such an arrogant prick."

She stormed off out of their house, back to her empty love nest.

Chapter 23

Life felt very empty for Pablo. The house was so empty. Not even a dog. He had fond memories of the place. He had enjoyed transforming the house from a dowdy three -bedroom bungalow, into a resplendent five bedroom split-level des-res. Now he had to shake off the notion that he would end his days there in glorious seclusion, so proud of his achievements, with his devoted wife by his side, interspersed with regular comfortable visits and stays by the family. Now the future held nothing but a sense of loss and uncertainty. He would just go and do the TEFL course and then see where that led. Essentially, for the time being, he wanted to be busy when he had to leave his home.

With only one week to go before the house sale completed during the beginning of October, Delilah came round to see him. It was tea time. He was in the garage, boxing up and labelling tools for storage. The garage was huge, big enough to house six cars, and he had a lot of boxes. As soon as she walked in, he could easily tell it spelled trouble. She moved quickly and purposefully, almost aggressively. He stood still and looked at her quizzically. He already knew that Troy had been down to hers for the day and that Sarah had joined them, mainly to catch up with her brother during his visit. Hadn't she had a lovely day with her two youngest children? She spoke fiercely.

"You couldn't make an allowance could you? Now Sarah is really upset. She was in tears. She feels so let down."

He didn't know what this had to do with him.

"Why?"

"Because I told her that I couldn't drive her to uni' after all."

He could see that Sarah becoming upset had really upset her too. Really, she was angry about the situation, but she wanted to take it out on him. Somehow, it was his fault.

"And that's my fault?"

"Yes. You weren't prepared to help us out."

"I told you why that was."

He didn't need to explain himself again. He had made his reasoning quite clear before. She seemed to be getting quite agitated, and instinctively he walked to the back of the garage as if to make it demonstrably obvious that he didn't want to engage in any kind of confrontation. He felt like he had been walking on eggshells all year long, and he had done that amazingly well. He hadn't transgressed her rules sufficiently for her to carry out her threat to have him arrested. He hadn't put his arm around her once, although he had told her occasionally that he still loved her very much. He didn't want to cock it all up now that they were in separate houses and he was relatively safe. She continued to hurl abuse at him about his selfishness and arrogance. For the twenty eight years that they had been happily married, he had never seen her angry or upset. Now that she was pursuing a much happier, more fulfilling life elsewhere, becoming extremely angry or upset was becoming commonplace, and it unsettled him. He really wanted to give her a big hug and comfort her, and remind her of his undying love for her, but he knew that was out of the question. That would definitely be a serious transgression. She began to actually sob and wilt. His heart reached out to her. He felt so sorry for her. He walked back to her wondering if he might be allowed to give her a loving hug, just this once. He stood a few feet away and looked at her compassionately asking her with his body language if she wanted a hug. Initially her eyes were shut, as she sobbed. Then she opened them, looked at him, and sort of exploded. She sprang up suddenly with gusto, and with fire from deep within her seemed to shoot out of her eyes. She grabbed a small metal caravan sink that lay conveniently close to her on top of a pile of boxes, she raised it over her head and stared at him half-crazed. In that moment, he saw that she hated him. He wasn't scared. He was deeply sad. She so wanted to hurt him, but she was half his size. It shocked him that his beloved wife wasn't content just to break his heart, she wanted to break his head open too. He instinctively gave her a small shove to one shoulder, just to remind her of his size and strength, but he had absolutely no desire to hurt her.

"Don't even think about it" he advised quietly but firmly.

She looked at him frustratedly, as the impossibility of a physical fight with him sank surely in. She dropped the sink and slowly slumped down the column of boxes behind her, sitting on her haunches. Her head dropped forward. She was crying. He was also frustrated, but only because he wanted to love her, and he wasn't allowed to. Instead he chose to remind her of the real reason for all this upset. He walked away backwards in order to leave the garage and the danger zone, repeating loudly several times

"You've got to stop fucking Roger!"

He exited the garage and went indoors, leaving her to compose herself. A few minutes later he observed her through a window leaving the garage and going home. He felt terrible. He just didn't know how to properly reach out to her in her time of need. He had never known her to be distraught like this before. A little later he texted her to say how sorry she was that she had become so upset and he only wanted to help her, but that couldn't include going in the car with her on a long journey.

The next day, he was awoken early by the doorbell. It was still dark! He looked at his watch. Five in the morning! Immediately the adrenalin raced through him. He instinctively knew his former colleagues were there to arrest him. He lay quietly still. He felt offended that they had turned out so early. That kind of treatment was supposed to be for offenders who were hard to locate or who regularly evaded capture. He, by contrast, was a sitting duck. He refused to answer the door or respond in any way, not at this time in the morning. After a few more rings, they left. He was flabbergasted. How could she do this to him? She had come round to make trouble for him, not the other way round. How could she be so spiteful? He struggled to believe that she was trying to get him into trouble with the law. He knew that the officers would be back, not necessarily the same day, and he would have to go through the stress of not knowing when they would return, and then the embarrassing process of justifying himself. He didn't have to wait long. They returned by midmorning. As he sat at his computer, he observed the squad car drive into his driveway. This time, at a reasonable time, he answered the door. One of the officers was a former colleague, and he wasted no time.

"I'm sorry Pablo, but we're here to arrest you for assaulting your wife yesterday." He was cautioned and led to the car.

"You've got to be joking. She assaulted me. All I did was give her a tiny push to bring her to her senses."

"You can tell them all about that in interview Pablo. We've only been sent to arrest you."

The journey to the custody centre at the central station took about half an hour. They spent little time talking. Pablo was feeling aggrieved and apprehensive, not sociable. On arrival at the police station he was led into the custody suite like a common criminal, and was laboriously processed onto the custody sergeant's computer. He was searched, booked in, asked lots of questions about his health, fingerprinted, photographed, and then dumped in an empty cell. He declined the offer of a solicitor. He had done nothing wrong. He had nothing to hide, and he felt that he would do a better job of defending himself than a solicitor would. The cell was bare and pure concrete. There was nothing to do, see, or listen to.

The next time an officer came to the wicket in the heavy steel door to check on him, he asked for something to read. He was bluntly told that they didn't have anything. He so wished that he had brought a book with him, but at the time of arrest his mind wasn't that focussed. The boredom was almost intolerable. He lay on the bench for what must have been well over two hours before finally he was fetched out for an interview. He was handed over to a man in plain clothes, aged about forty, who identified himself as a civilian investigator called Phil. He was led shoeless into one of several interview rooms. Obviously he was totally familiar with the interview process; the recording machine; the tapes. Again he was cautioned, and he declined the offer of a solicitor. He just wanted to get this thing over with.

Phil reminded him as to why he had been arrested and gave him the opportunity to speak. Pablo wasted no time in explaining the events of the past two years, all about the breakdown of his marriage and Delilah's affair. He made a special point of identifying Roger, his Federation Rep', as his wife's lover. He pointed out how angry Delilah was about him effectively bringing the affair to an end just a few weeks earlier by outing Roger to his wife. He went over the previous day's events in minute detail. He couldn't see how he could be charged with an offence because it was his word against Delilah's. There were no witnesses, and there were no injuries because he hadn't assaulted her apart from virtually holding her back as she prepared to attempt to split his head open. When he finished his long honest discourse Phil asked him a few routine questions, which he happily answered, and then Phil read out Delilah's statement.

Her account was that she simply came round to see him to ask him if he would accompany her in a few weeks' time to drive Sarah to university. She said that he then became agitated and aggressive and pushed her over. She then ran out of the garage and later that evening went to her sister Sirena's house. It was Sirena who was alarmed about Delilah being upset, and it was her who called the police. Delilah actually stated in her statement that when an officer arrived, she was told that they could only arrest Pablo if the alleged assault had resulted in an injury, no matter how minor. She and Sirena then went into a room in private where Delilah stripped and they looked for any potential marks. Apparently they found a small bruise on one of her legs, and alleged that he must have caused that. Pablo was shocked; what a contrivance! How obviously and blatantly disingenuous! The alleged injury didn't even marry up with her embroidered account of what happened. The only thing he was pleased about was that Delilah actually said in her statement that throughout their thirty plus years together he had never once used any violence against her. This allegation was the first and only instance. He thought that she said that to balance her guilt in making a false allegation against him. He mused on the bit about Sirena.

"Now that makes sense. I really didn't think that Delilah would have reported me. One of the witchsters put her up to it. Now it all makes sense."

He pointed out the factual errors in her statement and Phil had no more questions for him.

The interview ended and he was placed back in his cell. All the information now had to be sent off to the Crown Prosecution Service for a decision. That could take three or four hours. In the meantime he had to be locked up like a rabid dog. Some considerable time later, part of a face appeared at the small wicket in the door. A man identified himself as the custody inspector and stated that he was doing a review of his detention, and he kindly informed Pablo that he would be kept in custody until the CPS came back with a decision.

"Why is it taking so long?" Pablo enquired with obvious frustration in his voice.

"The CPS want more evidence, and an officer is trying to get that for them."

"What do you mean more evidence? There is no more evidence."

"I don't know. We'll have to wait and see."

This truly perplexed him. He asked for the time. He had been there for six hours. He asked for something to read. He was told again that they didn't have anything. He was very annoyed that he was supposed to amuse himself for hours on end in a bleak, barren, empty cell with absolutely nothing to do.

"Surely you have got some reading material out there?"

The inspector replied in bland illogical fashion.

"If we supplied reading material, we would have to be able to supply it in every language of the world, and obviously that's impossible."

"That's so fekin' illogical. This is England. Surely it would not be unreasonable to have some English reading material available."

"That would not be fair."

"But locking me up for hours and hours on end whilst some office-waller seems unable to decide on my fate is fair is it? Even though I've done nothing wrong?"

"Is there anything else I can help you with?"

"You said that like you've actually helped me with something."

The wicket closed, and Pablo was left alone. He was occasionally provided with a hot drink or water, and at some stage received a burger and chips in a mustard coloured polystyrene carton. The boredom was excruciating. He wasn't tired enough to sleep. It was daytime, and he hadn't expected to be there for so long after the interview had ended. Eventually the cell door opened and he was called out. He asked for the time. 11:00 pm. That was outrageous. He had been in solitary confinement for most of twelve hours. For what? He was led up to the custody sergeant behind his counter and computer. He actually used to work alongside this particular sergeant, but they both acted as if they didn't know each other.

"I'm afraid it's not good news" he announced, possibly slightly sympathetically.

"You're joking. They've got nothing on me."

"Well, I'm afraid that they want you charged with common assault."

"What a fucking waste of time. There's no way a court will find me guilty given what actually happened."

"That's for you to prove."

He was formally charged and released on bail to court with conditions not to go near his wife.

"She should be told to stay away from me. She's the one who comes round to my place to cause trouble. I've been doing my best to stay out of her way for the past year."

The bail date was for three weeks ahead.

"I can't be there for that date. I will be in the south of France. I'm doing a four week course there starting in a weeks' time."

"I'm sorry, I can't bail you for more than three weeks' time."

"I can't come back all the way from the south of France just to spend a minute pleading not guilty."

"I'm sorry, but you'll have to."

He was feeling that nothing was going right for him at the moment. He was very frustrated, but above all, he was very relieved to be about to get out of custody. Being locked up with nothing to do was awful. He was given his phone back and was discharged into the street. He had no money on him. He got straight on his phone.

"Fatboy?"

"Alright buddy? What's up?"

"I need you to pick me up?"

"Ok bruv. Are you at home?"

"No, I'm outside the police station in the city."

He immediately burst out laughing.

"Don't tell me you've got yourself into trouble!"

"I'll tell you all about it when you pick me up. Can you come straight away, Fatboy? I just want to get home."

"Of course mate. Don't tell me you got nicked!"

He laughed some more.

"I need to move. I'll be walking along the main road in your direction. Look out for me."

"Ok mate. See you soon."

Knowing that Tim was coming to his rescue gave him a comfortable sense of relief. It was great to have a friend like Tim. This particular little nightmare was nearly over for the time being. He walked energetically in the cool of the early night to work his frustrations out of his system.

Chapter 24

The south of France was still warm and sunny, and made a great change from the cloudy cold weather he had left behind. His little overloaded car had made the long journey quite happily. He was now staying in a very old extensive rambling townhouse near the sea. It's slight claim to fame was that Napoleon himself had stayed there occasionally during his many escapades. It was billed as a stay-with-a-family home, and as such he was hoping to brush up on his schoolboy French. In actual fact it proved to be no such thing. The house was divided up into family quarters and guest quarters, and there was virtually no contact between the guests and the French occupants, who were just two elderly sisters. They could barely speak any English anyway, and he hardly ever saw them. There was only one other guest in the guest suite, and he was also English, so the French language skills remained completely un-honed.

His own house sale had gone through without a hiccup a few days earlier, and both he and Delilah now had a considerable lump of cash in the bank. Exactly the same amount each, of course, to the penny. The only matter holding up the finalisation of their divorce was his ex-employer taking it's time to confirm pension details. Once that matter was confirmed, Delilah could send off that final tiny letter saying: 'please finalise the demise of my marriage'.

On the first day of the TEFL course he met the other twelve students. They were mostly quite young, and all English apart from one French girl. The teacher was herself French, yet she put all the English students to shame with her incredibly thorough knowledge of English grammar. As with any course, the participants formed a bond over the coming weeks through their shared goals and participation alongside each other. It was all very chummy. For the first time in just over two years, Pablo didn't cry every day. Only on most days, as he still contemplated his lost love. This was progress. He wrote to the court which he was bailed to attend, explaining his circumstances and asked for permission for his appearance to be delayed until after his course finished at the end of the first week of November. About a week later he received confirmation from the court that his proposal was acceptable, and he was given a new date to attend a few days after the end of his course. That was very helpful. The irony of course, was that Delilah wanted him right out of her life, and as far away as possible, and consequently he had gone abroad, hoping particularly to avoid any further complications with her, and yet now he was being required to return to her doorstep because of her spitefulness and a futile court case.

The course was enjoyable, and the weather remained warm and sunny throughout the entire four weeks that he was there. He amused himself in his spare time exploring the local area, and phoning his kids. He even went to a few salsa dancing lessons, but he found them more challenging than the modern jive that he was familiar with. During one of his evening forays he came across a kind of Hell's Angels bikers club. He was highly bemused as he watched big heavy bearded black-leather-clad biker-men arrive at the club and greet each other with kisses on both cheeks. It seemed incongruous.

He missed his kids, and his two granddaughters. The longer he was away, the more clearly he saw that his future was not going to be abroad. He couldn't allow his marital divorce to also divorce him from his own children and grandchildren as well. Maybe having to return so soon for the court case was a blessing in disguise. He had no choice about returning very soon. The course flew by. He got his certificate, as did all the other candidates, and each one was responsible for seeking out suitable teaching posts, which could be anywhere in the non-English-speaking world. His new colleagues were excitedly talking about the prospects of finding positions in various other countries. Some were happy to seek work there in the south of France, but he was simply planning to return to England to face criminal charges, yet again. He duly returned home, putting his poor little car through another one thousand mile journey, except that he no longer had a home to return to.

When he arrived back in England, he phoned some old friends, Alan and Margaret, a couple whom he and Delilah had been very close to during the many years they were all raising children together in the same locality. He hadn't seen them for about ten years since he and Delilah had moved away. They still lived in his old town, in the same house that he remembered. He explained his situation to them and rather cheekily asked if he could stay in one of their spare bedrooms for the time being. Margaret seemed fine with the idea, but Alan was reluctant. He told Pablo that he could only stay for up to two weeks whilst he found some longer term accommodation, but no more. Pablo was grateful for their assistance, although in all honesty, he was surprised and disappointed that Alan was being so stingy with his hospitality. He measured people by his own standards, and was often sorely disappointed. At least he had somewhere to call home for two weeks. It was about an hour and a half away from where Delilah currently lived, and two hours from the court.

The first day there, he busied himself on his phone. He had a catch up with his solicitor about the divorce. He had informed her of his arrest the day after he was released, and she had recommended a good criminal lawyer to him. Conveniently this criminal lawyer worked from an office in the same city as the court he had to appear in. Her name was Rebecca. The second morning at Alan's, he had to leave early to attend court. It was not the court he had attended for his data-protection case. It was the court local to his old home. He got there before 10:00 am and sat in the waiting area feeling rather weary of this pointless exercise that had so comprehensively interrupted his bigger plans. He knew that the case didn't have the legs to stand on, and this was only an administrative hearing anyway. The court would simply hear his plea, and as he would be pleading not guilty. He had given Delilah one guilty plea, and he wasn't going to do that again. A new date would be set for a hearing in a few weeks' time. There was all the usual activity going on around him; security guards searching people on entry, ancient ushers swanning around in their dusty old robes, solicitors emerging briefly out of private offices then disappearing again for long periods, and several groups of chatty young people either involved in cases, or supporting one of their number involved in a case. In due course he was summoned to enter the dock. Three middle-aged magistrates sat on the bench behind the clerk. They all examined him silently through their dark-rimmed spectacles as he stood there, as if trying to glean some insight into him. He was asked to confirm his name by the clerk, who then read out the assault charge against him.

"How do you plead, guilty or not guilty?"

He answered loudly and defiantly.

"Not guilty."

The clerk then looked towards the CPS solicitor and asked him if he would be ready to present the prosecution case at the next hearing. The Solicitor confirmed that he would be, and a date was fixed for two weeks' time on the 17th of November for a full hearing. Pablo was grateful that the new hearing was only two weeks away. The intervening time would be just dead time for him. He was released on bail with a warning of the consequences if he failed to appear. He had just driven over one thousand miles from the south of France to appear today. He was hardly likely to not attend on the next occasion from just two hours away. He left, returned to his car, and drove to the office of his new solicitor, Rebecca, with whom he had made a loose appointment for later that morning. He had to wait for half an hour before she was free, and then he had her undivided attention. She was a lot younger than his other solicitor, Sue. She was aged about late-thirties. She seemed knowledgeable, confident and friendly. He liked her. He briefly described the circumstances of the demise of his marriage and then explained the events leading up to his arrest. She asked him some questions, which he readily answered. She seemed to really believe in him, and was clearly very sceptical of Delilah's account. They talked about fees, and he had to sign a contract with her firm. She explained that she would be presenting a defence of reasonable defence to an assault by his wife. She asked if they could undermine her story of coming into the garage to make an arrangement to drive Sarah to university.

"Easily." he replied confidently.

"Sarah can testify that we'd had that conversation weeks earlier, and that on the day in question, she was upset because her mum had gone back on her word about driving her."

"Do you think she will be willing to attend court, and effectively testify against her mother's account?"

"Undoubtedly. My kids know what I am like, and they are horrified by what mum's doing. Sarah would definitely want to help protect me."

"Well, hopefully, we won't need her. I don't really want to drag your daughter into this."

She then considered another aspect of the case.

"In order to charge you they needed additional evidence to show a pattern of domestic violence, and they got a statement from one of Delilah's sisters. Do you know what that was about?"

"Total bull. She gave no specifics, just alleged that there had been lots of incidents over the years. I've got four kids who can testify that there's no truth in that. She probably felt obliged to make something up to help the case, as it was her who got me nicked in the first place. Anyway, Delilah herself put in her statement that I have never in all the time she has known me ever used or threatened violence against her."

"Really? That's in her statement?"

"Yep. You'll see it for yourself when you get all the papers from the CPS."

She shook her head slightly, probably in disbelief that this case had ever been prosecuted.

"Ok. I don't think we're going to have any problems. I'll see you in court on the 17th. Can you be there for 9:00 am so we have time to go over things?"

"Of course."

He walked out feeling much happier. It was always a nice feeling when you passed most of your responsibility for something onto someone else. He was very confident in her support.

He had little to do for the next two weeks. During the days, he researched the stock market and closely followed the live movements each day, determined to build up an understanding of how, why, and when the markets moved. He was convinced that over time one could build up an intuitiveness about the markets which could be very lucrative. Apart from that, he had to put feelers out for somewhere else to stay. Fortunately, some old friends with contacts arranged for him to be able to stay in a small self-contained unit at a nearby church conference centre. That was very kind of them, and he was grateful. He was given no ultimatums as to when he would have to leave, so he had time to find something longer term. He would move there when his time with Alan and Margaret came to an end.

He touched base with his best friend.

"Fatboy, how are you?"

"Fine mate, yeah fine. How are you buddy? Been locked up again yet?"

He laughed loudly. He was very amused by all this arrest and court stuff.

"I'm fine mate. Just been to court, to plead not guilty. Now I've got to hang around for two weeks for the trial."

"How are you feeling buddy?"

He always said that with such genuine feeling.

"Yeah, I'm ok mate. It's so weird though, being completely out of touch with Delilah now. We were side by side for thirty five years, all the time, and now she's engineered a situation where I'm not even allowed to phone her up. It's so horrible. What a sick way to end all that history together. It's so unnecessary. I just don't understand why she wants all this shite."

He surprised himself by starting to cry. The court case had briefly overlaid his emotions about Delilah, but now he was talking about her, the tears flowed freely, each one transferring an infinitesimal speck of pain out of his soul. Tim comforted him in a way nobody else could.

"It's ok mate. It will get better."

His voice was actually soothing.

"Yes Tim, I hope so."

Just before the next court date, he transferred his meagre belongings into his new temporary lodgings, which actually were rather nice; a converted animal pen. One of many, in a courtyard which was once a working farmyard. Hence it was quiet and in the countryside, and had some considerable character.

Then the 17th arrived, and he was out of his apartment early and en-route to court about two hours away. He arrived in plenty of time to have a meeting with Rebecca as arranged. She met him in the waiting area and led him into a private consultation room. They sat down. She had copies of all the documents in front of her.

"I've been through all the details" she said calmly. "I don't see how they can show beyond reasonable doubt that you assaulted your wife. Our defence is that you acted with great restraint and minimal force to defend yourself as she became emotionally unstable. There's nothing to show that you had any malevolent intent. There were no injuries. There were no witnesses, and the corroborative so-called evidence from Sirena is directly contradicted by Delilah's own statement. Frankly Pablo, it's a non-starter, and I'm going to suggest that the prosecution don't waste any more of the court's time."

He smiled. He liked her style, and he liked her faith in him.

"Sounds good to me" he replied cheerily.

"Just one word of warning though. If the case goes ahead, don't be surprised if Delilah gives her evidence from behind a screen, so you can't see each other."

This took him aback. The thought of it really upset him. He was close to tears.

"Why?"

"It's purely for effect. It helps to make her look like a victim. It helps to make you seem scary. I'm afraid it happens in court all the time now in domestic violence cases. The prosecution are entitled to ask for it, and so they do."

This thought really subdued him. That would be so unfair. It was absolutely unnecessary. It would be a complete farce, and it would upset him.

She led him back out into the waiting area and walked off confidently to discuss the case privately with the prosecution. Fifteen minutes later she was back, and sat next to him. There was nobody sitting close by, so she spoke quietly to him where he was.

"They've agreed to drop the case."

"Hallelujah!" he exclaimed quietly, but joyfully.

"There is a down side though" she added, now that he had heard the good news.

His heart sank a little. He couldn't imagine what the bad news might be.

"What?" he enquired, a little worried.

"They're going to ask for a restraining order."

"Why?"

"Because they can. She's probably been advised to get one whilst she's here and has the opportunity. And to some extent they're saving face."

"Can I argue against it?"

"You could, but seeing as you're realistically only days or weeks away from actually being divorced by her, it's unlikely that the court would attach any weight to your protestations."

He sat quietly for a few moments, mulling this blow over inside his head slowly, carefully. Communication was the only tool he had to try to win her back. He had used it continuously over the past two years, albeit totally unsuccessfully. It had been the only thing to keep his hopes alive. He really couldn't imagine not being allowed to reach out to her. She was still his wife and the love of his life, despite everything. Rebecca could see that he was really struggling with the concept. She showed him some compassion.

"I'm really sorry Pablo. You don't deserve this, but if this is where she's at, you've got to be strong and accept it."

"Ok." he said quietly and pensively.

"And you still have to appear in court for the charges to be dropped."

"Really?"

"Yes I'm afraid so. You're still on bail to the court, and you have to make an appearance, and the decision by the prosecution to drop the case has to be put to the court officially. So far it's just a discussion between them and me."

"Can you trust them?"

"Yes."

"Will Delilah be in court too?"

"I very much doubt it. She won't need to be if they're not prosecuting you, and if they're asking for a restraining order, she couldn't possibly stand being in the same room as you."

She said that last bit very sarcastically. It was all about creating the right illusion. Just then, he was called and he and Rebecca both entered the court.

He was escorted by the usher to the dock. He stood before three Justices of the Peace. He was asked to confirm his name and was reminded by the clerk of the charge. Before he was asked about his plea, the CPS solicitor got to his feet to interrupt the proceedings.

"Your worships, the prosecution are offering no evidence in this case."

There were mumblings on the bench, but before Pablo was released, the solicitor carried on.

"We are however asking for an injunction to be put in place preventing Mr Pilkington from contacting Mrs Pilkington."

More mumblings, then one of the magistrates asked the prosecution a question.

"Is that at the request of Mrs Pilkington?"

"Yes sir."

"Is she here?"

"She would rather not enter the courtroom sir."

"I see."

The magistrate was left to draw his own conclusions about that. Then he got down to practicalities.

"For how long?"

"Two years sir."

Two years? Pablo nearly swooned. Nobody mentioned two years. That was an enormously long time. He had presumed six months. She was actually still his wife. Who were these people to tell him that he was not allowed to communicate with his wife? He had done nothing wrong.

The JP chairman turned to Pablo.

"Mr Pilkington, do you have any objections?"

He was too upset to say anything. Tears began to roll down his cheeks. He literally couldn't speak. He was heart-broken, again. The magistrate could see that he was struggling to keep it together, and he repeated his question more quietly, as if it was less impacting if he asked quietly. Pablo had no fight left in him. He shook his head slightly as he stared at the floor, resisting sobbing.

The magistrates mumbled together again, then the chair announced

"Granted."

The clerk then did his bit and spoke directly to the quivering wreck of a broken man standing in front of him.

"Mr Pilkington, this court grants your wife Mrs Delilah Pilkington an injunction against you, known as a restraining order. You are ordered not to visit her at her place of residence or her place of work, and are banned from making any communication to her except through a solicitor for a period of two years from today. Do you understand?"

He felt like saying that he had just fucked off to France to possibly work abroad indefinitely, and he had only been dragged back because of this salacious allegation. His posture didn't change. He felt like, and looked like, a defeated confused man. He managed a slight nod of the head, and the Clerk took that as agreement. He then looked behind him at the magistrates. They all nodded. The clerk carried on.

"Mr Pilkington, you are released. The case against you has been dismissed due to lack of evidence. Details of the restraining order will be sent to you and to your solicitor."

With that, the usher shuffled up to Pablo to indicate with outstretched arm the way out of court. Pablo walked slowly. This was a terrible result. When he got out of the courtroom, he sat in a corner of the waiting room and quietly sobbed, his body arched forward over his lap. The thought of being unable to communicate with Delilah for two years was truly devastating. Before long

Rebecca appeared. She sat next to him and quietly placed her arm across his bent shoulders.

"I can tell you really love her, don't you? I'm so sorry."

He appreciated her kind words without acknowledging them. He cried for a few minutes and then composed himself.

"I need to give you my new address" he stated quietly, distracting his thoughts with practicalities.

"Oh yes. Thank you."

She took the details she needed.

"Are you going to be ok?"

She looked concerned.

"Don't worry" he assured her. "I'll survive. I've been like this for over two years."

She found that hard to believe, yet it was perfectly true. She left him rather reluctantly. She had a busy work schedule to get back to. A few minutes later he left the court building and stepped outside into the cold startling early winter air, very alone, but free. He got his mobile out and phoned Fatboy.

"Fatboy, I'm a free man. The case was dropped."

"That's great news. Praise God."

"The bad news is that the next two years are going to be very, very long indeed."

Chapter 25

The heavy steel door slammed shut with a shocking loud clash of metal on metal, accompanied simultaneously by the clatter of a lock cylinder driving a spring-loaded bolt firmly into a strike plate. It always sounded the same. Stern. Loud. Solid. Final. With a harsh echo around the big empty room. A door locking quietly wouldn't have the same demoralising effect. Pablo had heard that familiar noise many hundreds of times before from the other side, but only on one previous occasion from the inside.

Outside, it was a beautiful summer's day in mid July 2011. As he lay on the concrete bed, bathed in the glow of bright artificial light, with nothing to see or do, in absolute silence, apart from occasional random, inexplicable, shouting somewhere down the corridor.

He mused on the developments of the past half a year. On his return from France, he had stayed two weeks with his old friends Alan and Margaret whilst he awaited the court case for assault. He had been shocked at how they had aged considerably since he had last seen them, albeit ten years earlier. It wasn't so much about their physical ageing as a decrepitude of attitude and interests. They were content to sit in their armchairs all evening, every evening, watching television with little else in their lives to interest or simulate them. Their children had all grown up and left home, and they seemed to have done very little to replace their purpose. It was as if they had retired their zest for life, and it scared him.

Then he spent about three weeks at the church conference centre unit. Following the dismissal of Delilah's alleged assault case against him in court, he had decided to stay in England, and to find accommodation near his old town, so he was close to his middle son Lucian and his family. He would be able to babysit each week for them. That would give him some sense of purpose, and connection. He needed that. His old town was also safely an hour and a half away from Delilah, for whom he was now obsolete.

He had found new lodgings in an attic bedroom in a large rather plush country house set in an equestrian twenty acres. The residence was occupied by a small family of mum, dad, and two children aged seven and nine. He kept to his own space as much as possible, and only used the shared family kitchen when he was sure that he wouldn't be in anyone's way. He considered himself an ideal lodger. He was quiet and considerate, but most of all, he made himself scarce. Each week day, he went out to work, which in his case, was driving a few miles away to an office which he was renting in a converted farmyard, for a very modest rent, where he did his daily stock market trading. In the evenings, he was mostly out dancing, partly because he enjoyed dancing, of course, but mainly because he found the alternative of staying in as a single, formerly-married man, lonely and tiresome. He had spent thirty years sharing his evenings with his beloved Delilah, with four beautiful children in the background, and now, all alone, he needed lots of distraction to take away the pain of his loss.

He was lucky insofar that there were twenty one dancing events throughout the week which were no more than forty five minutes from where he lived. That was a lot of choice, and it kept him busy. Yes, it was rather spendthrift of him. Classes and dances all cost entrance money, not to mention the petrol costs, but he had a lot of money in the bank from his house sale, and his emotional and mental welfare took priority over any other sensible considerations, no expense spared. On weekends, he was mostly away visiting family. He felt he was as tiny a burden on his hosts as he could possibly be.

Whilst there he met Melanie. She occasionally cleaned and babysat for the household. She was in her late thirties, and was a nice friendly person, and she was rather on the large side to put it mildly, so she patently didn't appeal to him from a romantic point-of-view. After a few conversations with him, she had formed the opinion that he would be a suitable lodger for her spare room, and she offered it to him if he ever felt the need to change residence. At the time he thought this had been a strange offer, as he saw absolutely no reason to swap his nice big spacious comfortable house for a small bedroom in a small three-bedroom council house. Nevertheless, he retained her phone number out of politeness.

Things went well there for about three months, but then one early spring evening whilst he was sitting in the kitchen eating his evening meal, alone, as always, the landlady turfed him out of the kitchen because she had friends outside, and they were about to come in, and she clearly didn't want them discovering that she had a lodger, presumably because of the embarrassment of her needing a little extra income. He was sent to his room. He complied dutifully with her request to make himself scarce, but he was offended. He didn't appreciate being made to feel that small. He felt it was very undignified, and he wasn't willing to be an embarrassment to anyone. The next day, having firstly ensured that Melanie's room was still available, he gave his notice to quit. Hence, he ended up in Melanie's home after all, and that proved to be very comfortable and easy-going. She really did allow him to treat the house as his own. He was able to use the lounge freely at all times, and there were no restrictions on the use of the kitchen, which had its own little dining area. Melanie was a very considerate and gracious host.

Of course, at every possible opportunity, he spoke to her all about his beloved Delilah, and how he was waiting for the two year restraining order to end, so that he could win her back. She chuckled politely at him, telling him that it was never going to happen. Everybody said that, but nothing dented his determination and faith, even though he hadn't heard a whisper from her since the court order was made. He had sent her occasional cards, and a bunch of red roses on their wedding anniversary, but there had been no response. His best friend Tim had been horrified that he had sent her anything at all. He had chastised him.

"Mate, you're not supposed to be contacting her in any way. You'll get yourself in trouble again you plonker."

He was genuinely concerned, as always, because his default emotion was fear. Pablo had fought his corner, as always, because his default emotion was to defend and justify himself.

"Bud, I've done more than enough to comply with the court order. I've actually moved right away from her, geographically. I didn't have to do that. I just knew that if I stayed there and bumped into her innocently anywhere, she'd have me arrested again for alleged stalking or something stupid like that. I wasn't willing to give her that satisfaction. I don't think she's finished extracting her revenge for me interfering with the love of her life. I haven't texted her, or phoned her, or tried to see her. The kids only ever do anything with one or other of us. A few occasional cards here and there is just being civil."

"Why, you idiot?"

"You know why. I don't want her thinking I'm all bitter and twisted like she is."

"But you said it yourself. She hasn't finished getting her revenge. My ex is still angry at me, and she left me ten years ago!"

He'd laughed raucously.

As he lay in his cell, Pablo mused on that conversation. He had been wrong again. Tim had been right. He had underestimated Delilah's belligerence, and now he was in trouble, again.

The cell door opened up with almost as much clatter as it made when it shut. The custody sergeant strode in, with another officer standing in the doorway.

"This officer is going to take you for interview" he declared loudly and simply.

Pablo jumped to his feet. He was about to be interviewed about his criminal behaviour, and the sooner that was done, the sooner he'd be allowed out. He eagerly followed the plain-clothes officer to a nearby interview room. As usual he sat on the opposite side of the table to the door. The officer, Stuart, aged about forty, and with an enervated approach to the proceedings, explained about the interview and the tapes and the opportunity to have a solicitor present etc. He knew that Pablo was a former police officer, and that he would therefore know all these details well enough already, but he was duty-bound to go through all the correct procedures, or the evidence would become inadmissible. Pablo declined the assistance of a solicitor. He had nothing to hide. No games to play.

Stuart got Pablo to confirm his identity on tape, and then got on with the interview

"Pablo, you have been arrested because your ex-wife Delilah Pinkerton, has made a complaint that you have breached a court order made on the 17th of November 2010, restraining you from making any contact with her whatsoever, by sending her cards and flowers. Do you understand the allegation?"

"Yes, of course."

Stuart cautioned him. Pablo made no reply. Stuart then produced the items of evidence one by one, and challenged Pablo on each separate count. Firstly he produced a Christmas card covered in Pablo's distinct left-sloping handwriting.

"I am producing exhibit DP1 for the sake of the tape. Pablo, do you recognise this card?"

"Absolutely. I sent it to my wife last Christmas."

"Do you accept that this was in breach of a court order made against you on the 17th of November 2010 which banned you from making any contact with your wife for two years?"

"Of course, but I honestly didn't think it would bother her. It was just a Christmas card."

"But it's not just a Christmas card is it Pablo? You've written loads of messages in it declaring your undying love. Do you write that in all your Christmas cards?"

Pablo thought, 'careful Stuart, you're almost showing signs of some personality.' Then he answered him.

"No, only the one to my wife."

Stuart remonstrated with him.

"Your ex-wife!"

Pablo had the satisfaction of being right.

"Actually no. She was still my wife then. The divorce came through on the 17th of February this year."

That felt good. He had scored a point.

Stuart continued, matter-of-factly.

"I produce exhibit DP2 which for the sake of the tape, is a Valentine's Day card with what appears to be Pablo's handwriting in it, and signed by him. Pablo, do you recognise this card?"

"Absolutely. I sent it to my wife on Valentine's day." He emphasised the 'my wife' bit. She was going to be his wife for another three days.

"Again, do you accept that this was in breach of the same court order?"

"Of course, but again, I can't see why that would bother her. Anything I sent her was addressed in my personal distinctive handwriting. If she didn't want anything from me, she could have just put it straight in the bin without opening it."

Stuart mulled that over for a second, then blandly continued.

"Again, you wrote lots of messages in it to her declaring your undying love."

"Yes. I got a bit carried away. I was really missing her, and it was Valentine's day after all, and she was still actually my wife."

Pablo thought it worth emphasising that she was still his wife, again. Stuart continued staring at his notes as he said

"Then, towards the end of March, she received a bunch of red roses. They were anonymous, but she believes it was you who sent them, because it would have been your thirty second wedding anniversary."

He said that like it had been a really bad thing to do.

"Of course. I couldn't let our wedding anniversary pass without respecting it. We had only been divorced for a month, and we had been married for very nearly thirty two years."

Stuart barely looked up from his paperwork, ever, giving the impression that he was either unconfident, or not that interested. Then he read the next bit, still in perfunctory mode.

"I now produce exhibit DP3. It is a card with a picture on the front of a kingfisher sitting on a sign by a river saying: 'No Fishing', and the kingfisher has three little fish in his beak"

Pablo wondered if Stuart saw the humour in that picture. If he did, he didn't show it. That card had really amused Pablo, and even now, it brought a smile to his face.

"On the inside the writer, who uses the name Pablo, declares his undying love and affection for Delilah."

"Yeah. That would be me, funnily enough. I sent it to her just after my birthday at the end of May because I was sad that she hadn't sent me a birthday card for the first time in thirty five years."

"So effectively you are not disputing any of the evidence against you?"

"Nope."

"And you appreciate that all of these items were in breach of the court order."

"Yep."

"Is there anything you would like to add?"

"Only that she's making a mountain out of a molehill. I honestly don't think that my sending her an occasional card bothered her in the slightest. She's just taking advantage of the system and is only doing this to be spiteful."

Stuart looked at him blankly, and then announced that he was wrapping up the interview. Short and sweet and easy. Pablo was led back to his cell, and was incarcerated again for the evidence to be sent away to the Crown Prosecution Service for a judicial decision.

Four hours later, a weary, tired, and bored Pablo was aroused from his languor, and was escorted to the custody sergeant's desk. He stood in front of him, rather vacant and listless from the hours of inactivity and nothingness. He was duly charged with breaching the court order. He knew that he would be. Ex-coppers don't get cautions. He was bailed for a few weeks' time to appear at the Magistrate's court, and was released. It was 11:00 pm and his car was a long way away at the police station near Tim's, where he had surrendered himself at 9:00 am. He phoned his ever-loving friend Tim. Tim knew that he had surrendered to custody that morning. He always kept him in the loop.

"Fatboy! Can you collect me?"

"You complete plonker! Where are you?"

"I'll be walking along the main road from the police station, towards you, just like last time."

Tim gave his familiar raucous laugh.

"Ok Pablo. Try not to get arrested again before I get to rescue you, again, you complete tit."

Pablo strode on, wondering what the court would do to him.

Life settled down into a comfortable but quiet routine at Melanie's house. His objective in life was primarily to race through the next year and a half as quickly and smoothly as possible, without getting arrested again, hopefully, and without losing his hope of reconciliation.

He always cooked for himself in the evening before going out somewhere. He had bought an electric piano for his office, and was getting back into playing the piano, and for a social life, he relied upon his dancing, of course. He had come to know lots of local dancing ladies, but he really wasn't looking for a new partner. He wasn't using dancing as a dating game, just as a means of escape and fun. However, one partner really turned his head.

Stella had a very special air about her, and he couldn't help but be attracted to her. She was about five years younger than him, and was also divorced, and also had grown up kids, three of them. She was pretty, but what really attracted him to her was her personality. She was genuinely kind and gentle. She was mischievous and witty with bags of character. She was slim, which for him, was very attractive. He knew that he was shallow when it came to physical looks and sizes. He couldn't help that. He was programmed that way. They soon became dance partners, sharing a lift to all the dances which they went to. There was undeniably a strong, natural and mutual attraction between them. She became his confidant. He soon trusted her just as absolutely as he trusted Tim, and just like with Tim, he was often crying down the phone to her as he released his deepest emotions. He was still deeply upset about losing Delilah, and cried most days. Stella keenly accompanied him on family visits and walks in the countryside, but he stuck to his guns about Delilah. He made it clear that he couldn't commit to another woman whilst he had this restraining order hanging over his head. He had to wait for it to end, and then to find out where Delilah was emotionally, to see if she'd had a change of heart. That would be another year and a half. He seriously believed that at the end of the enforced two-year break she would want him back, and more than anything, he wanted to restore his family.

Everything with the family was so awkward now. When one of the grandkids had a birthday, their parents would only ask one of them to attend the celebrations. Technically, it didn't have to be that way. He was only banned from going to her home or place of work and communicating with her. He was free to attend all other places, but their kids interpreted the situation much more seriously than they needed to. Understandably, they considered it necessary that their warring parents were kept apart from each other because they didn't want to be the unwilling catalysts for more trouble. That meant in practice that for Pablo and Delilah, all contact with their family was diluted by half, at least. He most certainly didn't want this, and he couldn't believe for a moment that Delilah was happy with this either, and he hoped that these unwanted outcomes would help to reshape her thinking.

Stella herself initially didn't want to get involved in a relationship. She was nursing deep wounds from a recent relationship of two years herself, where she had discovered that she was being two-timed. Some men can be so greedy. So for her, having Pablo as a platonic soul-mate and dance-partner was ideal to start with, but as time went by, they were growing closer together emotionally, and there came a point where she wanted to be more important to Pablo than his absent, errant ex-wife, and that wasn't happening. This began to make her feel second-rate.

One day, after he returned from a week's holiday away without her, she told him that she preferred it when he was away. That stung and shocked him. He asked her why, and she explained about feeling second rate, and how the situation between the three of them was undermining her self-esteem. For Pablo, the timing was exquisite, because he had been starting to question his devotion to Delilah. He had actually considered whether this lovely new woman was worth ditching his dreams of a renewed join-up family. Now she had made his choice for him. He apologised for making her feel that way and told her that if he had inadvertently made her feel that way, they should stop seeing each other, which they did. It was awkward at first, as they both still attended the same dances, but after a few weeks, and because of their natural affection for each other, they re-established their friendship, but now they kept it casual with no illusions of future commitment. It remained a meaningful relationship for them both, but without any romantic connotations. Bizarrely her former two-timing boyfriend came back on the scene, and being the generous, kind and loving person that she was, she forgave him and took him back. Pablo made sure that for the next year and a half, he turned a blind eye to all the women around him, whilst remaining very good friends with Stella of course.

He used the opportunity of dancing to quiz lots of single older women as to why their relationships had broken down. Having misunderstood his own wife for so long, he thirsted for insight. Most of them initially presented stock deflecting answers like 'we grew apart', or 'I didn't love him anymore'. He usually pressed them further to get under the facade and find out what had really happened, or what had allowed the love to die. He also used the opportunity for his own therapeutic release by talking freely all about himself and Delilah if they gave him the chance to. The ladies almost exclusively seemed to empathise with him. He was therefore really taken aback when one particular worldly-wise lady reacted quite differently as he spoke to her on the side of the dance floor. Having spent some time protesting about the unfairness he had suffered at the hands of his former wife, and the madness of her choices she answered quietly but firmly.

"You're really conceited, aren't you?"

"Excuse me?" he replied a little stunned, as he checked what she had just called him.

"I said that you're conceited."

She was very direct. "You think she should come back to you. Therefore you must think you're better than anyone else she knows. Isn't that being conceited?"

She wasn't being jocular. There was an air of disdain in her voice and distaste in her expression. She clearly felt contemptuous towards him, and he felt distinctly embarrassed, and he initially stumbled for the words to respond with. Then, as he gathered his wits,

"It's got nothing to do with conceit. It's all about commitment. I agreed to love her and stand by her for the rest of my life, and she agreed the same thing. For better or worse."

"But she obviously doesn't like you anymore." He almost expected her to add that she didn't like him either. She continued.

"Why should she stand by a decision she made twenty years ago if she's changed her mind?"

"Twenty nine years ago."

"Twenty nine then. She must have been really young. She probably didn't know what she wanted at that age. She's grown up now and wants something different for herself, and you can't provide it. Why can't you accept that?"

He wasn't sure that trying to argue his corner was worth the effort. He didn't even know this woman, and he could tell that this lady had very fixed ideas about breakups and a woman's prerogative to walk away from commitment, but he proffered something of a defence, almost out of politeness. It was he after all who had steered the conversation down this road in the first place.

"Because of commitment. In a marriage you're supposed to work your way through problems and grow together as a couple."

He wondered if she had any respect for the sanctity of marriage at all.

"But you think you're better than this new bloke she's with, even though she obviously prefers him."

"I don't think I'm necessarily better than him" he said through gritted teeth, because this was the correct response in the circumstances, although he didn't believe it for one second.

"I think I am the father of her children. I think I will be the co-grandparent of all her future grandchildren for the rest of our lives. I think I am the one with shared memories over thirty years together, side by side. I think I am more relevant to her than some stranger she has just picked up because she has bought into a lie, and that we should still be loving each other and not experimenting with other people and each other's lives."

She looked at him piteously. She wasn't going to waste any more of her time listening to his pathetic complaints or points of view, and she walked off abruptly. It shocked him how shabbily some people treated true love.

Conversations with male dancers were never particularly fruitful. The men seemed to harbour such deep animosity towards their former partners. They had little constructive to say. Their love had mostly morphed into hatred, and all they wanted to do was express their contempt and resentment. They couldn't understand how he could possibly countenance a reunion with the wife who had betrayed him. When he tried to convince them of her uniqueness, they usually resorted to some bland platitude like 'there's plenty more fish in the sea'. That phrase particularly annoyed him, because it was so illusory. Fish might all seem identical to every other one of the same species, but with humans, it was very different. Everyone was so different. Original. Unique. Which meant that starting all over again really did mean starting all over again, getting used to a completely different person. He had little appetite for that. He still loved Delilah, deeply.

Chapter 26

The night before he was due in court, he stayed at Tim's house because it was only a half hour drive from the city, and he could get a train from there into the city for court in the morning. He couldn't take his car because he was fully expecting the court to make an example of him, and he didn't want the additional complications of his car getting towed away because it had been abandoned somewhere. He hadn't done anything particularly wrong behaviourally. He hadn't been threatening, abusive, insulting, violent, stalking or anything else unpleasant. All he had done was to remind his ex-wife that he still loved her even after she had been unfaithful to him, and even though she had got him arrested with a malicious complaint, and even though she had divorced him to be with her lover, and even though she had obtained a restraining order against him.

What he did expect though, was that the court would take a very dim view of the fact that he had disobeyed the court itself. He had breached their order, if only in a minor way, and he was afraid they would want to demonstrate their indignation at his disregard of their authority, by giving him a short sharp shock. Very likely, a week in prison, he thought. Maybe even two. He told Tim what he thought would happen. Tim was more worried than he was, as usual. He looked really shocked.

"Bruv, you don't deserve that. That's terrible."

"Well I have disobeyed their directive Fatboy, and they have to dish out a suitable punishment for that."

"But why prison?"

"Humiliation. Take me down a peg. A fine isn't going to hurt me is it? I've just sold my house, and I've got loads of cash just sitting in the bank doing nothing."

"Are you allowed to take anything with you?"

"I really don't know. I've memorised your phone number Fatboy. If I need anything, I'll phone you, ok moosh?"

"What, and I'll have to visit you in prison?"

He laughed. The idea amused him no end.

"I can't believe I'll be visiting you in prison bro."

Pablo got to court early. He didn't want to cause unnecessary complications. Delilah wouldn't need to be present because his intention to plead guilty had already been made known, so no witnesses were required. He met his solicitor Rebecca in the foyer. She had done a sterling job for him the last time he was in court for the spurious assault charge, and he had asked her to present mitigation for him this time. They had already met to discuss the case over a week earlier. She was going to show the court that he meant no harm, that he was just being polite, and that he was struggling to come to terms with the loss of a devoted wife after thirty solid years together, and of course, he wouldn't be sending her anymore cards, now that he knew how Delilah reacted, honestly.

"Pablo Pinkerton?" the usher hollered. Showtime!

Pablo marched into the dock. He confirmed his name. The charge was read out by the clerk. Pablo pleaded guilty. The prosecution was invited to sum up the case against him. As he did so, Pablo examined the three magistrates sitting high up to his left. They were all elderly gentlemen, dressed in conservatively dull, but smart, suits and ties. They all wore glasses. They all looked learned, earnest and dutiful. Real community stalwarts. What surprised him though, was the atmosphere. He could see no anger in their faces. Not even disapproval, or surprise. He sensed no animosity from them. They appeared to be listening half-heartedly to the prosecutor, as he relayed to the court the story of Pablo sending his ex-wife a card for Christmas, then for Valentines, oh, and then a bunch of red roses on their anniversary. They looked strangely disinterested. He got the impression that they were having difficulty resisting rolling their eyes at the so-called evidence. The prosecutor soon finished. The magistrates looked at each other, to see if anyone had any questions. Pablo couldn't help feeling that the only question on their minds was 'why the heck are we having to listen to this rubbish?' They expressed no questions.

Rebecca then got up and addressed the magistrates about what a fine upstanding family man Pablo was, and explained that he simply found his wife's abandonment so hard to come to terms with. The magistrates began to look a lot more alert. Pablo wasn't sure he could trust his instincts. This seemed to him to be going far better than he had expected. He felt that the magistrates' glances towards him conveyed sympathy, not condemnation. Maybe they would just hit him with a fine, or probation. It was a simple case, and Rebecca had soon finished saying her piece. Again, the magistrates looked at each other to see if any of them had any questions for Rebecca. None of them did, and they retired to form their judgment. They were only out for a couple of minutes. It was more like a quick comfort break. When they breezed back into court everyone stood. When they sat, the rest of the court sat, except for Pablo of course, who had to remain standing, as the guilty man. The chairman announced with barely a glance at Pablo;

"We give the defendant an absolute discharge."

Nothing more was said. Pablo's chin dropped a little. Wow! This was a slap in the face for the prosecution. Pablo felt that the magistrates were demonstrating their frustration at such an over-the-top case. They gave him no fine or punishment of any kind. They didn't even re-iterate the original court order, let alone extend it or make it more onerous. Pablo was led out of the dock by the court usher, and met Rebecca in the waiting area.

"That went surprisingly well" she announced with a big smile on her face, and that was an understatement. She was genuinely pleased for him, and he was elated.

"Yeah, I was so lucky I had three old gentleman magistrates. They seemed to feel for me. That was a great result, bearing in mind that I pleaded guilty."

"Definitely. An absolute discharge. That's a feather in your cap, but please, don't tempt fate. Don't send her any more cards. You won't be so lucky if there's a next time."

She looked at him with soft imploring eyes. She didn't want to see him getting into any more trouble. She liked him.

"No problem. If she wants to be the bitch from hell, I'll avoid giving her the opportunity to burn me."

"Good!" she said, with genuine satisfaction. She thanked him for his business, told him humorously that she hoped not to see him again, and left.

Pablo left the courthouse like he was walking on air. It was quite a big mental adjustment to make, realising that he was actually still a free man when not many minutes earlier, he was mentally preparing for incarceration in a prison. As soon as he got out he phoned Tim. As he told him the good news, the tears rolled down his face. The relief suddenly overwhelmed him, and he cried deeply.

Tim consoled him with his honeyed, quiet, voice.

"Mate. It's ok. It's over now. Come back to my place. I'll come home early. We can go for a pint to celebrate."

Tim was relieved for him, and he felt his emotion. Pablo hung up. He sat on a low wall alongside the pavement and cradled his head as he wept. So many emotions. Joy at being released. Sadness that Delilah was so bitter towards him. Frustration because his relationship with her had been banned. The overwhelming sense of loss. The lack of framework for his life now. Confusion. He removed his tie and jacket. It was far too warm a day to be wearing those. He walked to the train station, and joyfully bought a one way ticket out of there.

In the autumn of 2011, he was in church on the occasion of their third son's wedding. He thought how this event demonstrated how ridiculous the situation between him and Delilah was. He had no qualms about them both being there, and he knew that deep down she would want this to be as much of a family thing as it could be, with him present too. The situation was stupidly awkward, particularly for all of the children. She had recently had him arrested for sending her a Christmas card, but now they were back together, in church, celebrating the wedding of one of their sons, Troy, and yet there could be no contact between them. He was duty-bound not to speak to her, given her response to his cards, which he considered to be purely vindictive, and she had to maintain her distance on pain of diluting the order against him. On arrival, he was very warmly greeted by the rest of his family and he soon noticed Delilah flitting around, mixing with various family members from both parties. She looked a bit strange in a posh mauve dress-suit, because that wasn't something he'd ever seen her in before. It whispered quietly of her new life away from him. He thought that she looked as lovely as ever. She was closely flanked by two of her sisters, Morag and Sirena.

He would certainly have no time for them. Thankfully, Delilah didn't seem to have a male companion. This was good, because he didn't want to feel usurped at his own son's wedding.

There were lots of people present as it was a big public wedding, and it was easy for Pablo and Delilah to avoid each other, but as the start of service crept closer, Pablo decided to take his seat. He didn't want to be accused of deliberately sitting too close to his ex-wife, and to end up being arrested at his son's wedding for allegedly harassing his ex-wife. So he sat first. Parents and grandparents of the bride and groom had been allocated select seating in the choir pews, adjacent to where the action would take place, and at right angles to, and in front of, the main congregation. Dahlia's parents and grandparents were already sitting in the front row. Pablo positioned himself in the middle of the row behind them, which as yet, apart from him, was empty. With little time to spare before everyone sat quietly and orderly awaiting the regal arrival of the bride, Delilah strode into his row of pews. She squeezed past him with a 'Hi' and planted herself in the pew just two seats on from him. He responded with a polite 'hi' as she passed him, presuming that it was not illegal for him to respond in kind. He was pleased that she had chosen to sit so close to him. It was as if she was not denying their solidarity via their family when it really mattered, but there was of course no conversation. He stared straight ahead without looking at her. He didn't want to give her any ammunition. He didn't risk looking at her in a way which she might construe as breach of the no-contact order.

The wedding and reception were wonderful, and passed without incident. Morag pretended that he didn't exist, which suited him fine. Sirena tried to make a little small-talk with him at one point, but he regarded her phoney duplicity with utter contempt, and disregarded her as politely as he could manage in the circumstances. The wedding of one of your children is a marvellous event, but for Pablo at least, it was clouded by his turmoil over his beloved ex-wife. He felt so strongly that it was crazy that they weren't still together. He felt so deeply that they should be.

By November 2012, Pablo and Delilah had four grandchildren. Three with Lucian and Beatrice, and one with Reuben and Sharon. They had only shared the birth of the first one, which was the only one prior to the troubles. All the others they had visited separately. They had never had an opportunity not only to share visits, but also ideas, reactions and feelings with each other about their new progeny, or to make comparisons with their own babies of decades earlier. Pablo felt robbed. It wasn't the same, being a single grandparent. Everything to do with the most precious thing they had, their family, had been seriously diluted. He learnt from the kids that for the past two years their mother had become quite withdrawn from them all. They were almost as perplexed as he was by her. They had only relatively recently learned that she had formed a new relationship with a man much younger than her called Trevor. They had met him a few times, but they didn't seem comfortable talking to their dad about him. What Pablo did glean was that he seemed to be a nice, easy-going, ordinary chap, who was very caring towards Delilah. He was divorced with two young children whom he still saw regularly. He worked as a master thatcher and had his own business. Delilah had met him as soon as she had moved into her new love-nest at the end of 2010. He was actually working on the roof of her rented property when she got there. It seemed that she had only managed to be on her own for a few days. It also seemed that she was very happy with her new man. Pablo was only slightly disappointed by this news. He always knew that she wouldn't stay on her own for long. She hated the thought of being alone, and she was still an attractive lady with a lovely personality. The fact that she had now been in a steady relationship for two years would just add to the challenge he faced, and he never balked at a challenge. Surely this young thatcher with his own messed-up family history couldn't replace him in the long term?

Finally, after two long empty years, the 17th of November 2012 arrived. The restraining order expired. The life it had and its power to separate the inseparable for so long, withered suddenly, like a tiny flame in a violent storm. That horrible test that had been forced onto Pablo had been endured and conquered. His love and devotion to his ex-wife had remained solid. He felt like a warrior, trained, prepared, and honed for the next battle. There was nothing to prevent him from communicating with her again. How weird! He wondered how long he should wait before he messaged her for the first time in a year and a half. He had no idea what the etiquette for that was. Ultimately, he was too excited to wait for long. He was after all offering her an amnesty and renewed opportunity. He managed to hold off for one week. That was hard. Then the first text. A momentous occasion. He thought long and hard about what to write for such a significant event. He kept it simple.

"Hi Delilah. I constantly wonder how you are. I still love you with all of my heart. Always have. Always will. There is simply no room in my heart for another woman because no one could ever replace you. You are my childhood sweetheart and the mother of my children, and only you can restore our family. You can dishonour your marriage vows in every way you can imagine, but I don't believe that will make you happy. I pray each day for a miracle of restoration and fulfilment in each other. Please, talk to me xx"

He didn't know if she still had the same mobile number or not. He would leave that to fate. He didn't want to make anyone feel awkward by checking her phone number with them. Over the past four years, he had ensured that his children didn't get dragged into this mess more than was unavoidable, and he wasn't going to start trying to use them now. There was no response. He was disappointed. After two years of enforced separation, surely she could now at least acknowledge him? Maybe she really had changed her mobile number. He doubted that though. She would have been advised to, but he knew that she wasn't genuinely scared of him no matter what it suited her to pretend. He knew what had happened in the garage that fateful day. He knew that she wouldn't believe her own lies. Or would she? After all this time? In the absence of any responses he considered that it was reasonable to text her once a week. This he did on a Friday so she could muse on his message over the weekend when she wasn't so busy. A week later.

"Hi Delilah. Are you wondering why I am talking to you after all that has happened? Well, I want you to know that I forgive you. And I want to apologise. When you were threatening me with abandonment, I reacted by saying that if you did, you wouldn't see me for dust, implying that I would quickly find someone else. I'm sorry. That was merely hurt pride, and it was unreal, naïve, and unloving. I have discovered instead just how deeply I love you. My happiness and fulfilment derive from being a husband to you, a father, and a papa. I won't settle for a shallow substitute relationship which doesn't augment those roles. You are my true love, and I will wait for you. I know Sylvia undermined your relationship with me, and possibly your self-image, but I believe that in time, you will realise that she duped you just like Roger did. All she achieved for you was to steer you from a worthy lifestyle to a sordid emptier one. But you won't find a more significant or enduring love than mine xx"

The highlight of each week was his text to her. Number three:

"Delilah, our journey in life is about how we grow in our love together. You with me. Me with you. Nobody else will fit you. Nobody else will fit me. I am truly sorry for my shortcomings in loving you, but your absence has done nothing to diminish my love for you. I am full of hope for a future where we break through the glass walls and ceiling that limited our love. God has given me the grace and patience to wait for you. He hasn't done that for no purpose. You have given up so much for so little. I am inviting you to be an overcomer with me. Our hearts are two hearts that beat as one. We have a purpose together. Forgive me. Love me, and come back to my love. Xx"

Christmas arrived after four texts. He did exactly what he had done for the previous two Christmases. He visited each of his children in turn, usually staying overnight at least once to make the most of the protracted holiday and freedom from work, polished off with visits to his siblings. He saw nothing of Delilah. All the festivities were carefully arranged by everyone else involved to ensure the two of them didn't meet. He was not unduly disheartened.

2013 arrived in normal grey, wet, dark style. Everything was the same for him with life, work, and dancing as it had been for the past two years. He had rigorously stuck to his gym training, and he hoped his physique looked a little more honed than it had done prior to all that hard work, although in all honesty, he wasn't sure. To him, any changes were imperceptible. He still hoped that Delilah would respond. Surely she would want to talk to him? Yes, it would be hard, because she would have to swallow her pride. The initial absence of responses didn't deter him. He would continue to text her a short pithy message weekly. She just needed time and encouragement.

'Delilah, Sylvia taught you to resent your history, your role as a wife, and maybe even yourself. It was not an edifying lesson. Hatred only destroys, and its effects are further reaching than you would have ever imagined. To love and forgive is to create the opportunity to build and grow and create deeper relationships. You must have learned that cold hard lesson by now. Are you ready to swap the hatred consuming your heart for love yet?'

The messages didn't vary enormously. In effect he was just letting her know how deep and enduring his love for her was. Melanie genuinely thought he was crazy expecting any change at this stage, and wasted no opportunity in assuring him that he would get nowhere. Each time he proudly informed her about his latest message, she would laugh. Tim was dreadfully worried that he would get himself into trouble again. Pablo would remonstrate with him.

"What am I supposed to do? I have to catch up with where I was with her two years ago. The court order only postponed a conversation that had to happen and simply delayed the inevitable."

"Mate, she's with some other geezer now."

Tim felt exasperated by Pablo's determination and stubbornness.

"Fatboy, I'm just letting her know that I'm still here for her, that's all."

"Can't you find another babe with all that dancing you do mate?"

Pablo felt exasperated that nobody seemed to understand that his undying love for his childhood sweetheart was unique and irreplaceable. Why did he have to constantly justify himself?

"Nobody can replace her. I've loved her since I was seventeen years old. My eyes have never strayed but she thinks they have. I have to prove to her that I only have eyes for her, even now."

Tim relented as always, accepting his friend's determination, but still hoping that he really wouldn't get into any more trouble. The messages trickled out, week in, week out. Some challenged her about her disastrous affair with Roger. Some complained about being rejected and abandoned, but most just reiterated hope. He couldn't say anything about Trevor. He'd never met the man, and knew next to nothing about him. He could only hope that her relationship with him had been something of a convenience, and wouldn't have lasting strength. Time would tell. Sometimes he waxed lyrical.

"Love recognises no barriers. it jumps hurdles, leaps fences, and penetrates walls to arrive at its destination full of hope. Why do I prevail for you so? So much of why something precious has been thrown away is based on lies and deceptions. As time passes those lies will fade from memory, and the real memories they have been hiding will endure. That is the nature of life and love, and it gives me hope."

The weeks turned into months, but he still wanted her to know that he was not a flash in the pan. He would always be there for her. His gut instinct told him that she was reading his messages, but there were no replies. She had become a ghost.

Chapter 27

A spring-time dancing weekender called Well-Hot was on the horizon at the end of April 2013. It was particularly attractive insofar as it was only an hour and a half from where Pablo lived. Weekenders occurred every few months, but were usually at least three hours away, which was the main reason he didn't attend many of them. He had arranged to share a cabin at this one with Nicola. She was one of his local lady dancers that he had got to know quite well over the past two years. They had already shared occasional lifts to new dancing venues. They had a casual platonic friendship rooted in a love of dancing. She had shown a great deal of interest in his story, and had even made time to sit with him in her car after a dance, to learn more of how his marriage had ended so acrimoniously. She was amazed that talking about Delilah still brought him to the point of tears, after so much time. Four years!

Her own marriage had ended after more than twenty years, several years earlier, but she showed no remorse, and no emotion. Of course he quizzed her incisively as to why her marriage had failed. She routinely explained that as time had passed by, she had found her husband was becoming increasingly useless. She was having to take more and more responsibility for everything, and that meant managing the kids, running the home, doing all the cooking and cleaning, and even the DIY. He had become a beer-drinking, TV-watching, uninteresting and disinterested slob, and that wore her love for him away completely, to the point where she just felt that he was simply a burden, and one she felt no responsibility to carry any longer, and she kicked him out. She had a pleasant sensible nature, but she was very plain. Pablo liked her as a person, but was not attracted to her physically. She was too blokey for him. There was no chance of her becoming another Stella. She had been on her own for a number of years, and seemed to want friendship, but their weekend away was purely for the sake of convenience, and that was not unusual in the dancing community. Lots of casual dancing friends would share accommodation in order to be able to attend a weekender.

There were just the two of them in their three bedroom cabin, so of course they each had plenty of privacy. They drove to the venue separately as Nicola wanted to make the pre-event Friday lunchtime dinner at a local pub nearby, which Pablo couldn't make. He arrived later, in early evening, and that's when they touched base, in the chalet. Nicola told him all about the lovely atmospheric fun dinner, and Pablo told her all about the weary, frustrating rush-hour traffic. This pre-meet meal had become quite popular over recent years, and about forty dancers had attended. She had made good use of it to start making new friends prior to the main event.

The Friday evening dance finished late, at 3:00 am, and Nicola and Pablo became exhausted and retired at different stages in the early hours. They caught up over a late breakfast.

"Have you met those two ladies from the south coast? They seem really nice."

"Nicola, how am I supposed to know who you are talking about? There are about seven hundred people here."

"One of them is really pretty. I thought you might have noticed her last night. They were at yesterday's pub-lunch."

"You know I didn't make the lunch."

"Yes, I know. I just meant that I have already met them. They're nice."

"Hey, I'm glad you like them."

Pablo was emanating disinterest. There were a lot of ladies here, mostly aged between forty and sixty, but not many were particularly attractive, and he didn't think he was going to find anyone to turn his head. He was too busy ruminating on Delilah still. Nicola persisted.

"Don't tell me you didn't notice the little blond one last night? She's called Hellion."

"You know me. I spread myself around. I danced with all sorts of different women last night, but not necessarily all of them, and I never ask their names because I am crap at remembering them. You know that don't you, err..."

"She was wearing a light green dress. Shoulder length blond hair. Five foot two or three, beautifully delicate."

Nicola was obviously envious of the gorgeous Hellion, and she was right, he most definitely did recall seeing her. She was stunning, and she knew it. However, now that he was in his mid-fifties, he knew that he had to be realistic about his prospects, and not to act in a way that was embarrassing for himself or anyone else. He might cheekily ask for an occasional dance with a gorgeous, sexy, young babe, but he was far too sensible to allow himself to harbour any implausible fanciful ideas above his station, and he hadn't even approached the delectable Hellion. She was way out of his league.

"Nicola, she's about thirty five. I might just about appeal to a thirty five year-old if she's got a beard, or maybe a severe disability, or a very low IQ, or even worse eyesight, but not a gorgeous, fit one like her."

He was really quite dismissive, just as he had been the night before, when for the reasons he had just stated, he hadn't even risked asking her for a dance. He didn't want to give her the opportunity to reject him on grounds of age, looks, baldness, insufficient personality, or any other excuse she might reasonably come up with. Being rejected by a much younger dancer was not an uncommon occurrence for him, but he never relished it.

"I think she's much older than she looks. I agree she looks mid to late thirties, but actually, I think she's in her early fifties."

"What?"

He turned towards her, suddenly showing much more interest, but he was disbelieving.

"Surely not. I'm not kidding when I say she doesn't look a day over thirty five. That's why I ignored her. Far too young and gorgeous for me."

"No, really. It came up over lunch yesterday. I was equally surprised. She looks amazing for her age."

Pablo looked at her quizzically. The cogs in his brain were churning away.

"Are you sure?"

"Yes."

Nicola half looked at him, as if she was minding her own business really.

Pablo smiled.

"Game on!" he announced mischievously, smiling broadly. He still thought that she looked amazing, but if she was over fifty, then any tentative interest he was to show in her just might not be shunned out of hand immediately. He might summon up enough bravery to try to talk to her tonight.

That evening, after a long day of exhausting lessons, very little food, and an hour's cat-nap followed by a refreshing shower, he was stalking the dance floors, looking out for this ageless beauty. There were three dance rooms. The main one consistently played 'upbeat' contemporary music. The second room played various changing themes throughout the evening, ranging from Latin through soul to classic hits. The third room, Pablo's favourite, focussed on lower-beat, bluesy, funky tracks. That kind of music was acquiring various epitaphs in the dance world; silky, expressive, and smooth, but whatever it was called, it allowed for a slower, more expressive and creative style of dancing, and it was becoming increasingly popular, particularly with the more competent dancers who wanted to stretch themselves, and to continue to develop.

Pablo had to wait until about 11:00 pm before he spotted the gorgeous Hellion. He was pretty sure that she must have arrived fairly late. He didn't think that he would have missed her for too long. He had been flitting from room to room, looking out for her. A lot of dancers turned up late if they intended to survive into the wee small hours. Those who stayed on their feet right up until the last track were proudly called 'survivors', and there was often a 'survivors' group photo. The badge of honour. He spotted her in the main room. Her blond hair stood out in the dull light, and she had a pale yellow dress on which showed off her rather lovely, slight, figure. He really struggled to believe that she was over fifty. She had a much younger look about her. She moved gracefully. He observed that she wasn't one of the more energetic speedy dancers.

He grabbed a partner and got onto the floor. He politely focussed on his own dance and partner, but glanced occasionally towards Hellion. The lights were very low, and one could easily lose sight of someone as they manoeuvred around the floor. When that dance ended, he noticed that she was quickly grabbed by another man who had no doubt been preparing to catch her as soon as she came free. He stayed with his current partner. He usually liked to dance two or three times with the same partner in order for them both to get used to each other and to relax. At the end of his second dance, he thanked her, released her and walked off the floor. The same man kept hold of Hellion. From the side-lines Pablo watched, carefully biding his opportunity. He kept thinking how very lovely she looked, but he also wondered what she would be like as a person. Some gorgeous women were quite dismissive of men their own age, or were unpleasantly egocentric. As the current track was about to end, he walked onto the floor weaving in and out of the few couples between them. He wanted to grab her before anybody else did, but as the next track began, he had to concede that her current partner was not ready to relinquish his hold. He withdrew to the side-lines again and loitered in the shadows, avoiding as best he could, the risk of being grabbed by another lady. At the end of that track, he again weaved back onto the floor. To his relief Hellion released herself from her partner and started to walk towards the side. He deftly intercepted her.

"Dance?" he said hopefully and brightly.

She took his hand and they loosely embraced. The music was rather fast and loud. The atmosphere was energetic and inspired. He moved her around gently and sensitively. She was about half his weight, and he was careful not to come across as rough or insensitive. She appeared thoughtful and rather unemotional as she danced. He was concentrating on not putting a foot wrong, or messing up a move. He didn't engage in conversations on the dance floor. He found that he could either talk, or dance, but not both, effectively. After two dances, she put a hand on his chest and said she needed to go and get some water. He thanked her. The only thoughts swirling around his head were that she was truly pretty, and he wondered if during the weekend he might be able to get to know her a little. All he knew so far was that she had come with her friend Juliet, and appeared to be single, but that didn't mean that she actually was. Then he was checked by his common sense. She was too pretty for him, and if she looked thirty five, she might as well be. She was out of his reach. For the rest of the evening, he noticed her when she was on the same floor as him, but he didn't try to dance with her again. He could see that she was getting a lot of attention from other men, and he didn't really want to get into a competition. Deep down he didn't have the confidence for her.

The following day he was up at a reasonable time again so that he could attend classes, even though he still felt rather exhausted from the long day before. He didn't coincide with Nicola. She was probably very sensibly having a lay in. During the course of the day he would sit out of some of the classes to save energy, but would still benefit from just watching them. At lunchtime he attended the restaurant, alone, and treated himself to steak and chips. He felt that he needed the protein, and the calories, and anything else it could bolster him up with. It was going to be a long day with no other meals. When the classes ended he returned to his cabin for the compulsory recuperation-nap. Nicola was there, fussing around with her fancy dress costume, ready for later. Sunday evening was fancy-dress night, and everyone took it very seriously. There would be competitions in various categories, but the emphasis was definitely on the participation. He didn't particularly like fancy-dress, but here, you looked really out of place if you didn't sport one, so he had bought an off-the -shelf cheap-as-chips Roman Centurion outfit. All plastic and pastiche. He thought he looked a proper dick in it, but hey ho. It was the tiny little bit of effort that counted. Nicola was apparently going as a burlesque dancer. Quite a few ladies were dressing in similar fashion, and she had already arranged to team up with a few others to form a troupe. This would apparently include Hellion and Juliet.

At about 8:30 pm, he escorted Nicola to the main hall, or should that be said the other way round? She protected her modesty with a large dark coat. He protected his embarrassment with a bomber jacket which left his bare legs ridiculously exposed. At least it was dark. For that, he was thankful. The only thing worse than being in a cheesy fancy-dress costume, was being in a discordant mixture of a cheesy fancy-dress costume and proper clothes. The cabins were splayed out over a hundred acre site, and depending on the price of your cabin, the walk into the central buildings took anything from one minute to twenty. Their walk was about twelve minutes.

The main hall was already thronging with cowboys, spacemen, apes, Roman senators, strippers, vicars, pirates, flower-pot men, butterflies, bees, cats, dogs and anything else your imagination could remotely stretch to. Six hundred people randomly choosing fancy dress costumes meant that nothing was overlooked. He thought it incongruous that in this age of political correctness, the ladies mostly chose politically incorrect identities, exploiting their sexuality by dressing up as sexy schoolgirls, burlesque dancers, strippers, titivating half-clad nurses, sexy policewomen etc. He wondered who the event was designed to please, but in fact it wasn't steered by anyone, it was a free-for-all. The ladies seemed to relish the opportunity of transcending the politically correct restrictions of the modern era. This event seemed to serve as an ephemeral release for them, and it was all very tongue-in-cheek, and definitely contributed to the fun nature of this particular weekender.

Personally, he found that the whole protracted fancy-dress affair interfered enormously with what he was there for, the dancing. After all, nobody could dance very well bedecked within a giant chicken costume, or immersed somewhere deep within a huge, blow-up space alien outfit. For him, the only benefit was that his own costume showed off his muscular arms, and he didn't mind that. After the parades, performances and prize-giving, finally, people relaxed back to dancing. A lot would strip off most of the superfluous appendages, or change completely, in order to be able to dance. Now the dance floor was pock-marked with headless chickens, burlesque dancers minus their peacock feathers, and angels with their halos lowered around their necks, and their wings unceremoniously torn off and discarded on the side-lines. Pablo quickly took advantage of an opportunity to dance with Hellion. She was still in full regalia; corset, stockings, elbow length gloves, cheeky little bonnet. She looked fantastic. He managed to secure three dances with her before she asked to leave the floor for some water. She seemed very particular about drinking lots of water. She took his hand and led him off too. He willingly complied. He was chuffed that she was showing an interest in him. On the side-lines, on the non-dance side of a very messy row of tables and chairs, festooned with discarded feathers, bonnets, jackets, gorilla masks, etc, it was busy with yetis, red Indians and French maids jostling to find their way from one dance floor to another along the busy walkway. She wanted to find out a bit more about him. Next to her he felt huge. She was so delicate and petite, particularly against his sturdy muscular six-foot frame. He was filled with a sense of veneration. She was truly beautiful, delicate, feminine, and his emotions were churning a dizzy mixture of wonderment, admiration, awe and desire. He hadn't experienced those kinds of emotions since he'd been with Delilah.

She asked him several obvious questions about his circumstances and interests. He happily answered. He was praying fervently that she would find him interesting. Women weren't shallow like men. They didn't really focus on biceps and six-packs, much as they might pretend to. They wanted to know about motivation, skills, characteristics, personal attributes and achievements. At one point she had to turn around and move backwards to allow a particularly bulky foam sumo-wrestler to squeeze past them. Pablo pulled her back closely to him, his hands on her delicate bare shoulders. His shoulders were massive compared to hers. Her skin felt lovely. Warm, soft, firm. The wrestler wobbled precariously past, but after he had done so, Pablo held her there, closely in front of him. She happily stayed there, and he allowed his hands to move slowly up and down her upper arms as they quietly continued to engage in a seemingly perfunctory conversation. What felt important was that they were close to each other. As he spoke, he leaned down over her shoulder to speak closely at one side of her face. For their first encounter, this felt intimate, and it carried on for about ten minutes. His bliss was shattered when a rather presumptuous Arab sheik had the gall to ask her for a dance. For a moment he wished that the pathetic plastic sword tucked into his faux-leather skirt was a real one, and that he could act imperiously like a real Centurion. But it was only make-believe. She turned to look into his face briefly with a look of regret, but she felt duty-bound to accept the offer of a dance, even though she wasn't really in the dance-available zone. That was etiquette. He sadly watched her get led away by a man with a tea towel on his head, but he was nevertheless excited. There was chemistry between them. That elusive don't-know-how-to-explain-it feeling of something mysterious connecting them in a sort of spiritual way. He walked to the edge of the dance floor and grabbed a partner. He felt happy.

He didn't see her again until a lot later. They danced again. It felt good. It felt different. There was something metaphysical going on. He asked her when she was heading home. She told him that she and Juliet would stay there that night, and have breakfast in the restaurant the following morning before setting off home. He told her he would see her again at breakfast in the morning. That night, he was still excited. He wondered if he had actually met someone who could turn his heart away from its perpetual mourning.

He and Nicola were both up at a reasonable time. Chalets had to be vacated by 10:00 am, which was quite early when most occupants wouldn't have gone to bed much before 3:00-4:00 am, and they had to pack their belongings into their cars.

"I didn't know where to look last night" Nicola offered cheekily.

"What?" Pablo answered nonchalantly.

"I was sitting behind you when you got your hands on Hellion. You looked like you were going to peel her clothes off her there and then.'

He smiled broadly. "I felt like it! But she got rescued by a wealthy Arab. Anyway, how come I didn't notice you spying on me?"

"I don't think you'd have noticed a herd of wild elephants marauding through the place."

Pablo thought about that. It was probably true. He had been fixated with Hellion at the time."

She continued.

"I'm surprised that you allowed the Arab to take her away."

"I did consider cutting his hands off with my plastic sword, but decided it would take too long."

"So, did anything else happen I ought to know about?"

"Nicola, you know me. I'm a slow mover. All we did was to arrange to meet this morning in the restaurant."

"Oh! Can I come too?"

"Only if you're on your best behaviour!"

She threw a discarded plastic sword at him.

They drove their loaded cars up to the main car park, parked together, and entered the main building. Hellion wasn't there yet, so Nicola and he both went ahead and ordered a cooked breakfast. The restaurant had that de-mob, quiet feel about it. Most revellers had already set off home. Those still present were feeling very ordinary, dressed in ordinary clothes, preparing to return to their ordinary lives, and were grabbing one last coffee and conversation before driving back to normality and relative drabness. Nicola and Pablo had all but finished their breakfasts by the time Juliet and Hellion turned up. They sat elsewhere, and were shortly merely indulging in coffee and croissants. Nicola got up to go. Pablo stood too, and they hugged goodbye. Nicola then strolled over to Juliet and Hellion. He went with her. They all said their goodbyes, declaring how nice it had been to meet each other, and what a fabulous weekend it had been, and Nicola left. There were spare seats at their table, and Pablo asked for permission to sit with them. Of course that was ok. They made casual conversation about the weekend's events. The memories were fun, but Pablo had a sense of purpose about him. He wanted to somehow pursue Hellion. They were still in some kind of no-man's-land, despite the chemistry of the evening before. He summoned up the courage to directly ask her for her phone number. His request sounded rather corny and tacky, but he didn't think that would be a problem. It was.

"I don't give out my phone number."

She gave a little pained look, whilst Juliet adorned an expression of absolute empathy for her beautiful, troubled, best friend. He felt rather embarrassed. That was a rebuff he hadn't expected.

"Oh" was all he could manage on the spur of the moment, barely disguising his surprise.

She explained. "I'm having problems with my ex-boyfriend, and I don't want any more."

He felt rather insulted by the insinuation. He wasn't intending to be a problem of any kind. He just wanted them to be able to contact each other if they wanted to. She carried on.

"I'm being stalked."

He wasn't sure what she meant by that, but it sounded bad. He certainly didn't mean to imply that he was planning an additional stalking campaign.

"Oh, I'm sorry to hear that. I was just hoping that we could keep in touch, that's all. I don't intend to add to your list of stalkers."

"Yes I understand, but I'm not giving out my details at the moment."

She had a way about her that reminded him of Margret Thatcher in her heyday. She used to speak with an authority and certainty that made her opinion seem like a God-like proclamation, and of course, there was no possible alternative to what she thought. Hellion carried a similar strength of character and air of authority. He admired that, but it was also rather challenging. He didn't know what else to say. He was crest-fallen. They had finished their refreshments, and they all got up to leave. After a quick hug, and with no attempt to make any arrangements for the future, they said their goodbyes. As he watched her leave he felt somewhat confused. He was basically a simple man. The connection felt good, amazing really. Surely they should pursue it?